The HOLTS
An American Dynasty

W9-AEP-164

SHARE THE BREATHTAKING ADVENTURES OF THE HOLTS, THE SECOND GENERATION. THEIR DREAMS WERE AS VAST AS THE NEW HORIZONS OF A FAST-GROWING NATION. THEIR HERITAGE TIED THEM FOREVER TO THIS LAND, AND THEIR COURAGE DROVE THEM INTO THE FRAY, WHEREVER FREEDOM AND AMERICA'S PRECIOUS IDEALS WERE THREATENED . . . TO FIGHT, TO DIE, AND TO LOVE . . .

CAROLINA COURAGE

FROM THE LAWMAKING CHAMBERS OF GOVERNMENT TO THE BLOODSTAINED HILLS OF CAROLINA, THE HOLTS ARE A PART OF HISTORY AS AMERICA FACES THE TURMOIL OF RACIAL HATRED AND EMBRACES A FUTURE OF RIGHTEOUSNESS FOR ALL ITS PEOPLE.

JANESSA HOLT LAWRENCE

Very much Toby Holt's feisty daughter, this brilliant young doctor had always proudly called herself a Holt, forgetting her Cherokee mother's heritage. Now fate carried Janessa back to her birthplace . . . where, as Ka-nessa, her heart would be torn between two unexpected passions and her life threatened by an unknown enemy.

JOE CHEOH

Cherokee born and Indian proud, this bold lawyer defiantly challenged the mining companies and the law to save his people's land. But his passion for another man's wife could only bring heartbreak or shame to them both.

CHARLEY LAWRENCE

Dedicated to defeating the scourge of yellow fever, he followed his ideals even where caution warned of danger. Now he too could become a victim—of the disease he fought and of the dangerous sickness called jealousy.

SAM BRENTWOOD

Mad, wild, and ruining his marriage with liquor and women, this angry man shattered his world. There was only one way to pick up the pieces: Do the impossible—and go westward all the way to the Eden called Hawaii.

ANNIE MALONE BRENTWOOD

Marrying a younger man was supposed to be a lark, a way to thumb her nose at the world. But falling in love with him was foolish . . . especially now that an island rebellion could make them adversaries and forever drive them apart.

QUEEN LILIUOKALANI

Queen "Lydia" Dominis was too gentle and good to fight the men bent on greed and destruction. Now, this lovely, loving queen's future held foul betrayal from her friends and one bright beacon of hope: Henry Blake.

PILIKIA

Maddened by hate, driven by a blood lust against the intruders on his island home, he needed an American to capture and sacrifice to the volcano god Pele . . . a man named Sam Brentwood.

MIKE HOLT

Overprotected by his father Toby Holt, this young boy coming into manhood refused to accept the doctors' verdict—that his weakened heart meant sudden death at any time—for the Holt courage was his legacy to live fully . . . with passion and desire.

EDEN BRENTWOOD

Beautiful at sixteen, a blend of sensuality and innocence, she had already given her heart to Mike Holt, and she would follow him to the edge of doom itself if only to love him for a single hour.

MORTON BRIGGS

As porcine and greedy as a Carolina hog, this slippery mining company manager would grab whatever he wanted from the Cherokee. Nothing stood in his way . . . except one uppity Indian doctor named Janessa Lawrence.

HENRY BLAKE

Agent for the U.S. Government, he was a troubleshooter without equal. In the hills of Carolina or the sugar fields of Hawaii, his job was justice; his weapon was truth.

THE HOLTS: AN AMERICAN DYNASTY
VOLUME THREE

CAROLINA COURAGE

DANA FULLER ROSS

BANTAM BOOKS
NEW YORK • TORONTO • LONDON • SYDNEY • AUCKLAND

CAROLINA COURAGE

A Bantam Book / Book Creations, Inc.

Bantam edition / January 1991

Produced by Book Creations, Inc.
Lyle Kenyon Engel, Founder

ISBN 0-553-28756-7

Published simultaneously in the United States and Canada

Bantam Books are published by Bantam Books, a division of Bantam
Doubleday Dell Publishing Group, Inc. Its trademark, consisting of
the words "Bantam Books" and the portrayal of a rooster, is
Registered in U.S. Patent and Trademark Office and in other
countries. Marca Registrada. Bantam Books, 666 Fifth Avenue, New
York, New York 10103.

PRINTED IN THE UNITED STATES OF AMERICA

OPM   0 9 8 7 6 5 4 3 2 1

With a moan Andy pushed himself from the railing and into the water. The sea was cold beyond bearing, and he surfaced numb with shock. Desperately he began to swim toward Lydia. The roaring sea buffeted him, splashing his face with icy salt water. He tried to see Lydia but could only see the life preserver someone had thrown to him. ...

R. TOELKE '90

The moon ran out of the clouds to illuminate a terrifying tableau: Janessa lay motionless on the ground in a tangle of vines and briars. Sid stood above her and raised a large rock in both hands, about to send it crashing down on her head. Joe leaped toward them, waving his knife.

I

New York, August 1891

The wineglasses made a very loud crash as they went flying over the end of the bar.

"Here now, you'll have to pay for those." The bartender gave the three drunken young swells a disgusted look. *Boys*, he thought, *with more money than brains*.

"Yeah, sure," one of them said. Sam Brentwood counted the toppled glasses on the floor, then held out his hand to his companions. "That's three broken. Pay me." He jerked a thumb at the bartender. "You can pay him, too. Loser buys the glasses."

The men, in their twenties, were playing an impromptu form of ninepins, knocking down wineglasses with a wooden bowl, which they slid down the length of the bar. The man who knocked the most glasses down while breaking the fewest won.

"Try it again, Sam. That was simple luck, not skill." Dickie Merrill danced behind the bar and snatched up three more glasses while the bartender made a swipe at him with his hand. "Give us three more beers, too," he said, retreating.

"This ain't a bowling alley," the bartender said, but he put the drinks on the bar. The three men had spent a lot of money on beer. And they'd paid for the broken glasses. So far. He shook his head. Too much money. Too much time

1

on their hands. Too much everything. "You're a married man, Brentwood," he said. "Haven't *you* got anything better to do?"

Dickie cackled. "Sam's slipped his leash for the afternoon."

Sam Brentwood shook his dark hair back out of his eyes and aimed the wooden bowl down the bar. It whapped solidly into the glasses, and four of them toppled. One splintered into shards, but the rest rolled in semicircles on the bar. "Haven't lost my touch," he murmured. He held out his hand to the other two and pocketed the bills they gave him. After consulting his pocket watch, Sam pulled one bill back out and dropped it on the bar. He grinned at the bartender. "I like to go out a winner. As it happens, however, I do have something better to do."

Dickie Merrill chortled. "Annie taking you out for your evening walk?"

Sam swung his head around toward his friend. A certain dark light in his eyes made Dickie back off a pace.

"No," Sam said evenly. His voice was barely slurred. "As it happens, the honor of my presence is required at a wedding." He picked up his silk hat and set it on his head at a jaunty angle. His eyes crinkled, the bad temper fading. "My grandmother's getting married. I have to give the bride away." He sauntered out, hands in his pockets, spoiling the elegant lines of his coat.

His companions looked after him, shaking their heads. "In his condition?" Dickie asked.

The other man thought about it. "Sam's pretty much always drunk," he said sagely. "Maybe the old lady won't notice."

The old lady noticed. Claudia Brentwood, age eighty-two, narrowed her eyes at her grandson as they prepared to march sedately between rows of gilt chairs to the end of the small parlor in the Waldorf Hotel, where Howard Locke awaited her, with the minister. She didn't say anything, but the delicate hand she placed on Sam's wrist tightened perceptibly, and her green eyes bit into him.

Sam felt that his collar, comfortable a moment ago, had unaccountably grown tight. He straightened his back and ignored his wife's eyes, also boring into him from her place among the small group of wedding guests sitting upon the gilt chairs.

For her third wedding ("at my age," as Claudia had taken to remarking in tones of wonder that she was doing this at all), Claudia had decreed a simple ceremony in the hotel where she maintained a suite for herself and her fourteen-year-old granddaughter, Eden. Lydia Brentwood, Eden's mother and Claudia's daughter-in-law, had declared herself too ill to travel from Missouri, so she and Claudia's son, Andy, were not here. But Eden was, eyes bright with delight, as were Doctors Janessa and Charley Lawrence, courtesy kin to Claudia, who had come from the Marine Hospital Service headquarters on Staten Island. Claudia had remarked that should either member of the bridal couple succumb to old age at the altar, the doctors would come in handy. But she had been joking, and everyone knew it. Howard Locke, white hair neatly combed and a rose in his buttonhole, was the picture of health. He was looking at her with an expression that Claudia had never thought to see in a man's eyes again. As for Claudia, her stamina was family legend.

"Ready to tie the knot, Gran?" Sam whispered, and Claudia's eyes softened. He knew she wouldn't stay mad at him on her wedding day. A pianist at the upright in the corner struck up a march, and they sailed down the aisle on its music.

At the end of the ceremony, when the minister announced that the bridegroom might kiss the bride, Howard did so with gusto, and Janessa and Charley, not long married themselves, smiled mistily at each other. Sam's eyes slid toward his wife. She looked back at him with nostrils slightly flared as if she could smell the liquor on his breath from her seat.

You're supposed to get drunk at a wedding, Sam thought, surly again. *It's practically tradition. I just got a little head start on it.* He looked away from her. Annie hadn't used to be such a prig about it, either. She liked champagne, and he remembered the days when the two of them had put away a good deal of it together, laughing and scrambling after each other in her bed—and in a lot of other beds, too, halfway across Europe on their honeymoon. Since they'd come home, she had started to act as if she were his mother, and once his friends had found out that all the money was Annie's and that she was eleven years older than he was, too, they had started to make jokes about it.

Claudia and Howard were going back down the aisle, and Sam gave his arm to Annie. There was still the wedding dinner to get through. He had to do that much for his grandmother.

The Waldorf had outdone itself for Mrs. Brentwood, now Mrs. Locke, who had lived there for over two years in one of its most expensive suites and who tipped lavishly. Now she and Eden would go to live in Mr. Locke's brownstone on Madison Avenue. Management and staff had agreed among themselves that she should be sent off with a splash. The gas lamps were turned low, and in the center of each candlelit table a profusion of roses in a silver epergne spilled its blooms across the snowy linen.

Turtle soup was followed by veal cutlets and fresh peas. Then a wedding cake personally baked by the hotel's head pastry chef was carried out for the guests' admiration. A fine cabernet was followed by an equally spectacular French champagne while a string quartet in the background provided a buoyant undercurrent to the conversation.

The gathering had the air of a family party. Howard Locke had numerous children, grandchildren, and great-grandchildren, and all attended his nuptials. An old army man, he had never been able to spend as much time with his own children as he had wanted, and so, in his old age, he took delight in surrounding himself with these younger generations.

Janessa Lawrence laid her napkin in her lap and beamed sentimentally at the bride while the children fidgeted as quietly as they were capable of and waited for the cake. "Claudia, this is without a doubt the best dinner I have had in ages and the happiest occasion. Dad and Alexandra were so sorry they couldn't get away, but they send their love."

Claudia chuckled. "Enmeshed in political machinations, no doubt. Just tell him not to fight any more duels."

Janessa laughed, too. "Dad was horribly embarrassed about that. It wasn't his idea. He was challenged by an old flame's husband."

Claudia sipped her champagne, then asked her new husband, "You see what you have married into? Embarrassed, indeed! In my opinion, Toby did it because it was almost the only dangerous thing that he hadn't done yet. I knew his father, and Toby's just like him. Janessa comes of very stalwart stock—stubborn, too."

"It's been inherited," Charley said, grinning at Janessa, who was seated across the table from him. She responded by wrinkling her nose at him.

Howard's relatives regarded Janessa with patent curiosity. A woman doctor was enough of an oddity. One who spent her time on the government payroll fighting epidemics was nearly beyond their ken.

Janessa didn't appear to mind. She had become accustomed to being viewed by Claudia's upper-crust acquaintances with the same astonishment they might have accorded a two-headed calf. She turned to Sam, who was seated next to her, and said quietly, "I'm sorry not to see Andy. Is Lydia no better?"

"As compared to what?" Sam asked. "Lydia in Independence, Missouri, is greatly better than Lydia in New York. We might look at it that way."

"I meant her health," Janessa said, but she supposed that Sam had a point. Lydia was not an asset to a party, being inclined to doleful pronouncements interspersed with acid exchanges with her stepson, with whom she had a long relationship of mutual loathing. Lydia's ceaseless mourning for her own long-dead son had effectively kept her from being any sort of mother to her stepson. Nor for that matter had Eden fared any better with her mother, which was why the girl was now living with Claudia.

"Physically Lydia's probably as strong as an ox," Sam muttered. "Or she couldn't sustain all the vapors and tantrums." He poured himself some more champagne. "Gran says that my father's thinking of taking her to some doctor who specializes in mental diseases. Your suggestion, I believe?"

"It was," Janessa confirmed. "Do you disapprove?"

"I don't give tuppence, to tell you the truth." Sam studied her over the rim of his glass. "Shocked, Janessa?"

"I'm rarely shocked," she said equably. "Particularly when people are hoping I will be." She studied Sam in return. He had always been the Brentwood family bad boy, expelled from three colleges and possessed of a restless energy that had never been inclined to translate itself into any sort of work. Even though married, it was rumored that he cut a wide swath among the women. He was undeniably handsome, with a rakish charm and the light of the devil in his eyes.

Sam smiled at her suddenly, and Janessa was aware that he was turning that charm on her. She remained unimpressed.

"Do you think this doctor can prove that it all stems from a bilious stomach," Sam inquired, "and prescribe a tonic for it?"

"We know very little about the causes of obsession," Janessa said. "I suppose a bilious stomach might be as good a guess as any, but I doubt it."

"Female hysterics, then. The phases of the moon?"

Janessa raised her eyebrows at him. "If you are attempting to shock me with indelicate references," she commented, "I suppose I ought to warn you that it can't be done—a medical education is great protection against that. It's a prevailing theory, of course, largely propounded by male doctors. But it does not take into account the appearance of insanity in males."

"That's easy to explain," Sam said. "Insanity in males is brought on by the presence of females. The urge to procreate, frustrated by layers of religion and whalebone."

"An interesting theory." Janessa noted the strangled expression on one of Howard Locke's middle-aged granddaughters to Sam's left and Annie's furious eyes on him from across the table. "But you're being very childish. Now be quiet and mind your tongue while they cut the cake, or I'll explain the symptoms of cholera to you, and you won't want any dessert."

"Of all the infantile, vulgar remarks!" Annie unpinned her hat and smacked it down on her dressing table so hard that the plumes quivered furiously. "You were practically reeling with drink—and then to start talking like that at the dinner table!"

"Oh, don't act like an old lady." Sam pulled his shoes off. "You didn't used to worry so much about being vulgar."

"I am well aware that your whole family thinks I'm vulgar," Annie said icily. "So I have done my best to learn to be different. I let you pick my clothes; I listen to the way your grandmother talks and try to talk like her—"

"That's right," Sam snarled. "You've remade yourself into a little schoolmarm. You want to whap my knuckles with a ruler?"

Annie glared at him. The lovely face that used to be so exuberant and carefree was pinched with fury. "At least I don't drink like a fish."

"Ah, now we're getting to it, aren't we? You're not mad because I brought up the unmentionable subject of sex, you're mad because I was drunk."

"You wouldn't have talked like that if you weren't drunk. You know that was a shocking thing to say. You were brought up in good society; you know it better than I do. That wasn't some bar in Virginia City."

"Well, maybe I liked you better in Virginia City. You weren't so mealymouthed."

"You weren't drunk all the time!"

"You weren't acting like my mother!"

"I wasn't married to you then."

"And now you are. Well, God help us both, the collar is getting a little tight."

"Sam—"

"Please, Mama, can I have my allowance? Oh, thank you, Mama. Now I'll run away and play while you see to business."

"What do you want, Sam? A hand in my business? It's all investments, and you know you haven't any head for money. Why don't you learn to run your own family's business if you're so hot to be responsible?"

"Oh, no," Sam said. "Not allowed to. Bad, willful Sam is not to be trusted."

"Your father would give you a job in the shipping company if you asked him. You know he would."

Sam laughed sardonically and flung himself back in the chair. "Sweeping floors in the warehouse? Dad believes in a fellow's working his way up. Thank you, no."

Annie snatched her nightdress out of the bureau and banged the drawer shut.

Sam stood up. "You want me to unhook you?" His voice was a little slurred, but he wasn't too drunk nor too angry to be amorous. In fact, both conditions were inclined to increase his desire. Many of their arguments ended in bed, and neither one of them was ever sure, as they made love, that they weren't still fighting.

Annie tucked the nightdress under one arm. "Not tonight." She marched into the adjoining bathroom and banged that door shut, too.

A few minutes later she heard the heavy thud of the apartment door. Sam and she maintained a suite next door to the one lately occupied by Claudia. Annie came out of the bathroom, unhooked her own dress with considerable contortions, shook it out, and hung it in the big cherry wardrobe. The maid could have done it in the morning, but all the years of poverty Annie had suffered before she and her late first husband had hit a silver strike in the Comstock Lode had taught her to be careful with what she owned. This attitude had something to do, too, with why she had tied up her money so that Sam couldn't touch it. As she pulled the silk and lace nightgown over her head, Annie wondered if Sam would be happier with her if she had no money. Her mouth twisted. Like hell he would. He wouldn't have married her in the first place if she hadn't been rich.

Annie climbed into bed, but she didn't turn out the light. Instead she sat with her arms around her knees and looked at the big, fancy hotel bedroom. They had lived here for over two years, but it didn't look like home. Home was a house with all your own furniture and children. Annie sighed. She hadn't gotten pregnant yet, so maybe she wasn't ever going to. And with the state that things were in, it was probably just as well.

You ought to leave him, said a voice in the back of her mind. *Forget about how it would look and what his family would think. He'd be relieved.* Annie lay her head on her knees. She could even get a divorce—Lord knew Sam had given her plenty of grounds. She tried to picture herself actually going to see a lawyer and explaining that Sam fooled around with other women. The lawyer would demand proof, probably sending a detective to follow Sam. All to pull Sam's ring off her finger. All to say: Here's an end to hope. Here's what you get for marrying younger than you, for thinking it was just for fun and companionship and someone to take you around in high society. Here's what you get for thinking you wouldn't fall in love.

The music hall was as dim and smoky as the devil's antechamber, to which, Sam thought, waxing drunkenly poetic, it bore a certain resemblance. Cowes, the bouncer, could certainly have had horns underneath his bowler hat, and the muscular forearms folded across his chest could have wielded a pitchfork with the best of them. The girls on the stage, feet tapping automatically, smiles fixed—eyes fixed, too, on nothing—were as chained to their dreary lives as any sinner in hell. They welcomed new customers with the blank, glazed smiles of drug users.

Leaving a quarter on the table, Sam stood, then started up the stairs, where there were further temptations for souls tumbling along the rolling road to purgatory. With enough whiskey in him, a man could almost convince himself that sin was fun.

"Mr. Brentwood." One of Cowes's minions, a boy in his teens with bad teeth and the pasty look of premature dissipation, ushered him into the gambling room. Beyond the far tables a roulette wheel spun, black then red then black, clicking money out of the fingers of the foolish and unwary. It was rigged, Sam knew, but tonight he didn't care. Gambling was a way of passing time, confirming the convictions that everyone already held about him. He wanted to get back at Annie for not trusting him. Annie liked to be right, he thought savagely. Fine—he would give her proof. Bad Sam, losing his allowance. Well, if you don't like it, go jump in the lake; there's a price for being right.

The evening passed at the roulette wheel to the sound of click, click, and clatter, and the flashing, spinning red and black. His whiskey bottle was almost drained, his pockets nearly empty. Lolly, a girl from the music hall downstairs, clung to his arm, her eyes on his last ten dollars.

Sam put his arm around her and felt her lean against him, stumbling a little in her high, tight shoes. She smelled like smoke and whiskey.

She tugged him away from the table and led him to a room with a dented brass bed, an old, beat-up dresser, and a rag rug. The window shade had half fallen down and canted at an angle, allowing a view of the back wall of the tenement next door and dingy scraps of laundry on a line.

"S'a pigsty." Sam's eyes were bright and dark as polished marbles. He flung the window open and looked out. "City of the dead."

"You didn't mind last time."

He turned to face her, hands resting on the windowsill behind him. "I don't mind now. Just commenting on the decor."

Lolly didn't say anything, and soon he was pulling her dress off her shoulders.

"Careful! You'll tear it."

"Buy you a new one," Sam said stubbornly. The material split down the front as he pushed her onto the bed.

Sam woke in the morning to find himself still in Lolly's bed. She was trying to stitch up the tear in her dress and was near tears over it.

"Aw, hell," Sam said, pushing his hair out of his face. "Did I do that?"

"You said you'd buy me a new one," Lolly muttered.

Sam groaned. His head ached, and there was a horrible taste in his mouth. Annie would be as mad as fire. He sat up, and his head throbbed excruciatingly, pain pounding behind his eyes. He staggered to the dresser, found some water in the pitcher, poured it into the basin, and stuck his head in it. He heard Lolly leave, but in a minute she came back and put a tall glass of whiskey in his hand.

"Hair of the dog."

Sam took a swallow. The room turned blurry for a minute and then righted again.

"You look like you've been dug up," Lolly said.

"I couldn't feel this bad if I were dead," Sam groaned. "Must be alive." He drained the glass of whiskey and then took a drink from the pitcher.

"You said you'd buy me a dress, but you ain't got any money left."

"Checked, did you?" Sam pulled his pants on.

"I wasn't gonna roll you," Lolly protested indignantly.

"Just enough for the dress. You don't know what it's like not to have no money!" She flung the words at him as she pointed at the stained and torn taffeta dress on the bed. "I can't work in that. Bill's gonna kill me."

"Wasn't much to start with, was it?"

"It's all I got for work!"

Sam shrugged. He was beginning to feel comfortably drunk again, and the headache was fading, buffered by whiskey. *And I don't know what it's like not to have money?* he thought viciously. Now he would go home, hat in hand to Annie, and she would preach him a sermon. The hell with her, he thought. He might as well be hung for a sheep as a lamb.

"All right," he said, feeling vindictive. "I'll buy you a dress. But you have to come with me."

Lolly grabbed her handbag and followed Sam down the stairs.

Bill, the boss, was eating breakfast at the bar. "Where you going?" he said to Lolly. "You know you're not supposed to go out with customers in the daytime."

"We're going shopping," Sam said. "She had, uh, kind of an accident to her dress last night. Least I can do is get her a new one."

"Just pay me for it." Bill held out his hand.

Sam grinned. "Can't do that. Got to put it on my store account." He pulled his pockets inside out for proof.

"Put it on your bill and bring it back here," Bill said insistently. He stood up and pushed away his plate of steak and eggs. "She ain't going out with you."

Sam took a step forward. "Afraid she'll get her hands on some money you won't get a piece of? Afraid she won't come back? And you so kind to her and all?"

"Sam, don't." Lolly edged backward toward the stairs.

Sam glanced around the room and noted that Cowes, the bouncer, was off duty. "No fat-faced Irish pimp gives me orders."

Bill came around the bar with a roar. "I'm gonna shove your teeth down your throat. Lolly, get upstairs."

Sam dodged behind a table. "Irish pimp," he said again, since it had gotten such satisfactory results the first time. This time it produced a light of pure rage in the other man's eyes. Bill launched himself at Sam, swinging furiously, and his first blow sent Sam sprawling.

Maybe I should have left the Irish out of it, Sam thought, picking himself up and diving for cover. Bill came after him again, while Lolly shrieked from the stairs. Doors were popping open on the second floor, and other girls, wrapped in dirty kimonos, peered over the banister.

Bill swung again, and Sam managed to duck. He hit Bill solidly in the stomach and nearly broke his hand. Bill merely grunted and came after him, his big fists balled into mallets. He caught Sam with a clip on the shoulder, and Sam felt as if he had been kicked by a mule. He fell, rolled under a table, and came up on the other side.

"I'll teach you to bad-mouth the Irish, rich boy." Bill overturned the table and lunged at Sam. Bill was built like a tree trunk and didn't seem to have lost any muscle to middle age, but Sam was more wiry. Bill's fist slammed into Sam again, who retaliated by kicking the other man in the stomach. Bill doubled over, providing Sam with enough time to heave himself away.

"Go get Cowes!" one of the girls upstairs shouted.

Lolly, still standing on the stairs, whirled around. "You stay where you're at, or I'll pull your eyes out!"

Bill came at Sam, swinging. Sam twisted and managed to land the other man a good one across the ear, but Bill hit him anyway. Sam knew he wasn't going to win. In about another minute Bill was going to put him in the hospital, at best. Bill might also kill him. The pimp wouldn't think about the police and a murder charge until later, at which point he would dump Sam's body in an alley, and the girls would be too scared to tell on him.

Bill roared again and came at him, and Sam kicked at him desperately. Bill stumbled, and they fell into the wreckage of the overturned table. Sam jumped up first, a broken-off table leg in his hand.

Bill was just rising when Sam swung it. He was sixty pounds lighter than Bill, and he was drunk, but he had once played a fair game of sandlot baseball. The table leg connected with Bill's skull with a crack that dropped him like a fallen tree.

Sam grabbed Lolly's hand and pulled her out the door. They ran for a block and then slowed when no one came after them.

"Bill used to be a boxer," Lolly said, panting. "You could'a got killed."

"Yeah," Sam said ruefully. "That occurred to me." He got his breath back and rocked a little on the balls of his feet, shaking out aching muscles. Since Bill hadn't killed him and since he was still drunk, he felt pretty good. The sun was shining, and Lolly was looking at him with admiration.

She was a pretty thing, Sam thought, even in a shabby, badly made day dress. And she gazed at him with a look that Annie never bothered to give him, as if he were some kind of hero.

Sam smiled at her while she patted his clothes into place and brushed the dust off as well as she could, and then he held his arm out to her in a formal gesture. "Let us go shopping."

"You really mean it?"

"My dear, I just paid for the privilege."

He took her to Broadway, to the Ladies' Mile, where Annie had an account in every store. He took a vengeful satisfaction in charging to his wife's account a Chinese shawl, an extravagant hat of straw and shirred silk, kid boots and gloves, and, worse yet, an embroidered petticoat and a silk chemise. It added to his satisfaction that the merchants were well acquainted with Mrs. Brentwood and were well aware that she was not the thin girl in shabby sateen who was accompanying the still formally clad Mr. Brentwood.

Emerging from one store, laden with packages, they encountered Mrs. Meigs, a friend of Claudia's. Sam, in a cloud of whiskey—Lolly and he had stopped for a drink or

two along the way, in bars that would give him credit—
raised his hat to Mrs. Meigs, and the matron stiffened in
horror.

Sam chuckled as she swept away, and Lolly and he
continued their erratic course, stopping for oysters and
champagne at Delmonico's, where Annie also had an
account and where the maître d' very nearly didn't let them
in.

"I don't like it here," Lolly muttered, noting the stares
of the other patrons. "You're making yourself a scandal."

"I am a scandal," Sam agreed. "Get told so all the
time." He finished the champagne, then signed the bill
with a flourish and a wink at the waiter. "And we still have
to buy you that dress."

For that they had to go into the less fashionable
shopping district where ready-made clothes were to be
had. It was nearly five o'clock by the time Sam had cajoled
one of these lesser merchants to send the bill home.

"You been real good to me," Lolly said, looking at him
uncertainly as they left. "I didn't want to say anything when
you were being so nice—"

"And while I was still buying?" Sam suggested.

Lolly wrapped her arms around her packages. "I never
had nice things. You know that. But—"

"But what?"

"But where am I gonna go?" The words spilled out, her
thin little face determined but afraid. "I can't go back to
Bill. He'd kill me sure. And he wouldn't let me keep them."
Her arms tightened again around the paper parcels.

"You've got some nice clothes now. Go get yourself a
job in a decent music hall where you don't have to sleep
with the customers."

"I got no place to live."

"Save a Chinaman's life, you own him forever," Sam
muttered.

"I ain't no Chinaman," Lolly said, bewildered.

"Well, I don't want to own you." Sam's eyes lit up as

another idea came to him from the whiskey. "I can get you some rent money, though. Come on."

"Where are we going?" Lolly trotted after him as he pulled her along by the wrist.

Sam didn't answer for a moment; he just let himself enjoy his private joke. It was a good one. He couldn't get the girl any money at the bank—the bank had standing orders not to give him any. "I'm going to take you home with me," he said finally, with a sudden cackle of laughter.

Lolly tried to pull back. "You can't do that!"

"Annie's going to the theater," Sam said doggedly. "I've got the place all to myself. We can celebrate your new wardrobe."

The risk of it rippled around the edges of his mind like electricity, exciting and dangerous. Why not? Mrs. Meigs would report in anyway. Might as well do it up right.

Lolly balked again outside the Waldorf Hotel, but Sam pushed her through the front doors while the doorman stared at them. They went up in the elevator, Lolly cringing in a corner and Sam whistling cheerfully.

He unlocked the door of his suite, and Lolly gaped at its opulence and forgot her fear. Sam laughed. Everything looked very funny to him. He opened a cabinet and brought out a bottle of brandy and two glasses. He poured a splash in each and sat down at Annie's writing desk in the corner of the parlor. Her checkbook was in the pigeonhole where she always kept it, and Sam extracted it and picked up her fountain pen. He filled in the check with elaborate care, chuckling as he signed his wife's name. Annie didn't know he could duplicate her signature, but he'd been practicing. He blew on the ink to dry it—he didn't want to leave any evidence on the blotting paper—and decided the check ought to pass muster with the bank.

Lolly goggled at the signature, but she didn't say anything as she hurriedly stuffed it in her handbag.

Sam clinked his brandy glass against Lolly's and linked his elbow through hers so that they were drinking from each other's glass. Lolly giggled as Sam's glass shifted and more brandy went down than she had meant to swallow.

"You're awful," she said. "Are you always this bad and reckless?"

"Mad, bad, and dangerous to know," Sam said.

Lolly giggled again. "That's funny."

"Well, it's not original. A lady said it about Lord Byron."

"He a friend of yours?"

"Never mind. I educated one woman, and it got me a diamond poodle collar. I'm not going to start on you. I've got better things to do with you." He tickled her suddenly, and the brandy sloshed on the floor.

Lolly laughed. "I guess I owe you. Is the bedroom as pretty as the rest of this place? I never saw anything like this."

"Better," Sam murmured, his lips on her throat. "The bedroom's even better."

Within a minute, still dressed, they were on Annie's bed, the brandy bottle and glasses on the nightstand. It wasn't until the bedroom door had slammed shut with a crash that Sam jerked his head from Lolly's neck and spun around to confront the blazing eyes of his wife.

Drunk and defensive, he stared at her. "Why the hell aren't you at the theater?"

"I didn't feel well," Annie said in a monotone. "I stayed up most of last night waiting for you." Her voice broke suddenly into fury, and she picked up a picture frame and flung it at them. "In my *bed*, where you were going to tumble that *whore!*"

The frame missed them and shattered on the floor in an explosion of glass.

"Might as well tumble somebody in it," Sam snarled, "since you weren't interested."

Annie looked around for something else to throw, and Lolly, terrified and in tears, picked up her parcels and ran out of the suite.

"Get *out!*" Annie hurled an onyx paperweight after

her, which gouged a chunk out of the closing door. She picked up an inkpot and threw it at Sam, followed by a brass candlesnuffer from the mantel.

"Now, Annie—"

"You go to hell, Sam Brentwood! If I had a gun, I'd shoot you! I won't stay here another minute. You've humiliated me in front of the entire hotel, bringing that whore in. I hope you *rot!*" She snatched up her purse and as an afterthought the checkbook from the writing desk. He followed her through the parlor. She spun around, slapped him with vicious intensity across the face, and went on to the door.

"I'll send the porters up to clear out my things," was her parting shot. "And you'd better stay out of their way!"

Sam stood trying to get his breath back, his hand to his face. She wasn't supposed to be home, he thought angrily. And what right did she have to keep him from having any fun? He stumbled a little, more than half drunk, with adrenaline fueling his anger. Damn her. She'd be back. He snatched up a whiskey bottle, went back into the bedroom, slumped into a chair, and stared at the floor. The wreckage of the picture frame lay near his foot. Under the shards of smashed glass, his own portrait looked back at him.

He was still looking at it when the porters came in with an empty handcart.

Sam woke in the morning to find himself sprawled on the parlor rug, the drained brandy bottle beside him.

He sat up gingerly, and memories of the previous evening came back to him. He got up and stood uncertainly in the middle of the half-empty room, then staggered into the bedroom. The wardrobe gaped open, bare of all but his own clothes. Annie's dressing table was barren. *Well, that's that,* he thought. He felt no sadness, only a sense of relief. What they had both known was coming had happened.

"I hope you rot, too," he muttered. "Go drown in your money." He went into the bathroom, ran a tub of hot water, and swore because Annie had taken the bath brush, too.

II

Independence, Missouri, August 1891

Sam's father, Andrew Brentwood, looked at his wife with despair. He felt uncharacteristically baffled and ineffectual, wrestling with Lydia's demons in the big, old home that had been built by his parents to house a happy family.

"Mr. Brentwood, I cannot tell you that she will not try to do it again." The doctor looked up from Lydia's bedside and shook his head. "She is out of danger for now. That is all I can tell you."

Lydia's eyes were still closed, and her breathing was deep and even. The fine blond hair around her forehead was damp. Hattie, the housekeeper, had bathed her and washed away the sweat and vomit. An overdose of laudanum, the doctor had said. It had been a very near thing.

Feeling nearly dead himself, in mind as well as body, Andy wiped a hand across his forehead. "Thank you, Doctor. I'm grateful."

There wasn't very much else that could be said, although the thought brushed across his mind—and was pushed away immediately—that if Lydia had wanted death that badly, they should have let her have it.

After Andy had escorted the doctor to the front door, he walked into the front parlor and sat down stiffly, like a mechanical soldier. How had the love of their youth come to this tragic and foolish middle age? They *had* loved each other—of that alone was he certain now.

Andy had been a young army officer, recently widowed, attached to the American embassy in Switzerland. Lydia was the wife of a minor German duke with a connection to the Hapsburgs. The duke had a frail constitution and as a result could do little more than pursue his interests in literature and art. An elderly uncle, the Count von Lautzenberg, watched over the household, dealing with the daily matters that were beyond the duke's strength and keeping an eye on the duke's lovely young wife. Lydia had been married far too young to a man she had barely met, as was the way among the old European nobility, in an arrangement founded upon a careful matching of their respective pedigrees. Still, she was reasonably fond of her husband. Her longing for something more had not surfaced until she met Andy.

After that they were both lost. The old count, Machiavellian and family proud, had seen it coming and chose not to stop it because there must be an heir. And if the husband was incapable, the count was willing—as Andy had realized too late—to give the handsome young American a few months' amusement as a stud fee. The old man had never taken love into account; that emotion was for peasants.

When Franz was born, Andy and Lydia were consumed with guilt because they knew that he was Andy's son. The old man admitted knowing that, but his sole concern was that no one else should come by the knowledge. A year later the duke died, and Count von Lautzenberg planned to send Franz to the Hapsburg court to be raised. His mother was no longer a necessity but a liability.

She was free to marry Andy now, the old count had said, and to go with him to America . . . or to go home to her parents in Rumania.

We tried, Andy thought. *God knows we tried.* First they had kidnapped the child but had been caught, and the child was taken away. Andy and Lydia were lucky to have been expelled from Switzerland, not killed. Once in America, Andy, with his numerous connections, had pulled every string he could and spent untold amounts of money on European lawyers—all with no result. Eden had been born into the midst of this and became a neglected child while her mother tried to get Franz back. And Sam, eager at first to have this pretty young woman as his stepmother, had been totally ignored. Gradually his feelings changed into anger and resentment. .

Andy knew all this now, knew that Lydia had been obsessed with the child, and he had been obsessed with Lydia. Hindsight was a fine thing, but it didn't put cracked lives back together. By the time Franz died in Germany of scarlet fever, Lydia was too immersed in her own guilt to let him go. She transformed the house into a perpetual temple of mourning to Franz, then she became an imperious invalid who railed at Andy, even as she clung to him, for deserting her every time he left the house and for having brought her to a horrible and uncouth country.

Somewhere along the way, love had become duty to Andy, a strangling responsibility laid on him by his own conscience. Forced to resign from the army because Lydia couldn't be left alone, he had taken up the position at the head of the Brentwood Shipping Company, which had been founded by his father. He had gone to the office, come home, pampered Lydia with everything she asked for, and tried desperately to make up to her what could not be made up. Andy slowly came to realize that his wife had gone mad and that his son and daughter were lost to him. He himself had become a piece of machinery, putting one foot in front of the other, all emotions shut down in order to shield himself against Lydia's constant, irrational demands. That had worked reasonably well as a method of getting through the day until this afternoon, when he had come home for lunch and found Lydia sprawled in the parlor with an empty pharmacist's bottle beside her.

Andy stared into the dying fire and tried to sort out the complexities of his life. Was his anguish a punishment for the past—he was a reasonably religious man, but surely this torment was a harsh punishment for that long-ago sin of adultery—or only the consequence of Lydia's own nature, something bred into the beautiful child of aristocracy and privilege and triggered by a pain she wasn't strong enough to bear?

"Mr. Brentwood, you want anything else tonight?" Hattie, looking very somber, stood hesitantly by his chair.

"No, thank you. I'm only trying to figure things out."

"Mr. Brentwood, I'm sorry I wasn't there when—when she— I only went out to the market for a bit. . . ." She spread her hands in a helpless gesture.

"It's all right, Hattie. You couldn't know." Lydia regularly made her servants' lives miserable, but he thought that Hattie was genuinely concerned, and he was touched. "Nobody could have known, except maybe me—the more fool I. You go on home."

"All right, Mr. Brentwood." Hattie laid a hand on his shoulder. "It's always darkest before the dawn. Maybe she'll be glad to be alive now."

Would she be? Was there any way to give her back that joy in life? She had felt it once, and so had he. Perhaps the doctor that Janessa Lawrence had told his mother about could give it back. But maybe he couldn't. He was, however, their only hope. . . .

"Never!" Lydia's round blue eyes stared accusingly at her husband from her retreat in a wing chair in the parlor. She had her gloves and hat on, but she wasn't moving. She flattened herself against the chair. "You want to take me to this doctor so he can put me away in some asylum and you'll be rid of me! You should have let me die!"

"I don't want to be rid of you," Andy muttered. "I want our life to have some kind of sanity to it."

"Then you do think I'm insane." Lydia fluttered thin fingers at him, pushing away his unspoken accusation. "You all do. Your mother does, and that daughter of Toby Holt's. They don't understand. I'm not strong. They've never had grief to bear."

"They've had plenty of grief to bear," Andy said, trying to keep his voice level. "No one gets through life un-scathed, especially my mother, who's lost two husbands, and Janessa Lawrence, who lost her own mother under the most tragic circumstances."

"Janessa's mother was an Indian," Lydia retorted. "They are not a delicate race. They don't feel things as intensely as I do."

Andy's eyes flared. He took her by the wrist and pulled her from the chair. "You are coming. I've let this go on too long, and it was probably my fault from the start. You aren't strong enough to cope with things, and I should have seen that before I put you in a position where you had to. I was young and foolish, and I've paid for it ever since. But you are going to see this doctor. It's the only hope we have."

Lydia looked up at him, her eyes welling over with tears. "You hurt my wrist," she whimpered.

Andy let go of it. "Lydia, you drank a bottle of laudanum. What do you expect me to do? Just go on with my life, wondering if you're going to do it again?"

She walked to the window and stared out. It was raining, and the gray light outside made her seem even slimmer and more delicate than usual, frail enough to wash away in the rain. "I don't know," she said, and seemed really to be trying to give him an honest answer. "I thought if I could see Franz, I could explain to him why I left him."

"Lydia, for God's sake—" But he thought that perhaps she meant it. He also thought that before she took the laudanum she had pictured her husband weeping over her lifeless form, guilty forever, but there seemed little point in saying that. This time he took her gently by the wrist and walked her to the waiting carriage.

Dr. Freer removed his spectacles from his nose and polished them carefully. He adjusted them, put the tips of his fingers together, and studied Andy Brentwood while Andy fidgeted. He had been confined to the waiting room during Dr. Freer's interview with Lydia, and now Lydia was nowhere to be seen. The doctor billed himself as a specialist in disorders of the mind. But from Andy's point of view, the doctor was offering intangible cures for intangible diseases.

"Where is my wife?" he demanded finally, since Freer remained silent.

"Mrs. Brentwood is resting in the next room," Freer replied, folding his hands in his lap. "I thought it best that I speak with you alone."

"All right," Andy agreed. "What's wrong with her? I mean, I know what's wrong with her, but what can you do about it?"

Dr. Freer shook his head. "The study of disorders of the mind is not an exact science, Mr. Brentwood. I can give you no magic potion."

"Then what, if I may ask, am I paying you for?" Andy tried to keep the impatience out of his voice but without success. Now that he had made up his mind that Lydia should see Freer, he expected something from it—yea or nay, kill or cure.

"You are paying me for advice, Mr. Brentwood. For a diagnosis that may perhaps let you and your wife effect a cure."

"If I could have effected a cure, I would have done it!" Andy said. "For— All right, just tell me what you think I ought to do."

Dr. Freer put the tips of his fingers together again, a habit that Andy found maddening. "First I must tell you what the problem is."

"I know what the problem is!"

"Mr. Brentwood, please. Your wife's illness stems from a nervous constitution and a burden of guilt, as I am sure you have surmised. It also stems from a denial of the consequences of her own actions in succumbing to a physical desire that led her into adultery."

Andy looked at the floor, embarrassed.

"To have reached such a demoralized state preys on her mind," Freer continued. "Your wife's female psyche is delicate and, when sexual forces are brought into play, easily overset. Gently bred females have no sexuality unless they are naturally degenerate or, in this case, have a weak constitution of the mind, making them capable of being unnaturally aroused." Dr. Freer tapped his steepled fingers together again. "Did you say something, Mr. Brentwood?"

"I said 'hogwash,'" Andy said.

Dr. Freer smiled. "This is commonly accepted wisdom in my field, Mr. Brentwood. I sense a certain denial in your own attitude. Naturally, no man likes to think of his wife being capable of debased behavior, even if it is brought on by his own actions. However, *your* conscience is not of concern here. Mrs. Brentwood's difficulty is in admitting the actual loss of her child. Had it not been for the child, she might have recovered from the sexual shock to her psyche in the normal context of marriage—or at least found an outlet for unhealthy desires so that they did not derange her."

Andy glowered at him.

"Mr. Brentwood, if I am to help you, you will have to accept the truth of the human psyche as discovered by science and demonstrated by many men more learned than I. Let us get to practicalities. Your wife's maternal instinct, warped by her experiences, makes her unable to face the loss of the child, not only to his, er, supposed paternal relatives but to death. She is unwilling to admit the fact that he is now irretrievable. She *must* be brought to face that before she can hope to put the past behind her."

"That's the first intelligent thing you've said," Andy remarked. "How do you propose I do that?"

"By forcing her to face it literally," Freer said. "Take her to—Germany, I believe it is?—and bring her to the child's grave."

Andy sat up slowly. "I hadn't thought of that. Do you think it would work?" He hadn't a lot of confidence in Freer's diagnosis, but his suggested cure might still be a good one. And it was certainly more than he himself had been able to come up with.

"If I did not think it would work," Dr. Freer said, smiling slightly, "I would not have suggested it. Your wife, I might add, has given me her complete confidence."

"My wife would give you her complete confidence if you suggested self-flagellation," Andy snapped. "She's *trying* to punish herself. Why do you think she took laudanum?" He sighed. "And given her upbringing and the state she's in, she'd probably even swallow your damnfool theories about sex."

Dr. Freer stroked his chin whiskers. "Perhaps I understand women better than you think," he commented.

"I think it's possible to arrive at the truth through your muddle," Andy said. "I'll take her to Germany."

New York

Sam read the short, terse letter from his father, then tossed it in the wastebasket. He didn't know why the old man had bothered to tell him, since the only possible interest Sam could have in the venture was if his father took Lydia to Germany and left her there. A pity she hadn't drunk more laudanum, he thought vengefully.

He stood up and paced uncertainly about the suite, now littered with dirty clothes, a miscellany of empty bottles, playing cards, and overflowing ashtrays filled with cigarette stubs and half-smoked cigars. Dickie Merrill and a couple of other cronies had come over the previous evening for a poker game. Sam had won enough from them to pay the hotel bill awhile longer, and there were still plenty of things he could sell: a gold cigarette case, his signet ring, a set of diamond shirt studs. . . . Annie had been generous with her presents.

Maybe he would go out again that night, he thought. There was a new show at Weber and Fields that Dickie was hot to see. Dickie had telephoned earlier to sing its praises: "Best-looking chorus in town. Well-fed, long-stem beauties, and they're not above slipping out the stage door afterward for a drink, either."

Sam poked through the debris on the parlor table and found a stale biscuit in a dish. Moodily, he bit into it. *Fancy free, that's me*, he thought. *No more dog collar, and I still have money in my pockets*. So why wasn't it more fun? And what was he going to do to kill the afternoon until he could go out and not have fun? He looked at the mantel clock, but it had stopped because no one had bothered to wind it. He opened his pocket watch, and Annie's face stared back at him from the miniature frame inside the lid: smiling, beautiful, and with a glint in her eyes like granite.

Still looking at the watch, Sam sat down in a chair. He hadn't heard from Annie in a week, not since she had left. The porters, for five dollars apiece, had told him that they had taken her things to the Fifth Avenue Hotel.

The telephone rang, and he got up and lifted the receiver. It was only Dickie Merrill again.

"It's all set, old boy. Two of the little darlings are going to meet us afterward for dinner. Prettiest pair of the lot, too."

It didn't seem worth the trouble. "Count me out tonight," Sam said. "Maybe next time."

"Are you all right?" Dickie's asked, surprised. "You don't sound well."

"Maybe I'm coming down with something," Sam muttered.

"Well, put a mustard plaster on it," Dickie said. "Or a little champagne inside it. That's the ticket."

"Yeah, I'll do that."

"Well, the girls will be disappointed."

The girls would find another stage-door Johnny with no trouble, Sam thought. *Dime a dozen, that's me. Annie will find someone, too*, he supposed. The thought rolled over his mind like a wave of nausea, and he threw his head back, startled at the intensity of his reaction. *Oh, God, Annie . . .*

"I wasn't supposed to miss you!" he shouted at the empty room.

The hotel maid, coming in to clean, took one look at his

face and backed out again. Sam swept the debris of the previous night's game off the table with one arm, cards and ashes spilling to the floor.

Let her clean that up, he thought savagely.

Annie . . .   She wasn't coming back, or she would have returned by now. And he wasn't fool enough to think that it wouldn't all start up again if she did. His father was taking Lydia to look at Franz's grave, in an attempt to cure her, but there wasn't any cure for Sam and Annie.

He found a whiskey bottle that, miraculously, still had something in it and took a swallow. Nausea receded into a faint ache and then numbness. Sam went into the bedroom, taking the bottle with him, and rummaged through his jewelry case. There was a pawnshop on Thirty-fourth Street that would give him enough for the shirt studs to buy a lot of whiskey. He couldn't think of anything else he wanted, except Annie.

He looked up at the mirror over the dresser. There were dark circles under his eyes. He picked up his hat and set it at a jaunty angle, mocking the reflection. "Good-time Sam," he said. "Always a barrel of laughs."

"Well, my dear, I just thought I ought to tell you, since Claudia is still in New Orleans with Mr. Locke and Eden—" Mrs. Meigs's voice came piercingly through the telephone receiver, and Janessa silently cursed the machine's invention. Normally she considered progress to be a boon, but not when it allowed Mrs. Meigs to call her and complain about Sam's deportment.

"Mrs. Meigs," Janessa said firmly, "it's really none of my business. I'm sure you'll report to Claudia when she comes home. And now I'm afraid I have a patient to see. Quite a distressing case—a form of plague, we think, very unpleasant in its last stages. I should advise you to stay indoors."

Mrs. Meigs rang off, and Charley raised his eyebrows. "Plague?" he inquired.

"A plague of gossip," Janessa said. "The old witch."

"I take it she was referring to your feckless courtesy cousin Sam?"

"He ought to be hung up by his thumbs," Janessa said, "but she's lost her mind if she thinks I'm going to go talk to him. Annie can do any hanging that's necessary. It sounds as if she already has. I hope they patch it up before Claudia gets home, but I honestly doubt it. I'm surprised Annie put up with it as long as she did."

"I imagine women might put up with a lot for a man who looks like Sam," Charley remarked.

Janessa inspected her husband's plain but pleasant square face, gray eyes, his unruly brown hair, and his compact, muscular body with its air of solidity. "Handsome is as handsome does," she remarked tartly. "I wouldn't be married to Sam for all the tea in China." She put her arms around her husband's waist and looked up at him affectionately. His shirtfront smelled faintly of carbolic acid. "Have I told you lately how glad I am to be married to you?"

"Not lately," Charley allowed.

"Well, I am. What if I'd gone completely crazy and married someone like Sam?"

"Such as dear old Brice?" Charley suggested.

Janessa tilted her head up and kissed the end of his nose. Brice, who had golden curls and Apollo's profile and who had jilted her years ago, was now making money hand over fist as a fashionable physician in Washington. Janessa believed that a woman had never had a luckier escape. "Dear old Brice wasn't even in the running," she said.

"So now you have me," Charley said. "Shall we go see patients, treading hand in hand together among the microbes?"

Janessa grinned. "I married you because you're so silly."

Charley's arms tightened a little around her. "That all?" he asked. He leaned down and kissed her.

"*Mmmm*. No. No, that's not all."

Charley inspected her. "Do you know that when you're feeling affectionate it does the oddest things to that nice straightforward Holt face? All the Cherokee in you seems to come out."

Janessa's lips formed a faint, secretive smile. "Elemental longings," she murmured. "Unexplored depths."

"Let's explore a little."

They were late for their hospital rounds and received a dressing-down from the chief of staff, tempered somewhat by his private amusement. Their sheepish expressions made it very plain what the doctors Lawrence had been up to.

From the porthole of Andrew Brentwood's stateroom, the North Atlantic Sea looked greasy with white foam as it rolled and swelled against the steel hull of the *Germania* with an unending motion that had reduced Lydia to quivering misery and made Andy wish he had not eaten breakfast. He would not have chosen a November crossing, but it had taken a full two months before he could arrange his business affairs to a point at which he could be comfortable leaving them in the hands of his vice-presidents for an extended period. And Lydia's life, he knew, might not be safe until spring, even with Hattie to stay by her every moment.

She was as thin as a wraith, and her eyes shone with a feverish blue glow that unnerved him. He didn't think she had eaten a full meal since they boarded the *Germania*, even though he had decided against the master's stateroom on one of his own company's sturdy cargo vessels in favor of the opulence and comfort of a Cunard liner. The cabin blazed with electric light, and there was a fresh bowl of hothouse roses on the table. Her face was shadowed with demons.

"Would you like to go out on deck?" he asked. "A breath of air always helps."

Lydia was lying, propped up with pillows on a berth, a lap robe across her legs. "No. I must just endure it."

"In God's name, why? You'll want a hair shirt next. Lydia, you must realize that what happened to Franz was . . . fate. We did everything we could. And you know he might well have died even if he had been with us. Scarlet fever isn't confined to Germany." They had been through it all so many times before. He looked at her without much hope. When she didn't answer, he said, "Lydia, if I could turn time back and do it differently, I would."

"If I could turn time back, I would not have lived out my life in an uncultured country where everyone hates me!" Lydia snapped.

Andy sighed. "They don't hate you. But you haven't made it very easy to love you," he said bluntly.

"Even you don't love me." Her voice was doleful and set his teeth on edge.

"I did," Andy said. "I do," he amended. "And you haven't lived out your life. We have a lot of good years ahead. And they could be happy years. Think of our daughter."

"Your mother has taken her away, just as the count took Franz."

Andy sighed. "We didn't do very well by Eden. Mother was right."

Lydia sat up straight and pushed the lap robe away. "You never loved Franz! You had Sam. You never cared that I had lost Franz!" Her voice was rising hysterically. "Well, see what Sam has become. And married to that *woman*! Bringing her to our house and flaunting her!"

Andy winced at the memory of what had probably been the most unpleasant Christmas of his life, when Sam had brought his bride home. Annie Malone, now Brentwood, was not the wife that even Andy, who was no snob, would have picked for his son: She was undeniably common, Sam's senior by more than a decade, and had, since her first marriage and widowhood, "seen life," as the ladies' journals phrased it. She had brought with her ten trunks of clothes that were still being talked about in conservative circles in Independence and unsuitable presents for Eden—notably a parrot, which had belonged to a miner

and had been taught to screech "Fire in the hole!" at
unnerving moments. Lydia had banished Eden to her room
for fear of corruption and taken to her own bed with a sick
headache in the most pointed manner possible. Sam and
Annie had not stayed long.

Andy ran his hands through his hair. "Annie has a good
heart," he muttered. He had learned that much by now.
"And Sam's our fault, too. He may be past reaching now,
and I blame myself for that. It was no way for him to grow
up, shunted aside while we were trying to get Franz back."

Lydia's eyes spilled over. "You didn't love him, did
you? Because he was a child of my—sin and degradation!"

"Oh, for Christ's sake!" Andy exploded. Lydia quailed,
and he tried to modulate his voice. "You've been listening
to that idiot Freer and his half-baked theories."

"Oohhh . . ." Lydia curled herself into a ball on the
berth, her moods as unpredictable as the rolling of the ship.
"You never loved him, but I loved him. Why won't you let
me go to my baby?"

"That's where I'm taking you," Andy said grimly,
almost to himself. Lydia wasn't listening. "I wish to God I
thought it would work."

He got up and put his coat and hat on. "I'm going out
for air," he said as gently as he could. "I'll be back soon."

The night air was icy outside on the promenade deck.
Wisps of cloud scudded before the wind, and the stars were
flung among them like the lights of distant houses. Andy
leaned against the rail and pounded his fists on it. Strollers
passed by him—a courting couple, an elderly gentleman
dressed in a greatcoat and puffing a cigar. On the deck
below, he could hear the notes of a concertina and the
laughing voices of dancers warming themselves to its
music.

What would happen when they actually got to Germany? he wondered. Unexpected tears, as cold and salty as
the sea spray, ran down his face for Franz, whom he had
loved. But it had been so long ago, and eventually their

desperate quest had obliterated all feeling but determination. What would Lydia do when actually faced with his grave? It was a gamble; Freer had admitted as much. Andy wished that the doctor, even with all his pompous, unproven theories, were there to tell him what to do next.

Repeated visions crossed his mind: Lydia, shocked to sanity, growing gradually well again, welcoming their daughter home, encouraging him to make his peace with Sam; Lydia, driven over the brink, mad and uncontrollable, being dragged back to the States in a straitjacket . . .

He looked up at the stars again as if their cold light might spell out some answer. As the ship rolled, the salt spray lashed his face. The wind was coming up, and the sea was swelling. He turned to go in and saw a white figure slip like a ghost along the railing. In his despondent mood he almost thought it was a ghost—some past happiness fleeing from him. Then he lurched forward.

"Lydia!"

The figure turned toward him, waved him back, and began to climb the rail, her pale skirts gleaming in the moonlight.

"Lydia, no!" Andy began to run. The ship rolled, pitching him from side to side. He heard someone screaming at the other end of the deck. He stretched out his hands, stumbling. He was too far away.

She scaled the top of the rail, then balanced precariously astride it, eyes turned to his, unspeaking. Then slowly she toppled over the side.

He reached her just in time to feel her skirt brush against his fingertips. People were rushing to the rail, shouting agitated queries and orders at each other.

"What is it?"

"She's gone overboard! A woman's gone overboard!"

Andy snatched a life preserver hanging from the railing and hurled it, its tether line uncoiling into the darkness. Lydia was floundering in the water, buoyed up for the moment by air trapped in her heavy skirts and petticoats—a tangle of clothing that would sink her as soon as it was wet through. People were still shouting orders, and a ship's officer had appeared. The steady clatter of the engines slowed and stopped, and a siren was shrilling.

The ship's officer was ordering a boat lowered, but Andy knew it would not be in time. Already Lydia was slipping away in the liner's wake into the icy darkness. Her white skirts floated eerily on the water. She made no move toward the life preserver and might not have been able to grasp it in that frigid water if she had wanted to.

Oh, God. Andy looked up for a moment at the night sky, some desperate, unspoken prayer on his lips. She had wanted death, and he knew how much easier his life would be if she found it. And who would blame him in that raging North Atlantic sea for leaving her rescue to the ship's crew, who knew their business?

But with an agonized cry he tore off his coat and ran to the stern. Hands pulled at his arms.

"Get back, sir!"

"You'll drown for sure."

The lifeboat was halfway down the side. Lydia was only a pale splotch, like a pool of moonlight on the water, the spreading skirts beginning to sink around her.

"Get *back!*" Someone tried to drag him from the rail, and he lashed out at the unseen face before climbing over the side. If Lydia drowned it would be an unutterable relief to him. And because he knew that, he could not let her, could not face his God in some later judgment if he let her drown.

Andy pushed himself from the railing and dropped into the water. The sea was frigid beyond bearing, and he surfaced nearly numb with shock. Desperately he began to swim toward that floating patch of white. The lifeboat was behind him. The roaring sea buffeted him, slashing his face with icy water and forcing it down his throat. He choked and floundered, trying to make his limbs obey as his muscles cramped from the terrible cold.

The swell of the liner's wake rolled him under and lifted him again, eyes blinded with salt. He tried to see

Lydia but could see only the life preserver that someone had thrown to him. He put out a hand for it, but already his cramped muscles had gone numb and would not move. His hand brushed against something wet and as dank as seaweed, and Andy clutched at it; his hand entwined with Lydia's tresses. She lay facedown in the water, unmoving; a single pocket of air beneath her petticoats holding up the almost-weightless body. As the lifeboat struggled toward them, Andy tried to lift her from the water, but the swells rolled him under again, turning him over and over into the endless icy sea.

The ship's crew pulled Lydia's body from the water, and the other boats that had been lowered hunted on a zigzag course throughout the night, searching for her husband. At dawn they gave up.

"Fool," the captain said, shivering with cold. "Damn fool! What was he thinking of?"

"Of his wife," the chaplain said. "Poor man. He must have loved her very much."

They stood in a solemn group around Lydia's canvas-wrapped corpse, and the chaplain read from his prayer book. When the little ceremony was over, they committed her body back to the sea that had claimed Andy—and to the grave she had chosen for herself.

III

New York, November 1891

Three months' honeymoon in lighthearted New Orleans, bracketed at either end by the leisurely romance of a riverboat trip, had left Eden and Claudia both blissfully happy and, as Howard said, almost terminally lazy. The sultry, languid atmosphere of New Orleans had gotten under their skin. He beamed at them proudly as the carriage rolled up to his house—their house, now—and referred to them impartially as "my girls."

As the driver set the trunks down, a subdued housekeeper handed Claudia the telegram from Independence, where the news had been sent to Brentwood Shipping Company vice-presidents via transatlantic cable. "It came this morning, Mrs. Locke."

"I've put Eden to bed," Claudia said wearily. "I think she will sleep now."

Howard put his arm around her. "How is she taking it?"

"It's hard to say. I don't know whether or not she can honestly mourn her mother. And if she can't, of course, that will be dreadful for her, too. I know she's grieving for Andrew, despite the distance he put between them. My poor Andy. What a wasted life at the end."

Howard brushed the top of her head, his fingers

36

lingering on the white hair. "Perhaps not. He died doing a brave thing."

Claudia laid her head against his chest. "It's a fearful thing to outlive one's children. I remember him so well as a baby. Such a happy child." She straightened in the circle of his arm. "And now find me my cane, dear. I must go and tell Sam."

"Do you want me to go with you?"

"I do, but you mustn't. Eden may wake and need someone to comfort her."

"All right." Howard fetched the cane and her wrap and sent a maid for the coachman. He watched his wife with admiration as she stepped into the coach, her back straight and chin up under the glow of the streetlights. He was an old soldier, with two wars behind him, but he thought he had never known another soul as valiant as she. He climbed the steps again, a little short of breath with all that had happened, and then, more slowly, the stairs to the second floor to look in on Eden.

As he stood in the doorway watching her, he thought she was sleeping, but after a moment she opened her eyes and beckoned to him. He walked into the room and sat on the edge of her bed. She lay amid a tumble of lace-trimmed comforters and looked pathetically younger than her fourteen years, with her corn-colored hair skinned back into its nighttime braid. She had taken to bed with her an ancient rag doll that he had thought would have been long since consigned to the painted chest that held her cast-off toys.

"I thought you were sleeping, child."

"I couldn't." Eden bit her lip. "Grandpa Howard?"

"Yes?" He saw that her face was tear streaked.

"Grandpa Howard, is it a sin if you didn't love someone who you were supposed to?" she whispered.

Howard sighed. "No, dear, that's . . . life. Some people don't let you love them, I think. God doesn't hold it against you if you did your part."

"I tried to love Mama," Eden said. "It seems so wicked of me not to, now that she's dead. I miss Papa more, but I can't help thinking how he always put her first. Oh, Grandpa Howard, I feel terrible inside!"

She burst into tears. Howard put his arms around her and held her and did something that he himself had always considered a sin—he cursed the dead.

Sam let Claudia in. In her grief it took her a few moments to see that the suite was a shambles and that he was drunk. "Oh, Sam!"

"I wasn't expecting company," he said defensively. "Uh, sit down. You just get back?"

Claudia took a deep breath. It wasn't in her to rail at him for being drunk. "Sam, your father is dead."

Sam stopped in the midst of sweeping newspapers off the settee. Slowly he straightened up. "How did it happen?"

She told him as gently as she could manage and saw his mouth twist when she came to Lydia's part in it.

"He should have let that she-devil drown," he said viciously.

"Sam, don't. It won't do any good."

"Nor any harm." He moved restlessly but seemed half-shocked into sobriety. "How's Eden taking it?"

"Badly."

"Poor kid."

"I'm afraid she feels much as you do but has more conscience about it." She tried to gather her thoughts. "Sam, I've seen Andrew's will. There's a trust for Eden, but everything else, including his share of the company, goes to you." Sam closed his eyes for a moment, and she looked at him doubtfully. "Sam, where's Annie?"

"Visiting. Friends."

"You'll need her, Sam. Your father always managed the company. It has to be run, and I'm too old to do it. Andrew didn't expect you to have to, yet, and he hoped—"

"That I'd turn out better?" Sam suggested.

"Oh, don't, Sam. You know you've always been my darling, from the time you were a baby. You've taken the wrong road somewhere, but now you've got to turn back. I'll teach you as much as I can about the business, but Annie will help if you'll let her. You're going to need her."

He needed her all right, Sam thought, staring gloomily into the latest box of papers and accounts to arrive by insured express freight from Independence. The three vice-presidents wanted him to go there, and he supposed he would have to after Christmas, but in the meantime the three interim managers of Brentwood Shipping were sending him box after box of paperwork. He felt he was drowning in the minutiae of the shipping business: account books that he had to hire a bookkeeper to explain to him and yearly cost projections for everything from rivets and coal to dry-dock space and the salaries of the cook's boys. He was going to learn the business from the bottom up, the vice-presidents implied, and then if he let it slip through his fingers, as he knew they expected him to do, they wouldn't be blamed.

Ironically, the vice-presidents' clear expectation of his failure had accomplished something that his father had never achieved: Sam hadn't had a drink in three weeks, and he *was* learning. He was also learning that he hated it.

Andrew Brentwood had complained often enough that to be tied to a desk and account books was a burden, but Sam, with the blithe assumption of youth that parents never do anything they don't wish to, had paid no attention. Now he wondered just what it had cost his father to resign from the army for Lydia and stay home with the business.

Sam shoved the newest box aside and put his head down on the desk. What else hadn't he known about his father? Possibly quite a lot, it seemed to him, now that the knowing was beyond reach. Could there have been a reconciliation, or would his father have remained perpetually dissatisfied with him, as Lydia had been, simply because he wasn't Franz? There was no knowing now and no going back to ask, diving through those black waters with his unanswered questions. *"Full fathom five thy father lies; of his bones are coral made. . . ."* Sam turned his head toward the window, where a white December snow was falling, and began to cry.

"It's a risky proposition, Mr. Brentwood, and as I happened to be in New York," said Mr. Fingall, the eldest of the three vice-presidents, "I did feel the decision should be yours."

So it's my fault if the blasted deal lands us belly-up, Sam thought, but he knew that his father would have made the decision. "What about insurance?" he asked Fingall.

"I'm afraid that no one wants to insure livestock of such exorbitant value and in that delicate condition."

The livestock in question was racehorses, three of them mares well into foal, being shipped down the Mississippi from Minnesota to the Gulf of Mexico and on to Brazil by an owner who wanted Brentwood Shipping to bear the risk. But the breeder was willing to pay an astronomical shipping fee, and if the transport was successful, he promised a great deal of further business. And no, the owner was not willing to wait until spring—something to do with regulations and upcoming races.

"Oh, hell," Sam said, and ignored Fingall's raised eyebrows. He looked at his watch. He could call his grandmother and see what she thought, but he wasn't willing to do it under Fingall's beetle-browed gaze. "All right, do it," he said abruptly.

"If you're certain . . ." Fingall said.

"If you didn't want to ship the horses," Sam said, "you wouldn't have come here to ask me about it; you'd have turned him down. So do it."

When Fingall had departed, Sam looked at the latest set of account books and tried to figure how bad it would be if the horses were injured midvoyage. It made his head ache and he thought wistfully that Annie would have nosed through those account books like a beagle and told him a figure—*and* what the figure meant—in two minutes.

Annie . . . Whenever someone told him a joke, he

thought about how Annie would have laughed. While shopping for a Christmas present for Eden, he saw hats that would have suited Annie. He saw a dud of a play and knew how Annie would have described it; he rode through the full spectrum of autumn leaves and thought how Annie would have loved it.

Sober and with plenty of money in his pockets, he still missed Annie. Was there any way to tell her that it wasn't the money, it was her? And would she believe him if he did? It was not the kind of problem that Sam, in his wayward life, had ever wrestled with before, and he had his first drink in weeks to bolster his courage as he reached for a pen and notepaper.

Her answer, all of one line long and postmarked Virginia City, arrived on New Year's Day, and the paper was spattered with ink as if she had gouged it with the pen. *So much for auld lang syne*, he thought bitterly, and threw the crumpled note into the fire.

He was in a tricky mood when he arrived at his grandmother's house for New Year's dinner and took in her somber expression. He poured himself a cup of eggnog and added a stiff dollop of whiskey to it.

"Sam, I must talk to you privately. Please don't drink that."

He put the cup down and stared at her. There was more agony in her eyes than the last time he had seen her. Grief should be fading, not growing stronger. Or was it the season? It had been a dismal Christmas.

"Come in here before Eden sees you."

He followed her, wondering, into her sitting room and stood dutifully in front of the fire as she closed the door. She motioned him to sit.

"Sam, is Annie coming home soon?"

"Yes, I think so." *No, she's never coming home; how can I tell you that?*

"Thank goodness. There's been gossip, I know, but

people are dreadfully spiteful. Sam, I've got to lay another burden on you, and on Annie."

He looked closely at her and saw that her eyes were hollow and dark circled. For the first time he could remember, she looked her true age. "Gran—"

"It's Eden," Claudia said. "I want you to take her to live with you and Annie. No, hear me out. If I don't go ahead, I'll break down. Howard has a degenerative heart condition. He's been complaining of shortness of breath, and today the doctor—a dear, good man to come out on a holiday—became convinced of it. I don't grasp all the medical details, but we don't know how long he has." Her voice quavered, and she put her hands to her face for a moment. Howard's sapphire ring, the only item she wore that was not the dismal black of mourning, quivered on her finger. "I've been so happy with him."

"Does he know?" Sam whispered.

"Yes, but Eden doesn't yet. She loves him, Sam. I cannot bear to have her watch him die, not after losing her parents. And I'm nearly eighty-three. I want her guardians to be young, young enough to give her something to cling to."

"Gran, I'm not—"

"You are. I've watched you these last six weeks."

"Six weeks?" Sam stared at her, shaken. "Six weeks against how many years? What makes you think I'll stay sober?"

"You probably won't," Claudia said with a touch of her old spirit. "Not all the time. But I truly believe you've reached a turning point. Eden needs you, and maybe you need her. Responsibility seems to do you good. And she'll have Annie, too."

Sam groaned. "Gran, I can't—"

"You can. There's more, Sam. I am going to take Howard on an extended tour of Europe. We may not come back until—" Her voice broke. "He says . . . he says he has no wish to spend the time that's left being pushed around in a bath chair; that wasn't why he married me. It's what he wants. Thank the Lord he isn't in any pain."

Sam stared at her, then stared past her into the fire, trapped.

It was a dreadful dinner. Eden, looking wan and lifeless in a horrible black dress, must have sensed that something new was amiss. Claudia was determinedly matter-of-fact and cheerful, but her movements were quick and too brittle. Howard had a look of calm resignation, and Sam ate what was put before him mechanically, so that he might have been eating paste. After dinner they broke the news to Eden. Tentative plans were made: In two weeks Claudia and Howard would sail for England, and Sam and Eden would take a train for Independence.

Independence, 1892

"Miss Eden! Mr. Sam!" Hattie came down the steps as the carriage rolled up in front of the three-story frame house, wrapped around with a two-sided veranda and set above a sloping green lawn.

The front of the house looked shuttered and dismal. It wasn't much better inside. All the furniture was draped in dust sheets.

"I'd of had these off," Hattie said, "but you didn't say if you'd be staying."

Sam sighed. The house held no pleasant memories for him—and just now some very unpleasant ones—but his half sister had to have a solid footing somewhere. He'd decided that on the train.

"We're staying," he said, and saw Eden's stiff shoulders relax a little in relief. "And you can get that down, too," he said suddenly, pointing to the portrait of Franz, aged one, that hung above the parlor mantel, wreathed in dusty crepe.

"Yes, sir."

"And open those shutters. The place smells like a tomb."

"Mr. Sam, I got a home to go to. I couldn't be staying here all the time, not knowing if anyone was coming back to it."

"No, I know you couldn't. But for God's sake, let's let some life into the place."

"There'll be plenty of that," Hattie predicted, "when folks find out you're back."

"I didn't know I was so popular," Sam remarked. "I'd rather expected offers to ride me out of town on a rail."

"Your circumstances have changed some," Hattie said cryptically. "You'll find out."

The next morning the vice-presidents were lying in wait for Sam. As he stepped through the office door they encircled him, looking like octopi, waving contracts and bills of lading, round bespectacled eyes peering at him solemnly through clouds of ink. He spent the morning at his father's desk, feeling unpleasantly small for Andy's shoes. He made his escape at two and went home to find Eden sitting morosely in her mother's bedroom.

"You look awful," Sam said. "The first thing we have to do is get you out of those black dresses."

"I can't," she told him. "I have to wear them for a year."

"Well, they're hideous."

"Sam, don't you know anything? Maybe I can wear white or lavender by the summer, but not till then."

"You're too young to look like an old crow. I hate mourning," Sam muttered. He twitched the folds of crepe trim that added a further note of gloom to Eden's dress. "Are you sure?"

"I think so," Eden said doubtfully. "I wish Annie were here. I need some more stationery, too. There'll be more notes to answer now that we're home."

"Your mother must have had something you can use."

"It has to have a black border," Eden explained.

"Oh, for—"

"And I have to have some new—" she looked embarrassed—"well, chemises. I've outgrown all mine."

"Do they have to have a black border, too?" Sam demanded, exasperated.

"No, of course not."

"Well, maybe Hattie can take you." Sam went to find the housekeeper, encountered her coming up the stairs to fetch him, and explained the situation briefly.

"I got this house to straighten out," Hattie said. "You want some ladies' help with Eden, you got plenty in the parlor."

"What do you mean?"

"Ladies come to call on you and your sister," Hattie said. "I told you so."

Sam went back upstairs to tell Eden they had company. They came down to find the parlor inhabited by what appeared to Sam to be half the matrons in Independence, accompanied by their daughters. The mothers pressed his hand condolingly and called him "dear boy," while the daughters fluttered around Eden, sympathizing solemnly and casting bright-eyed glances over their shoulders at her half brother. All were older than Eden, girls in their first season or well beyond. There were several whom Sam distinctly remembered had not been permitted to dance with his wicked self some years before.

He wondered briefly if his new status as owner of Brentwood Shipping cast an aura of respectability about him, and then realized that it was also the absence of his wife that had brought out not only the mamas but also their hopeful daughters. The mothers sounded him out delicately.

"Mrs. Brentwood is not with you?" They tut-tutted and patted his hand. "Poor boy, such a dreadful time for you. But we're all so glad to have you among us again. Do you plan to reside here? I was saying to my Betty—she's just 'out,' you know—that we must do all we can to make you feel at home. And dear Eden, too, of course—Betty has always thought of her as a little sister."

They had all heard about Sam and Annie's separation, that much was plain, and there was no use in wondering how. Some matron either had a friend in New York or a cousin who had visited in Virginia City, and any news as interesting as Sam Brentwood's unsuitable wife's having left him would travel at top speed. He gathered that a divorce was considered imminent. Shocking, of course, but he was only a boy and was not to be held permanently to blame for youthful mistakes.

They stayed no more than the requisite fifteen minutes but departed with considerable groundwork having been laid. The restrictions on gentlemen during mourning were not so confining as those imposed upon women, and Sam found himself pressed with warm invitations to small teas, musicales—"dear Betty" or "dear Susan" was always scheduled to sing—and sleighing expeditions that "would do Eden so much good."

As winter faded into spring, Sam accepted all wholesome invitations extended to Eden and him, hopeful that the girl's spirits would lift. His experience of fifteen-year-old girls had been confined to putting mice in their desks when he had been fifteen, too. He couldn't tell what Eden wanted or should have, and as the months passed he felt himself on swampy ground when it came to her wardrobe and her schooling, the necessity for piano and art lessons, and whether she should be allowed to put up her hair, as she assured him—truthfully, he suspected—that it was quite permissible nowadays for a girl her age to do.

And she wasn't happy. She was thin, and her expression was often bereft and bewildered, despite the efforts of the older girls to make a pet of her and the introductions they offered to their own little sisters.

If I can't cope with her now, Sam thought desperately, *what am I going to do with her when she's old enough to court?* He narrowed his eyes at a pair of sixteen-year-old boys, guests at an afternoon picnic party, who were offering Eden a ride in their donkey cart. To Sam, they radiated illicit urges from every fiber of their adolescent bodies. He shot them both a look of warning, and they pulled uncomfortably at their collars and sat a little farther away from Eden on the cart's seat.

"Aren't they cute?" Susan Millhouse sat down beside him on the grass, carefully arranging her flowered muslin skirts. It was the first nice day of spring, and the girls' bright ginghams and muslins made Eden's black look drearier than ever. "Mama says," Susan confided, "that it would be quite proper for Eden to wear some plain light colors in June when it gets so hot. I'd be glad to take her to Mama's dressmaker. After all"—a musical laugh—"men can't be expected to understand all our feminine fripperies."

"That's nice of you," Sam said. *And how indebted do I want to be to you and your dear mama?* He looked at her sideways, and she flashed him a look that wasn't quite demure. *You're far too pretty.*

"I feel so restless," Susan said. "Spring always makes me feel that way."

She had the look of a girl who could be inveigled into a walk behind the summerhouse, and Sam thought he could kiss her if he wanted to—and probably a little more than that. No one even inquired about Annie anymore, and he thought that most of the hopeful mamas had consulted their respective husbands on the intricacies and probable timetable of the expected divorce. So far he hadn't had any word from Annie about that, but he knew he would hear from her about it eventually. He was as sure of that as Susan and her mama were.

Since that was the case, why shouldn't he kiss a willing girl behind the summerhouse? Because, he thought wearily, if he did, he would either end up engaged to her or create a scandal that would affect Eden. Those same reasons had kept him from going out at night looking for even more willing and less respectable company. Sam shifted uncomfortably on the ground. He had never put a curb on his physical impulses before, and he was finding it something of a trial.

Eden regarded her brother thoughtfully as they rode home in their carriage through the gathering dusk.

"Sam?"

"Yes, honey?"

"Why are all those girls flirting with you?"

"Don't be silly," Sam said grumpily. "They aren't flirting with me."

"Yes, they are," Eden said. "And they're all being just as nicey-nice to me as they can, and I can't abide it. Don't they know you're married? I told Susan Millhouse you were married, and she looked at me as if I were stupid."

"Don't pay any attention to Susan Millhouse," Sam said. "She wants to take you shopping, though," he added. "Her mother says it's all right for you to go into colors in June. I guess you'd better let her. *I* don't know anything."

"Annie can take me shopping when she gets here." Eden looked at Sam's face to see how that registered.

He didn't say anything.

Eden's expression turned sad. "Annie isn't coming, is she, Sam?"

"No, I guess she's not," Sam admitted. "I didn't have the nerve to tell Gran."

"What did you do to her?" Eden demanded.

"I am not," Sam said distinctly, "going to discuss my marriage with a fifteen-year-old."

"You went out with other women," Eden said knowledgeably. "I bet that was it."

Sam pulled his hat over his eyes. "There was a little more to it than that," he muttered. Then he turned and looked at Eden. "And don't ask."

Eden sat at the desk in her bedroom and chewed the end of her pencil. She was supposed to be studying French irregular verbs, but the book spread open on the desk was

Miss Evangeline Esmond's *Etiquette for All Occasions*.
Under the heading of "Correspondence," Miss Esmond had
a great deal to say on the choice of stationery, acceptable
and unacceptable uses of the postal card, and the proper
address for persons of title, but she was understandably
silent on the question of how to ask one's sister-in-law to
return to one's brother. In Miss Esmond's world, social
controversies of that sort apparently did not exist.

Eden's wastepaper basket was full of balled-up attempts to plead Sam's case, and she flung the latest effort
irritably after them. There was no way to cast Sam as an
innocent penitent and not lie through her teeth, and Eden
knew it. With quick decision, she took another sheet of
stationery from the box and picked up her fountain pen—a
pen was so much more definite. She might as well just tell
the truth and see what would come of it, Eden decided.
That was what her grandmother always advised.

> Dear Annie,
>   I am writing to ask you to come home to us in
> Independence. You probably know that Papa and
> Mama are dead, but now there is worse. Grandpa
> Howard is very ill, and Gran has sent me to live
> with Sam. I miss you dreadfully, and I know that
> Sam does, too, because he was too ashamed of
> himself to tell Gran that you left. Also because
> everybody in Independence thinks that you are
> going to divorce Sam, and all the girls are making
> eyes at him, but he doesn't seem interested in
> them. Maybe you could come for a little while and
> see what you think about it.
>
>   All my love,
>   Eden

"Mrs. Brentwood's here." Hattie made the announcement from the doorway with a theatricality that she might
ordinarily have reserved for the news that the kitchen was
on fire.

Sam looked up from the dinner table in confusion. "Gran?"

Hattie shook her head, and Eden's eyes blazed with delight.

"Annie!" Eden pushed her chair back and shot out of the room to hurl herself at the woman in the parlor. "Oh, Annie, you came!"

"Of course I came," Annie said briskly, but then she dropped her handbag and pulled Eden to her. "Of course I did," she murmured. She looked over Eden's shoulder and met Sam's eyes. He was standing in the doorway, his napkin still in his hand. "I will talk to you later," she told him. "In the meantime, you might ask Mrs. Bellow"—she nodded at Hattie—"to make up a room for me."

"Make up a room for you?" Sam grimaced at Annie when they were eventually alone in the parlor, Eden having gone ecstatically but reluctantly to bed. "Do I take it from that that I owe your presence purely to my sister's machinations?"

"You do," Annie said. Hattie had provided them with a tray of sherry and biscuits, and Annie poured herself a glass, then raised a questioning eyebrow at Sam.

"No, I don't want any."

"You'll strain something, Sam, if you put on airs for me," Annie commented.

"Damn it, Annie—"

"You listen to me," she said. "I am here because I feel desperately sorry for Eden with all the losses she has endured, and I can't square it with my conscience to leave her to be brought up by a drunken idiot who'll fill the house with chorus girls and not pay any attention to her."

"I do pay attention to her!" Sam said, stung. "She's going to school, and she has the right clothes and—"

"Yes, I gathered that you've had plenty of help with that. But she doesn't seem to fancy any of your admirers as a confidante. I suppose *you're* going to talk to her about female matters and tell her the facts of life and so on?"

Annie raised her eyebrows at him again in sarcastic question.

"God forbid," Sam said, shuddering. "I've had enough to do trying to learn about clothes and music lessons and how much she ought to put in the plate at church. And there haven't been any chorus girls," he added, harkening back to her earlier accusation. "I haven't had time."

"You won't have time now, either," Annie said, "if I'm going to stay. This is for Eden, and you needn't think she doesn't notice things. She's nearly grown now, and she's not a nincompoop. If you don't behave like a saint, I'll make you sorry you were ever born."

Sam slumped in his chair. "This is for Eden?" he inquired. "Just for Eden?" He smiled slowly, his mouth curving into the old rakish grin. "Don't I get some reward for all this rectitude?"

He thought he saw her waver for a moment, but then she pushed herself firmly back into her chair. "I wouldn't touch you with a barge pole. And if you have any ideas about slipping into my room some night to try to change my mind, I'll split your skull open with the poker."

"Well, that's frank," Sam snapped, the smile gone. "And how long am I supposed to behave like a monk under your benign tutelage?"

"Until Eden is grown and married," Annie said. "And furthermore, she isn't to know that. She needs a stable home right now more than either of us needs our freedom. After she's married, you can do as you please."

"What if she's an old maid?" Sam asked.

Annie smiled finally. "I don't think you need to worry. Have you looked at her lately? She's a beautiful young lady."

Sam stood up. "Fine. All right. Whatever you say. I know Eden needs you, so I don't suppose I have much choice. What a delightful time we're going to have for the next few years, to be sure." He stalked out, his shoulders rigid. But when he got to his bedroom, he cast a lingering look at the open door of Annie's room across the hall, where Hattie was unpacking her trunk.

She's back! he thought jubilantly. And he'd get around her. He'd always been able to get around Annie before.

The Brentwoods appeared in church the following morning and caused a wave of comment that hummed down every telephone line in Independence. Mrs. Millhouse called up Mrs. Cleery, and dear Susan and dear Betty ruthlessly directed their little sisters to attend that evening's ice-cream social and pump Eden for information.

While they were doing so, their mamas formed ranks to assess the situation.

"How nice to see you in Independence, Mrs. Brentwood." Mrs. Cleery handed Annie a dish of strawberry ice cream. "Will you be staying with us long?"

Annie inspected Mrs. Cleery and Mrs. Cleery's daughter, who hovered just within earshot. "That remains to be seen," she said.

Sam escorted his wife a few paces away and looked at the ice cream with a wicked grin. "Better not eat it," he said. "It might be poisoned."

Eden joined them. "Adelaide Millhouse says Susan and her mother and father had a terrible fight this afternoon. Her father said he *told* her mother she should have had more sense, and Susan was yelling that now she looked like a fool, and it was her mother's fault if she ended up an old maid. Adelaide says she went up to her room and slammed the door and threw all her hair ribbons on the floor."

Annie glared at Sam, who appeared to be choking on his ice cream. "Adelaide Millhouse has no business gossiping about her sister," she said, since Sam seemed incapable of speech. "And neither do you." But she bestowed a charitable smile, touched with ill-concealed enjoyment, on the unfortunate Susan, who was across the room sulking.

"This won't do, Sam," Annie said at breakfast the next morning after Eden had departed for school.

Sam looked up from his newspaper without comment.
"Sam—"

"I heard you," he said. "I am awaiting your next edict."

Annie folded her napkin and laid it on the table. "I mean to try to get along with you, Sam. I'm sorry if I seem arbitrary." She bent over the table toward him. "But honest to God, you would try the patience of a saint!"

"Which you are not!"

"I never claimed to be. *I*, however, do not have hordes of disappointed suitors throwing their hair ribbons on the floor."

"I guess she's too juvenile for me at that," Sam said. "I like older women."

Annie didn't rise to the bait, although it appeared to cost her some effort.

"All right," Sam surrendered. "What won't do?"

"Independence. This isn't good for Eden. We meant to give her a stable homelife, and all we've done is get ourselves talked about."

"*You* left *me*," Sam pointed out.

"And you—" Annie bit her lip. "Never mind. I'm not going to sit here and fling spite at you. But we've got to go somewhere else. Eden's going to have a normal life if it kills me."

"It may kill us both." Sam hadn't had much sleep. He had lain awake, thinking about going to Annie's room last night, but he hadn't had the nerve. He glared at her, frustrated. "All right, where do you suggest we go?"

"I don't care," she said. "You have your company to think of. You decide that. As long as it's a fresh start. Not New York and not Virginia City."

Sam stared at her. "Anywhere else? My choice?" He looked at the newspaper again, then back at Annie.

"Anywhere."

"Hawaii," Sam said.

"*What?*"

"You said I could choose," Sam said. "Are you going to take it back?"

"No, but—"

"All right then, Hawaii. Look at this." He held out the travel pages to her. "Tropical paradise. No unpleasant associations. Americans are getting rich over there, planting sugarcane."

Annie blinked at him. "What about your company?"

"I hate my company," Sam said in a low voice, and the look in his eyes lent truth to that statement. "I loathe it. I have a squadron of vice-presidents waiting with bated breath for me to foul it up, and I'm going blind from reading account books and reports. I'm going to sell the damned thing."

"And you think there won't be any account books on a sugar plantation?" Annie asked. "You don't even know how to grow sugarcane. What makes you think you won't hate that, too?"

"I couldn't possibly hate it as much as I hate this," he replied. Suddenly he was possessed of a fierce desire, born that very minute, to pack up Annie and Eden and what few hopes he had left and go, to sink Brentwood Shipping—and his attempts to take over—as deep as the grave his father lay in.

Annie stared at him, taken aback. "Your money," she finally said faintly. "I don't know anything about sugar. We use your money, not mine."

Sam nodded. "My money."

IV

New York, June 1892

"They're going where?" Charley Lawrence burst into laughter at his wife's announcement. Janessa was a dedicated letter writer who kept her far-flung family in touch with one another, and as such she was always the first to know the news. Charley thought that this particular piece of information had stunned even Janessa. He shook his head in mock outrage. "Hawaii? As in the Sandwich Islands? Sam Brentwood misbehaves in the most spectacular fashion possible, then inherits a fortune and lands on a tropical beach in the Sandwich Islands? And where do we, practically models of rectitude, get sent?"

"Fargo, North Dakota!" Janessa burst out laughing, too. "Life isn't fair, chum." She sat in Charley's lap with a certain amount of care, since the chair he was occupying was as rickety as most of the furniture in their apartment near the Marine Hospital. They had been back for three days from a hellish stint with a cholera epidemic in Fargo and had only just unpacked and gotten the place put to rights. No amount of furniture polish, however, was going to make it appear palatial.

"We could go into private practice, you know," Janessa said. "You could be a swell and wear spats."

"No, I just like to grouse a little. We're doing some good, and there isn't a better opportunity anywhere to do field research." He looked at her seriously. "Unless *you* want to? Is it getting you down?" Charley was used to not having much money. His mother and his lawyer stepfather in Richmond were only moderately well-off, and Charley had paid his own way through medical school. Janessa, on the other hand, had from the time she was nine led a charmed life, at least financially, as the daughter of Toby Holt, one of the wealthiest men in Oregon. Even with some financial reverses a few years back, Toby kept a household that Charley could not hope to imitate. "What about it, Janessa? Are you sick to death of it?"

"No!" She looked horrified. "This is what *I* wanted to do. I just don't want you doing it for me and pining for, well, for the Sandwich Islands."

"If I'd wanted that, I would have married a Hawaiian," Charley said.

"Mmmm." Janessa looked at him sideways. "Instead you got a half-Cherokee. Which brings me to another subject. Dr. McCallum cornered me today in the hall and after a lot of hemming and hawing got around to saying he wants to send us out again this week."

"No wonder he cornered you," Charley said indignantly. "He knew what I'd have told him! We're supposed to get some leave." As commissioned officers in the Marine Hospital Service, a government corps that dealt far more often with landlocked epidemics than seamen's maladies, the Lawrences were supposed to go where they were sent. They were also supposed to have a break between assignments. "I hope you blasted his side-whiskers."

"I didn't," Janessa said ruefully. "There are extenuating circumstances, and he wanted me particularly."

"Indeed?"

"It's yellow fever. In the Cherokee settlement at Qualla Boundary in North Carolina. I can still speak a little Cherokee, and he thinks they might accept me more easily than other doctors. I gather the Cherokee have a certain amount of suspicion of government doctors."

"Not without reason, I imagine," Charley muttered.

More than fifty years before, the federal government had allowed the expulsion of most of the Cherokee from their native lands in the South, sending them along the Trail of Tears to Oklahoma. The eastern band of Cherokee in the Qualla Boundary were the few pitiful remnants of those who had managed to stay behind.

"They're my mother's people," Janessa said quietly, more to herself than to Charley, who had heard the story years before. "I never lived there, but that's where she came from. We lived in Memphis until she got sick and brought me to Dad."

Mary White Owl had been a Union nurse in a hospital in Washington, D.C. She and Toby Holt had had one of those brief wartime romances that so many people fell into in the chaos of those days. Toby had healed from his wound, departed, and never known that he had left Mary pregnant. Dying of tuberculosis nearly ten years later, Mary had taken Janessa to Toby in Oregon. Charley knew that Janessa could now barely remember her mother. He wondered how much that bothered her and began to suspect that it might be quite a lot.

"You want to go, don't you?" he asked.

"Yes, I do. My mother must not have had any close relatives, or she wouldn't have been desperate enough to take me all the way to Dad. All I know of being Cherokee is what I learned from her, and it's faded so. All these years, it's just been something in my blood that has made people sneer at me or think, 'Oh, how exotic,' but I haven't identified much with the Cherokee. These people are probably desperately poor, and I could so easily have been one of them."

"Instead of Toby Holt's daughter? Do you feel guilty about that?"

"Not guilty exactly, but . . ."

"Driven to make it up somehow?"

"Driven to find the other half of me, maybe," Janessa said. "Maybe I'm just curious. I don't know. I do know that I want to go."

"Then go we shall," Charley said.

"You don't mind?"

"It's my considered opinion that the Cherokee have had a raw deal and are owed a little doctoring by the government, your own unbalanced racial urges aside. Furthermore, I want to get my hands on another yellow-fever epidemic. If we could just pin down the cause of it, we could do more for medicine than anything since the discovery of the smallpox vaccination. Yellow fever has always been endemic to the South. When I was little I saw an epidemic lay Richmond flat. How far has this one spread?"

"Dr. McCallum says so far it's confined to the Cherokee population. The local authorities are in a swivet to get it stopped there. They're afraid of trouble erupting between the whites and the Cherokee if it spreads. People are brainless!" Janessa said angrily. "As if you could blame someone for catching yellow fever!"

"That won't be the only trouble we'll have if it spreads," Charley murmured. "If McCallum thinks the Cherokee will be recalcitrant and suspicious of the government, he hasn't met the white population in those mountains. And neither have you, my innocent little Oregonian."

Janessa thought about that for a moment, then nodded. "Qualla Boundary is in the Appalachians. That's where that woman Rosebay Ware, whose husband works for my brother Tim, comes from. Tim says it's a whole different world there."

"That it is," Charley agreed. "Some of the people who live in those mountain hollows are so isolated, you'd swear they hadn't seen the outside world since the seventeen hundreds. They're very proud, very individualistic; they keep to themselves, and God help the man who goes where he doesn't belong."

Janessa chuckled. "Sounds like parts of Richmond."

"Yankee snob," Charley said, unoffended. "Just you wait. It's the most beautiful country you ever saw, though. I'll give it that."

North Carolina, June 1892

As the train steamed south through the Shenandoah Valley and began to climb into the mountains, Janessa had to admit that Charley was right. The mountains were breathtaking—blue-green in the distance, and then, up close, a clear, brilliant emerald, splotched with the smoky clouds of mountain laurel in bloom. They had brought with them a third doctor, Steve Jurgen, who had been at medical school with the Lawrences, plus a team of five nurses and half a dozen orderlies. They would assess the situation and wire New York for more assistance if they thought it necessary. The youngest of the nurses, on her first assignment, peered out the open window, oblivious to the smoke and cinders.

"You'll blind yourself," Charley warned. "What on earth are you looking for?"

"An Indian. I want to see an Indian."

Janessa laughed. "Don't expect paint and feathers. They're going to look a lot like me. The Cherokee started intermarrying with white settlers a century ago, and they're very like them in their ways."

The young nurse, Eileen Riley, looked disappointed.

The train climbed higher into the mountains, switchbacking around hairpin curves and shooting like a bullet over the wooden trestles that spanned the gorges. The Appalachians were old mountains—not mountains at all by western standards, but atop a railroad trestle and traveling at sixty miles an hour, they seemed high enough.

Steve Jurgen, Janessa noted, was humming "The Wreck of the C&O," and she poked him. "Stop that."

The train rocketed off the trestle, and the group breathed a mutual sigh of relief.

"It looks very wild," Janessa said as the wheels shrieked and climbed another switchback, through green forests that appeared nearly untouched. Only the smoke of a chimney somewhere on a ridge above them proclaimed human habitation. "Charley, what do they do here? I mean, how do they make a living?"

"Subsistence farming mostly," he answered. "They hunt. They grow a little tobacco and corn." He grinned. "They make a fair amount of whiskey, legal and otherwise. Mainly otherwise."

"Not in Qualla Boundary, surely?" Whiskey was strictly illegal on Indian land, most Indians having, in the government's opinion, no tolerance for it and too much leisure time to drink it. Janessa's mother had said that it was an acknowledged problem among her people and was rooted in their despair.

"I expect it finds its way in," Charley said. "Drunken patients will be the least of our problems."

Janessa nodded. They all knew they were "whistling past the graveyard," talking of moonshine whiskey and the vagaries of the local economy—anything but yellow fever, the ancient dreaded "yellow jack," which turned its victims saffron, made them retch black vomit, and killed anywhere from twenty to eighty-five out of a hundred patients despite anything the doctors could do.

It came from no one knew where, up out of hell maybe, and stayed until the first frosts of fall. It jumped erratically from house to house, or even from town to town, only to return a few weeks later to its starting point and break out anew. No one could identify the bacillus that caused it, or if it even was a bacillus. Juan Carlos Finlay of Cuba claimed that mosquitoes were involved, but he was generally held to be a crank. Medical wisdom on prevention ranged from fumigating the house and possessions of the victims to burning the properties to the ground. Even more maddening, the disease seemed not to care whether one was clean or dirty, whether one hid in the house or went abroad, or even whether one touched or did not touch friends whose families had the disease. The doctors and their staff were well aware that at least one or two of their number would inevitably come down with it.

Steve Jurgen began to sing "The Wreck of the C&O" again, and no one stopped him.

The depot at Quallatown, on a spur line that looked as if it had not been repaired in years, was a boxy wooden building devoid of platform or any other amenities. A mail crane with a limp sack of mail on its arm arced over the cindered railbed, and a water tower loomed beyond it, throwing a long shadow over the tracks. The sun was going down blindingly just on the crest of the western mountains, and Janessa blinked in its glare and looked around for whoever had come to meet them.

It took a moment before she saw the woman in the depot doorway. She had dark and obviously Cherokee features, but her black hair was hidden under a scarf, and she wore a calico dress and apron of the sort that might be seen on any mountain woman. Eileen Riley was going to be disappointed, Janessa thought. Since there wasn't anyone else in sight except for the railroad crew unloading the medical team's baggage, Janessa assumed the woman to be their welcoming committee and took a few steps toward her.

"I am Dr. Lawrence." Janessa held out her hand, and the Cherokee woman took it dubiously. Up close Janessa could see that she was middle-aged, maybe older. It was hard to tell.

"I am Walini Smith," she announced in excellent English. "And the government agent told us the doctor was to be Cherokee."

At least she wasn't complaining that the doctor wasn't a man, Janessa thought. Many of the native practitioners among the Cherokee were women, and thank goodness for that. "I'm afraid you'll have to settle for me," Janessa said. "I am half-Cherokee. My mother was from this area. She named me Ka-nessa, Dawn Star," she added, stumbling a little over the no longer familiar pronunciation.

Walini seemed ready to make some retort to that, but she closed her mouth again and looked over Janessa's shoulder at Charley and Steve, who were coming to join them.

"This is my husband, Dr. Charles Lawrence," Janessa said. "And Dr. Steve Jurgen. We have also brought nurses and orderlies and sufficient tents for our housing and a field hospital for the worst cases. Are you—pardon me, but I have lived with my father, who is a white man, since I was nine, and I don't know your customs—are you in charge?"

Walini snorted. "I am not the chief. But the chief does not know medicine."

"And you do?" Janessa asked. Something in the older woman's face informed Janessa that she and this Cherokee "wise woman" might be going to butt heads.

"Not enough to cure yellow jack," Walini said. "Can you?"

"Cure it, no. But we can try to stop its spread and give the patients the best care possible. The rest is up to the strength of their constitutions."

"Very well, Ka-nessa. I have brought wagons. Can you drive a wagon? The man who drove it here will not be coming back with us."

"Certainly," Janessa said, deciding that if she had forgotten how, she would die trying to remember.

"When you have pitched your tents," Walini said, "the council will wish to speak with you."

"I don't doubt it," Janessa muttered.

Since the railroad crew considered their duty done when the baggage was off the train, the medical team pitched their belongings into the wagons, the orderlies carefully stowing the cases containing glass vials of medicine and Charley's precious microscope. Mercifully, Janessa was not called upon to make good on her claim that she could drive a mule team, since one of the orderlies, who appeared to have a way with mules, took over one of the wagons, with half the medical crew crowded into the back. The rest piled into the other, driven by Walini. Janessa sat beside the Cherokee woman, and they lurched over a rutted dirt road. The faint flowering of lights from scattered cabins could be seen in the distance. It was dark by the time they came to the field that had been set aside for them in the Cherokee town of Yellow Hill.

"We thought it better," Walini said, "to have the hospital within Qualla Boundary. Less trouble from outside that way, maybe."

"I thought that Quallatown was within Cherokee lands," Janessa said.

"It is, and it isn't," Walini said. "We are neither fish nor fowl here. Much like you."

Janessa thought she heard a faint chuckle in the darkness.

"No one knows quite what we are," Walini said. "We are citizens of North Carolina. We vote and pay taxes. We fought in the white man's War Between the States. On the losing side, naturally," she added with asperity. "Only, North Carolina will not *say* that we are citizens, except to collect our taxes, and the government in Washington puts us under its protection when it suits someone to meddle in our doings. No one knows what to do with us. But Qualla Boundary is tribal land, and Quallatown is Cherokee but not in Qualla Boundary."

"It sounds very confusing," Janessa ventured.

"It confuses the judges when some white man makes a claim to Cherokee land," Walini said. "They consider it unobliging of us not to have gone to Oklahoma when the rest of the Cherokee Nation did."

Walini brought the mules to a stop, and they found themselves on a flat common. Fireflies drifted lazily over the grass and in the trees that bordered it. They could hear from somewhere beyond the trees the faint whistle of a train passing, skirting the Oconaluftee River. The railroad company hadn't bothered with a depot at Yellow Hill. There was a half-moon in the sky, and by its light Janessa could see several men coming toward them.

"We will put your house tents here," Walini said, "and the hospital on the other side of the trees over there." She pointed. "We have no suitable buildings for so many people."

"That will be fine," Charley said, climbing down from the other wagon and stretching out his muscles. "It's better to be in the open, and a tent is cheaper to burn than a house when the epidemic is over."

He sighed, and Janessa knew what he was thinking: They didn't know whether it did any good to burn anything. They all felt as if they were fighting invisible devils.

"How bad is it now?" Charley asked. "How many cases do you have?"

"More than a hundred, counting those who have died. Probably more." Walini pressed the small of her back as if it ached. "Some of them don't send for anyone. They just stay at home and die."

"And you are treating all of these people yourself?"

Walini shrugged. "I am immune. I had yellow fever when I was small. There are others to help me, but not many. That is why we asked the government for you."

"All right. Let us get our tents pitched, and we'll make plans."

Walini motioned to the Indian men who had approached them silently, and they and the medical crew unloaded the wagons. They pitched the tents by lantern light, moving sleepily among the ropes: a tent for Charley and Janessa, one for Steve Jurgen, and two dormitory tents for the orderlies and the nurses. The latter looked longingly at their cots, but Janessa was having none of that. She climbed into the wagon that still held the bundled hospital tent and its supplies, and they climbed in behind her, grumbling.

"It has to go up tonight," Janessa told them, "or we'll be pitching it on top of patients in the morning." As soon as the people in outlying towns knew that the team was there, they would begin to bring their sick in a doleful and unending stream that would last as long as the epidemic.

Charley cradled his crated microscope between his knees. A smaller tent beside the hospital would serve as a laboratory annex. Hospital-service doctors were sent not only to cure but also to discover, and each epidemic brought the hope that this time its cause might be found and the disease vanquished.

They were reeling with weariness by the time the hospital tent was up, its cots and cupboards in place. Janessa took pity on her nurses and orderlies.

"Go to bed. We'll need you in the morning."

Eileen Riley looked at her dubiously. "What about you? There are circles under your eyes."

"Eventually," Janessa said. "Shoo—unless you want to hang around and gawk at Indians."

"I can gawk better in the daylight," Eileen replied. "Good night."

Steve and Charley came over, and the three doctors went to meet with Walini and what was plainly a tribal reception committee. Janessa hadn't tried to sort out the Cherokee men helping them with the tents, but now as they filed behind Walini into the lantern-lit hospital, she saw that they had been joined by several others, presumably the tribal elders—"elder" being a term of respect rather than necessarily one of age. Stillwell Saunooka, the principal chief of the eastern band, was only middle-aged, and a number of the councilmen were younger. The Reverend Nimrod Jackson of Big Cove didn't look much more than thirty and would have been a tremendous disappointment to Eileen, since his hair was the color of Janessa's and his eyes were hazel. Joe Cheoah from Yellow Hill was about Jackson's age but plainly a full-blooded Cherokee, as was Wesley Calhoun of Bird Town.

Walini Smith introduced them all, and they greeted the doctors with expressions ranging from relief (Stillwell Saunooka) to suspicion (Joe Cheoah). Most of them spoke excellent English, with varying degrees of accent.

"You will stay as long as you are needed?" the chief asked.

"That is what we are here for," Janessa affirmed.

"What if the sickness spreads to the white towns?"

"We'll try to contain it, but that's always a possibility."

"You will need two hospitals then," Joe Cheoah muttered.

"Yellow fever has no interest in a person's ancestry, and neither have I!" Janessa snapped, irritated by his unfriendly glare.

"You will if the patients all try to kill one another," Cheoah said.

He did not elaborate, and Janessa looked at Walini, who, at any rate, was friendly. "Is it as bad as that between you and the whites?"

"It isn't the sickness only," Walini explained, giving Cheoah an aggravated look. "If they catch it, they will blame us, but it will only give them something else to be angry about. There are troubles over land just now, but it isn't something for you to worry about."

She would have to worry about it, Janessa thought, if it made all the Cherokee act like Joe Cheoah. She studied him surreptitiously while Charley and Steve Jurgen arranged with Stillwell Saunooka to let the outlying towns know that the doctors had come. Joe Cheoah was a handsome man by any race's standards. He had a strong-boned face and thick, straight black hair and dark mustache. His features were prominent and pleasing, and faintly piratical, as if he ought to have a gold ring in his ear. His speech was educated and without a trace of accent. Walini Smith had said he was a lawyer. He stood stolidly, arms folded, as Charley gave the chief a list of hygenic precautions that might help to arrest the disease.

"It's probably best if there is as little contact as possible between households. I would advise against any large public gatherings."

"What about the schools?" Joe Cheoah leaned forward now, challenging.

"I'd suspend classes," Charley suggested. "But that's up to you folks."

"Our children have to go to school!" Cheoah snapped. He turned to the chief. "If we are going to survive—"

"Do you have children of your own, Mr. Cheoah?" Janessa asked him.

"No. I am not married."

"Then perhaps you haven't got the right perspective to decide that question," she retorted.

Walini gave them both a look that she might have accorded to bad children. "If you argue with this man, Ka-nessa, you will be up all night, and he will still claim to have won."

"No doubt," Janessa said briskly. "We will be ready by seven in the morning. Any help that you and others with medical training can give us will be of great use."

She swept off, followed by Steve and Charley, who raised their eyebrows at each other and tried not to grin.

In their tent, Janessa set the lantern down on the camp table and drew the flaps. She began to unbutton the brass buttons of her uniform jacket and frowned into the mirror that hung from a post above the clothes trunk. She unknotted her tie and hung her braided cap, adorned with the hospital-service badge, on a nail.

"One of us has to go to the nearest white town and make sure they haven't had any cases there and let them know we're here," Charley said.

"You work it out," Janessa said irritably. "I'm only nominally in charge because I happen to speak Cherokee— as Dr. McCallum so painstakingly explained to you!"

"He's worried about my manly pride," Charley said. "Are you snapping at me because that Cheoah fellow got your dander up?"

"Probably," Janessa admitted. She hung her jacket up and stepped out of her heavy serge skirt. "Blast him. If there's trouble between the Cherokee and the whites, I'm willing to bet he hasn't helped it any. He's pigheaded and resentful and—"

"Probably thinks he's immune to yellow fever from sheer force of character," Charley said. "He strikes me as the forceful type."

"I don't like him because he doesn't like me," Janessa

muttered. "I'm too sleepy to be logical. In the morning I'll ignore him."

"Good," Charley approved. "Now will you come to bed?"

In the morning Janessa had ample opportunity to ignore Joe Cheoah. As the medical team made its way along the quarter-mile path that bordered the railroad spur line, they could see people already waiting for them, clustered around an assemblage of wagons and buggies. An old man on a mule held a small boy in his arms. A woman knelt at some distance from the others, heaving up black vomit into the dirt. Her skin, where Janessa could see it under the dark fall of hair, was a bright saffron color, and the two women who had accompanied her watched her fearfully. It was obvious that they had walked, for their feet and the hems of their ragged skirts were coated with dirt.

As the woman sat back on her haunches, shoulders shaking with the hiccups that also accompanied the disease, Janessa motioned to two of the orderlies to pick her up and take her into the hospital tent.

She was the first of an endless flow of the sick, some near death. Those who were capable of taking notice of their surroundings looked at the government doctors in their uniforms with mingled hope and fear, the latter allayed somewhat when Janessa spoke to them in halting Cherokee. At noon, with thirty-five patients in the hospital, she thought that the influx had ended. She nearly sobbed with despair when just as many arrived in the afternoon.

"They have found out you are Cherokee, Ka-nessa," Walini said. "So they come."

They were also sending for her, she soon discovered. There were families living in isolated hollows of the mountains, too ill or too far away to travel. At least every half an hour, a weary woman and man would arrive, or a solemn child, to say that Grandmam or Brother was sick and would the Cherokee doctor come? Always they asked for the Cherokee doctor. It seemed that Dr. McCallum had been right. How many would have come at all without the dubious assurance of her long-denied bloodline?

"They'll have to accept Charley or Steve," Janessa said desperately to Walini. "I can't go to all of them. You tell me which ones." She and the older woman would confer, and Walini would decide who would see any doctor if they were sick enough, who would see only the Cherokee doctor, no matter how thin her blood, and who might put more stock in their doctor's being male rather than a half-Cherokee woman. For the first time in her life, Janessa found herself actually grateful for that attitude. Using a map, they divided Qualla Boundary into three sectors according to the preponderance in the population of each category. Patients whose opinions placed them in the wrong district would have to put up with it, Janessa said brusquely, and Walini nodded. At six o'clock the doctors, each with a nurse accompanying them, set out to make home visits.

"You look like hell," Charley said. "Get back as soon as you can."

"You don't look so good yourself," Janessa muttered. She kissed him, and they went their separate ways.

Janessa watched Nurse Riley's face as they rode the horses provided for their use by the tribal council. Janessa's was an unprepossessing animal, with one blue eye and a piebald coat that looked as if someone had tossed a bucket of paint at it. Riley's wasn't much better.

Eileen Riley was all business now; in fact, she had never been as flighty as she looked. She held the small girl who had come to fetch them in the crook of her arm and handled the reins with her free hand.

"Lord, it's beautiful, isn't it?" Eileen asked as they ascended the trace that slanted up the mountain under overhanging oaks. The laurel blossoms glowed in the sun, and a redbird was chirruping on a branch.

Janessa nodded, glad for a moment of peace to soak up the cool greenness of the mountains. A little creek bubbled along beside them: Stillhouse Fork, the child had said.

The trace narrowed, and the horses' hooves clattered

on a tumble of rock. The little girl stuck her fingers in her mouth and gave a shrill whistle. A boy of fourteen dropped from an oak tree ten yards ahead with such swiftness that the horses snorted and Janessa jumped.

"I brought her," the girl said in Cherokee. "How is Mamaw?"

"Bad," the boy replied. He didn't say anything else, just ran ahead of them toward the house that came into view at the top of the trace. It was built of logs, with a pitched roof and a wide porch on which a bed had been made in the open for the old woman. A man sat beside the mattress, and Janessa, faintly startled, saw that it was Joe Cheoah.

"You took your time," he complained.

I am not going to quarrel with this man. "We have nearly seventy people in the hospital." She forced her voice to sound as even as possible, although she knew that it still had an edge to it.

"She is too old to move," Cheoah said. He spoke in English as his hand moved gently over the old woman's. Her eyes were closed, and Janessa couldn't tell if she even heard.

"Do you live here?"

He ignored the question. "She's my grandmother."

"Pap lives here," the little girl said. "Mostly." Her English wasn't as good as Joe's, but she had a pretty, clear voice.

"You bite your tongue, Lottie," the boy said to her in Cherokee, and Janessa decided not to ask where Pap was now. From the empty whiskey bottle under the porch, she had a reasonably good idea.

"These are my cousins," Joe muttered. "My uncle Walker's kids." He looked balefully at Janessa. "I tried to persuade her to move down from here, but she wouldn't have it," he said defensively. "She won't go to the hospital, either."

Janessa dismounted, unstrapped her bag from behind the saddle, and Eileen followed her. Joe Cheoah didn't move away, and Janessa knelt by the woman's other side. Her skin was chilly; the jaundice showed clearly even with her dark complexion. Her thin gray hair was lifeless, her pulse slow, and there was an overpowering odor of sickness surrounding her even in the open air.

When Janessa had examined her, she looked Joe Cheoah in the eyes. "She's very old and weak, and malnourished, I think. I can't tell you what the prognosis will be, but she needs to be kept clean and dry and given any nourishing food that she can hold down. Soups, meat broth, and juice if she can't hold down fruit. Protect her from extremes in temperature. Don't let anyone else eat off her dishes or use her bedding." Goaded and weary, she added, "And if you think these children should be in school, then don't let them come back here—one place or the other, but not both. We're trying to contain this." She slapped a mosquito off her wrist with more force than was necessary, partly out of a desire to slap Joe, and got up. "I have other patients to see now. I'll try to send a nurse to look at her again tomorrow."

He didn't answer. He just looked uncertainly at the children and then around him as if for someone else. Possibly Pap, whom Janessa surmised to be his uncle. Joe Cheoah struck her as almost a changeling in this mountain family, which might account for his bad temper. Whatever his views on progress and education, he didn't appear to have been able to instill them into his own family.

Janessa and Eileen mounted their horses. As they turned the horses around, Janessa looked over her shoulder. The little girl stood, bare toes turned in and her thumb in her mouth, waving away the bugs that swarmed in the hot, sticky air around the sick woman.

"Wait!" Cheoah shouted suddenly.

Janessa drew her rein and raised her eyebrows.

"I'll come with you."

"That isn't necessary."

Cheoah got up anyway. "You stay till your pap comes home," he told the boy. He began to trot down the trace toward Janessa. "This isn't the place for strangers to wander around in the dark," he said as he passed her and began to stride down the mountain. He didn't wait to hear what else she might have to say.

With twilight the woods became a place of almost impenetrable gloom, and the path seemed to vanish under their feet. Janessa gave up trying to see it and followed their guide's white shirt instead. She had to admit that without him they would probably have gotten lost. Charley's tales came back to her, of the mountains and of mountaineers who liked their privacy. She wondered what Cheoah thought they might stumble upon in the darkness, and the answer came to her as they forded Stillhouse Fork. The endeavor that had given the creek its name was probably still in existence, or somebody else's was, nearby.

At the foot of the trace, Cheoah left them. "I'm going to go back up and tell a few people you'll be bumbling around here for a while. That way you won't get shot by accident." Janessa thought he looked amused, but his face was half-masked by shadow.

"That is an impossible man," she said to the nurse as he vanished.

"He's very handsome," Eileen said thoughtfully.

"Hmmph!" Janessa dug her heels into the horse's flank. She hadn't been in a saddle in a long time, and she was riding astride, since the saddle did not offer any other options. The animal had a remarkably rough gait. In the morning she was going to feel as if the horse had ridden her.

They rode into the hospital encampment to find that Charley had returned before them and was now brooding over blood samples in the laboratory tent. Steve Jurgen was talking to a plump, gray-haired white man in a plain, black suit. The stranger rose as Janessa came in.

"This is Mr. Spray," Steve said. "He runs the Quaker school here. I met him over in Ela when I went to see if there have been any cases outside the Cherokee settlements."

"I went trying to talk some sense into hotheads, but as thee saw, Jurgen, it didn't take." Spray looked as if that hadn't surprised him.

"The usual outcome of trying to talk sense to hotheads, I'm afraid," Janessa said, with Joe Cheoah on her mind. "Were there any cases?"

"Not yet," Steve answered. "But I got the impression they're eagerly awaiting one so they can complain about it. But Mr. Spray here has come to help in the hospital."

"The tribal council has decided to close the school," Spray said. "So I thought to turn my hand to help where I could."

"They've closed the school?" Janessa goggled at him.

Spray nodded. "Joe Cheoah pushed the vote through."

The devil he did, Janessa thought. "I saw him today. He didn't tell me. His grandmother has the fever, I'm afraid."

"Poor old woman." Spray looked concerned. "No, I wouldn't think he would mention it. That's a strange family, and Joe isn't exactly forthcoming. I'm afraid thee may not be quite Cherokee enough for him, Dr. Lawrence."

"No, I suppose I'm learning that I'm hardly Cherokee at all anymore," Janessa said. "But Mr. Cheoah will just have to understand that my primary function here is that of a doctor."

Charley looked up from his microscope and gave Mr. Spray a tired grin. "She was the best the hospital service could do. We do have a one-eighth Apache," he added helpfully, "but the poor devil managed to catch malaria on assignment, and he's in the hospital in New York, feeling sorry for himself."

Spray smiled. "Thee have a dedicated service." Janessa thought he knew that they made light of catching what they had been sent to cure because there was no other way to deal with it. He looked at her admiringly. "And thee's a brave woman, Dr. Lawrence."

"I'm not," she said uncomfortably. "It's my job." She was beginning to feel that Mr. Spray was considerably braver than she was—and it wasn't his job. And that Joe Cheoah might be, too.

She thought of him, sitting in that desolate cabin with a dying grandmother, waiting for a drunken uncle to show up, if and when . . . balancing his tribe's health against its hope for the future, which was embodied in that school. She went to bed resolved to try to start off on a better foot with Joe Cheoah when she met him next.

V

"This is all they have, and you want to burn it!" Walini Smith stood in front of a cabin doorway, feet planted defensively on the sagging porch. They had, as Janessa had predicted, butted heads over hygiene. Walini was an incongruous picture, in work boots and a calico dress, with her long black hair hanging below her waist and an expression on her face that meant business.

"Extreme measures are the safest," Janessa explained again, but the pathetic cabin, with its buckling walls and its only living occupant staring at her miserably from the window, tore at her heart. "You could fumigate with sulfur instead," she said reluctantly. "But—"

"Is there any proof, have you and your husband with his microscope got any proof at all, that sulfur doesn't do as well?" Walini demanded.

They didn't have any proof that either worked at all—only that infection lingered somewhere, and the logical place was in the possessions of the dead.

When Janessa didn't answer, Walini said to the face in the window, "Burn the boy's bed and his clothes and smoke out the house with sulfur."

Janessa turned wearily away, and Walini called after her, "You have lived with white men too long, Ka-nessa. With rich white men."

Janessa spun around. "I didn't have any place else to go!"

Walini's expression softened. They had been working side by side all day, and worse, they had just lost the child that Janessa had been so sure would get well. His jaundice had even faded. But then his heart had stopped. They could hear the sobbing of his mother inside the cabin.

"Come," Walini said. She took Janessa's hand and pushed her into the buggy that the doctors used in town. "You need to eat. I'll give you food and some herbal tea that is good for the liver. Keeps it strong. We can't afford to lose you, Ka-nessa, and I want to talk with you."

Since they hadn't done anything for the last week but talk—or argue—over cases, Janessa looked at her curiously, but she let Walini take the reins and head the horse for the small log house where Walini lived in Yellow Hill. Despite their differences, she liked Walini, and to turn down food and a placatory gesture would be insufferably rude.

They spoke little during the ride. When they reached Walini's house, Janessa saw that the windows and door were thrown wide to let in any breeze. The herbs and dried plants hanging from the rafters were pungent in the heat, and the smell of them washed over Janessa like a wave, acrid and tinged with remembrance. Their shapes and colors hovered just on the edge of her conscious memory, and she was startled to feel tears well in her eyes.

As Walini turned away to put a kettle on the stove and poke up the fire, Janessa, with streaming eyes, half lifted her hands as if to touch the clusters of snakeroot and pokeberry leaves.

"What do you see, Ka-nessa?" Walini asked, turning.

"My mother's house," Janessa whispered. "I had almost forgotten."

"Tell me about your mother." Walini sat down, content to wait for the kettle to boil, and lit a corncob pipe. She put her boots on a footstool and looked at her guest with expectant eyes.

Janessa sat, too, and wiped her eyes with a handkerchief from her uniform jacket. A fine linen handkerchief, monogrammed JHL. Claudia Brentwood had sent her three dozen of them as a wedding present. Janessa cast her mind back to the days before linen handkerchiefs, to the days before she had, for that matter, possessed a last name to put on one.

"She was a medicine woman like you. She trained me, but I was only nine when she died, and there wasn't anyone to help me keep my memories fresh. My father lived in Portland, and I studied medicine with a wonderful old doctor there, but he didn't know Cherokee medicine, and gradually I just lost it."

"And how did you come to Portland, then? That is a very great distance."

"There was nowhere else to go." Somewhat to her surprise, Janessa began to tell Walini the whole story. "We lived in Memphis, you see. My mother didn't have any family left. She made a living for us, barely, as a midwife, and doctoring people's farm animals. No one would trust her to do more—a Cherokee woman with an illegitimate daughter who was all too plainly a white man's child. . . . When she knew she was dying, she took me to him. She died of tuberculosis. She knew what it was and knew she didn't have much time left."

The kettle boiled, and Walini rose and made tea. "And where is she buried?" The woman's voice sounded off-handed, but as she handed the cup to her guest, the tea slopped over the rim, splattering Janessa's already stained skirt. The heat seeped through her petticoats.

"On my father's ranch." The memory bit into her like the hot tea. "I didn't know how old she was. The stone just says 'Mary White Owl.'"

Walini bowed her head over her own cup. "I was going to ask you her name," she said after a moment, "but then I found that I couldn't, quite. She was my sister, Ka-nessa."

Janessa stared, trying to see something of her mother in the dark face bent above the cup, clawing through faded memory for that vanished image. "She couldn't have been. She had no family."

Walini looked up at that, dark eyes meeting Janessa's blue ones. "No one tells everything to a child of nine. Particularly if they don't *wish* to go home. Shall I finish the story for you, Ka-nessa? I've been nearly sure since you told me your name."

"Ka-nessa? Surely I can't be the only Cherokee child with that name." She found, with a kind of agonized frustration, that she both wanted to be Walini's niece and fervently hoped she wasn't. Her hands began to shake so much that she had to put the tea down on the table. It tasted dreadful, medicinal, and at the same time familiar. She could almost remember that taste . . . remember her mother, briskly stirring a pot with a whisk and listing its many benefits for a reluctant daughter whose face was screwed up into a grimace.

"Homecoming is a fearful thing." Walini seemed to have wrapped some control around her own emotions so that her voice had a story-telling tone that soothed and yet demanded to be heard. "A fearful thing, particularly if one is unprepared or rebellious and if the home is unyielding. Your mother couldn't do it."

Janessa realized that Walini was speaking not of her but of Mary White Owl.

"Mary was what the Yankees called her," Walini said, "when she went north to work in their hospital during the war. I said she was rebellious. She was two years older than I, and when she took a notion in her head, you couldn't dislodge it with a stick. Our men fought for the Confederacy, but Mary said when the federal government sent our people west on the Trail of Tears it was because the Southerners wanted it, not the Yankees. It was Southerners who had wanted our land, and so she decided to move to the North. It wasn't a popular notion. Our foothold in North Carolina was shaky then—as shaky as it is now—and we wanted mightily to prove we were loyal to the state. Our father tried to lock her up, but Mary went her own way, and we didn't see her for nearly a year. While our own boys were dying for lack of drugs that couldn't be smuggled through the Yankee blockade, Mary was aiding and abetting the enemy—or that's how it seemed to us then.

"At the end of a year she came home pregnant, and our father raged and roared around the house, and she raged and roared right back at him. He tried to make her marry—there was a man who wanted her, even with the baby. It was Joe Cheoah's father—he's dead now, too, poor man. But Mary wouldn't have him, wouldn't bend. She was prideful, you see, and thought he'd throw it up to her and wouldn't love the baby. She loved the baby's father and wouldn't speak a word against him, wouldn't be ashamed.

"It was like a battlefield in the house. You could hear her screaming at someone and them screaming at her every time they crossed paths. I thought she was wrong, but I was young then and sick to death with tending wounded men for our side. It all boiled up like a festering sore, and half the family wouldn't speak to her and the other half only to speak spite. After she had the baby—you, Ka-nessa—she lit out one night for Memphis, and never came home again. Our father never forgave her, but the rest of us, the young ones, didn't have enough spite to cling to, and it seemed like when Mary left she took some kind of life with her that we couldn't get back. Before she went north she'd been the gayest of us, the liveliest, the one who made things fun. In a few months I was crying my heart out for her, but I knew she wouldn't come back."

The room had grown dim with twilight, and a firefly was circling lazily about the pokeweed leaves, winking on and off, green-gold in the dusk.

What do you do, Janessa wondered, *when you find a family? What do they, poor souls, do when they find you?* And how many of them were there? Had she tended one and unknowingly watched him or her die in the last week?

She looked at Walini, a little frightened. "Do you want me to go away again? They'll send another doctor if you ask."

Walini shook her head. "No. You don't belong to us anymore, Ka-nessa, and maybe that's just as well, for you. But you are *of* us. We are half your blood. Stay and learn about us." She smiled crookedly. "And maybe you won't cry when you smell healing herbs again."

"How many of you are there?" Janessa asked tentatively, trying to envision unknown faces, cousins and uncles and aunts. "You're my *aunt*," she said, revelation sinking in. The Holts were a close-knit family, inclined to take in without question any who belonged to them, but this—

"You have," Walini said, counting on her fingers, "three cousins, an aunt-by-marriage, a great-uncle, several first cousins once removed, and five second cousins. Including the boy who just died."

"Oh, God." Janessa put her head to her hands.

"That was when I knew I had to tell you."

"Do the others know?" Janessa spoke through her fingers, not lifting her head.

"The ones who are old enough to remember. Now I will tell the rest."

So I can watch them slip through my fingers, Janessa thought, panicked, *like that boy today.* She remembered now: Walini had said that his father, dead already of the fever, had been Walini's cousin. A new thought came to her, as frightening as the first. "What if they don't want me?" she whispered.

"They have you," Walini said. "You have them. Blood is blood."

Janessa lifted her face and saw the other woman's eyes on her, troubled but determined. She hesitated a moment, and then she was at Walini's feet, her arms around her waist, holding her tightly, with Walini's dark curtain of hair falling around them both. Her own was coming out of its pins, absurdly pale against Walini's. She twisted some strands around her fingers and saw that Walini's was streaked with gray, the gray that her mother hadn't lived long enough to grow.

By the time Janessa returned to the hospital, she felt reassembled but precarious, as if the pins with which she had redone her hair were the only things holding her together. Loosen them and she might shatter into small pieces like glass breaking.

She found Charley in his laboratory, attempting to give yellow fever to guinea pigs while Elliot Spray, the Quaker schoolmaster, was looking over his shoulder. What Charley was trying couldn't be done, or at least no one else had ever been able to do it, but he kept at it, injecting the animals with blood and other bodily secretions taken from his patients. It was one of the infuriating factors of yellow-fever research: It didn't seem to affect anything but man, which left doctors with nothing to experiment on. Charley scooped a guinea pig out of its wicker basket and glared at it while it squealed at him in a temper.

"You could be a hero," he informed it, "if you weren't so healthy."

"And how does thee diagnose jaundice in a guinea pig?" Spray asked. He was eternally curious.

"You shave its stomach," Charley replied. Except for faint traces of soapsuds, the guinea pig's bare abdomen was maddeningly pink.

Janessa took Mr. Spray by the shoulders. "You oughtn't to be in here. It's not awfully safe."

"Only for guinea pigs," Charley muttered in disgust. "She's right, though. You take enough risks in the hospital."

"I suppose thee's right." Spray let Janessa hustle him out the tent door, but he looked back wistfully.

"I've never met anyone so curious," Charley said. "The man's a walking encyclopedia. He knows the darnedest stuff."

"Curiosity killed the cat," Janessa said. She slumped moodily into a chair. The tent looked odd to her suddenly, as if she were viewing it at some oblique and unfamiliar angle. "Charley . . ."

He looked up, eyes narrowed, focusing now on her distraught expression. "What's up?"

"I got more than I bargained for," Janessa said. "Walini is my mother's sister." She picked another guinea pig out of the basket and put it in her lap to play with, for something to do with her hands.

Charley stared at her. After a moment he put his own guinea pig away. "Good God," he murmured. "Here, don't play with those."

"If they can't get it from us, I doubt I'll get it from them."

"You'll mess up the control of the experiment," Charley said. "Twiddle your thumbs or something instead. Are you serious about Walini?"

Janessa nodded. "I don't think there's any doubt at all. She's been practically sure since I told her my name. I ought to be ecstatic over finding my family. I'm probably related to half the people in Qualla Boundary. But somehow I just feel numb. And sort of demented."

"Perfectly reasonable for someone who hasn't had any sleep in a week." Charley took the guinea pig out of her lap and put it back in the basket. "Get sick, blast you," he told it.

"Where's Steve?" Janessa tried to focus her mind on business, to prevent it from straying down new paths suddenly opened and possibly dangerous. This recent discovery could only be assimilated slowly, she felt. When she thought too hard about it, she wanted to cry again.

"Steve's gone to bed. He's on call tonight, so he's catching some sleep while he can." If there was a crisis with a patient, it almost always occurred in the small hours of the morning.

"I want to take a quick look in the hospital," Janessa said. She felt driven to see if she could sense who among the dying might now belong to her.

"I'll come with you." Charley seemed to sense her jagged mood.

Eileen Riley was on night duty, bathing a feverish woman's forehead in the dim glow of a turned-down lamp.

"All's quiet," the nurse murmured, "for now." Even in the grip of disease, the body's natural rhythms would eventually let the patients sleep, although some might not wake.

Janessa and Charley moved quietly between the rows of cots. The beds were draped for the night with filmy sheets of mosquito netting, their folds reflecting faint ribbons of lamplight so that the room might have been the lair of some giant, sleeping spider. There was no sound but the thin breathing of the sick and the insect chorus that screeched and buzzed in the summer night, outside the canvas walls. Janessa let the familiar hospital calm settle over her and attuned her senses to the business at hand. The panic-stricken urge to know who was her kin began to fade. They were all sick, all in her charge, and that was all that mattered. The rest she could deal with by daylight when the surrounding shadows weren't quite so thick.

They had nearly finished their rounds when the quiet was broken by Eileen's outraged voice.

"You can't come in here!" The nurse was at the door, trying to block entrance to a man far taller than she. He wore a dark suit and a bowler hat, and his shoes were polished and slick. His pale eyes slid over Eileen and scanned the darkened tent.

"Where's Dr. Lawrence?" he demanded.

"I'm Dr. Lawrence," Charley and Janessa said together, and Janessa added, "Will you be quiet? These people are sleeping!"

The man surveyed them both and decided on Charley. "Morton Briggs, Superior Coal Company." He held out his hand. "I want to know what you folks are doing to keep these Indians' diseases from spreading to the white folks. I got some worried people back in Ela."

Charley took his hand with every evidence of dislike.

"My wife is head of this team, not I. But you can be sure that we are doing everything we can."

"Glad to hear that." Briggs looked around. "Uh, you mind if we step back outside? I don't want to take any chances I don't have to. But I promised to look into it. When Superior promises to take care of folks, we keep our promise."

Charley and Janessa ushered him outside.

"Now, Dr. Lawrence—" he said to Charley.

"My wife is in charge, Mr. Briggs. Dr. Janessa Lawrence."

"That right? Well, well." Briggs tipped his hat. "Well, little lady, if you can give me some assurance that—"

Janessa was annoyed. Morton Briggs was too sleek, and his chubbiness was unappealing, like an underdone ham. She made a flying grab at her temper. "Mr. Briggs, I can't give you any assurances at all."

"Well, now, my company is going to want more help from the government than that. Aren't you folks supposed to be protecting us? Keeping these infected Indians confined? I saw two of them today in Ela, as bold as brass, including that savage who thinks he's a lawyer, and I'll tell you—"

"Your company? What exactly does your company have to do with this? Do you live in Ela?"

"You might say I've kind of settled in for a while. We've got plans for this part of the country—big plans. And your Indians have given us just about enough trouble. If they don't watch their step, things could get ugly. Just a word to the wise, little lady. You keep them locked up. It's for their own good."

"These people aren't criminals!" Janessa hissed, trying to keep her voice down. "They are sick, and if it spreads, it won't be anybody's fault but nature's. If you want to stay healthy, my best advice to you is *not* to settle in at Ela!"

"I've got business in Ela. And I'll be frank with you—these Indians up here have been a thorn in my side. We've tried to do right by them, but they're too dumb to know progress when it's offered. I've got white men eager for jobs down in Ela, and these Indians are holding it all up. It's bad enough having savages strutting around putting on airs. Now they're bringing in filth and disease. You keep them out of Ela, and you keep this sickness confined, or I won't answer for what happens!"

Janessa's temper boiled over. "Get out! If you show your face around my hospital again, I'll have you *thrown* out!"

Briggs shrugged. "I heard you were half-Indian, but you don't look it. Guess they were right, though." He tapped his hat more firmly on his head and mounted his horse. He glanced down at Charley. "You ought to keep her on a tighter rein, bud."

The horse cantered away into the darkness, and Janessa glared after it, quivering with fury.

"An unpleasant and porcine fellow," Charley commented, slipping an arm around her. "Do you want me to call him out for you?"

Janessa chuckled in spite of herself. "Oh, would that you could. . . . No, I'll just hope he breaks his neck in the dark. What do you suppose he's up to, he and his coal company?"

"As a guess," Charley said, "I'd suppose he smells coal in these mountains and wants to root for it. As another guess, I'd say he wants to do it on Cherokee land."

"That must be what Walini meant about troubles over land."

"If there's trouble, that would do it. My stepfather, who has thirty years as a lawyer to back him up, says that any suit can invariably be traced back to a grievance over someone's family, his dog, or a foot of land."

And how long could the Cherokee hold out against a big company? Janessa wondered. Her anger flared again, and with it a certain understanding dawned regarding Joe Cheoah's dislike and mistrust of anyone white. Over the past week, she had begun to see what Walini had meant by saying that these Cherokee were neither fish nor fowl. They

dressed like the white mountain folk of these parts, in many
cases spoke like them, and had many of the same concerns
in wresting a precarious agricultural living from the mountains. But they didn't look like the whites and weren't like
them. The Cherokee had adopted white ways very early in
the country's history, intermarrying, becoming landhold-
ers, and, in the more prosperous states farther south, even
slave owners before the Civil War. Tragically, this accul-
turation had gained them very little security when it came
to the white settlers' desire to take over their land, and now
the remaining Cherokee were torn between two factions:
those who felt that the whiter they looked and acted, the
better and more likely they were to be left alone; and those
like Joe Cheoah, who felt that their only hope lay in holding
to their Cherokee heritage, forcing the government to
make good on its promises, acquiring sufficient education to
accomplish this task for themselves, and trusting no one
else to do it for them. In these parts, that philosophy led to
some of the Cherokee having more education than most of
their white neighbors, and it wasn't surprising that there
were those among whites and Cherokee both who felt that
Joe was giving himself airs.

And what was she, Janessa wondered, in light of
Walini's revelation? Cherokee or white? Ka-nessa or Janessa?

"You're a doctor," Charley said when she repeated
some of her musings aloud to him.

"Meaning I should stay out of it?" Janessa asked.

"Yes, but you probably won't."

Janessa linked an arm through his and stared around
her at the dark bowl of the mountains. "I'm ignorant," she
said. "I don't know enough to butt in, even if they'd let me."

They walked slowly along the path back toward their
sleeping tent. Below was a sharp drop, the spur line that
ran toward Quallatown, hugging the mountain. Still farther
below, the Oconaluftee River flowed, and the rich scent of
water came up on the air, mingled with the cinder smell of
the railbed.

"I was born *here*," Janessa said suddenly. "Not in Memphis." Somehow that seemed as strange as all the rest of Walini's revelations put together. To have been here before, even unknowingly, seemed to provide a tie of blood to this piece of ground—her foot of land. It was to these mountains that her mother had come home, rebellious and unrepentant, to have her baby and quarrel with her father and leave again, never to return. According to Walini's calculations, Mary White Owl had been younger when she died than Janessa was now. How strange to be older than your mother.

She glanced uncertainly at Charley. How did he really feel about all this? When he had married her, he had bargained on the Holts for relatives. How did he feel about having the Cherokee of Qualla Boundary suddenly included in the equation not merely as a bloodline but in the flesh? It was impossible to tell.

We're all looking at each other, Janessa thought the next morning, as if we were exotic oddities, like the tigers in the zoo. There was, however, serious uncertainty as to which one of them was the tiger. Walini had spread the word, and cousins, second cousins, first cousins once removed, even the great-uncle had begun to appear at the hospital to have another look at this government doctor who was Mary White Owl's baby.

They seemed happy to see her, even the great-uncle, Wolf Mooney, who had been her grandfather's brother and was a Confederate veteran who held no great opinion of Mary White Owl's rebellious antics. He was a tall, gaunt reprobate, a gray-haired old man with a limp he had carried since the war. Wolf lived with his daughter Rebecca in a cabin far up on a fork of the Oconaluftee called Yowling Branch. He watched Janessa solemnly and said only, "It's time you came home," but Rebecca had baked her a cake.

Janessa began to write their names down in her journal, struggling to keep them straight. The relationships were as tangled as those of the Holt clan, complicated by the fact that among the Cherokee, marriage was often mainly a matter of mutual arrangement rather than a legal agreement, and the arrangements tended to change. Walini, she had learned, had two sons by different husbands, neither of whom she was married to now. One son was Wesley Calhoun, the councilman from Bird Town; the other was Parker Smith, whom Janessa had not met before, but who came down from his farm near Big Cove and went to the hospital tent to have a look at her.

He was a tall, rangy man, lighter skinned than his half brother, and wore tattered overalls and a slouch hat. He shook his head and said, "I hope Mother knows what she's doing, telling you all this."

"I don't see how she could not tell me," Janessa said. She was kneeling by the hospital door, washing her hands in a pail with carbolic soap. "Does the idea bother you?"

"Hell, no," Parker said. "I always figure the more kin the better. I just wasn't sure how you'd take to the lot of us. You don't strike me as a country girl. I hear your daddy's a senator in Washington."

Janessa laughed. She liked Parker. He was the most forthcoming of all of them. "My daddy's a country boy, if it comes to that. But you're right. This is new to me. You'll have to forgive my ignorance."

"You got the knowledge *we* need right now," Parker said, gesturing with his thumb at the hospital ward. "When this sickness is over, you bring your husband and the rest of them to a corn-shucking party, let us say thank you."

Janessa sighed. She stood up and wiped her hands on a clean towel. "We don't know as much as you think."

"You know more than we do," Parker said. "Even Mother can't do anything with yellow jack. We got to hang on here. It's all we got."

"There was a man here last night from Ela," Janessa said. "Somebody named Morton Briggs. He said he was with a coal company."

"Him." Parker spat. "The devil take him and the horse he rode in on. That company's got the whites all fired up,

promising them jobs and chicken every Sunday if the
company can mine coal out of these mountains. But Briggs
can't start up unless he can get our land, too, and the coal
company has been in court trying to prove we don't own it
legal. I don't understand land law. This was ours to start
with, and then we bought some of it again to make it
certain, but this company keeps going back to old records
and saying it can prove it's not ours or finding sales that
weren't written up right."

The air was heavy and oppressive, and a faint flash of
lightning blinked at them over the mountains. Parker put
his hat on. "I think I'll go dig in at Mother's—it's going to
storm. Don't you worry about Morton Briggs. He's our
problem. You just try to keep enough of us alive to fight
him."

Janessa watched him ride away as raindrops began to
spatter down and a crack of thunder shook the air. She
lashed down a flapping corner of the tent's front canopy.
The tents, wood floored and set up on high ground, could
weather a storm—it rained nearly every other day—but
this one seemed more ominous than most, rolling in on a
black sweep of cloud that was shot through with fire, ready
to set the mountains ablaze, burning like the coal that was
inside them would burn. Blast Morton Briggs and his
company! How could she not worry about him, now that
she knew what she knew? To come here as a doctor, to heal
and then leave—she could have done that yesterday morning, not now.

Another horseman was riding through the gathering
storm, and Janessa, oblivious to the weather, shielded her
eyes and stared through the rain. It was Joe Cheoah, his
dripping hat pulled low over his eyes. He was leading the
piebald horse that Janessa rode on her rounds.

"I need you!" he shouted. "Mamaw's worse, and I think
Lottie has it, too. I got to get them out of there before it
floods. If Stillhouse Fork runs over, you can't get down off
that mountain."

"I can't leave! My husband and Dr. Jurgen are out on rounds. Can't you find one of them?"

"They're scared of anyone but you." Cheoah slid off his horse. "They're all alone up there, and *I* don't know what to do!" He glared at her as if that angered him.

"Can you bring them to me? What about the children's father?"

"I don't know where he is. And if I find him, I'm gonna kill him." He stared at Janessa, his mouth hard. "Never mind, then."

"No, wait." Janessa pulled the tent flap open. "Eileen! Charley's due back in an hour. Can you cope till then?"

The nurse hurried over, her wide eyes taking in Joe Cheoah's angry face. "There are three of us, and the orderlies," the nurse said. "We can cope."

Janessa brushed by her and picked up her bag. "Tell Charley I've gone up to Stillhouse Fork," she said as she came out. "I'm going to bring Mr. Cheoah's grandmother and the little girl back with me."

"In this?" The thunder boomed and rattled.

Janessa pulled her slicker on. "I don't melt," she said. She lashed her bag to the back of the piebald's saddle and swung herself up before Joe could help her—if he had been going to, which she doubted.

He rode silently, setting his horse into a splashing gallop that churned up mud in her face, so she kicked the piebald into step beside him. The wind had come up, whipping the trees into a fury, and she shouted at him over it. "Why didn't you get me *sooner*?"

"I was in Ela all morning!" he barked. "Arguing with white men."

"It might be better if you could stay out of Ela," Janessa said. "If you're worried about trouble."

"If I thought my going to Ela would give them all yellow fever, I'd live in Ela!"

The fury in his voice battered at her ears like the storm. "I can't share your sentiments," Janessa said stiffly. "I'm a doctor. You don't use disease for a weapon."

"I'd use anything I could," Cheoah said. "But this is a stupid conversation, since you don't know how it spreads."

"You started it," Janessa said, feeling that that was childish and inadequate. So much for getting off on a better foot with Joe. Every time he talked to her, he infuriated her.

"Why did you come here?" he shouted at her over the storm. "Walini told me about you, but you still don't belong. You don't know anything about us!"

Janessa pulled the hood of her slicker down farther. She was already soaked to the skin, even with her slicker on. "My alternative assignment was examining immigrants at Ellis Island," she informed him. "I'm beginning to think it might have been more pleasant."

"For all of us," Joe agreed. They started up the trace toward Stillhouse Fork, and he reined his horse ahead of hers to lead the way, splattering her with mud again.

"You're lucky I did come!" Janessa shouted after him. "No one else would put up with you!"

"*I'm* not kin to you!" Cheoah shouted back.

The piebald slid and stumbled on the muddy trace. A wet tree branch smacked Janessa in the eyes, and she lost her temper. "If you're anything like your father," she yelled after his disappearing back, "it's no wonder my mother wouldn't marry him!"

He didn't answer; he just plunged on up the trace while Janessa followed, wet and seething.

The path grew steadily more slippery, the red clay turning to slick mud. Where the trace crossed Stillhouse Fork, the brown water bubbled past the horses' bellies. Janessa kicked her feet loose from the stirrups and tried to draw her thick skirts up out of the current as the piebald plunged through, floundering and snorting. Another flash of lightning shimmered above them, followed within a half second by the crack of thunder. The piebald lunged up the far bank of the fork, slid backward on its haunches, and then scrambled its way up again. The rain was coming down in sheets now, driven by a gale-force wind. The piebald lurched up the trace, driven as much by terror as by Janessa's urging.

Why am I doing this for you? Janessa wondered grimly as another flare illuminated Joe lashing his own horse up the mountain ahead of her. She gritted her teeth. She wasn't doing it for him; she was doing it for the sick woman and the child, alone in their cabin in the midst of this. Another thunderclap deafened her, and the mountain was lit by an unearthly blaze of light. The earth shook as if the mountain were trying to blast the human interlopers off its face, and Janessa looked upward, terror stricken, to see a giant pine split open and fall. It came downward in a cloud of steam, trailing ripples of blue fire that crackled through its branches. She screamed and kicked the piebald forward, and the pine came down behind them, spitting and smoking, close enough to brush the piebald's tail.

The horse reared and shrieked, and Janessa, sliding back toward the horse's rump, clawed frantically at the saddle with one hand, trying to steady the piebald with the other. Joe had turned around and was looking back at her, his face nearly as white as the lightning flare. He began to rein his horse around on the narrow trace, and she waved at him to go on.

"I'm all right!" Janessa dragged herself forward and into the saddle, pulling the piebald's head around until its nose was nearly on her knee and it stopped its terrified lunging. It went on, quivering and ears flattened, when she loosened the rein.

When they came to the spot where the boy had met them before, there was no one in sight. Streams of water rushed down the trace from the muddy yard around the cabin and poured from the slanting roof of the porch, creating gullies in the red earth. Someone had attempted to dig a ditch to take the runoff away from the foundation but had given up, leaving the shovel standing abandoned in the mud.

They tied their horses under the porch overhang, then Joe took the steps two at a time and flung the door open.

Janessa wrestled her bag off the piebald's saddle and ran after him. It was so dim inside that it took her eyes a moment to find the boy Billy sitting cross-legged by the unlit hearth, his little sister in his arms. The old woman lay on an iron bedstead in the corner.

"How's Mamaw?" Cheoah demanded.

"She's dead," the boy said. His eyes were wide and frightened. "And I'm skeered. I can't wake up Lottie."

VI

Janessa dropped to her knees beside the girl. "Get me some light," she told Joe, and she put a hand on the child's forehead while she heard him fumbling with a lamp. Lottie's skin was damp, but that was natural in this climate—even the storm hadn't lowered the temperature appreciably, only raised the humidity. And the girl's skin temperature felt normal to Janessa's touch.

Joe struck a match, and the lamp flowered into light, illuminating the grimy cabin. The only furniture consisted of the bed on which the old woman lay; three pallets on the floor, covered with ragged quilts; a scarred wooden table; a pair of cane-backed chairs; and an ancient iron stove. Janessa looked at the child's skin, sallow but not really jaundiced, and pulled back Lottie's lips to examine her gums.

"How long has she been like this?"

"I don't rightly know." Billy looked down at his little sister helplessly. "She had been peaked a day or two, but we was tending to Mamaw, and she seemed to get around all right. Then she got mighty poorly about the time I sent to find Joe."

"Has she been vomiting?"

"Naw. But she was shaky. And then Mamaw died."

Billy snuffled and rubbed his hand across his face. "And then Lottie got like this."

"What has she had to eat?"

"Corn pone," Billy said. "That's all I know to cook. All there is, too," he muttered.

"What about your grandmother?"

"Joe sent some pork and vegetables. We made 'em into broth, but Mamaw couldn't get it down anyways. Most of it got spilt."

Janessa gave Joe a hard look. "How long has it been since you've been up here?"

"I've been in Ela," he said. "I sent—"

"I don't care what you sent or where you've been! Where is their father?"

Billy shrugged, and Joe's mouth tightened.

"Is Lottie gonna die, too?" Billy whispered.

"I don't think so," Janessa said, "but we have to get her out of here." Furious, she looked up at Joe. "As far as I can tell, she doesn't have yellow fever. She has scurvy, from malnutrition! She needs food—fruit and vegetables, not corn pone. If she's dying, it's from neglect. This isn't something that comes on in a day or two!"

Joe set the lamp on the floor and sat down beside it with an angry groan. Janessa opened her bag and rummaged in it, producing an apple, a lemon, and a glass jar of tea, part of the picnic meal she made it a habit to carry with her on her rounds. "Get me some cold water," she said, and Joe got up again, grabbed a bucket, and disappeared into the storm. He came back dripping, the bucket filled with well water. Janessa dipped her handkerchief in the bucket and sponged the child's forehead, trying to wake her. She handed the lemon and the jar to Cheoah. "Cut that and squeeze about half of it into the tea."

Janessa pulled Lottie up so that she was sitting in Billy's arms and felt how thin the girl's body was under her homespun dress. "Have you got a garden?"

"It's pretty well gone to seed since Mamaw got sick. Pap doesn't take much of a hand with it."

Janessa sponged more cool water on Lottie's face. The dark lashes fluttered a little. "Come on, Lottie. You have to wake up and eat something."

Joe came back with the tea, and Janessa put the jar to the little girl's lips. Some of it went down, and Lottie spluttered and made a face at the sour lemon taste. "Awful, isn't it?" Janessa said encouragingly. "But it will fix you up. Come on, Lottie, you have to drink it."

They managed to get the rest of it down her, and Joe squeezed the other half of the lemon into more water to follow it. They peeled a piece of the apple and cut it into thin strips, and Lottie obediently ate that, too; but her eyes remained heavy lidded and dull, and she didn't even wince as the thunder cracked over the house.

"That will do for now," Janessa said. "But she's going to need more food and decent care."

Billy lifted the little girl and laid her down on one of the pallets against the far wall. She didn't look more than six, and Janessa was possessed of a desire to find the father and strangle him with her bare hands. She held the light to Billy's face and made him open his mouth so that she could check his gums. She handed him the rest of the apple strips. "You eat those."

She got a grip on her temper and turned to find Joe Cheoah watching her, his dark eyes glowing with a fury that she realized was no longer for her but for poverty in general and for his uncle in particular. "We've got to get them out of here," she said.

"Can't," Joe said. "While you were feeding her, I went out and had a look. The water in the fork's come up since we went across, and the storm's getting worse. With that tree across the trace, we'll never get back."

As he spoke the cabin shook with another thunderclap, and Janessa went to the door and stood looking out into the storm. He was right. Even the two of them alone might not make it. Riding double, with Lottie as sick as she was— never.

Janessa turned back and looked unhappily at the old

woman on the bed. "You know that we'll have to move her,"
she said. "I'm sorry."

Joe nodded. "I don't expect she cares anymore." He
went to the bed and gently began to wrap his grandmother's
body in a ragged quilt. Janessa helped him, smoothing the
gray hair and crossing the woman's worn hands on her
breast. She drew the quilt across the yellowed face, and Joe
lifted the body in his arms. It was light, hardly heavier than
the quilt.

"I'll put her on the porch," he said, "while I dig the
grave."

"I'll help you," Janessa offered.

"You don't have to."

She followed him anyway and found another shovel
leaning against the side of the cabin. An empty jug rolled
away as she lifted the shovel, and furious, she kicked at it.

As the wind whipped the rain around them, Joe led the
way to the burial ground, then drove his shovel into the
sodden earth. He turned up a shovelful of mud. His face
was a mask of anguish under his hat.

"You loved her, didn't you?" Janessa asked.

"I *tried* to get her to move away and to take those kids
with her." Janessa could hear the loss and frustration in his
voice, mingled with guilt.

They dug side by side, and the light was nearly gone
by the time they had gotten deep enough into the sticky
clay. Joe stuck the shovel in the mud and went to get his
grandmother's body. When he returned, the grave was
already filling with water. They laid her in it, and he bowed
his head.

"I don't know what to say, Lord," he said after a
moment. "She was a good woman. She did her best. Please,
God, take her to You and give her some ease now."

They filled in the grave without speaking, then leaned,
exhausted, on the shovels, almost too tired to move. Joe
straightened up. "You're going to catch pneumonia," he
said. "Let's get back to the house."

Another flare of lightning illuminated the sodden yard,

but the boom of thunder that followed it was not as close as it had been.

"Where's the garden?" Janessa asked him.

"You won't get anything out of it. What the rabbits and the bugs and the weeds didn't get will be flattened in this."

"There's always something," Janessa said. Men never looked past the weeds. "How long until that stream goes down?"

"Tomorrow maybe," Joe replied.

"And maybe not? Where's the garden?"

"Oh, for— All right, damn it." He pointed. "It's to that side of the cabin."

Janessa plowed through a tangle of wild morning glory and sodden honeysuckle and dug in the mud, rain dripping in her eyes. At first she thought Joe had gone, but after a moment he was back again with a covered lantern. They found a few flattened cabbage leaves and a handful of onions going to flower. Janessa pulled up a fold of her muddy skirt to hold them. Joe gave her the lantern and put his foot on the shovel in a snarl of weeds. He unearthed a scattering of potatoes, all rotten but one, and put the good one in her skirt.

"That do you?" he inquired. "This lantern's about out."

"It will have to," Janessa said. She felt ready to drop, battered with the storm and weariness and the weight of her wet clothes.

"I'll get a fire going," Joe said. "If there's any dry wood," he added.

As they came into the cabin, Billy looked up from the corner by his sister's bed. "She's asleep," he said. He was shamefaced. "I should've helped, but I fell asleep, too."

Janessa put the vegetables on the table and pushed him back down, drawing a thin quilt over him. "You've done just fine. You sleep some more, and I'll make us some soup."

Joe looked up from the woodbin. "I hate to bring this up," he said, "but you've got to get out of those clothes." He sneezed.

"So do you." Janessa unbuttoned and removed her uniform jacket, then dragged her muddy, dripping skirt off and hung them both over one of the chairs. Her chemise and petticoats were wet, too, but without the heavy serge over them, she knew they might dry. She pulled her boots off and set them on the hearth, defying him to make any remarks.

Joe shrugged and stripped down to his long underwear. He set about lighting the fire while the rain hammered on the tin roof and the children slept.

Janessa made soup with the well water and her meager collection of vegetables. The provisions in her bag also included a ham sandwich, and she took the slice of thick country ham out of its soggy bread and put it in the soup, too, for what flavor it might provide.

The fire in the stove was out, and a look in the firebox revealed nothing but clinkers. Janessa cursed the children's absent father again, aloud this time, and hung the kettle on the hook in the fireplace. She peered at it dubiously. Cooking had never been one of her strong points, but any nourishment just now was better than none, especially for Lottie.

"It won't boil if you watch it," Joe commented, and Janessa sat down grumpily on the hearth to wait and try to dry her petticoats. Neither she nor Joe referred to the fact that they were both in their underwear, maintaining modesty by ignoring it. All the same Janessa looked down uncomfortably at the thin pin-tucked batiste that covered her breasts—barely—but not her arms and shoulders. She unpinned her long hair, which was as wet as her clothes, and spread it around her shoulders to dry. *Lady Godiva in the mountains*, she thought, and experienced a certain amount of amusement. She doubted she had much to worry about from Joe Cheoah. He didn't even like her.

She looked sideways at him. He was sitting opposite her on the hearth, barefooted and in his long johns, which fitted very much like a second skin and gave him rather the

look of a man about to go bathing. His thick, dark hair hung
damply around his face.

Eventually the soup boiled despite Janessa's concen-
tration on it, and when she could poke a fork through the
potato and the onions, Janessa ladled it into the assortment
of cracked bowls she had found on a shelf. By this time the
aroma had awakened Billy, and he wolfed down his portion
with the appetite of a starving animal. Janessa saw how thin
he was, too.

Lottie had to be awakened, but she drank the soup
obediently and ate the vegetables. Janessa waited to make
certain that the food would stay down, then she stuck a
thermometer in the girl's mouth. Still no fever. She took
Billy's temperature, too, for good measure, and by the time
she had shaken the thermometer down again, Lottie had
curled back into her quilt with a little sigh and closed her
eyes.

"I don't like that," Joe said. "Should she be out like that
all the time?"

"In addition to having scurvy, Mr. Cheoah," Janessa
responded, "she's anemic. Exhaustion is symptomatic of
anemia." She cleaned the thermometer again and advanced
on Joe with it.

"I'm fine."

"How do you know? And this house needs to be
smoked out with sulfur, at the very least."

"Not while I'm in it," Joe said. "Take your own
temperature."

"I don't need to. I have sense enough to know when
I'm sick."

"You don't have sense enough to come in out of the
rain." He laughed suddenly. "I'll take my temperature if
you'll take yours, you pigheaded woman."

Janessa jammed the thermometer in her mouth. Billy
finished a second bowl of soup and got up to go outside,
"Don't go out in that storm," she told him around the
thermometer. "Pee off the porch." She looked at Joe. "I'm
not as fine haired as you think."

"Neither is Billy," Joe said. "He probably always pees off the porch—when it's dark, anyway. There might be a copperhead in the outhouse."

Janessa narrowed her eyes at Joe. She thought he was teasing her in advance of her own inevitable trip to the outhouse, but she wished now she hadn't drunk quite so much soup. She cleaned the thermometer and presented it to Joe as Billy came back in. "I'm taking the lamp," she announced.

When she came back, Billy had curled up next to Lottie and seemed to be sleeping, too. Joe looked up as Janessa set the lamp on the table again and wrung fresh rainwater out of her petticoats.

"I'm sorry I got you out here," he said.

"You needed me," Janessa said. "I'm a doctor. It's what I'm supposed to do." Since he seemed to have mellowed slightly, she refrained from remarking that the Hippocratic Oath did not include putting up with his bad temper. "What are you going to do about the children?" she asked, keeping her voice low.

He motioned her over to the hearth, and she sat down beside him, spreading her skirts to dry again, bare toes to the fire.

"I reckon I'll take them to Walini," he said, "if she'll have them. They can't stay here without Mamaw, that's certain." His mouth twisted. "I can't bring up the kids. Half the time I'm not home."

"You don't live up here?"

"Of course not. You think I would have let it get like this if I did? No, I got out as soon as I was old enough. Mamaw was all that held us together when I was little, but after that I couldn't stomach it even for her."

There didn't seem to be any answer to make to that, so she waited silently to see if he was going to tell her more.

Joe sat cross-legged on the floor, snapping a piece of kindling into progressively smaller fragments with his long fingers. Eventually he said, "My pa fought with everybody. He fought with me, he fought with my ma, he fought with my uncle Walker—those kids' pa. Pa beat me every time he thought about it. I could have stood that, but not the constant shouting. They all fought with each other, too, but most times Pa was the poison that got it going. Mamaw said he never got over the way he felt when your ma wouldn't marry him."

"And you blame her for the way he was?"

"Maybe. Yeah, I do. He married my ma on the rebound, and it didn't work out. Then he caught her with my uncle—Walker's a shiftless layabout; he probably just didn't have anything better to do right then—and my pa killed her and shot himself. That wasn't long after I left home. A kid's got to have someone to blame for something like that."

Janessa noted that Joe's father had not shot Walker, which might have been more to the point, but she was too horror-stricken by the story to say so. She looked at Joe's brooding face and the way that his fingers were still snapping the kindling into pieces and thought about what it would have been like to grow up here with him. She hadn't had a bad life in Memphis at that, she decided.

"My mother's dead now," she said gently. "And she and your father wouldn't have worked out, either. Do you think he would have been able to forgive her for having another man's baby?"

"Not a white Yankee's baby," Joe said. "But she got off scot-free, and he committed murder."

The wind battered the shutters, wrenching one of them open. A white flare of lightning lit the room for an instant, freezing his face in immobility, harsh planes of light and darkness. Thunder boomed, and Joe got up and wrestled the shutter closed against the wind. His shoulders slumped. He looked down at her. Under Joe's scrutiny Janessa felt very aware of her father's blood: Her brown hair was growing paler as it dried, and her blue eyes still blinked from the sudden light.

"I wasn't going to tell you that," he said abruptly.

"Why did you?"

"I don't know. I figured I owed you. I watched you with Lottie. . . ." His voice trailed off. "I'm sorry for the way I said it. I've had it up to here with white men right now."

"I'm not—"

"Yeah, yeah, I know. But it's not your Indian blood, it's how you're raised. People raised white don't see things the same way we do. Land's all we've got. Land's all that's ever counted. This coal company wants to take our land and gut it like a dead animal."

"Parker Smith told me about them."

"Did he tell you they're going to do it?"

"But I thought you—"

"I've done all I can. Unless we get some outside help, I'm finished. When it comes down to it, no judge is going to listen to me. I'm just a damn, dumb Cherokee lawyer!" His fists clenched, and he slowly forced them open. "I'm not riled at you." He stood looking at her while the firelight flickered up and down her long hair and the tangle of white petticoats around her knees, and his expression softened. "They told me you threw Briggs out of the hospital. I want to thank you for that."

"He hadn't any business there," Janessa said quietly.

"No, and I don't—" He broke off. "You get some sleep while you can. We'll try the fork in the morning if the rain lets up. You take that other pallet. I'll roll up here on the floor." He pulled a quilt around him and gave her another. "Best not to sleep in the bed, I expect."

"No, best not." Janessa took the quilt and stretched out with it. She looked back at Joe.

He gave her a rueful smile. It was the first time she had seen him smile. "Good night, Ka-nessa," he said.

Janessa smiled, too. "Good night, Joe." She wrapped herself in the quilt. Charley would be worried to death about her, she thought sleepily.

By morning the storm had passed, leaving behind it bent and broken trees and a sea of mud. Joe Cheoah

dressed before Janessa awoke, and slipped out to look at the
fork. The water was down enough to ford it, and he thought
he could see a way around the split, charred tree. A faint
regret crossed his mind, and he pushed it away. Lottie
needed care. And he needed to get out of there before he
made some kind of fool of himself like his father had done.

By the time he got back, Janessa was dressed, too, with
her boots on and her hair braided up under her uniform
cap. The boots made a solid, no-nonsense tread on the
cabin floor. Joe bundled up Lottie and put her on the
piebald with Janessa. Billy climbed on behind Joe's saddle,
and slowly they made their way down the trace.

Charley and Walini met them halfway, with twin looks
of relief, and told them what else the storm had brought:
Gardens were ruined and shacks blown down; old Wolf
Mooney had sprained his ankle trying to catch his cow;
Nimrod Jackson had been hurt when a tree went through
his church roof—and Walker Cheoah had been found
facedown in the lower reaches of Stillhouse Fork, with his
bottle still in his hand.

"He must have fallen in the storm," Walini told Joe,
mincing no words, "and been just too flat drunk to get up
again."

Billy's mouth quivered, and he looked at her with
confusion. "Mamaw's dead, too," he said.

Janessa bent toward Walini. "The little girl's got
scurvy," she said, "not yellow fever. She'll be all right, but
she needs decent food and care, and a fever hospital's no
place for her. We thought maybe you would—"

"Of course I will." Walini put out a hand toward Billy.
"You come with me, too. I could use a good boy like you to
help me."

Billy's face shone with relief.

When they had left the children at Walini's house in
town, Janessa knew the children would be all right. She
wished she could feel the same assurance for Joe Cheoah.

She watched him ride away, his hand lifted in farewell and his face bleak, to bury his uncle's body.

"Charley, I can't bear this. We've got to help them somehow."

"When I've recovered from the attack of stark terror you gave me," Charley said, "I'll consider other problems. Besides, I thought we *were* helping them."

Janessa smiled and took his hand as they rode side by side. "My poor darling, I knew you'd be worried. But I was referring to the threat of Mr. Briggs and the Superior Coal Company. These people are at the end of their rope."

"It isn't going to get any better," Charley said grimly. "There are two cases of yellow fever in Ela this morning. I was saving that grisly bit of news until you'd rested, but you might as well know now. I've sent someone down to the depot to wire New York for two more doctors and as many staff as they can send us. Danforth has it, too, I'm afraid."

"Oh, no." Danforth was one of the orderlies. "How is he?"

"I can't tell yet. And I can't think about this coal company right now." He slapped a mosquito off his wrist. "Blast! I thought the storm had blown these little devils away. Do you want to rest? Someone has to go into Ela."

"I'll go," Janessa offered. "I want to see what's going on there."

She continued to brood while she changed into a clean uniform and drove the hospital buggy to Ela. *Outside help,* Joe Cheoah had said. *Well, I'm no use.* The complications of law, especially land law, were a mystery to her. And it sounded as if they were going to need someone with more clout and money than the coal company, thus eliminating a pair of government doctors right away. It did not, however, Janessa mused as she climbed down from the buggy outside the Ela Hotel, eliminate the government itself. The Cherokee were, or should be, a federal responsibility, and it didn't sound to her as if the Bureau of Indian Affairs had been living up to it. The local office, as far as Janessa could tell, appeared to be snarled in its own red tape and indecision.

Janessa tied up the horse and, bag in hand, mounted the steps of the hotel, abandoning further speculation as the landlady pounced on her at the door.

"I'm telling you, he can't stay here. I've got my other boarders to think of." The landlady followed Janessa upstairs to the patient, expostulating loudly. "And I may as well say, *Doctor* Lawrence, I don't think you're doing us any good, coming here from those filthy Indians and bringing the sickness with you, like as not. We don't need you—we've got a good doctor in Ela. This poor man wouldn't have took sick if you'd kept your Indians away—"

"Your doctor sent for me," Janessa said evenly. "He can't handle an epidemic single-handedly, and that's probably what you're going to have. And you can't blame the Cherokee. They were just unlucky enough to be in the first path of the disease. Now excuse me." She shut the door firmly in the landlady's face, leaving her shouting in the hall.

The patient, an official of the coal company, was vomiting into a basin and shaking with hiccups and spasms. Janessa made him as comfortable as she could and wrote notes for Charley's journal on the onset of the disease and his previous activities. Additional information was provided by Miles Fentress, the Ela doctor, who slipped in past the landlady and a gathering delegation in the hallway.

"He does have to be moved," Janessa whispered. "That old harridan is right about that."

"I've set up a temporary clinic in my office," Fentress said, "until your people can get here."

Neither of them suggested taking patients to Yellow Hill. Joe Cheoah had been right about that: Doing so would create a riot. She followed Fentress to the house of the second patient, with a growing segment of Ela's citizenry trailing the buggy, outraged. Janessa heard more than one protest about the "half-breed doctor."

The patient was a woman with a frightened, angry

husband and three little children. "I'm gonna shoot me the
next Indian what comes into this town," he threatened,
glaring at Janessa. "Nor I don't want you here again."

"Button up, Tom," Dr. Fentress said. "Dr. Lawrence
has more experience with yellow fever than I do. We need
all the help we can get."

"We don't need Indians. I been poor as spit all my life,
and this Superior Coal could be a salvation for us iffen it
weren't for them dirty Indians squattin' on the land. Now
they bring in disease, and my wife's took sick, and I don't
want no goddamned Indian quack tending to her!"

His wife looked up weakly from the bed while Janessa
was bathing her face. "Leave her be, Tom. I can't bear it."

Dr. Fentress pushed him into the next room, and
Janessa heard them arguing.

"I can send another doctor next time," Janessa said.

"Won't matter. Not if he comes from up in Quallatown,
even if he's white." She lay back limply. "You don't *look*
Indian. I guess you can't never tell. Can't you do anything
with them Cherokee, bein' one of them and all? This town
needs that coal mine bad. If we don't get it, I don't know
how Tom's gonna make enough to get along."

"I wouldn't put all my faith in the coal company,"
Janessa said. "They're a business proposition. They aren't
here to make *you* rich, whatever they say. My brother was
a miner once. He said it was brutal."

"It don't seem to me like no place for a man to work,
down under the ground like a mole." She sighed, moving
her head restlessly on the pillow. "But Tom and them all
want it. Lord, I feel so sick I just don't know."

"Try to rest," Janessa said. She knew she couldn't
change anyone's mind in Ela. "You need to rest to get well.
Have you got anyone to help with the children?"

"Sulie's my oldest. She's nine. She'll just have to make
out. I can tell her what to do."

"I want to move you to the clinic," Janessa said. "We
must try to protect your children. I'll discuss it with Dr.
Fentress."

The woman burst into sobs, hands pressed to lips that were scarlet with fever, her bleary, congested eyes squeezing out tears. "Oh, the devil take them Indians!"

There was a sizable crowd waiting in the street when Janessa came out onto the porch with Dr. Fentress. She took a deep breath and tried to speak with the voice of reason.

"We want to contain this as much as we can. But please don't blame the sick. As Dr. Fentress will tell you, no one has been able to discover the organism that causes yellow fever or how it travels. It is advisable not to go out in crowds, but we have no proof at all that it can be spread by casual contact. The Cherokee did not bring this on you."

"No one took sick till that Indian started coming here all the time!" someone shouted.

"If you mean Mr. Cheoah," Janessa said, "he does not have the disease himself, so it is unlikely that these people could have caught it from him. And the Cherokee have always done business here. They're your customers, your neighbors—"

"You're wasting your breath," Dr. Fentress muttered. "The Cherokee haven't set foot in Ela since this trouble started—except for Joe Cheoah, the damn fool. These folks are mad and scared. You aren't going to get anywhere. I've already tried."

A man pushed to the front of the crowd. Janessa recognized Morton Briggs. "If you want to help, Dr. Lawrence, you go on back and make your Indians listen to reason—before these good people take matters into their own hands."

"That's right!" A chorus of shouts and raised fists followed her as she swept down the stairs to the buggy. "We're gonna put those land-stealin' Indians right outta this state like the government shoulda done a long time ago!" A rock smacked into the back of the buggy as Janessa shook out the reins.

* * *

"He's a rabble-rouser!" Janessa paced furiously through the laboratory, her skirts swishing like a tiger's tail.

Charley watched her sympathetically. "All right. Granted. What are you going to do?"

Janessa stopped pacing and snatched up Charley's notebook and a pen. "Call in the cavalry," she said. "And you are going to help."

"I don't know any cavalry."

"You know a lawyer. That's the next best thing. And *I* know a senator." She sat down and started to write.

By the end of the day, a series of furious and urgent telegrams had begun to click along the wires from the depot in Quallatown.

Janessa, once she had set her mind on a matter, rarely took no for an answer, as her father, Senator Toby Holt, had had occasion to remark. This time, because he thought she was in the right—also because he may have been troubled by a guilty conscience over the matter of her mother—Toby corralled a few influential friends, made a well-received speech in the Senate on the subject of governmental honor, and spent a convivial evening playing poker with the head of the Bureau of Indian Affairs. As a final diplomatic maneuver, he telephoned his sister, Cindy, because, as a result of Toby's actions, her husband would be leaving Washington on assignment.

Figuratively speaking, the cavalry arrived a week later on the morning train in the person of Colonel Henry Blake, special agent and professional investigator for the United States government—and brother-in-law of Senator Holt.

Following him down the steps was Janessa's second plan of attack: Charley's lawyer stepfather, Vernon Hughes. He was a mild-mannered, graying man. He had married Charley's widowed mother after the Civil War, and his original New Jersey accent had been overlaid through the years with a Richmond drawl. His associates occasionally ragged him for being a carpetbagger, but they no longer meant it, and he was accounted to be an excellent candidate for the next judgeship to become available. Charley was very fond of him.

"We met on the train," Henry Blake said. He was tall and muscular with observant green eyes and a parade-ground carriage. He walked with the brisk stride of a man used to looking into things and straightening them out. A faded scar down his left cheek indicated that the straightening had occasionally been physical.

"This should be interesting," Vernon Hughes said. "I've never worked with the government before."

Janessa linked arms with both men to lead them to the buggy. "Oh, thank you for coming! I knew you'd help!"

"Now, Janessa," Henry warned, "I'm here to conduct an investigation for the government, not to take sides."

Hughes smiled. "Fortunately, I am under no such constraint. I am here to sue the so-and-so's."

Janessa grinned at them both. "Henry, when you've *seen* what that company is trying to do, I don't have any doubts at all about what side you'll be on."

"You're trying to prejudice a government official," Henry remarked mildly. "Watch yourself." But he hugged her before he helped her into the buggy. "I've been down-and-out myself. I know how they must feel."

"Uncle Henry has a past," Janessa whispered to Vernon. She gave Henry a teasing smile. Now that they had arrived, she felt almost lighthearted. Surely something good would come of it.

"Damn and blast that meddling woman!" Morton Briggs glowered at his company lawyer over the ham steak on his breakfast plate while the housekeeper hovered nervously in the background with the coffeepot. "I'll tell you, Scoggins, I don't know what this country's coming to when a company can't make an honest living without some sob sister getting in the way, bleating about a bunch of Indians. And her being a government doctor, too."

"I've written to her commander to complain," Scoggins said, forking another slice of ham. "But I don't know that he'll do much. I've a low opinion of a man who'd let a woman into government service in the first place."

"That's just what I mean." Briggs wiped his mouth and swallowed the last of his coffee. "The government's been getting a sight too many notions like that lately. Bunch of freethinkers and anarchists. Country's going to hell in a hand basket, if you ask me." He held out his cup. "Give me some more of that."

"I heard," the housekeeper said, pouring, "that he's her cousin or uncle or some such. And the lawyer's her father-in-law."

"There," Briggs said. "It just goes to show what the whole family's like. Intermarrying with Indians!"

"*I* heard," the housekeeper went on, "that they wasn't married. Her daddy and her Indian ma." She sniffed. "Nice doings."

"Indeed," Morton Briggs said.

"Morton, you're getting off the track here," Scoggins said. "The point is, what are we going to do about it? This Blake has been nosing around everywhere, like a damned government ferret. And Hughes has filed three appeals and a countersuit so far. This judge is on our side—these are his folks here in Ela—but I still don't like it."

"Well, you're a lawyer, aren't you?"

Scoggins gave his employer a look of infinite patience. "Certainly. As your lawyer, I'm advising you to quit carrying on about the state of the world and do something about Dr. Lawrence."

"It's Blake and Hughes I'm worried about."

Scoggins sighed. Morton Briggs was a reasonably inventive man once you got him on the right track, but sometimes it took awhile. "*She* got them here. They're her kin. How long do you think they'd stay interested if *she* wasn't around?"

* * *

Morton Briggs, with his lawyer's flea in his ear, proceeded to work on that theory, but he was hampered by the full-blown epidemic of yellow fever that had, as Janessa had predicted, finally come to Ela. The Marine Hospital Service sent three more doctors to staff a separate hospital for whites, and as July turned to August and the heat grew ever more stifling and the air more sultry, the new hospital filled to overflowing. Morton Briggs came down with it himself, leaving Scoggins in a fury of frustration—Scoggins was not a man to make a risky move on his own.

Henry Blake, attempting to interview anyone with any knowledge of old land transactions, found half his subjects sick or dying. The courthouses, where the records were kept, were staffed by one or two bewildered clerks, if at all. Soon Henry was nearly tearing his hair out in frustration.

To further complicate matters, a great deal of land, both white and Cherokee, had been sold for unpaid taxes after the Civil War. Some had been bought back; some had not; some had been bought by people who had lost other tracts of land. All had been recorded with a high degree of confusion, sharp dealing, and ambiguity. Henry was hampered by the fact that those who had lost land during Reconstruction were now disinclined to cooperate with a representative of that selfsame government. Old wounds had healed uneasily in these mountains, the more so since many of the mountain people, unlike the more prosperous politicians and cotton planters to the southeast, considered themselves to have been caught up in a war they had not wanted in the first place.

By the end of August Henry Blake presented an interim progress report, but he wasn't happy about it. Janessa, Charley, Chief Stillwell Saunooka, and Joe Cheoah met with Henry and Vernon Hughes at the boardinghouse in Quallatown where Henry and Vernon had set up their headquarters.

"About all I can report so far," Henry said gloomily, "is that whoever deserves title to this land Briggs is after, it is not the Superior Coal Company—which we knew already. They're just trying to buy it. But I can say, and have reported officially, that until Vernon has traced all the legal tangles back to their source, no sales to Superior Coal should be allowed by anyone claiming title to the land, Cherokee included."

"The Cherokee don't want to sell," Stillwell Saunooka said.

"They may if they get scared enough," Joe said. "Right now everyone's too sick to fight. But . . ." He spread his hands and didn't bother to go on. Everyone already knew what he meant. There had been threats and counterthreats for two months, until no Cherokee went to Ela or white man to Qualla Boundary without an armed guard. The fever was all that kept outright violence at bay. When the fever lifted, there might well be some among the Cherokee who would give in because of fear, for their families if not for themselves.

"I've talked to the judge," Vernon said. "At least as much as he's willing to talk to me. I think he's an honest man, but his sympathies are with Ela. He was born here."

"At least Briggs is out of commission," Joe said with satisfaction. He glanced at Janessa. He knew what she, with her doctor's training, thought about wishing disease on enemies.

"Don't get your hopes up," was all Janessa said. "The Ela clinic tells me he's nearly recovered." She gave Joe a half smile. "And holds us both personally responsible for his ailment."

Stillwell Saunooka rose. "You have done much for us." He included the doctors and Henry and Vernon in his glance. "Whatever the outcome, we are grateful."

The rest of them stood, too, wearily. For the doctors four hours sleep a night had begun to seem almost normal. Janessa had nearly quit looking in the mirror, knowing that the face that looked back at her was thin and ragged. Charley looked almost worse.

Joe bent his head toward Janessa's as they approached

the doorway. "I want to thank you, too, Ka-nessa." He looked as if he wanted to say something more, and his dark eyes caught and held hers for a moment. But they were creating a bottleneck in the doorway. The others pressed around them, and Joe moved away.

Outside, the Lawrences climbed into their buggy, Janessa half looking over her shoulder at Joe mounting his horse. He was a strange, intense man—a driven man certainly, and with good reason. But he was not the guarded and hate-filled person he had once been—not with her at any rate. She had begun to like him, although there was something . . . well, not disturbing exactly. *Unsettling* might be the word.

Charley handed the reins to Janessa. "You drive. I don't know what it is, I just feel beat. I've got an awful headache."

He slumped against her, and Janessa snapped her head around. All thoughts of Joe Cheoah fled. Charley's body felt hot against hers, too hot even for an August night in which the valley seemed to compress the heat and fold it around them. She put a hand to his forehead and found it dry and burning.

Oh, no. Oh God, please no. Janessa shook out the reins and smacked the horse into a trot. "Why didn't you tell me you were sick?"

"I'm not sick." Charley's voice sounded more determined that he should not be sick than certain of it.

Janessa didn't argue with him. There was not any point to it. She drove toward Yellow Hill and the hospital as fast as she dared in the dark, knowing that was pointless, too. The hospital had no miraculous cure to offer. No one knew better than she that nothing cured yellow fever but the body's own strength; a patient was either stronger than the disease or he wasn't. And Charley, like the rest of the doctors, had already expended his own strength trying to save others.

The trip was a nightmare, through hot, wet darkness, out of which all her personal demons, past and present, seemed to loom at her: fear of loss and of not belonging, the dreadful weight of being different from everyone else, and the terror of losing the love she had found. Charley had cured her of all that. Charley was her anchor. If she lost him, she would find herself spinning helplessly into some dreadful void.

She pulled the buggy up in front of the hospital, shouting for Steve Jurgen and for Eileen Riley. They came running, wide-eyed at the panic in her voice.

"He has it!" Janessa said desperately. "Steve, he's sick!"

"I'm not sick," Charley insisted doggedly as Steve helped him down, but he slumped and would have fallen if Steve hadn't held him up.

"That's fine," Steve said soothingly. "You just get some rest then, and we'll see."

"Not sick," Charley muttered. They got him into the hospital and onto a bed. In the light of the lamp that Eileen held high, they saw that his cheeks and lips were flushed scarlet.

"All right, old man, just relax. We'll take your temperature and get a urine sample. Janessa, will you for God's sake go away?" Steve said over his shoulder.

Janessa paced restlessly through the silent ward, among the other patients—some sleeping, some half-awake and plucking at the bedclothes, their fingers moving ceaselessly, driven by the unconscious urges of delirium. She knew she would be of no use to Charley in this state. Panic-stricken, she wanted only to drop to her knees and howl in terror.

Finally Steve came over to her. "I don't think there's much doubt. His temperature's nearly a hundred and four. There's a lot of albumin in the urine. I'm afraid he's in for a rough time."

"Oh, Steve!"

Steve put his arms around her and stroked her hair. "Don't throw in the towel now, you hear? More people than not pull through. Look at Nurse Steinman and how sick she was."

Janessa nodded and tried to pin her hopes on Nurse Steinman. She, too, had been stricken, but they had put her on the train for home finally, weak but recovered. But Danforth the orderly had taken sick at almost the same time. They hadn't put Danforth on the train. They had buried him in the Cherokee cemetery at Yellow Hill.

VII

The next days became a kind of nightmare for Janessa, from which only her surface self emerged to tend the sick, to confer with Henry Blake, Charley's stepfather Vernon Hughes, her aunt Walini, and Joe Cheoah, and to drive periodically into Ela to oversee the hospital there. She made these trips in stone-faced silence, ignoring the looks and insults that followed her, not even caring anymore.

After three days Charley's temperature dropped rapidly to well below normal, and he began to vomit, the fluid at first clear and then dark with blood. His skin grew steadily more jaundiced as the disease attacked his liver and kidneys. His pulse rate slowed as if his heart fought to keep beating. Janessa spent every possible moment at his bedside, consumed with the terror that if she left him, he would die. She believed that her hand on his, feeling the slow, faint trip of his heart was all that tethered him to life.

Charley's laboratory was abandoned except for the orderly who cared for the guinea pigs. No one but Janessa could decipher Charley's notes enough to continue his experiments, and she had no heart for it. But he would wake, sometimes rational, sometimes delirious, and ask about the laboratory. He had grown thin because he could not keep food down. His eyes were dull and sunken, his brown hair as lifeless as straw. Clutching her hand, he would shake with spasms and fret endlessly over his experiments.

Finally, a week after Charley had taken sick, Janessa crept into the laboratory tent and began to set it to rights. Charley's notebooks were scattered, and his pen lay across an open page. The lamp had guttered out. Janessa refilled it and gathered the notebooks into a stack while the guinea pigs chirped and rustled in their baskets. She sat down and began to read. If Charley died, this was all that would be left of him, and it mattered enough to him to torment him even through his illness. Slowly she turned the pages, notebook after notebook, written in his minute and illegible hand. Janessa hugged them to her, leaving the ones yet to read piled in her lap, as if here, too, she might somehow hold on to Charley.

There was no solid evidence, but it looked as if he had begun to think that Carlos Finlay, that crazy old doctor in Havana, might have been on the right track about mosquitoes. He hadn't mentioned it to her. It was only a faint suspicion, and Charley was a scientist, a man with a penchant for proof and order. But the mosquito theory jibed with the erratic progress of the disease and its ability to jump from house to house. But which mosquito? Or all mosquitoes? And was it endemic to that mosquito, or must it first bite an infected patient? The hospital cots were netted for the comfort of the patients, but few of the Cherokee cabins contained mosquito netting for their beds. And where was the bacillus? No one, Charley included, had been able to find it in the blood of yellow-fever patients, and Finlay hadn't been able to find it in his mosquitoes, either.

Janessa put her head in her hands, trying to sort out the meager and scattered evidence. She was a doctor. She treated the sick. It was Charley who had the researcher's passion, carried around baskets of guinea pigs, and wheedled blood samples from healthy citizens to compare with those of the sick. It was Charley who might make some sense of all this—if he lived. *Oh, Charley*. Bereft, Janessa took one of her husband's guinea pigs from its basket and cuddled it, crying into its fur.

Steve Jurgen came in. "You'll get fleas." He took the guinea pig and looked at it. "*I* don't know what to do with these. Are you making any headway with Charley's notes? He's sleeping again, but when he's awake, the poor man is nearly in a frenzy over them."

"I don't know," Janessa said mournfully. "As far as I can tell, he's been trying to correlate mosquito bites with the onset of fever. But we've all been bitten by mosquitoes. Every bare inch of skin looks like I've got hives. And we aren't all sick."

"Old crackpot Finlay's hypothesis? I heard him lecture. The audience nearly threw tomatoes."

"All the same, I think we ought to advise people to try to keep mosquitoes out of the house. Fumigating with sulfur does seem to keep other people in the same house from getting it, and that makes sense if we're dealing with mosquitoes."

"They just come back in again," Steve said.

"But not infected ones?" Janessa asked. "It's worth a try. You know the fever dies out after the first frost. That fits the mosquito theory, too."

Steve scratched his head, the guinea pig under one arm. "You want to tell these people keep mosquitoes out of these shacks they live in? We can't even keep them out of our tents."

"Right now I'll try anything," Janessa said. "I have to do something, or I'll go mad."

Steve looked at her somberly, his eyes sympathetic. Charley was his friend. They were both his friends. "I know, kid," was all he could say.

Janessa looked at him, bewildered. She held out her hands for the guinea pig and stroked it mechanically, finding little comfort in the silky fur except for the fact that the creature was Charley's. "Steve, what am I going to do? I can't get by without him."

"You can if you have to," Steve said. "I'm not going to

give you permission to fall apart. You're tough. You've always been tough."

"Not so tough now," Janessa whispered, feeling close to the edge.

"You want to talk up your mosquito theory?" Steve asked. "Now's a good time. There's a kind of delegation here to see you. That's what I came to tell you."

"Delegation?"

"Your great-uncle, that old reprobate Wolf Mooney. And Cheoah. And your aunt Walini and her sons."

Janessa wiped her eyes. "Tell them to come in here."

They filed in solemnly. Wolf Mooney held out a basket. "Rebecca baked you a crumb cake," he said. "How's Dr. Charley?"

"He's very sick. I don't know."

"We come to ask after him," Parker Smith said. "Tell you how sorry we are."

"He's a good man," Wesley Calhoun added. "Reverend Jackson led us in prayer for him."

"That's kind of you," Janessa said, touched at their coming, their wrapping around her the blanket of kinship, and their letting her know she was not alone. Vernon Hughes was as frantic as she was and was too terrified to write to Charley's mother for fear she would come to Qualla Boundary herself and catch the fever.

"We're grateful to Mr. Hughes," Walini said. "Joe tells me he's a good lawyer—the best at land law Joe's seen. And a fine Christian soul to take on our troubles when his boy's so sick."

"And you to come asking after him," Janessa said. She smiled tiredly at them all. "I've been feeling so alone. I can't tell you what it means to have family about me." She looked at Joe, who was not family and who had not said anything, to include him, too.

"And you, Ka-nessa," Joe said. "Are you keeping well? Maybe I should take your temperature," he suggested with a half smile.

"Probably bust the thermometer," Wolf Mooney told

him, "if you're still as ham-fisted as you were the last time you laid hands on me."

Janessa had learned from her aunt that Joe, with Walini's instructions, had gone up to Wolf's farm and taped his sprained ankle for him.

"You're on your feet, aren't you?" Joe asked. "If you hadn't been too pigheaded to let Rebecca at it, you old devil, I wouldn't have had to come up there and hold you down."

"All it needed was a little goose grease," Wolf said.

"And a splint," Joe retorted. He came closer to Janessa and stroked the guinea pig in her lap. "Are you really all right?" he asked softly.

"Yes," Janessa said. "As well as I can be until Charley gets better." She couldn't admit, even to Joe, the possibility that he might not.

"You love him very much, don't you?" Joe's fingers brushed hers, and she felt the muscles of his hand contract as if shocked by some current.

She nodded silently, and he stepped back.

"You keep up hope," Parker Smith said. "Hope's worth a lot."

They gathered themselves to leave.

"Wait!" Janessa said. "Before you go—I've been going over Charley's notes, his journals of the fever. There's a theory that it's spread by mosquitoes. It's unproven, but if there is any way to keep them out, it might be useful for you to try."

"Mosquiters?" Wolf Mooney stared at her. "Bugs?"

"It's a theory," Janessa said defensively. It sounded unlikely to her, too. There were mosquitoes every summer, but not yellow fever. But epidemiology was full of startling revelations, and you had only to look into a microscope to know that the world could be divided into much smaller increments than you had imagined. "It may not be true. But the fever comes from somewhere. Why not take the precaution?"

"That's like trying to keep out the rain," Walini said.

"But we'll try it. For you, Ka-nessa." Their expressions indicated that they thought she was grasping at straws.

"You need sleep," Wolf told her.

"I want to go sit with Charley," Janessa said. "The nurses can't be everywhere. I can't bear to leave him alone."

"For an hour," Walini said. "Then I'll come back and sit. And you will go to bed." She nodded briskly as if that settled that and shepherded the visitors out. "An hour," she repeated from the doorway, pausing to prod Joe ahead of her.

Joe looked at Janessa over Walini's shoulder, with eyes nearly as haunted as her own, and then turned away abruptly. Janessa put the guinea pig in its basket as the rattle of hooves and wagon wheels faded into the twilight outside. She was beginning to have an uneasy suspicion about Joe, but in her weariness and preoccupation she couldn't hold the thought long enough to concentrate on it. She walked out into the hot, misty air and into the hospital tent to sit beside Charley and hold his thin hand in hers.

Joe kicked his horse into a gallop, trying to blow away his unwanted thoughts with the wind of his going, but they rose unbidden. Janessa drying her hair by the fire. Janessa helping him to dig a grave in the storm. Janessa cradling Lottie in her arms and bringing a crate of oranges she had sent clear to Asheville for to Walini's. Lottie was fine now with Walini—clear-eyed and healthy and learning to pick herbs in the woods. And Billy, without his father to come home and beat him every time the man got a skinful, was studying his books against the time that the school opened again.

Janessa had done all that. Joe knew that he should have done it himself, but he hadn't. He'd just plain hated to go up there any more than he had had to, and he'd been too caught up in this land fight that Vernon Hughes was helping him with now. That had been Janessa's doing, too, as had bringing in that uncle of hers, Colonel Henry Blake, who had the look of a gunslinger about him despite his rank and who had Morton Briggs in such a state. Briggs wasn't being quiet about his anger at Blake's intervention—and Joe thought that was a good sign: If a person was mad, he was probably worried.

If it hadn't been for Senator Toby Holt—a man Joe had counted on hating permanently for what his brief affair with Mary White Owl had cost Joe's family—Colonel Blake wouldn't be here. And if it hadn't been for Janessa, Toby Holt wouldn't have bothered. It all came back to Janessa, and Joe was wrenched by the knowledge that he was more than just grateful to her—he ached for her. Not for what she had done, but for who she was. For the memory of her face in the firelight. For things that he couldn't put his finger on but that added up to misery for him and a troubled conscience. It was bad enough to set your sights on another man's wife when he'd been good to you, but to do it when the other man might be dying. . . .

Joe reined in his horse and turned it away from Yellow Hill, down the track that led to Mabry Forge. He didn't drink much, but tonight he wanted one, and he didn't feel like running into folk he knew. Mabry Forge wasn't a town; it was just a place on an old wagon road, half a mile off the route between Quallatown and Ela. It had a saloon and a shanty store that sold mostly cornmeal and sugar and didn't ask questions such as what could a man do with that much sugar except make whiskey with it? A lot of the whiskey found its way back into the saloon. Mabry Forge was a kind of no-man's-land, neither white nor Cherokee, frequented by the elements of both who liked to keep themselves and their doings private or who came for the pair of tired, sad-faced women who, for fifty cents, slept with the customers in the shed out back. Joe wasn't interested in them, but he wanted to drink and be miserable, and Mabry Forge was a fine place for that.

He urged the horse down the track and had to rein it past two men who loomed up out of the twilight around a curve of the mountain.

One of them made a lunge at him, but the other, an older man, grabbed his companion by the arm. "That's that Cheoah feller. I seen him before. Damn it, ain't you got any sense?"

Joe went on, burning with a quick flicker of fury that came of his own despair and cursing them just for being there.

"Dumb Indian near run me down!"

"You got about enough brains to make a jaybird fly crooked, Sid, you know that?" The older man gave him a shove up the track toward Yellow Hill.

"Don't take no crap from no Indians," Sid Walley growled. "That's what you allus said, Pap."

"An' what did Mr. Morton Briggs say? Don't draw no attention to ourselves, that's what he said. That means we better not get caught if we want to get paid and don't want to get strung up instead. So we don't need that Indian nosin' around afterward, rememberin' us."

"I'll get him later," Sid said venomously.

His father, Eamon Walley, picked up a rock and hefted it. "You give me any more lip, I'll chuck this rock at you and bust your head in. Now let's go."

Sid considered it. He was nineteen now and broad in the shoulders. He was of the opinion that he could take his pap on and win, but he hadn't tried it yet. His pap was a mean son of a bitch and handy with a rock.

"You're mighty worried about one little woman, Pap," he said scornfully. "Seems to me we could do her in in about a minute. What you skeered of?"

"I ain't skeered. I want to get paid. If it don't look like a accident, there'll be a big investigation. This Blake and this Hughes feller ain't gonna go off all grief struck. They're gonna hang around gunnin' for whoever done it. Blake's got a quick hand with a gun, too. I watched him pottin' bottles off a fence yesterday."

"Hell, he ain't so tough." Sid was in a mood to fight

somebody. Cheoah's horse had kicked up dirt in his face. "Mebbe I'll just take him on."

"You shut your trap, or I'll take you on." His father advanced on him and caught him in the rear with the toe of his boot. "I knowed I should of taken someone else along, but I figured we'd keep the money in the family. Don't prove me stupid, boy. Now git!"

Sid turned around snarling and then thought better of it. Morton Briggs had promised them a whole lot of money, more than Sid had ever seen in one chunk. Once they had taken care of this doctor lady, maybe he could cut loose from his pap, go somewhere else, and live high. Everybody else was so set on having this mine, but Sid thought he'd just as soon stay poor as dig dirt out of a hole in the ground. He went on up the track still in a fury, but he was quiet about it.

The job ought to be easy, he thought. You couldn't gun down a government agent—the government would just send three more. But word had it that this one was kin to that Indian doctor who'd stirred it all up and that Blake would probably lose interest if she wasn't around to push him. Sid grinned in the darkness. His teeth weren't good, and they gave him a feral look. Old Briggs was in a hell of a bad mood. He hadn't liked having the yellow jack, and he'd come out of it spitting fire. He'd laid it all out with his weaselly little lawyer Scoggins and a couple of company thugs in the background to see that Pap got it straight—no guns, no knives, no weapon. Just a nasty little accident on the rail line. The night mail train was as regular as clockwork.

Joe Cheoah pushed open the door to the saloon at Mabry Forge. The saloon didn't have a name, just a sign hanging sideways by one nail that said No Spitting on the Floor. By the look of the floor, the warning had been left by a previous proprietor.

"Give me a whiskey."

The bartender set a glass in front of him, and Joe,

suspicious, tasted it to make sure it wasn't moonshine colored with molasses. The local product would take paint off a board.

He sipped it moodily, not paying any more attention than he could help to the men around him. Some were Cherokee, some white, but all were hard-bitten men out of the mountains, with poverty ground into them. Several wore guns or had a rifle leaning against the bar or the edge of their tables. Their guns were a part of them, like their horses.

There were fights regularly at Mabry Forge, but they were fought outside. That was the one rule that was enforced. Nor were the fights generally over race relations, even in those troubled times, but over more personal matters: a bad debt or thievery or a daughter courting the wrong man. It was a place where Cherokee and white could meet and conduct shadowy and often unsavory business together. In Mabry Forge, the doings of the outside world were of less matter.

A few white men, recognizing him as a troublemaker, gave him cold stares, but Joe ignored them. Most of the Cherokee in here weren't people he wanted to know, either. He hunched over his whiskey, thinking that Mabry Forge was everything he wanted to fix about the mountains, everything he wanted to change, so that kids like Billy didn't grow up running white liquor over the mountains at night and get shot in the back over vengeful pride or a deal gone sour. Change would come with time and prayer, Elliot Spray said, but Joe didn't have the Quaker schoolmaster's patience. *Maybe I'll just give up and leave,* Joe thought, *before it drives me crazy.*

Vernon Hughes might lend him a hand to find a place in a law firm in Richmond that would take on a Cherokee. And if that meant that Janessa Lawrence might cross his path now and again. . . . Joe told himself irritably that that wasn't why he was considering it. He ordered another whiskey and drank it, miserably aware that he could never do it—he couldn't leave Qualla Boundary, as much as he hated it, as much as he felt trapped by it. Not if he was going to live with himself afterward.

Gradually he became aware that someone else had entered, someone as out of place as he. He turned slowly to see two white men, beefy and well dressed, tight collars loosened and hats a little awry after an evening's drinking. Coal company thugs. He'd seen them before. He turned away as they staggered boisterously to the bar. Joe thought that they had better watch out. Like him, they did not belong in Mabry Forge, but unlike him, they didn't appear to realize it and had no local roots to make their presence tolerated. Mabry Forge didn't take well to strangers who threw their weight around.

He was prodded out of his thoughts by the slurred and cocky voice of one of them.

"Hey, it's that fancy-pants Indian lawyer."

"Daggone if it ain't. What're you doing in here, Running Bear?"

Joe gave him a long look. "Beat it." He went back to his drink.

"What'sa matter, Little Fawn? Can't get a date? And we was counting on you to find us a little mountain quail."

Joe spun around, his black mood growing. He thought that if he took this son of a bitch apart, it might make him feel better in a whole lot of ways. He tried to scotch that notion and get his temper under control, but all control had flown. "You get out of here before you push me too far," he said between his teeth.

"Aw, he thinks he's tough."

"All these hillbillies think they're tough."

Joe saw that the other drinkers had turned silently to watch them. He knew from the look in their eyes that they might take care of these two after their own fashion later but that they wouldn't help him now. This was his fight.

"Get outside," the bartender told them.

Joe measured the distance between him and the thugs. He knew he held an advantage, even though there were two of them. They were beefy but soft and staggering drunk, or they wouldn't have been dumb enough to show up in a place like this and insult the locals. He didn't care. Right now he wanted nothing more than to beat the hell out of someone, and two loudmouths from the Superior Coal Company were a God-given opportunity. He launched himself at the bigger of the two and knocked him sprawling through the door.

In a rage the other man staggered after them. Joe spun to his feet and punched the first man as hard as he could in the stomach and then in the jaw. He turned and ducked as the second man jumped him from behind; but he was not quite fast enough. A fist slammed into Joe's shoulder and sent him backward, scrabbling for balance. The man came after him.

All the same, Joe wasn't in trouble. He was wiry and strong, and he had grown up fighting. In the scraps of his youth there had been no rules, and he wasn't inclined to employ any now. His heart pounded with the old insane rage he had felt when his father used to beat and taunt him, poisoning the peace with his shouting. Joe stuck out a foot and tripped the comer, then hit him as he came up—once and then twice and a third time while the man flailed his arms and slumped down. The first man was still writhing on the ground. Joe jumped onto the second one's chest and pounded his head over and over in the dirt. It wasn't until he saw blood running from the man's mouth and nose that some trace of sanity crept in. His breath coming in gasps, Joe let go of the man and stood up.

The first man was crouched ten feet away, spitting out his teeth.

"Get out of here," Joe growled. "Before I kill you."

The man spat another mouthful of blood into the dirt. He looked queasy from the alcohol and the beating, and he glared dully at Joe. "You think you're so high and mighty," he gasped, then bent over, retching. "You think you're as good as a white man. But you aren't. You been hiding behind that lady doctor's skirts, but you're gonna get it."

"I said get out of here." Joe's rage was ebbing, and in

the fight's aftermath he felt only a dismal depression. "If I don't kill you, those boys in there will." And where had his high hopes for change and education gone, when he'd set out to work off his anger by beating a man to a pulp?

The man wasn't listening. "You're gonna get it," he repeated doggedly. "Your lady doctor ain't gonna be around to help you. Someone got tired of her strutting around and acting like a man. Damn Indian bitch," he mumbled.

"What do you mean?" Joe snapped, lunging forward and grabbing the man's collar.

The man's eyes were glassy, but he gave Joe a vitriolic stare and a bark of laughter. "You might say she's gonna take a train." Joe pushed him away, and he bent over again, drooling blood. "I hope she burns in hell."

As Joe stared at him, a queasy feeling crept into his own stomach. The moon was up, moving through the scudding clouds, as round as a headlamp. He thought of Janessa walking back to her tent from the hospital, through the menacing shadows of the trees along the path that bordered the railbed, and he remembered the men he had nearly ridden down. They had been coming up the track toward Yellow Hill. What business did white men have in Yellow Hill these days? He ran for his horse, leaving the bigger man lurching across the dirt toward his partner.

"Go home," Walini urged. "I will sit with Charley. I will wake you if I need you. I will wake you if *he* needs you."

Janessa bent to kiss Charley's forehead. His skin felt clammy. Despite the fact that she bathed him herself three times a day, he smelled of sickness. His eyes were closed and his hands uncharacteristically slack on top of the sheet. He was as thin as bone, and limp, as if his skeleton had no power to support him. Janessa drew the mosquito netting around the cot and murmured a prayer. She prayed constantly these days, in her mind and under her breath. It was all she could think of to do. With so much anguish behind her prayers, surely God would hear them.

"Go *home*," Walini said again. She turned Janessa toward the door. "Do you want to be dead yourself when he recovers?"

Janessa felt half-dead already and believed that if Charley died, the rest of her would go with him in spirit if not in body. She pushed the tent flap open, took a deep breath of the steaming air, hot even at this hour, and forced herself to move, to walk, to cover the quarter mile to her own bed.

Her legs carried her mechanically along the well-worn path. The night seemed as somber as death. The trees that bordered the path were thick with shadows, broken only here and there with silver streaks of moonlight. The clouded moon etched the trees dimly against the sky and made the weight of their leaves a menacing canopy.

"Though I walk through the valley of the shadow of death . . ." It was no use. The shadow of death flickered all around her, and she feared it dreadfully, petrified of the thing she could not see—the organism that brought the yellow fever. Never seen, never captured, its presence was visible only in the destruction left in its wake.

Wrapped as she was in her horror of the insubstantial, she never noticed the human forms lurking in the trees until their arms reached out and caught her.

She struggled, heart pounding, almost convinced at first that they were the embodiment of the disease itself, some power come out of hell to overwhelm her. Irrational fear subsided in an instant, however, to be replaced with true terror. One of the men had his hand over her mouth, and was fighting to drag her into the trees toward the precipice above the railbed. The other gripped a rock in his hand.

She fought them, thrashing frantically, as one tried to wrestle her arms behind her back. "Hit her with the rock, damn it, and get her over!" he ordered.

Janessa dug her heels into the ground and ducked her head to avoid the blow. The hand over her mouth and nose was cutting off her breath. Her feet tangled with her captor's, and they stumbled together as the other man lunged at her.

"Come on! We got to get her over before that train comes!"

A fist with a rock in it smacked against the side of her head, and she slumped.

Joe pushed his horse at a dead gallop through the darkness, praying against a groundhog burrow. He could see something moving in the shadows ahead, and he lashed with the end of the reins at the horse's flank. He leaned forward over its neck.

Now he could see an amorphous form that coalesced in a few more strides into two men dragging something into the trees. He reined the horse in on its haunches and hurled himself through the air. Joe came down on top of the two men with a force that sent them reeling.

As he staggered to his feet, the moon ran out of the clouds to illuminate a terrifying tableau: Janessa lay motionless on the ground in a tangle of vines and briars, her cap gone, her hair falling among the blackberry canes. As Joe caught his breath one of the men grabbed hold of her again, frantic to finish the job while the other dealt with their attacker. Joe saw her hand move feebly, batting at the man's arm. He felt a sense of relief; she wasn't dead.

The man now illuminated by the pale moon lunged at Joe. Joe turned and hit him in the face, then tried to push past him. But the man came at him again, and Joe knocked him aside, then lashed out with his boot. But the man's fist caught him in the stomach and nearly doubled him over. These were men bred in the same mountains as Joe, fighters all their lives, and he knew, because he had seen their faces, that they had fear to drive them. But Joe had fury and terror for Janessa to give him strength. The older man battered at him, and Joe swung again and sent him spinning against a tree. His head cracked against the bark.

Joe pivoted toward Janessa. The younger man was trying to drag her from the clinging spikes of the blackberry thorns, and she had revived and was fighting him. But he had her nearly to the ravine's edge, and as Joe ran toward them he saw the man stand above her and raise a rock in both his hands.

Joe leaped across the last ten feet, one hand at his belt. The man saw the gleam of the knife and tried to twist away, but it was too late. With Joe's full momentum behind it, unstoppable now, the knife was driven into the man's chest to the hilt.

There was a crashing in the undergrowth as the older man began to flee. "Get out, Sid! It's no good now!"

But Sid wasn't going anywhere. He lay on his back in the cold moonlight, eyes open to nothing and blood pooling on his chest.

Joe, crouching in the briars, lifted Janessa in his arms. She tried to fight him, and he said, "It's me, Ka-nessa. It's me."

"Joe? Ohhhh . . ." She leaned against him, clutching his shirtfront, just holding on. "They were going to push me over." She was shaking uncontrollably. "Onto the tracks."

"I know." He tightened his arms around her and held her.

"How did you know?" she whispered.

He told her, and she pulled herself together and sat up, staring at him in horror.

"I never thought Briggs would stoop to murder."

"It's been my experience that a man like that'll stoop to anything." Gently he freed her skirt from the thorns and pulled her protectively to him again.

Janessa's eyes flashed, and some of her old spirit returned. "I'm going for the law. Now."

Joe looked at her somberly. "I killed one of them."

"Oh, no!" Janessa struggled out of his arms and went to look at the body. Joe bent to retrieve his knife, then wiped the blade on the grass as Janessa watched.

"No law," she whispered.

They both knew that no amount of testimony from her would erase the fact that Joe was a Cherokee who had killed a white man. With the Superior Coal Company's money and lawyers to seize the chance to rid themselves of Joe Cheoah, the court would be under pressure to hang him. Even Henry Blake would not be able to intervene in time.

"What then?" Joe asked. "He's dead, Ka-nessa. You can't hide that."

A train whistle screamed in the distance. Janessa got to her feet. "We're going to put him where he was going to put me," she said grimly.

They took the man by the arms and dragged him toward the ravine as the distant roar of the train grew nearer. The drop to the spur line was only somewhat steep at first, then precipitous. They scrambled down as far as they could. Joe, having found a foothold, lifted the body and threw it. It arced out dreadfully, arms spread, and landed with a thud across the tracks. Janessa stared at it, hands to her mouth, as the whistle shrieked up the ravine.

"Get back!" Joe grabbed her wrists and pulled her up the slope.

The engine's headlight filled the ravine and cast a misty gleam on the river beyond the tracks. They heard a whistle and a scream of brakes that would be too late; it was a fast mail train, eighty tons in weight. And then the train thundered through.

Janessa shuddered convulsively, and Joe wrapped his arms around her once more. "He was dead already, Ka-nessa." He stroked her hair and turned her so that she couldn't see the light swinging down the track. The train had stopped finally and sent a brakeman back to see what they had hit. Sometimes boys put a dummy on the track to scare the engineer, but they weren't going to find a dummy this time. The brakeman was shouting now, and voices answered from farther down the line. Joe drew Janessa away into the trees, never letting her go. She shivered again. "He was dead, Ka-nessa. He didn't feel it." Joe's urge to comfort her was almost as strong as the desire to go on holding her.

"I know," she whispered. "And it could have been me. I suppose the trainmen will think he got drunk and fell. I don't imagine Morton Briggs will argue with them." She tried to make her voice level, to discuss calmly what they would say, while the creak of an approaching handcar drifted from the railbed below.

"The other one ran," Joe said.

"Oh, no." She looked at him wildly. "He saw you, didn't he?"

"Yes, and you saw him. I expect Briggs would be happy enough to throw him to the wolves, but I think your attacker knows that, too. I don't think he'll come forward. He'll lie low. There are plenty of places to do that for a man who knows the mountains." Joe put more assurance in his tone than he felt. "Mexican standoff," he said lightly.

They heard more voices, this time from the town behind them. Joe stiffened. "We'd better get going. Folks who live by the tracks set their watches by that mail train. They know when something's wrong. There'll be a crowd here in a minute." Janessa's skirt was muddy and covered with leaves, and her hands and face were scratched in deep, red lines from the briars. Joe bent to pick up her cap, and they ran through the darkness toward the medical team's encampment. They slowed as they came near and went swiftly and silently between Steve Jurgen's tent and the nurses'. A lantern flashed nearby, and Joe pulled Janessa into the shadow of her own tent. Eileen had come out in her dressing gown to see what the fuss was. She cocked her head at the shouting and heard the words "run down." Joe let his breath out as Eileen set off, lantern swinging, to see what she could do.

"Tell them you slept through it," Joe whispered to Janessa.

She lifted her hand to his face. He had a cut down one

cheek, and there was mud in his hair. "Thank you for what you did for me," she whispered back.

He bent his face toward hers and then stopped. His eyes looked past her into the darkness of her tent. "I'd better go." He kissed her swiftly, then turned and vanished into the night before temptation and desire overwhelmed him.

VIII

Oahu, July 1892

At about the same time that Janessa was first discovering her kin among the Cherokee, the Brentwoods' ship docked in Honolulu Harbor. Annie, who was still of the opinion that Sam had lost his mind, looked suspiciously at the crowd on the docks, but Eden was enchanted.

The clean, cool trade wind, thick with the scent of salt and the lushness of the islands, blew across her face. Sea and sky were brilliant blue, and every wave flashed silver in the sunlight. The surf ran milky white over the outer coral reef, sounding its deep, booming thunder against the cries of sea birds.

As the ship passed through the channel and into the harbor, coral fishers in canoes and outriggers rode the waves around it. Their wet brown skin gleamed and sparkled, and Eden thought they were the most beautiful people she had ever seen. The channel was an intricate passage of indigo water, entering upon a calm harbor of aquamarine. Inside the harbor, British and American naval vessels rode at anchor, and the inter-island steamer *Likelike* was just setting out for Hawaii, the Big Island.

Above Oahu there rose volcanic peaks of gray and red, cut by chasms of forest green and streaked white with falling water. Punchbowl Hill, an extinct crater of red volcanic ash, blazed against the emerald of the mountains.

136

Along the bright sea sand, on a strip of soft grass, wooden
and grass huts with deep verandas sat under banana trees
and feathery coconut palms. Behind them, almost hidden
in the dense greenery, were the church spires and roofs of
Honolulu, capital of this island kingdom.

"Oh, Annie," Eden breathed, "I feel just like Sara
Crewe when she found the Indian gentleman's presents in
her room!" Mrs. Burnett's novel was a favorite of hers.

"Sara Crewe, indeed." Annie chuckled. "You haven't
been exactly impoverished. But I know what you mean. It
looks almost magical, doesn't it?"

Annie softened visibly as they stepped down the
gangplank and a man in white trousers and a bright red
shirt threw a garland of scarlet and orange flowers about her
neck.

"Aloha, pretty wahine," he said with a smile that made
the comment not at all forward. "And you, too, little
wahine." He tossed another lei over Eden's head and stuck
a fallen flower in the band of her straw boater.

"Oh, look at Sam!" Eden giggled at the sight of her
brother with his own necklace of blooms.

Flowers grew in lush profusion here, brilliant tropical
blossoms that Eden had never seen before, and everyone,
men and women alike, wore them knotted together with
fern and sweet-scented vines. Even the foreigners—the
haoles in their white summer suits and pale muslin dresses,
and the naval officers in their uniforms—wore them. If you
didn't have on a lei, someone was sure to give you one. The
natives had wavy, shiny black hair, and the women wore
holokus, the Hawaiian version of a Mother Hubbard,
imported seventy years earlier by missionaries who had
thrown up their Christian hands in horror at the women's
dress, which had consisted of a skirt of kapa cloth and not
much else. If their intention had been to make these
women less alluring, it had backfired. The holokus, in
brilliant colors, accented women's long, abundant hair and
ideally suited their ample figures. Corpulence was regarded as a sign of beauty here, and some of the older

women were of a size that was amazing. Eden thought she knew a few American women who might have benefited from the elegant, concealing folds of the holoku.

The Brentwoods spent the first night in the Royal Hawaiian Hotel near the cream-colored cupolas and colonnades of the Iolani Palace, and word soon got around that these haoles were planning to stay.

Sam and Annie had settled on purchasing a city house in Honolulu and a farm on the Big Island in the lush land around Kilauea. Before negotiations had been concluded for either, they found themselves deluged with invitations from both haole planters and the native royal family. Hawaiians, it seemed, liked to have parties, and any occasion—a birthday, a visitor, or simply the urge to socialize—called for a celebration. Eden was agog at the prospect of a luau, a kind of Hawaiian picnic on the beach, hosted by Queen Liliuokalani herself. The fifty-three-year-old queen, who the year before had lost her Hawaiian-born haole husband, John Dominis, had never lost her love for parties, and now that she had begun to entertain again, she happily included the Brentwoods in the scores of invitations that were hand delivered, a hibiscus flower tied to each, by her household staff.

Starting school seemed to Eden nearly as exotic as the coming luau. The day school was next door to the missionary-run Royal School, where the royal family's children were educated. A few older pupils at both schools were studying in the summer, preparing for college entrance exams, and Annie had decided that Eden should, too, not so much for her education's sake as to make friends. Many of the students were the haole or half-haole sons and daughters of planters whose own parents had first come to the islands as missionaries.

There seemed no local prejudice on either side against intermarriage, and the *hapa-haole*, or half-haole, children were to Eden as exotic as the full-blooded Hawaiians. Better still were the children at the Royal School next door, who boarded there except during vacations. Eden and her classmates could scramble up the adobe wall between the schools and look down on these fascinating beings. The royal children didn't seem to mind. They smiled and, when their teachers weren't looking, tossed flowers up.

The day of the luau came just as the Brentwoods finished moving into the new house on Beretania Street, not far from Liliuokalani's private house, Washington Place. The queen sent a bouquet of fresh flowers and a basket of mangoes with a personally written note, in her delicate copperplate hand, saying how delighted she was to have such charming neighbors.

Annie blinked as she read it. Her experience with queens was admittedly slight, but she had never even heard of one who acted like this.

"We're in the tropics," Sam explained, slicing a mango. "Everything is different here." He seemed different himself, rather dashing and Hawaiian in a white summer suit and a straw hat with a hibiscus in its band. He looked at Annie hopefully to see if the tropical friendliness had rubbed off on her.

She gave him a glance more suitable to the Arctic and said, "The land agent is here about the farm." Then she swept out to oversee her newly hired Hawaiian maid, who was upstairs unpacking trunks.

Sam sighed. Annie liked the Hawaiians—she was friendly with the neighbors already—but the balmy climate didn't seem to have defrosted her any, where he was concerned. On the nine-day voyage from San Francisco, they had had two staterooms, one of which Annie had shared with Eden and one in which Sam slept alone. There were numerous bedrooms in the new house. Annie had taken the largest, which opened on to the second-story veranda, and after claiming it for her own, she shut the door in his face. Sam's bedroom opened on to the same veranda, but he hadn't set foot on it yet; he wasn't quite sure where Annie's territorial demands ended.

To Sam's surprise, the Hawaiian women, although pleasant to look at, enticed him no more than did the young ladies of Independence. Celibacy left him restless but unwilling to look elsewhere, and as a diversion, he turned to the plans for his farm. He had bought it from an American woman whose husband had died, and she was going back to the States. The acreage was already planted in cane, although from a preliminary inspection, there would be a good deal of work to be done on it. The land agent said that the Hawaiian crew was inclined to be casual about their tasks when no one kept an eye on them. Sam had sold his interest in Brentwood Shipping to his grandmother via a series of transatlantic cables (hers had expressed her surprise at the developments). The vice-presidents who had made his life a burden now ran the company for her.

Everything Sam owned was tied up in the plantation, and he knew he had better get out there fast. The rambling farmhouse was being repainted and repaired, and the insect life discouraged—every conceivable variety of bug flourished in this tropical clime, some of them in amazing proportions. As soon as the house was ready, Sam planned to move into it. He fervently hoped Annie was coming with him. That had been their original plan, but she was settling into the city house in Honolulu with a thoroughness that included a complete redesign of the gardens and an expensive rug for the parlor. Sam had not quite the nerve to ask her if she would be accompanying him; he felt as if he were balancing on a cannonball—one that might prove to be still inside the cannon.

What on earth, Annie wondered, *does one wear to meet the queen? And what does one wear to a luau?*

She finally asked her maid, who giggled and said, "Something cool and comfortable. And take a bathing dress if you want to swim."

Heavens, Annie thought. She settled on the dressiest of her light muslins and put Eden into a similar costume. The party was at the queen's beach house at Waikiki, and the Brentwoods' carriage joined a throng of others in the sweet-scented night, rolling down the road amid a crowd of laughing riders on horseback and a number of Hawaiians in gaudily painted carts drawn by servants. A tropical moon hung in the sky, making a shimmering silver path along the water, where the surf rolled for a full mile from the coral reef to the white sand.

They alighted as the steaming *imus*, Hawaiian underground ovens, were opened, and the pungent aroma of roasted meat filled the air, mingling with the perfume of the flowers.

"Aloha! Aloha!" Leis were thrown around their shoulders, and coconut shells of fruit juice were pressed into their hands. A naval officer winked and tipped a splash from a hip flask into Sam's. The partygoers milled around them to the haunting sound of guitars and taro-patch fiddles, the little ukuleles that Hawaiians had recently adopted as their own.

Sound and color swirled around Annie in the lantern light until she felt as breathless and excited as if she were Eden's age. Even her stiff anger at Sam began to bend. She still wasn't going to have anything to do with him, but she could relent and be beguiled by the island he had chosen.

"Mrs. Brentwood, I have so wanted to meet you. You must forgive me that I have been occupied with tiresome ministers with equally tiresome business."

Annie turned to find a tall, plump woman with a coronet of flowers in thick, graying black hair. She wore a black gown cut in the European style, but her smiling Hawaiian face was instantly recognizable from the royal portraits that hung everywhere.

"Your Majesty!" Annie managed a curtsy.

"Come away from all this commotion for a moment, and let us get acquainted, since we are neighbors," Liliuokalani said. "Your little sister is in good hands."

Eden was already surrounded by a group of young people whom she knew from school, although Annie noted that some of the younger naval officers were eyeing her admiringly. As Annie followed the queen into a fragrant nook of the beach-house gardens, she decided to continue to resist Eden's pleas to let down her skirts. Eden still wore the short frocks of a girl not yet "out," and among respectable men those short skirts were a safeguard as effective as a barbed-wire fence. Eden was getting prettier all the time.

Liliuokalani remarked on the girl's beauty as she settled herself in a high-backed wicker chair and gestured for Annie to do likewise.

"She is lovely, isn't she?" Annie said proudly. "She's had a difficult time—she lost both her parents in a tragic accident at sea. We brought her here for a complete change of scene, and the island seems to agree with her. One couldn't ask for a more peaceful, beautiful place."

"Poor thing." The queen was instantly sympathetic. Children were much valued among the Hawaiians, to the extent that childless families "borrowed" readily from kinsmen who had plenty. The queen herself had been adopted at birth by a high-ranking kinsman and had barely known her real parents. "My first clear memory of my real father," she said, laughing, to Annie, "was when I was nine, and my older brother James died in an epidemic of measles. My father came to our house and made me shave my head in mourning—the old customs, you know. He wanted me to knock my front teeth out with a rock, too. My foster father, Paki, was furious, but he let my father talk him into just filing them into points. Paki gave me a new cart to ride to school in as a reward for not making a fuss."

"Goodness," Annie said. "Still, it would be nice," she added thoughtfully, "to think that someone would grieve that much over you." She thought of Andrew and Lydia, without even a grave.

"I don't think," the queen remarked, chuckling, "that your little sister would be improved by pointed teeth. I suppose she could use them to bite unwanted suitors. She will certainly have plenty."

Annie chuckled, too. This woman was a darling, like no queen of Annie's imagining. Annie had made a few close women friends in the old days before her first husband had struck it rich. But then, as a silver nabob's wife, and shortly after that as a widow, it had been harder—and complicated by an affair with Sam, which had scandalized even a boomtown society. She had begun to feel close to Sam's grandmother, Claudia, and she liked Toby Holt's wife, Alexandra, but she did not have the kind of woman friend to whom one could pour out all her confidences and find sympathy without judgment.

"Tell me about yourself," Liliuokalani invited, and Annie, somewhat to her surprise, found herself doing so, editing Sam just a little. She thought that maybe the queen, set apart as she was by her rank and with almost none of her own family still living, might feel much the same lack. They talked as the music and laughter went on around them.

"Adoption as a custom is dying out now," Liliuokalani said when the subject came around to children again. "So few these days reach maturity. We have no resistance, you see, to haole diseases. The measles that your children usually survive kill ours so quickly. It began with the missionaries. One can't hold them to blame, but it does seem ironic that the people who brought us God also brought death."

"It's a wonder that you tolerate us," Annie said, shocked.

"It isn't the haoles only. We have leprosy here now—a dreadful plague. That came from China with the coolies imported by the planters to work the cane fields." She sighed. "So I suppose that *was* the haoles. But my husband, my darling John, was a haole. If there hadn't been haoles, I wouldn't have had him."

"You must have loved him very much, Your Majesty."

"Oh, I did. But you must call me Lydia, as we are neighbors. My mother named me Liliuokalani as a baby, and a queen must have a Hawaiian name. But I was always called Lydia as a child. My dear John called me that, and all the people that I loved. We are a very informal people among our friends."

"I should like that very much," Annie said, touched and amazed at how this dear woman had with such a simple

and artless request erased the thoroughgoing dislike that
Annie had always held for that name. "My own name is
Annie," she added. "Annie Laurie, actually." She laughed.
"My mother was a romantic. It's from an old Scottish song."

"I know that!" the queen said, delighted. She began to
sing it in a clear, beautiful voice:

> "Maxwelton's braes are bonnie,
> Where early fa's the dew,
> And it's there that Annie Laurie
> Gave me her promise true."

"Sam used to sing me that when we were courting,"
Annie murmured, then felt annoyed that she had thought of
that. "You have a beautiful voice," she said.

"I have always been musical. I wrote 'Aloha Oe,' you
know. That's what they are playing now."

Annie listened as the haunting melody lilted across the
beach, melancholy and beautiful, commemorating two
lovers' parting. It was played everywhere. She had even
heard it in the States. Liliuokalani was certainly a most
unusual queen.

"I wrote our national anthem, too," the queen said.
"But 'Aloha Oe' has become more popular. It speaks to
something in our blood, I think. These days it grows
difficult for us to cling to the things that are Hawaiian, that
are exclusively ours. I wish my haole legislators would
listen to it more closely."

Annie thought she heard an acerbic note in the queen's
voice that was at odds with her gentle personality. She
decided there might be a good deal of steel inside that
plump figure.

"Are all your legislators haole?" Annie asked.

"All the ones who count," Liliuokalani said grimly.
Then she raised a hand, and a servant scurried over. "But
dinner is ready, and this is not a night for my guests to
trouble themselves with politics. This is a party. My

ministers will do what they want to, and I will do what I have to, and I suppose we will muddle through."

While the luau continued under the shimmering moon, Sam found himself at the other end of what he and Annie were discovering to be the troubled Hawaiian political spectrum.

"Brentwood, good to see you again." Lorrin Thurston clapped Sam on the back and held out his hand. Thurston was the dark-bearded lawyer whose firm had handled the farm purchase. "I hear you're getting ready to take up plantation life. Always good for the owner to hang around. If you don't, it all gets done on Hawaiian time."

"Hawaiian time stops every quarter hour to play the fiddle," another man said. "It makes lunch end up around, oh, five o'clock."

"You know Judge Dole, don't you?" Thurston asked.

Sam and the judge shook hands.

"I was just saying," Thurston went on, "we've got to get you a membership in the Planters Club. That's where you'll pick up anything you need to know about the sugar business. Best poker game in Honolulu, too."

"I'll be grateful for any tips you gentlemen can give me," Sam said. "I'm new at this, but I intend to make a go of it."

"Sugarcane's easy to make a go of," Dole said. "Everything grows like weeds out here. You plant some jessamine around your house, and the next thing you know, you can't tell what's vine and what's house. Lush. There's nothing like it. Grows year-round. The main thing is to keep your ear to the ground politically. The queen's got some independent notions, bless her. No head for business or progress. Of course none of the Hawaiians have. If they didn't have guidance, they'd still be catching a fish for supper when they got hungry and the rest of the time snoozing under the breadfruit tree."

They carried their plates, filled with steaming, pungent slices of pork, spiced pineapple, and other concoctions that Sam could not identify, to a circle of chairs beyond a fire pit where Liliuokalani's servants were roasting freshly caught fish on sticks.

"Now that's Hawaii for you," Thurston said, pointing at the water, where a laughing, middle-aged man in a *malo*, a native loincloth, walked into the surf. On his shoulder he was carrying a long, flat board. "That's one of the queen's cabinet. Not ten minutes ago I was having a serious conversation with him, then one of his cousins comes by with a surfboard, and the next thing I know he's taking off his clothes." Thurston shook his head. "No attention span. If he isn't careful, he's going to get a surprise when the legislature opens in September."

"How's that?" Sam asked, but his eyes were on the man in the water. He had paddled his board out beyond the first reef, and as he knelt facing the shore, he rose and fell as the waves rolled under him.

"We're having a little trouble with Her Majesty's cabinet," Thurston said. "They're making noises about retracting David Kalakaua's constitution, and we can't have that."

"David Kalakaua was king before Liliuokalani," Dole explained. "Not a solid man at all. Easily led. It finally came down to forcing a constitution on him that would give us some stability—election reform to put the vote in the hands of solid citizens. Now only qualified voters will elect the upper assembly of the legislature. And we've disallowed dismissal of cabinet members on silly whims. That was no way to run a government. We have too much invested in these islands to let that kind of thing go on. They're a fine people, but they're like children."

"Are you two at it again?" Harvey Sessions, who farmed a plantation next to the one Sam had bought, came by with a drink in his hand and shook his head pityingly at Sam. "This is too nice a night to let these two bend your ear about politics. Take a break, and come out on the water."

Dole grinned. "You go, Harvey. I have no intention of getting wet."

"How about it, Brentwood? Ever been out in a canoe?"

"Go on," Thurston urged. "It's an experience. Once."

Sam got up. The moonlit water was irresistible. He turned and shook hands with Thurston and Dole. They knew the situation in the islands and were well respected. If he wanted to be a success, Sam thought, he had better listen to them.

"You won't find a sounder man than Judge Dole." Sessions echoed this thought. "But he does prose on at parties."

There were several outrigger canoes beached on the sand, and Sessions appropriated one. He set his coconut-shell cup in the sand, and he and Sam took off their shoes and rolled up their trousers.

"Form's sake." Sessions laughed. "You'll get wet anyway."

"Is this yours?" Sam asked him as they ran the canoe into the water. The surf bubbled enticingly around his ankles.

"No, but they know I'll bring it back. Where am I going to go in it? Paddle to Kauai? The Hawaiians do, you know," he added as they settled themselves in the canoe. "A hundred miles at least. They have races. Old Kamehameha the First conquered the islands in these things. We mostly travel by steamer now, of course, but if you want the real island flavor, hire a canoe."

The real island flavor was very wet and salty, but Sam found it exhilarating. The slender canoe shot over the water like a dragonfly, although the sheer size of the breakers they were crossing gave Sam a few qualms. He realized, as Harvey began to sing "Aloha Oe" loudly and considerably off-key, that Harvey's cup of fruit punch had been spiked with alcohol, and it hadn't been his first drink. Sam wondered how drunk you could be and still paddle a canoe. Pretty drunk he decided, listening to Harvey.

"You ever overturn one of these things?" he shouted to Harvey over the roar of the surf.

"Never!" Harvey shouted back cheerfully. "Can't. I can't swim."

Oh, very good. "Well, I can!" Sam shouted. "But don't let it go to your head!"

The nearby surfers on their boards seemed to be enjoying themselves. They rode the monstrous swells gracefully, and when one big enough to suit them came along, they paddled furiously and let the wave pick them up. Then they rose to stand with one foot in front of the other, arms outstretched, flying toward shore. As they shot past the canoe they waved cheerfully, although a couple of them turned their heads for an instant as if in concern. Then the surfers were gone.

"You need to go out farther for a good canoe ride," Harvey said, panting. Looking behind him, Sam could see the surfers paddling out again. He and Harvey plied their paddles through the sparkling, inky water. The black surface looked rime-encrusted in the moonlight, but it rose and swelled and broke in long combers that showered diamond sparks around them. *Magic*, Sam thought. He decided that you probably couldn't turn over an outrigger canoe; the long bar that sat well out in the water to one side gave it balance. Harvey didn't seem worried. They paddled over the top of a long swell and out past the surfers waiting on their boards. The music from the luau on the beach was lost in the roar of the surf.

"This is good!" Harvey called. "Now we turn in and just enjoy the ride back!"

They began to swing the canoe around, Harvey laughing and waving his paddle at the surfers. One of them shouted something at him that was lost in the sound of the surf. Sam looked uneasily at the incoming swells that were now broadside to them.

"Hey!" he yelled at Harvey.

Harvey looked around at him and then at the rapidly rising water coming landward toward them from the ocean. He dug his paddle into the water, bumped his chin on it as

a smaller swell rocked them sideways, and lost his grip on
it. He gave a muffled curse.

A bigger wave was nearly on them, and the magic had
gone out of the moonlit water in a hurry. Its roaring
blackness made Sam think of an approaching train, and
even the silver moon looked ominous, drawing that mountain of water inexorably down upon them. Sam paddled
desperately, but without Harvey's paddle the canoe was
cumbersome and difficult to control. Sam realized with a
flicker of terror that the canoe, hard to overturn, could still
be swamped, pressed downward by the sheer weight of the
water.

Sam could not turn it in time. Harvey was staggering
up now, panic-stricken, sending the craft lurching off-
balance. The wave came down on them like a landslide,
rolling Sam under, choking him with salt water. The flying
bar of the outrigger caught him across the jaw as he rose,
and he went down again, deeper into salty darkness, with
his father's ghost howling in his ears.

It was the thought of his father's drowning that sent
Sam fighting frantically to the surface. He took a breath of
air into seared lungs and saw the empty canoe, its outrigger
bar swinging toward him like a battering ram. Sam dived as
the canoe shot over him, then clawed his way up to the
surface again. His eyes were blinded with the salt and the
blackness, and he couldn't see Harvey anywhere. Another
wave slammed into him, pushed him down, and then
something caught his wrist and pulled.

Sam struggled, thinking that he had caught his hand
somehow in the canoe's outrigger, but whatever it was
didn't let go. It grabbed him by the collar and yanked him
above the surface. He found himself pushed facedown
across a board, with a voice in his ear yelling at him to be
still.

"Hang on!"

Sam hung, clinging to the board with both hands. He
could just see a man's bare back ahead of him, bent low over
the board, paddling with both hands. The board picked up

speed, rose on a swell, and shot down the other side like a rocket toward the shore. Its rider gradually maneuvered himself to a standing position, guiding the board by some method unknown to Sam, who was, in any case, too busy hugging it with both arms to care.

Their wet, hell-for-leather ride ended with the board bobbing in the rippling shallow surf and Sam, with his teeth clenched tight, still lying flat, a piece of kelp plastered across his nose.

His rescuer unceremoniously hauled him upright, but the fellow steadied him while Sam bent, head over knees, and retched up salt water. Little waves tickled his feet.

"Our canoes take some practice," the man commented.

Sam retched again and straightened up. He discovered a very small crab in his shirt pocket and flung it away. "Apparently." His chest felt as if it were on fire. He looked around. "There was a man with me," he said, coughing.

His rescuer pointed toward the beach. With relief Sam saw Harvey Sessions staggering over the sand with another Hawaiian, who carried his own board on his shoulder.

"Thank you," Sam said. "My father drowned at sea," he added with a shiver that was at odds with the warm night.

The Hawaiian looked at him closely. "You're Brentwood, aren't you?" the man asked. "I'm Peter Aikanaka."

He held out his hand, and Sam shook it solemnly. The gesture lent to their meeting a peculiar sense of formality that intensified the phantasmagoric qualities of the night and the sea.

"I'm glad to meet you," Sam said. "I thought for a minute there I was going to follow my old man."

"Well, you might have. We shouted at you to watch that reef—it breeds huge waves. But I guess you couldn't hear us."

They waded through the last yards of surf and up the beach toward Harvey. Then Peter Aikanaka disappeared.

Harvey was wringing out his trouser cuffs. "Well, that

was a ride," he said. "I guess I'm going to have to pay for that canoe."

Sam didn't think that Harvey's ride had sobered him up much. He looked out toward the water. "Maybe not." Sam saw now that Peter and his companion had swum out and righted the vessel. The paddles were gone, but they dipped their hands in the water and caught a wave to ride.

"Gave me a bit of a jolt," Harvey admitted. "I'll have to send the old boy a nice present."

Sam saw that the other man in the outrigger had white hair, which was startling against his brown skin, and was sixty years old if he was a day. "It gave me more than a jolt," he muttered. "Look at the old devil! If I can do that when I'm his age, I'll count myself lucky."

"Well, they don't do much else, you know," Harvey said cheerfully. "It's just a matter of practice. I could probably do it myself if I didn't have business to attend to. That fellow who picked you up—he's one of Liliuokalani's cabinet ministers. You'd think he'd have a better pastime than fooling around with a surfboard, but that's a Hawaiian for you."

"You sound like Thurston," Sam said.

"Oh, Thurston's right," Harvey told him. "Childlike, endearing people. I'm fond of them. My wife's Hawaiian. Cute as a button." He grinned. "But traits that are endearing in the little woman aren't what you want in your government."

He ambled away, presumably to assure the little woman that he hadn't drowned, and left Sam sitting on the beach. Sam wondered vaguely if he ought to go tell Annie the same, but he decided that she probably hadn't noticed. There hadn't seemed to be much commotion over their rescue. Peter Aikanaka and the old man had simply lifted the haoles out of the water by the scruffs of their necks and slung them onto surfboards.

Sam couldn't rid himself of the disquieting feeling that he had actually seen and heard his father, or some drifting piece of his angry spirit, out there in the water. It hovered wraithlike and stubborn just on the edge of his memory and wouldn't go away.

"The kahunas say that if the sea doesn't get you the first time it tries, you'll be safe for five years before it tries again," Peter Aikanaka said, coming to sit beside him. "This would be a good night to learn to surf."

Sam looked at him suspiciously to see if Peter might be making fun of him. Peter's face was bland, but Sam decided he probably was. "Standing up, you mean?" Sam inquired. He felt embarrassed and irritable, but he'd be damned if he'd admit it.

"It's much more pleasant," Peter said with a low chuckle. "Not so much seaweed in the mouth."

Sam also thought that this man who swam so well was challenging him. He wondered if Peter Aikanaka had any idea that it wasn't so much the water Sam feared as what he might find in it. Did the kahunas believe that drowned men haunted the sea in Hawaii? The notion that his father's body might have tumbled in the waves from one ocean to another in relentless condemnation of things left undone had begun to take hold of him. He stood up defiantly.

"All right."

Peter held out a malo, and Sam stripped off his wet shirt and trousers in the shadow of the beached outriggers and wrapped the loincloth around him. Peter showed him how to straddle the board and then got on behind him as the water deepened. They began to paddle, with Peter guiding the board. When they had reached the other surfers, out again and waiting for the right wave, they turned the board around, expertly this time.

"Wait till I tell you," Peter said.

"How do you know which wave?" The board rose and fell as swells, apparently not the right ones, rolled under them.

"We feel it," Peter answered. "We know. We'll give you a good ride this time and take the taste of the last one out of your mouth."

Sam heard a low laugh behind him in the darkness.

"Sure," he said. "Why not?" His voice was cocksure—carefully so—but his eyes were riveted on the water. The Hawaiians believed in ghosts—the "night marchers," a spirit procession of lights or shadows, were often seen along the ancient trails, or so it was said—and kahunas were consulted before new houses were built, to be sure the structures were not in the path of these wandering shades. Could you call up the dead by your own belief? Sam shuttered his mind against that thought. *I'm sorry. Please go away. I didn't drown you.*

You didn't care, either, some voice came back to him. *Do you care enough for anything to drown for it if you have to?*

I don't know.

Peter Aikanaka tensed behind him. "Get ready."

"Welakahao!" someone shouted, and the rest took up the cry.

"Welakahao!"

They began to paddle furiously to gain speed, and suddenly Sam felt the board rise as if some ocean giant had come up beneath it to lift it on his shoulders. It plunged forward, and Peter rose to his feet, pulling Sam up with him. He steadied Sam with two strong hands around his rib cage, and they soared.

Peter shifted his feet slightly, and the board turned at an oblique angle to the wave. It moved faster and faster, always ahead of the breaking crest of the wave. It was like flight, with the spindrift in his face and the salt wind whispering past his ears. This is how the frigate birds dipping above the sea must feel, he thought.

They shot toward the bonfires on the beach, back into the music and the laughter. Sam found himself on the water's edge again, heart pounding, startled at the swiftness of the moment. He wanted to thumb his nose at the ocean, at whatever might be in it, to let it know that he had beaten it and could outrun it.

"I want to learn to do that," he said suddenly to Peter Aikanaka. "By myself."

"Not at night." Peter's grin glinted through the darkness at Sam. "Let's not push the sea too far."

"Tomorrow then," Sam said.

"It's not as easy as it looks," Peter murmured. "I've been surfing since I was a child."

"I don't care," Sam said. "I want to learn. I'll pay you to teach me."

Peter shook his head, startled now himself. "You haoles are a mystery. I would not expect anyone to pay for lessons. I *like* to surf. If you want to learn, just come down to the beach tomorrow morning."

"Tomorrow," Sam said. He picked up his wet clothing and walked up the sand, back toward the fires.

Peter Aikanaka looked after him wonderingly. Brentwood seemed to him more mystifying than most. Peter was beginning not to like haoles very much. He had overheard Harvey Sessions's remarks to Brentwood and had not liked the tenor of the conversation.

The missionaries had brought peace and God, and Peter, a devout churchgoer and descendant of a long line of chieftains whose oral tradition still told of bloody inter-island wars, knew himself blessed by both. But the missionaries' children had turned to more lucrative pursuits as planters and Honolulu businessmen, and they considered themselves also to have done Hawaii a fine favor with their land reform and new economic system. The land reform had left most of the native Hawaiians landless because they had not understood the new concept of individual ownership. And the economic system wasn't making anyone but the haoles rich.

Still, they were a familiar presence, and Peter knew what they wanted even if he found himself unable to fathom why. Who, for instance, needed more money than that which would allow him to live in a fine house and wear elegant clothes and give parties? Haoles always seemed to want more, and what would they do with it if they had it?

Sam Brentwood was another matter, Peter thought.

He had come to the islands on a whim, it was said, and it might be to make money, but he was different somehow. He was restless like all haoles, but there was more to him than that. He was edgy and volatile, like Kilauea the volcano on the Big Island when she began to wake up and send long molten fingers searching down the slopes. Peter looked up the beach at Sam, standing on wet sand with his eyes sliding between the water and the luau, and wondered if *he* knew what he was looking for.

IX

Annie narrowed her eyes suspiciously—an expression she had adopted as permanent where Sam was concerned—and asked, "Are you going out like that?"

"I'm going to the beach, not the Royal Hawaiian Hotel. Why don't you come with me?" Sam invited.

"I am having tea. With the queen."

"Oh, la. Very high circles."

"If you're going to the beach, put on a bathing costume!"

"This is one."

"Not for a gentleman." Annie sniffed, nose in the air.

Sam struck a pose in her sitting-room mirror. "I think I look rather well in it."

"You look like a cart boy," Annie snapped.

"And if you get much more refined," Sam retorted, "Mrs. Astor will be able to take lessons from you."

The truth was, he had fancied himself in the malo that Peter Aikanaka had lent him and had bought several in Honolulu during the last few days before they were to move the household to the Big Island for the rest of the growing season before the winter cane harvest. Since the accepted masculine bathing costume in the States demanded knee-length knitted breeches and a chest decently hidden by a matching jersey, the brightly patterned native loincloth

156

gave him a raffish look that, he knew, annoyed Annie on more counts than one. She considered it undignified, and Annie was very concerned about dignity just now. Worse, he looked far too good in it. His bare chest was tanned nearly as brown as a Hawaiian's. Paddling a surfboard out among the combers off Waikiki, he might have been one. Up close, you could tell by the fine-boned features of his face that he was haole, but his back and shoulders had grown more muscular from his newly adopted hobby, and he had acquired a lazy, loose-limbed gait that seemed to belong to the islands. Sam had always had a tomcat sensuality to his movements, and the malo did nothing to hide it.

"If you are going to come into my sitting room," Annie said, "I would appreciate it if you would put some clothes on."

Sam stood looking at her without answering, until she turned her eyes away. Then he plucked a gardenia, which was floating in a glass bowl beside her, stuck it behind his ear, and sauntered out, whistling.

When he was out of sight, however, he stopped and looked back angrily. Tea with the queen, indeed. There had been a time when Annie wouldn't have wasted her afternoon with a fat old woman when she could have come out with him. He smacked his fist into the fine teakwood paneling in the parlor, then stalked out the front door, shouting for someone to bring him his horse. Annie wouldn't like his riding through Honolulu in a malo, either, although it probably wouldn't have shocked her fat friend the queen. Liliuokalani was more Hawaiian than not, despite her corsets and her tendency to sign bills as "Lydia Dominis" when she wasn't thinking about it. Annie had no more sense than some goody-goody old church lady, Sam thought grumpily. And there was no telling what Liliuokalani was filling her head with. Annie didn't understand politics. She let sentiment rule her.

He remembered the time in Virginia City when she had given five hundred dollars to the miners' union strike

fund, although she'd still had some of her money invested
in the mining corporations. It came from growing up poor,
he supposed. Poverty made some people greedy; it had just
made Annie a soft touch. She had said she was ashamed of
him when she'd found out that Sam had been spying on the
union for the mine owners. She had married him anyway,
though. She had been a soft touch for Sam, too, in those
days. Now she was chummier with the queen than she was
with him.

A houseboy handed Sam the reins, and he swung
himself up into the big Mexican saddle. Hawaiian horses
were a sorry lot, but the natives made up for that with their
saddles—high cantled, with huge wooden stirrups, silver
bosses, and bright saddlecloths. Hawaiians loved to ride
and went everywhere on horseback, men and women alike
riding astride, usually at a gallop, black hair flying. Sam
kicked the beast into a reluctant trot and left his houseboy
to bring the surfboard in a cart. He intended to make the
most of the afternoon. Once he took over the plantation, he
wouldn't have much chance to indulge in this new hobby.

The streets of Honolulu were tree shaded and lush.
Houses of every description, from native thatch to adobe
and New England clapboard, were hidden behind rampant
greenery: umbrella trees, bamboo, monkey pod, banana—
a canopy so dense that the afternoon sunlight barely
trickled through, and nothing could be seen past the next
bend in the road. Once past the last house, Sam kicked the
horse into a jolting gallop down the beach road to Waikiki.

Despite his determination to enjoy himself, he
couldn't stop thinking about the plantation. He was going to
make it pay and force Annie to eat every word she'd said
about it.

Sam understood politics; he grasped the necessity for
believing that Judge Dole, Lorrin Thurston, and even that
drunken idiot Harvey Sessions were right. The sugar
industry demanded a steady economy, and that meant a
stable government, one that didn't run on Hawaiian time.
Hawaiian sugar had to be taken seriously in the world

market, taken seriously in the States. The States were what counted—that was where the sugar went. Annie could afford to be naive; it wasn't her money.

At Waikiki Sam tethered the horse to a banana tree and waited, looking irritably at his watch, for the houseboy and his board to arrive. He could have pulled the blasted cart quicker himself, he thought, fidgeting. He was in a hurry. Everything seemed urgent to him now, even proving whatever it was that he was proving by mastering the ocean.

By the time the cart arrived he was well into a good burst of temper, but he stifled it when he saw Eden sitting beside the board. She had on a bathing dress of the elaborate sort that haole women wore. It consisted of a middy blouse with a big white sailor collar, a knee-length serge skirt over voluminous bloomers, black stockings, and canvas shoes. A straw hat covered her gold curls.

"Why aren't you in school?"

"Summer term has been over for a week. If you were ever home, you'd have noticed," Eden said.

"Indeed," Sam said. "And are you under the impression that I'm going to take you out with me?"

Eden hopped down from the cart. "I came to protect you from all the pretty wahines. You might as well take me out."

"I don't need any protection." Sam laughed, his mood improving in spite of himself.

"Well, you don't have much resistance," Eden said doubtfully.

"You're much too young to be keeping track of my resistance," Sam informed her. "All right, I'll take you out. But you have to take off those shoes and that silly hat."

Eden sat down on the sand and began to pull off her stockings. "I know. This was just to get past Annie."

"How was Annie?"

"Tricky," Eden said, rolling up her stockings and stuffing them into the toes of her shoes. "I think she misses you, but she's still mad." They had long ago given up any pretense that Eden didn't know what was going on. "If you ask me, you ought to court her some."

"What do you mean by that?"

"Flowers. Candy. Take her out to dinner and a concert."

"I'm going to have a plantation to run," Sam protested. "Starting tomorrow. It's not going to be easy, beginning in the middle of the season. The land agent says the farm's been let go, and we're going to have to put our backs into it."

"Annie knows a lot about Hawaii."

Sam picked up the surfboard and set it on his shoulder. They waded into the waves. "Not about sugarcane. And all she knows about Hawaii is what the old lady tells her. She ought to hang around the Planters Club. She'd have her eyes opened. A lot of them think Liliuokalani went too far when she got rid of David Kalakaua's cabinet and put in her own." With the water up to their waists, he steadied Eden on the board and straddled it behind her. "There's beginning to be talk of deposition."

Eden turned a shocked face around to him, eyes wide. "Sam! You wouldn't do something like that! That's a revolution!"

"Of course not," Sam said. "Really now, can you see old Judge Dole as a bomb-throwing anarchist? Nobody will do anything that's not constitutional. Now quit worrying and pay attention to what you're doing here. If you play your cards right, I may see if we can't find another board and let you try it by yourself today."

Eden squealed excitedly and gave her attention to the blue, rolling water. Nothing was as much fun as being out with Sam. They caught a perfect wave, and she managed to rise to her feet without his help, her arms spread wide. A pelican flew slowly by them with a fish in its beak and dipped its wings in what might have been a greeting as it wheeled past.

* * *

"To annexation." Lorrin Thurston drained his glass and thumped it down on the tablecloth. He poured himself more port and nodded at Sam. "I'm glad you've joined us, Brentwood. I felt you were a sound man."

"I've sunk everything I've got into sugar," Sam said. "I'm for whatever stabilizes prices."

"Precisely the point. They've been depressed ever since the McKinley Tariff was enacted two years ago. Lost us our favored position, and there's only one way to recoup."

Sam nodded. A reciprocity treaty negotiated in 1876 had allowed Hawaiian sugar to enter the States duty free. The McKinley Tariff had allowed all sugar, from whatever source, into the States duty free but paid domestic producers a bounty of two cents a pound. The Honolulu Planters Club, and its sub rosa committee, the Annexation Club, took a dim view of that.

Thurston coughed delicately. "I understand your wife has become a confidante of the queen," he said, sipping port. "Very useful."

"Probably not," Sam said. He grinned, embarrassed. "She doesn't talk to me about it. Doesn't talk to me about a lot, if it comes to that. She's not pleased with me at the moment."

"Ah, the ladies . . ." Judge Dole chuckled. "We've all been in that spot. Still, I'm sure you can bring her around. I'm afraid Her Majesty is preparing to do something very unwise."

"Fine talk from you, Judge," Thurston muttered. "Your court upheld her when she replaced David Kalakaua's cabinet."

"I upheld the constitution," Dole said. "It says the reigning monarch can't dismiss his ministers without a vote of the legislature. Unfortunately, it doesn't say that a new monarch has to reappoint the old one's ministers."

"Shortsighted, that," someone murmured. Most of the

men in the room had been involved in writing that
constitution.

"Well, yes," Dole allowed.

"What about the new men she's chosen?" Sam asked,
thinking of Peter Aikanaka.

"She appoints them, they're installed, and the legislature votes them out," Thurston said. "It's been like a
revolving door since last May. In another couple of months,
there won't be a man left in Hawaii who hasn't been a
cabinet minister for at least fifteen minutes."

Sam decided Peter Aikanaka probably wasn't going to
have much longevity. He took a sip of his port, then asked,
"How does the legislature stand now on annexation?"

"They're not quite as biddable there," Thurston admitted. "They won't stand for the queen being the absolute
power here, but they're pussyfooting around about the only
possible way to deal with her."

"Come now," Dole said. "Many of them are natives.
You can't expect them—"

"I can expect them to see the inevitable!" Thurston
exclaimed. "Hawaii can't go back to being an all-powerful
monarchy. Hawaii has been civilized for nearly seventy
years. That cannot be turned around!"

"You'll catch the curtains on fire." Dole smiled. Thurston had been gesturing with his cigar, to the danger of the
draperies behind him.

"Well! The point is, someone has to take charge."
Thurston put out his cigar in an ashtray, but he continued
to wave it to make his point. "Now, I went to the States
earlier this year. I spoke with the secretary of the navy and,
through him, with President Harrison. Harrison's a cau-
tious devil. I let him know that we have no intention of
precipitating any action but that the queen is expected to
attempt an absolutist constitution that is bound to meet
resistance. I came away quite satisfied that the President
will be exceedingly sympathetic toward us if that should
happen."

Sam nodded. This was heady talk and exciting. He

liked being a part of it. But it was grounded in common sense. The annexationists were businessmen, in the business that he had bought into. "I take it you foresee a peaceable changeover?" he asked.

"Certainly." Thurston stabbed the air with his cigar again. "The United States wouldn't stand for anything else, you know. And just among us in this room, we have Stevens to advise us." John Stevens was the United States minister to Hawaii. "He's a close friend of Secretary Blaine's, and they're both scared to death of the British."

"Wonderful bugaboo, the British," Dole confided. "One has only to hint to Mr. Stevens that they are gaining influence at the palace, and he fires off another report to the President. The one thing no American wants is to have the English annex us instead."

Sam looked startled. "Is that a possibility?"

"I very much doubt it," Dole said. "America's had a naval base at Pearl Harbor since 1887. But Her Majesty has a soft spot for the British. And in any case, politics are largely a matter of playing upon what people *don't* want, as well as what they do. We like to keep Mr. Stevens worried—it makes him so much more efficient."

"I see," Sam said, and thought he did.

"Just a word to the wise, Brentwood," Thurston added. "Although your wife's friendship with the queen could be very valuable to us, don't let her get in too deep. In the eventuality that it became necessary to, er, discredit Her Majesty, you wouldn't want that to spill over."

"No, I'll remember that," Sam said, feeling a little uneasy for the first time. These men had no idea how little control he could exercise over Annie. And while Annie might just now be an enigma to him, he understood perfectly what Thurston was getting at.

In the morning the Brentwoods left by the inter-island steamer *Pele* for the Big Island. They were accompanied by two houseboys and one of their maids from Honolulu. The steamer was jammed, crowded on every deck with sight-

seers on picnic expeditions, bowler-hatted importers and
exporters bound around the islands on business, people of
every race and description—English, Scots, Americans,
Portuguese, Hawaiians and hapa-haoles, Chinese going to
work on the sugar plantations, and newly arrived Japanese.
They had recently been recruited to fill the endless need
for field hands and, so it was hoped, compensate for the
tendency of the Chinese to drift toward the towns after a
season's labor in the cane fields. An enormous woman in
a red and orange holoku sat down next to them. She had a
hen under one arm and a straw bag over the other. The
hen, seemingly resigned to the crossing, peered beadily
over the woman's arm. The woman offered Eden a banana
from her straw bag, and Eden tried out her minimal but
improving Hawaiian on her, to shrieks of laughter from
them both.

That brought neglected matters to Sam's mind. "What
about her lessons?" he asked Annie. "I thought you were
going to get her a governess." He looked around as if in
search of the governess.

Annie sighed elaborately. "She will arrive on the next
packet from San Francisco. She comes with excellent
recommendations. I told you that last week."

"You may have muttered it as you whisked by," Sam
said. "I can't say we had a heart-to-heart talk about it."

"Possibly because you were either on a surfboard or at
the Planters Club."

"It beats standing around waiting for the thaw to set
in," Sam retorted. Noting that their fellow passengers were
regarding them with interest, Sam grew quiet and gave his
attention to the passing scenery. A summer shower had
begun to fall, splattering the bright canvas canopy above
them, and the afternoon sun was spanned by a brace of
rainbows—not the pale, dim lines he was used to seeing at
home but bright bands of color.

Those passengers who had paid for first-class accommodations would spend the night in their cabins, but for
now everyone was on deck to catch the breeze and

socialize. Those travelers who had bought only deck space were settled with their mats, blankets, pipes, ukuleles, hampers of fruit, and pots of poi, a native staple made from taro root. Sam thought it tasted like fermented library paste, but it was reputed to be highly nutritious. You could live for weeks on it, Judge Dole had assured him. If you had to.

Some six hours out from Honolulu, as dusk was falling, the steamer approached Molokai. As the *Pele* began to turn down the southern coast of the island toward Kaunakakai, she overtook a smaller ship turning north around the fish ponds at Laau Point. There were no passengers on deck— only sacks and crates and a single figure sitting motionless in the stern.

"For the leper colony at Kalaupapa," said the fat woman with the chicken. "Poor souls."

Leprosy had come to the islands in 1852. By 1866 the government, fighting a desperate battle with the disease and its terrified victims, had founded the leper colony to which all tickets were one-way.

"How dreadful," Annie murmured. She bent her head toward Sam's and spoke softly. "Lydia went there to visit them, before she was queen. Her husband didn't want her to, but she felt she must. I really think that Lydia is the most amazing woman."

"Don't call her by that name!" Sam snapped. This time it was he who turned away.

Eden went on talking with the fat woman and stroking the chicken, which seemed to be quite tame (she hoped it was kept for eggs and not for dinner), but she heard. Sam and Annie were like two magnets, she thought, turned the wrong way around. When one approached, the other slid away.

Dinner, taken in their cabin from a hamper packed by Annie, was somewhat strained. None of the three was prone to seasickness, but neither was the combined mood conducive to good digestion. They went up on deck again to

look at the moonlight but were driven below by a summer
gale beginning to blow up.

Finally they slept fitfully in their clothes in the narrow
bunks that ran along each side of the low-ceilinged cabin.
The accommodations were not as unprepossessing as those
that Mark Twain had described twenty-five years earlier
("Rather larger than a hearse and as dark as a vault"), but
they were not palatial, either. Eden, with her toes sticking
off the end of her bunk, could have enjoyed herself
anyway—it was an adventure—had the atmosphere of
mutual recrimination not sparked so visibly between Annie
and Sam. In her inexperience, Eden wondered sadly how
they could bear to remain at odds like this.

In the morning the sky had cleared to misty sunlight,
and rain dogs—little patches of rainbow—drifted through
the air like multicolored clouds. The ship was approaching
Hawaii. They could see the peak of Mauna Loa, rising
nearly fourteen thousand feet to an ice-capped summit. The
mountain swept down through temperate elevations to
eternal summer at its base.

The ship put in at Kailua Bay and then skirted the
orange and coffee region of the Kona coast, stopping
periodically to let passengers disembark. The fat woman
with the chicken waddled ashore at Honuapo Bay, looking
as if she had slept perfectly well, followed by the Brentwoods, who did not.

Hoakina, the resident plantation foreman whose name
proclaimed his Mexican heritage, met them in an oxcart
and drove them deftly through the crowd around the docks.
Many in the gathering appeared to be dressed as Mexican
bandidos. The *paniolos*, Hawaiian cowboys, had adopted
from the Mexicans who had trained them—and intermar-
ried with them—their elaborate black and white lariats,
bandannas, serapes, and red-fringed Spanish sashes. There
was less cattle ranching on the island than there had been
before, but everyone wanted to look like a paniolo. It was
the fashion.

The cart lurched along some ten miles up the coast and

inland toward Pahala, with Sam and Annie jolting on the seat beside Hoakina. Sitting in the back with Eden were the two houseboys and the maid. They had slept on deck all night but seemed none the worse for it. The maid waved at a paniolo galloping by and threw him a flower from her hair, and one of the houseboys took his ukulele off his back and began to sing. Eden found them far better company than Sam and Annie, whose stiff backs made it evident that they were ignoring each other as well as Hoakina's recitation of the local sights.

"Those are the tree molds. Kilauea covered the forest here with lava, oh, long ago, and you can see the bark on the sides of the holes where the trunks rotted away. Farther up are the Footprints, where a great chieftain's army was buried by Kilauea. They say that Queen Kapiolani taunted the goddess Pele at her own temple on Kilauea to prove that the Christian god was more powerful. Me, I wouldn't go that far. But you can picnic on Kilauea and cook eggs on the cracks in the earth. All the haole tourists like to do that."

"Thank you, Hoakina, but I am more interested in putting my own kitchen to rights," Annie said.

Eden thought you could probably cook an egg on Annie, too. With relief the girl saw the farmhouse come into view; it was freshly painted and had two stories of graceful verandas among a sea of pale-green cane. The cane waved shoulder high on either side of the road, which sloped up toward the house. Beyond it were the white outlines of the barns, the sugarhouse, and the cabins of the field hands. At first there seemed to be very few workers in sight, but heads popped up hurriedly out of the cane as the wagon approached, and by the time it had passed, a dozen men were shoveling busily in a half-dug ditch by the road.

"What were they doing?" Sam inquired.

"Sleeping in the cane," Hoakina answered cheerfully. "I give them what for as soon as I get you settled."

"I'll give it to them myself," Sam said grimly. "But you can come with me."

"What for" proved to take some time, primarily because it had to be translated into several languages. Most of the *lunas*, the bosses, were Hawaiians or Portuguese from the Madeira Islands and the Azores. There were fewer Hawaiians among the field hands because of their dwindling numbers among the general population of the islands. It was this scarcity of labor that had prompted many of the mass immigrations. Agents bearing contracts and large promises had scoured every likely looking country on the planters' behalf, and Sam found that his work force—some under a contract purchased with the plantation, some newly signed—also included Chinese, Japanese, one Norwegian, and a German.

Norwegians and Germans had both been imported in considerable numbers some twenty years back, but it had not worked out: The Norwegians had insisted on butter and Irish potatoes with their meals, while the Germans had gone on strike for beer and bratwurst. Both nationalities had written so many complaining letters home that the press had begun to picture Hawaii as a second Devil's Island. The planters had given up and gone back to hiring coolies, who put up with more, despite the fears of Hawaiians and haoles alike that the Chinese were going to inundate the islands.

These disparate nationalities made an uneasy amalgam. The Asians wanted to better themselves and showed a tendency to head for town and more profitable jobs at the first opportunity; the Europeans were ethnocentric and touchy about being down on their luck enough to work in the cane fields; and the Portuguese were the touchiest of the lot, feeling themselves above the Hawaiians but aware that they were not considered true haoles.

Out of the fields, they all kept to themselves in separate enclaves, and an insult to one of their number by another nationality was considered an insult to all and addressed as such, occasionally with a cane knife.

By the time that Sam had spoken to them all, with translations by Hoakina, which he suspected might be

largely unintelligible, they were eyeing him with grave
suspicion. Since the departure of their widowed mistress,
no specific orders other than to grow sugarcane had been
given. Since sugarcane largely grew itself, that had suited
everyone. Nothing had been done about clogged irrigation
ditches, the holes in the roof of the sugarhouse, the weeds
in the kitchen garden, or the oranges and coffee that grew
on the higher terraces that climbed the slopes of Mauna
Loa. Now it appeared that this new American owner was
upset.

"There are holes in our roof, too," one of the Chinese
informed him, aggrieved.

The next morning, the holes were patched, those in
the sugarhouse first. Some of the women were set to
sweeping the four-inch-long cockroaches out of it. The
roaches scuttled off in a fury into the cane but came back
again that night. Sam rode out on horseback with Hoakina
and the lunas. The plantation had been named by its former
owners Aloha Malihini, "Welcome Stranger," but if it
offered Sam Brentwood a welcome, it was the grudging,
stubborn one of a place that will test the stranger first and
will wait and see, before it confers belonging.

The lower field that the former owner had intended to
plant in seed cane had run riot instead and was nearly
engulfed with blooming creepers, strange ferns uncoiling
beneath young banana trees, and lumbering vines for which
Sam had no name but that seemed ready to cover him if he
stood there too long. He set a crew with machetes to clear
the field and then to plow, with the women walking behind
the plow to pull the roots loose from the clinging earth.
Cane could be planted at any time and would grow
year-round here. It was best to plant it now, before another
season's growth turned the field into impenetrable jungle.
Already Sam could hardly tell that it had ever been cleared.

The other fields were "rattoons," regrowth from the
roots of the previous season's crop. In Hawaii, cane did not
have to be replanted each year, only hoed until the new
sprouts were tall enough to choke out the weeds. That

these fields had not been hoed was obvious. Creepers
climbed the cane stalks like snakes, their heads waving
above the tops.

"Bad for the cane," Hoakina said, shaking his head.
"They choke the sugar out."

Sam had no idea of the botanical exactness of that
statement, but he knew that if the creepers weren't pulled
out now, they would have to be separated when the cane
was cut and milled, and that would be even harder. He set
another crew to untangling five hundred acres that were
snarled like a basket of knitting wool. He glared at Hoakina
and asked why it hadn't been done before.

Hoakina looked sorrowful. "They don't work so well for
me when there is no big boss to stop their pay."

Oh, splendid. I've been paying them all this time.

"Also I have been busy supervising the repairs to your
house," Hoakina volunteered.

Probably from a chair on the veranda, Sam thought.
Or worse, underfoot, countermanding the carpenters' orders. Sam had already discovered that haoles wanted a
great many things that Hawaiians saw no sense in.

"It wasn't necessary that you supervise my house. You
are hired to be a *field* foreman."

"Oh, I did not mind. They get lazy, you know, if no one
is here to watch them."

Sam gave up, and they rode on, to see what, if
anything, had survived in the kitchen garden. This plot was
a "kitchen" garden only in the sense that its produce was
destined for the plantation tables. It covered a good five
acres and grew enough to feed the field crews as well as the
master's household. It contained melons, sweet potatoes,
strawberries—ripe all year—and peas, carrots, turnips,
asparagus, lettuce, and celery. There was a patch of *hala-
kahiki*—pineapples—which some farmers were experi-
menting with exporting to the States . . . if only they
could solve the fruit's tendency to rot when shipped green
and blow up when canned. Beyond that was a taro patch of
little hillocks, each with its crown of large, bright-green

leaves. The roots made poi, for such of the field hands as could be induced to eat it. Sam noted irritably that only the taro patch was free of weeds.

"I want all hands to put in half an hour in this garden when their shift is over until I can tell the melons from the creepers. And then start on the bugs. This isn't a beetle farm." As he spoke, a large spotted one, chewing lazily, looked up at him from a pea pod.

"They won't like that," Hoakina informed him. "That's not in their contract."

"They've been snoozing in the cane with a whiskey bottle for three months," Sam replied. "That's not in their contract, either."

He went into the house in search of his lunch while Hoakina delivered the news to his doleful crew. The flame-colored bougainvillea that covered the verandas had been trimmed back so that the verandas could be repaired and painted, and Sam found Annie tying the remaining branches onto the lattice so that they would climb the roof again.

"The bathroom doesn't work," she informed him.

The bathroom was new, added to the old-fashioned house on Sam's orders. "It worked last night."

"Well, it doesn't work now." Plainly Annie did not consider the plumbing to be part of her province. She finished with the bougainvillea and plopped into a wicker chair, her garden snips and coil of twine still in her hand.

"I'll see about it," Sam said. He'd fix it himself if he had to. There was no one more aggravated than a woman, in several layers of pantalettes, petticoats, and muslin skirts, who was deprived of her indoor plumbing. "You look nice in that dress," he offered. "It suits you."

Annie was always dressed to the nines, even in a checked gingham housedress. The latest fashion was for enormous sleeves, puffed up on each shoulder like monstrous cabbages. In Sam's estimation, they made some women look like football players, but Annie's slender, full-bosomed figure carried them admirably. She appeared, however, impervious to compliments.

"Cook has lunch on the table," she informed him. "But you'll have to wash under the pump."

At lunch he tried another tack. "I'm sorry I snapped at you on the boat about the queen," he murmured, passing Annie the bread basket. He thought of his conversation at the Planters Club and decided to kill two birds with one stone. "I'd like to hear your views on her. I'm afraid some people are beginning to take a dim view of her notions of government."

"She takes a dim view of what has happened to her country." Annie looked at him earnestly, not angry now but trying to make him understand. "White men's diseases have devastated the population. White men brought about the *mahele*—the land division. The whites said it was to give the peasants their own plot, but the Hawaiians were afraid to buy land that had belonged to their chieftain. Now the haoles have it all, and no one can vote but landowners. The missionaries meant for the best, but they've given these people a civilization that demands a kind of thinking that the Hawaiian culture doesn't prepare them for. Foreigners run everything."

"Foreigners have to, or it wouldn't be run at all. Even David Kalakaua, the queen's late, lamented brother the king, was totally irresponsible. He spent money like a sailor on shore leave. He drank like a fish. He took bribes from *two* separate Chinese syndicates to allow them an exclusive franchise to import *opium*—he even cheated *them*—and—"

"Under the influence of Walter Gibson, a haole adviser," Annie said hotly. "I know all about that. If—"

"If responsible haoles hadn't forced the new constitution, the islands would still be under the control of the irresponsible ones. The haoles are here, Annie. They aren't going to go away. If we all moved out, others would take our place—opportunists and sharks like Walter Gibson. We have to protect these people."

"You make them sound like children!"

"They are."

"Fine words from Sam Brentwood, the most irresponsible man ever to walk the face of the earth!"

"Maybe I grew up some. Ever think of that?" He put his napkin down. "I've had all the lunch I want."

He had had all the cane he wanted, too, by week's end, but he wasn't going to admit it. He was aware that Annie was grudgingly impressed with the hours he put in in the fields. In any case, he had no choice but to swim or sink in a sea of debt. A year ago he might not have cared, but now he had a point to prove, and Eden to provide for. Their father had left a trust fund for her, but Sam knew perfectly well that to have an acknowledged wastrel for a brother wasn't going to improve her eligibility. He spent his days, from sunup to dusk, either on a horse or later, when the harvest began, cutting cane himself because they were getting behind, and Hoakina and the other lunas wouldn't cut cane if he didn't—it was a matter of their pride.

In the evening he pored over sugar prices and account books and cursed the McKinley Tariff Act that was making California beet farmers rich instead of him. He tried to figure where they could cut corners. It wasn't going to be by asking Annie to curtail household expenses—he'd sell his clothes and walk around in a malo before he did that. He had said the venture would be on his money, and he wasn't going to take a dime from Annie under any circumstances . . . not that she had offered.

He also followed the erratic course of the Hawaiian legislature with an uneasy eye. Pending legislation and appropriations were stalled while the wrangle over the queen's cabinet went on until Harvey Sessions, paying the Brentwoods a neighborly call, swore furiously to Sam over a rum punch on the veranda that nothing was ever going to get done as long as that woman was on the throne.

Harvey was loud and full of liquor, and Sam looked around uncomfortably for Annie. When he heard shouting

from the field hands' quarters, he nearly snatched Harvey
up bodily in relief.

"I'd better go see about that," Sam said, shoving
Harvey down the steps. "Come with me. Maybe you can
translate."

Harvey looked mildly surprised to find Sam so interested, but he followed anyway. They discovered a fight
brewing between the Japanese contingent, the Portuguese,
and a shouting Hawaiian luna, Pilikia. There were nearly
two dozen men on the Portuguese and Japanese sides,
glaring at each other and hurling unintelligible threats and
counterthreats. Between them, a Hawaiian girl whom Sam
had never seen before was having a furious fight with a
Chinese man while the luna, Pilikia, screamed at her over
his shoulder. The rest of the Hawaiians and the Chinese
were chattering agitatedly in separate groups, and the
German and the Norwegian were complaining loudly about
the noise. Hoakina was hopping up and down in the middle
of it all, trying to get someone to listen to him. Sam arrived
in time to see the Hawaiian girl break her ukulele over the
Chinaman's head.

For some reason this seemed to infuriate the Portuguese and Japanese, and they rushed at each other. Sam
saw the flicker of a machete in someone's hand and the
equally sinister glint of a cane knife in Pilikia's.

Sam grabbed Harvey, frisked him for the pistol that he
knew Harvey would be carrying for the solitary ride back to
his own farm, and fired it in the air.

The men stumbled to a halt, blinking into the twilight,
but when no one seemed to be shot, they surged forward
again, the Hawaiian girl still screaming imprecations at the
Chinese man in the midst of it all.

"Maybe you should shoot one," Harvey suggested.
"Get their attention."

Sam considered shooting Harvey instead, then stuck
the pistol in his pocket and snatched Hoakina's blacksnake
whip off his belt. He swung it, and it coiled around Pilikia's
ankles. Swearing, Pilikia went down, and Hoakina hopped

on his chest and took away his weapon. Pilikia glared and spat at him. His name, Hoakina had said, meant "Born to Trouble," and Sam decided that was probably reasonably accurate. Sam snapped the whip again and extracted the machete-wielding Portuguese, the leader of the Japanese, and finally the unfortunate Chinese man with the ukulele frame around his neck.

The fight muddled to a stop. All the lunas carried whips to encourage recalcitrant workers, and Sam had made it clear that while he might not use a pistol, he meant business with the whip. Sam gestured at the Hawaiian girl with it, and she came forward haughtily to indicate that force was not necessary and that in any case she was the aggrieved party.

"Mother of God," Sam muttered. He looked at Hoakina. "What the hell is going on?"

Hoakina climbed off Pilikia. "My cousin has been very bad," Hoakina said. He looked at the girl, then at the ground.

The Hawaiian girl began to protest indignantly, and Sam collared her and put his hand over her mouth. "You'll get a turn."

"She tells this Chinaman she will marry him," Hoakina said. "But then she goes off with another man."

"Then why was *she* hitting *him*?"

"Because he tried to beat her."

"Then why were these other three fighting?" Sam's head was beginning to ache.

"Well, she went off with two men actually," Hoakina said. He dug his toe in the dirt. "Not at the same time, you understand, but they find out. Also she is engaged to Pilikia."

"Sam Brentwood, what in the name of mercy is going on?" Annie bustled between the thatched huts and stood, hands on hips. "I heard gunshots!"

"Er, courtship customs," Sam murmured. "Rather different from ours."

"Really!"

The Hawaiian girl, sensing a champion, began to cry piteously.

Annie gathered the girl in her arms. "You poor thing."

Pilikia pushed himself up from the ground and pulled the girl away. He spun her around to face him and swung his open hand across her face. Before she could move, he took her by the throat. "Dirty! Dirty bitch! Go with haoles and coolies! You are *Hawaiian!*"

Sam lunged forward and jerked Pilikia's arms away from the girl and pinned them behind his back. Pilikia's face was contorted with anger.

"You're fired," Sam said. "If I see your face on Aloha Malihini again, I'll bust your head open!" He let go of Pilikia and gave him a push, and the man staggered toward the road. The other Hawaiians were silent, watching him with shocked eyes.

"He is drunk," Hoakina said, as if to make some excuse. Sam realized that Pilikia had embarrassed them.

The girl sniffled. "He is always drunk. That is why I don't want to be engaged to him anymore."

Annie put an arm around her again. The other Hawaiians crowded around sympathetically, while the Japanese, Portuguese, and Chinese all began to talk at once.

"Will you *shut up!*" Sam bellowed. In the small pool of silence that followed, he jabbed a finger at each of the other three suitors in turn. "You, stay away from another man's girl. And you, too. And you, never try to beat a woman who outweighs you." He turned to the girl. "And you, young lady, I don't want to see you on this farm again unless I see you in church first, getting a ring on your finger."

"She got no place to live, boss," Hoakina said. "I let her live with me."

"Since when?"

"Since she run away from a haole lady she work for. Not a nice lady at all."

"Then you marry her," Sam snarled.

"Sam Brentwood, you ought to be ashamed." Annie

fixed him with a look that would have opened an oyster.
"What's your name, child?" she asked the girl.

"Koana, ma'am."

"Very well, Koana. It so happens that I need another
maid. One girl can't do for me and my sister-in-law both."

"Annie . . ." Sam thought of frustrated suitors chop-
ping each other up with machetes nightly outside Koana's
window.

Annie ignored him. "Would you like to work for me?
Live in the big house?"

"Oh, yes, ma'am!"

"Very well. And there is no need to make up your
mind about any of these men just yet. An ill-judged
marriage is a great mistake."

"You bet your boots it is!" Sam shouted, but Annie and
Koana were already headed for the house. The field hands
took one look at the boss's expression and melted into the
night.

"And now I've got that siren living in my house," Sam
muttered.

Harvey Sessions, who had been sitting on a log and
silently watching the entire scene with the look of a slightly
drunken operagoer, appeared to come to life.

"Her antics may keep the little woman busy," he
suggested.

"I don't want her busy. And I don't want a resident
hula-hula girl waiting on my sister."

"I'll take her," Harvey said happily. "Nice little wahine."

"The hell you will."

"Dog in the manger."

Sam considered punching Harvey, but it was just too
much trouble. "I'm too old for that," he snarled. "And too
tired." He sat down on a log. A cockroach scuttled out and
waved its feelers at him. Sam tried to stomp it, but it ran
under the log again.

"Where's my pistol?" Harvey asked.

Sam gave it back to him. The cockroach rustled out

again, and Harvey fired at it point-blank, blowing it into
another world. Sam sprawled backward off the log, blood
draining out of his face.

"I'm going to kill you, Harvey!"

Harvey stuck the pistol in his pocket as Sam struggled
upright. Harvey's brow creased, and he rummaged deeper
in the pocket. "Knew there was something I needed to do."
He produced an envelope. "Was in Honolulu yesterday.
Sanford Dole sent you this."

Sam snatched the envelope. His heart was still pounding as he tore open the flap. In the dusk he had to squint to
read the letter. "The queen gave in! She's named a cabinet
the Planters Club will agree to!"

"I was going to tell you that," Harvey said plaintively,
"before we got interrupted."

"Then why were you in such a swivet?" Sam peered at
the letter again. "And why does Dole want me in Honolulu?"

Harvey looked at him with the expression he might
have accorded a slow child. "Because now that she's named
them, she's stuck with them. And we can take the next
step."

"What's that?"

"I'm not drunk enough to tell you that out here,"
Harvey said. "You can think about it on the boat to
Honolulu. You'd better go. Dole thinks he needs you." He
hiccuped. "I'm not reliable, you know."

And I am? Sam thought. *That's a novelty.*

Harvey shook his finger at Sam with an expression of
owlish reproof. "Told you you might be glad of li'l Koana
Hula-hula. Give Mrs. Brentwood something else to get her
teeth into. I don't think she's gonna like this." He chuckled
to himself and fell off his log. He looked up at Sam with a
sly smile. "Not a bit."

X

Qualla Boundary, September 1892

Janessa found that her world, which had narrowed itself to Charley's bedside, was imperceptibly expanding to include Joe Cheoah. When she was not tending the people of Qualla Boundary or making grim, and now terrifying, trips to Ela, she spent every waking moment at Charley's side, bathing him or just holding his hands . . . hands that when he slept were limp and lifeless and when he woke moved restlessly over the sheet. Sometimes she wasn't sure he realized she was there at all. She studied his chart constantly, eyes intent on Steve Jurgen's scribbled figures, as if her very urgency might somehow bend those bleak notations into a different form. But every night when she rose bleary-eyed to stumble back to her own tent and sleep, she would find Joe waiting outside the hospital for her.

He never came into the hospital or intruded upon her vigil over Charley, but every night he walked her to her tent, along the path above the railroad tracks, with a shotgun under his arm. He brought her a small covered pot of hot stew, which he made her eat, or a flask of Walini's tea. When he saw that she had worn her boots through and hadn't had time to have them mended, he brought her a pair of Walini's to wear and took hers to the cobbler. Sometimes when she crawled into bed, weary past exhaustion, and lay awake, open-eyed in the darkness, she knew that he was still standing there outside.

"You watch over me like a mother hen," she told him the next evening, and he only said, "Drink your tea."

"No one has so much as said boo to me."

"That's the idea, and I want to keep it that way. I've been doing some asking around. The man I— the man on the tracks was Sid Walley, a no-account by anyone's standards. Now it seems his old man, Eamon, has disappeared, or at least they couldn't find him when they laid out Sid. No one seems real upset about that, either, but the point is, we don't know where Eamon is."

Janessa looked around her at the night. She could have discussed the situation with Henry Blake, who would have arranged for an armed escort to accompany her everywhere she went, but that would mean telling about Joe. Janessa trusted Henry but— No. Joe had killed a man for her. She couldn't tell anyone and take the chance. When Eamon Walley was caught—when Henry Blake went looking for a man, he generally found him—Walley would try to pin the blame on Joe.

"You said you thought he would lie low," she whispered to Joe.

"I still do," Joe said, "unless he was fonder of Sid than folks give him credit for. Still, Sid was kin, and people up here can get real angry about kin. Blood feud's what you might call a social tradition up here."

"Then you'd better look out for yourself," Janessa murmured.

"I am." She noted that in addition to carrying a shotgun, he wore a pistol on his hip as well as a knife in his belt. "I reckon Eamon Walley knows enough not to mess with me," Joe said, his eyes sparking. "But I'm not taking any chances when it comes to you. Morton Briggs must have been behind the first attack on you, and I don't trust him not to have something else up his sleeve. When your uncle finishes his report, you'll be safe. Until then I'll just go on seeing you home."

"If Briggs thinks my uncle would back off if I got killed, he doesn't know Henry Blake very well," Janessa said indignantly.

Joe smiled at her. "You were getting to be a real nuisance to Briggs, you know. You're pretty stubborn. If the coal company managers could get rid of you, they probably figured your father-in-law would lose interest, too, especially if—" Joe stopped, biting his tongue.

"If Charley dies," Janessa said.

"How is he?"

"The same."

The tears that started so easily came again, and Joe wiped them away, gently brushing her cheek with one finger. "I'm sorry I-I wouldn't hang around if I—" He looked at her bleakly. "Ah hell, I know I would. But you would chase me away if you didn't want me around."

Would I? Janessa wondered uneasily. *Would I want to?* She studied Joe's face, with the dark angles that shifted with the shadows. Some of the old anger seemed to be back in it. Did her constant presence rub him raw? Charley had never felt that way about her—but she had not been married and off limits when she had met Charley. If she had been, Charley, she knew, would simply have backed away, and she would never have known how he felt about her. Janessa couldn't deny that there was something seductive about the torment she was putting Joe through, about being desired so much by a man. Nor could she deny the response that that elicited in her. Even in repose, every inch of him emitted a sexual tension, which set her humming in reply. His air of intensity and danger stirred something in Janessa that she was reluctant to confront. She examined him from odd angles or in minute detail, as if through a microscope, and looked only reluctantly at the whole man. Because when she did see Joe head-on, the impact left her breathing hard.

In addition, he was kin to her—not literally, but in the blood, kin to the Cherokee half of her, the recently discovered, rich heritage that her exiled mother had not

given to her. Joe was part of her homecoming, with all the
conflicting sense of familiarity and danger of an old lover
newly chanced upon.

They had reached the outskirts of the medical team's
encampment. Little pools of light splashed the darkness
ahead of them. The night shift was getting up, murmuring
sleepily to one another. Janessa stopped in the edge of the
shadows and let herself look at Joe.

"It doesn't matter what I would want," she whispered
finally. "Things are the way they are. We'll have to take
them like that."

"I'll take what I can get," Joe whispered back, and her
eyes met his for far longer than she had meant them to.

Janessa slept uneasily that night. Strange dreams
flickered through her sleep: herself on a train, speeding
somewhere, with the headlight as straight as a bright lance,
picking out someone on the tracks . . . Charley and her in
a sleeping car, relentlessly tending a patient who had
already died and rotted and who was transformed into a
mangled body as the train wheels rolled over something. "It
wasn't yellow fever at all," Charley said. "He's been
stabbed."

When Janessa woke with the first daylight, wisps of the
dream still clung to her. She climbed out of bed to wash
them away in the bowl on her dresser. The water was very
cold. The nights were beginning to chill now, and she
shivered into her uniform skirt and jacket and into boots
that were stiff with the plunging temperature. She stared at
herself in the mirror, at hollow eyes and pinched cheeks,
and tried to read her own mind in the glass.

"Who are you?" she asked. "Do you know what you're
doing?"

When she got to the hospital, Steve Jurgen was just
coming off his shift. He was only supposed to be on call at
night, but the calls were so frequent that he now slept on a
cot in Charley's laboratory.

"Just a minute before you go in . . ." Steve said.

Janessa's hands flew to her mouth. *Oh, no! Charley!*

"He's better," Steve said hastily. "He's better. That's what I wanted to tell you. Damn it, don't faint."

"I never faint," Janessa said weakly, with Steve's arm under hers. "I'm just . . ."

"You're just about done in," Steve said. "Look, honey, I don't want you to get your hopes too high, but he is better. He's had one of the worst cases I've ever seen, but I honestly do think he's going to make it. You know you're not supposed to treat your own, so do what I say and don't get too excited. His system won't take anything but absolute rest right now, and when you get all worked up, it's contagious."

"I'll be careful," Janessa said, her heart thumping. "Is he really better?"

"He's awake, and he knows who I am," Steve said. "His heart rate and his temperature are both up some. There's still a lot of blood in the urine, but the quantity of urine is way up. Now take a deep breath before you go in there."

Janessa nodded. She put her hands to her chest, drawing the cold, crisp air into her lungs, forcing her hammering heartbeat to slow, suppressing the urge to run to Charley.

"I'm all right." She went into the hospital, careful to move quietly, as if nothing very important were happening, and saw that Charley's eyes were open, watching for her from behind the blur of mosquito netting.

She drew it aside, and he smiled at her. "I think you're still stuck with me," he whispered.

"Oh, my darling." She sat down on the stool by his cot and took his hand. It looked fragile enough to break in hers.

"I may go to sleep on you," he said. "I seem to be sort of in and out of things."

"But you truly feel better?"

"Truly." His eyes crinkled a little in another smile. "I've read my chart to make sure I'm not imagining it."

"You aren't supposed to do that," Janessa said severely.

"I thought maybe I felt better because I was about to

die," Charley admitted. His eyes were sober now. "I've seen that happen."

"It's not going to happen to you. Can you eat something?"

"I've eaten. Eileen spoon-fed me personally. It tasted like week-old oatmeal, but it stayed down."

"'Pease porridge in the pot, nine days old,'" Janessa murmured. She knew the nurse's gruel and hoped she never had to eat it.

"There was also a tea from your aunt Walini. I'm not sure I can describe the flavor. *Bizarre* is the word that comes to mind."

"It's strengthening," Janessa said, chuckling. "She's been making me drink it, too."

Charley narrowed his eyes at her, focusing wearily on her face. "You've really been through it, haven't you? You aren't getting sick? Every time I've been rational, that's what I've been afraid of."

"No, I'm all right. And we're nearing the end. There'll be a frost soon, and that always stops it. I read your notes, and we've told people to try to keep mosquitoes out. I don't know whether it's helped or not. I don't even know if they've done it. We have no way to keep a check."

"It's just a—theory," Charley said. He sounded sleepy. "Only a theory. When I'm better, maybe I can reconstruct . . ."

"Sleep, darling," Janessa said. "It's all right." She leaned close and laid her head on his chest, listening to his heartbeat, still a little too slow but regular. The faint, steady thump-thump sounded like a triumphant drum in her ear. *I'm not going to lose him.* Nothing else mattered. The heartbeat washed away all fear of Morton Briggs, all thought of Joe Cheoah. "You'll be all right now," she whispered. "Everything will be all right."

Only it wasn't that simple. Three days later, Charley moved from the hospital into their own tent. Within the week—much too soon, Janessa said frantically, trying to force him into the bed again—Charley got up and dressed.

"You aren't well yet!"

His skin was still jaundiced, although it had lost the brilliant saffron color that came with the worst of the disease. And there was still blood in his urine, despite the gallons of water that he drank daily to flush out the last of the sickness.

"I'm well enough," he insisted, tugging on one of his boots. His uniform trousers hung on him, and she thought they would have fallen over the sharp bones of his hips if he hadn't had on suspenders. His hair, which she had cut for him the day before at his insistence, still looked brittle. His hands were so thin she could see the wedding band slide loosely between the knuckle and the joint.

"Charley, I'll make Steve come and sit on you if you don't get back in that bed."

"You won't have any luck," Charley said. "You need me. Steve knows it. We *haven't* had a frost yet, and there are still new cases coming in. You'd do better to go back to bed yourself. I'm immune now, and you and Steve aren't. I'm not going to let you run yourself down to the point that you'd die of the sniffles if you got them."

"Charley, I told you, we've cleared away all the standing water, and we've netted all our beds."

"But maybe it isn't mosquitoes," Charley said, dragging on the other boot. "That's just Finlay's theory. Maybe I'm as crazy as he is. I got sick before I could do any work on it."

"And now you want to go out and try to make up for it and have a relapse! I nearly lost you! How can you risk yourself now when you aren't well?" She tried to take his jacket out of his hands, and he pulled it back.

"I'm a doctor, damn it."

"So am I. You wouldn't let *me* up out of bed too soon."

"I would if you wanted to get up," Charley said solemnly. "I have never held you back from risk, and I never will. Don't you try to do it to me."

"It isn't the same thing!"

"Oh, it isn't? And exactly how do you figure that?"

"Well, I—I'm not sick."

"No? Between treating patients and your personal war with the Superior Coal Company, you're just exhausted to the point of looking like a week-old corpse."

"And sitting up with you!"

"I know that, too, Janessa. I knew you were there. I think it's what got me through. But I've been sat with, and I don't need sitting anymore."

"You need to be tied to your bed!" she said. The weeks of agony over his life boiled up with the thought that now he was going to go out and risk it again. He *was* a doctor, and she knew in the back of her mind that she had no right to try to keep him from his work, but she couldn't keep her anger from rising to the surface. "How can I work when I'll be sick with worry over you?" She was almost yelling. "You don't know what it's been like!"

Charley's eyes flashed. "Take the energy you're spending trying to hoist Morton Briggs with his own petard. You can use that to worry over me. It'll loosen up your schedule a little."

"These are my people. They need my help."

"They need you to be a doctor, not a free-lance counsel for Cheoah. You leave that to my stepfather. I saw him yesterday. He says it's becoming an obsession with you."

Janessa's eyes widened. "Well, thank Vernon very much for me."

"He's worried about you, Janessa."

"He wouldn't have to be if he made some headway himself." Janessa sniffed. "He's got forty-five volumes of notes and only two cases into the courts. Maybe we'd get somewhere if he didn't stop to pick everything apart with a toothpick."

"If he didn't, the case wouldn't stand up in court. Damn it, you know that judge."

"Well, Joe says that at this rate, it won't matter if it stands up in court because there won't be anything left here to save but a hole in the ground. Briggs won't wait forever while lawyers tiptoe around. He'll just go in and do it and see who can stop him."

"Joe says that, does he?" Charley glared at her, his own temper slipping. "It doesn't seem to me that Henry Blake has done an awful lot better!"

Janessa obligingly took up the Henry Blake question, her eyes flashing. "He's made a report, hasn't he? And a hefty one at that—I saw it."

"Are you putting your faith in a government report?"

"I'm putting my faith in the government. Why shouldn't I? Henry's documented I-don't-know-how-many instances of Superior Coal's lies and intimidation."

"All of which will be read by some moron in Washington who's more interested in taking his afternoon nap or feeding in some restaurant with a coal lobbyist."

Janessa was outraged. "Are you implying that my father—"

"I'm not implying anything about your father! But it's been my experience that the federal government's never helped any Southerner yet unless it suited its bankbook or someone's reelection campaign."

"Charley, that's absolutely unfair."

"You didn't grow up here, kiddo. I did. Reconstruction was a vendetta carried on by the Union against the South; and it was aided and abetted by hyenas with money to invest and an eye to opportunity. After my father was killed, we lost our house and our farm for taxes that were set so high we couldn't pay them. There were plenty of reports sent to Washington about that," Charley said bitterly. "I imagine they're still in somebody's desk drawer."

"Things have changed since then. I've never heard you talk like this." To Janessa the Civil War was part of a misty past she had taken no part in.

"That's because your father was a Yankee officer, and I like him," Charley retorted. "And I don't like picking at old scabs. But don't give me any horse manure about the benevolent federal government. My mother was snooted on the street for marrying a Yankee, but we'd have gone under if it hadn't been for Vernon—who's busting his tail for free for these people while your precious uncle Henry writes reports no one's going to read."

Janessa glared at him. "Joe says they'll be read. Joe thinks—"

"Joe can go take a flying leap!" Charley shouted. "If Joe Cheoah hadn't antagonized every white man within fifty miles, Vernon might have an easier time in court." He pulled on his uniform jacket and began to button it.

"If it weren't for Joe Cheoah—" Janessa bit her lip. She couldn't tell Charley that, either, at least not while he was in such a mood. "It's Superior Coal that's been encouraging white men to beat up Cherokee and threaten them and blame them for the fever!"

"Well, the white men are just as sick as the Cherokee now," Charley grumbled. "And that's what I'm supposed to be attending to. I've got my notes to go over, and I hope you've been saving case histories if you weren't too busy playing politics." Having discovered that he had buttoned his jacket one button off, he swore.

"You aren't going out there." Janessa planted herself in the doorway.

Charley strode over to her. "I'm going wherever I damn well want to," he said distinctly. He took her by the shoulders, pushed her to one side, and stalked out, his jacket flapping around him.

Charley spent the next week in the laboratory, reading case histories. He took his meals on a tray in there, like a fox dragging its dinner into its den, and Janessa suspected that if the tent flap had been a door with a lock, he would have locked it. She, too, was still furious and took it out in monitoring his pulse and temperature whenever she could lay hands on him.

"Your temperature's a degree low," she announced.

"My temperature's always a degree low," Charley

muttered. "You can write and ask my mother. Hand me that notebook from over there."

Janessa slapped it down on the desk. "At least put a blanket on your lap."

"I don't need one."

"You have no right to take chances with your health this way."

Charley yanked his cap off and flung it across the tent, provoking a startled *eeping* from the guinea pigs. "Janessa, will you get out of here and let me work?"

She left in an icy swish of skirts and went to the hospital tent to take Steve Jurgen's temperature instead, convinced beyond all reason that somebody was going to get sick.

"Will you cut that out," Steve said, pushing the thermometer back at her. "If anyone's going to collapse, it's you. You look flushed."

"I don't know why he's being so obstinate," Janessa complained. "We've never quarreled like this before."

"You've been turtle doves," Steve agreed.

"Then what's the matter with him? Just because I want him to take care of himself."

Steve looked wary. "Maybe you aren't fighting about what you think you're fighting about," he suggested. "If you want my medical opinion, I'd say old Charley's jealous."

"What?"

"He's never had any competition for you before. Now you're spending a whole lot of time with Cheoah. Charley's not about to make accusations he knows aren't true or go punch Cheoah in the nose. That's not Charley's style. So he's working it out by keeping his nose in a notebook. And don't get me in the middle of it, you hellcat," Steve added, backing off. "Go work it out for yourself."

"Of all the unreasonable, insulting—" Janessa's fists were clenched at her sides. "You're lucky I'm not armed."

"I didn't say I thought you were canoodling with Cheoah," Steve said. "I think I'll go make rounds now." He vanished.

Janessa watched him retreat to the protection of his patients. She became aware of Eileen Riley's interested face and turned away abruptly, picking up her bag as she went outside. She slung the bag into the gig and shook the horse into a trot.

Her irritation seemed to feed off Charley's, and Charley's off hers, she realized, and she had to admit that their silly argument over Vernon Hughes and Henry Blake had held a treacherous undercurrent. It *was* like Charley just to back off. How far would he retreat if he were unhappy enough? Janessa wished fervently that she had never met Joe Cheoah, and by the time she had seen three patients, the prospect of losing Charley over him had so terrified her that she had half convinced herself that she didn't care at all for Joe. She shouldn't have let him walk her home all those nights, she thought, uncomfortably aware that if she had tried hard enough, she could have arranged for another escort. Her conviction faded. Joe's pensive face, dark and attractive, seemed anchored in her mind's eye. It didn't matter—she did care for Joe, but she cared more for Charley. She remembered, with an edgy sense of balancing on a precipice, that Joe and she were to meet with Henry that afternoon to hear the gist of his third and final report. Joe was going to drive her to Henry's boardinghouse headquarters in Quallatown. Oh, Lord . . .

On the way to Quallatown, Janessa sat as far away from Joe on the buggy's bench as she could get and made brisk conversation about the weather. Charley did not see them off.

She thought that she might possibly sound demented. Joe was giving her an odd look, and the earth appeared slightly tilted as if the plates that had formed the surrounding mountains had shifted in the night. The sense of unreality intensified when she found herself saying brightly, "Well! I'm sure Uncle Henry will have good news for us."

"I'm sure he will," Joe said, cocking his head at her speculatively.

I don't talk like that. I never talk like that. I sound like I'm going to a tea party. "That is, I hope he will. . . ." Her voice trailed off, and she looked edgily at the mountains, as if they might disappear if she didn't watch them.

Henry Blake, when he greeted Janessa and Joe, was forceful and normal. He thumped the stack of papers on the table. "This won't be finished for a few more weeks yet. I have to have a fair copy made. But I've wired Toby the gist of it, and I'll give it to you."

The report, in Henry's bold handwriting, was a good three inches thick. He tapped it with two fingers, enumerating its points.

"One: Superior Coal has indulged in illegal tactics including intimidation, blackmail, and incitement to riot. Two: They have made promises regarding future prosperity that are very hard to justify given the facts as stated in the company's brochure for investors and the current economy. Three: They have committed perjury or encouraged others to do so.

"That's a summation. The rest of this is documentation." He tapped the report again. "Mind you, none of this has been proved in court, so it's just my opinion. But my opinion is that they're as guilty as hell, and I've said so. Furthermore, I don't think a mining operation in these mountains is going to benefit anyone but Superior Coal."

"Did you say that in the report?" Joe inquired.

"I did," Henry answered. "But that isn't going to count. If people want to sell Superior their land, no one can stop them. All we can try to do is prevent them from taking any land against the owner's will."

"I think you're right," Janessa said, distressed. "Those poor people aren't going to be any better off if they let this company in. They don't know what mining is like. And what happens to them when the coal is gone?" She thought about what Tim had said about the Virginia City miners when the silver failed. Those men hadn't had anything to start with; but *these* people had their land, and they would end up owning nothing. "Can't you do anything?"

"Not about how they'll be treated when the coal's gone." Henry straightened the stack of papers and put his hands in his pockets. "I'm an investigator. It isn't my decision what's done with the information I provide." He nodded at them both. "And I must tell you that since I have given you the substance of this report prior to submitting it officially, I am obligated to give it to Mr. Briggs as well."

"Uncle Henry! You're just warning them. Then they'll try to move faster."

"I'm a federal investigator, Janessa. I can't play favorites. If I do, Superior Coal will have a legitimate complaint."

"Superior Coal hasn't got anything legitimate about it," Janessa said, outraged. She crossed her arms, lips compressed, as if she meant to dig in and stay until she changed his mind. She was ignoring the fact that no one had ever changed Henry Blake's mind—not on a matter of principle.

Joe sighed. He put a hand on her arm. "He's right, Ka-nessa. If the investigator looks prejudiced, it impugns the credibility of the report." He glanced at Henry Blake. "And he's going to do it anyway, so we might as well practice restraint gracefully."

Henry gave him a rueful smile of acknowledgment.

Janessa stood, defeated. "I wasn't aware that restraint was your strong point," she murmured to Joe.

"It isn't," Joe said. "But I'm learning. Good afternoon, Colonel Blake. Thank you for your efforts on our behalf."

He helped Janessa into the buggy, and they drove toward Yellow Hill. For the first few miles, they were silent.

Finally Joe said, "I'm not sure I want to know the answer to this, Ka-nessa, but what's the matter with you? You look—"

"Worse than usual," Janessa muttered. "Everyone's been telling me so."

Joe grinned at her. "Fishing for compliments?"

"No!"

"I'll give you one anyway. You're beautiful."

Janessa hunched over, chin in her hands. "I'm stupid. I'm too old to be as naive as I am."

"And a doctor to boot," Joe said, smiling. "What have you done?"

She looked at him with such a miserable expression that he stopped teasing her, and some of the light went out of his eyes. They drove in silence again until they came to the hospital encampment at Yellow Hill. Halfway along the track between the sleeping tents and the hospital, he halted the buggy.

Joe wrapped the reins around the whip socket and climbed out. He walked deliberately around the back of the buggy and helped Janessa down.

They stood very close together, and Janessa put her hand on his chest. She could feel his heart under it, could feel a current running through her fingers from him.

"I'm sorry," she said. "I didn't know what I was stirring up."

"You sound as if you deliberately set out to seduce me," Joe said. "It's not your fault that I fell in love."

There, she thought. *The unspoken is spoken*. It didn't seem to make things any easier. "I should have stopped it, when I knew." She found it hard to let him look her in the eyes. There might be too much to be seen there.

"I doubt that you could have." Joe slid his arms around her waist. "I tried to. It was like trying to outrun dawn—or winter. It couldn't be done." He took her cap off and leaned his face against her hair. "Silly hat. Makes you look like a conductor." His voice was a low, warm murmur. "You could have run, you know. Why didn't you?"

"I'm going to now." But she didn't move.

"You've come home to us, Ka-nessa. Couldn't you stay?"

She shook her head and felt his lips move across her temple.

"We need you here. There aren't enough doctors among us." His voice was still a whisper. "You could do as much good here as in the Hospital Service. More, maybe."

Janessa felt her eyes well with tears. Most men would have talked of the home they could give her, of the comforts they could provide. Instead Joe had offered what he knew to be nearer her heart. His lips brushed her hair.

"You aren't a flirt," he whispered. "You wouldn't be here if you didn't love me."

"I'm married," Janessa said desperately, "to someone else."

Joe lifted his head. "I have some conscience to let that trouble me, but not enough." His eyes met hers. "I'm in too deep."

Janessa spread her hands in anguish, and then she pushed him away. "Nobody told me you could love two people at once! It's not right."

"I imagine it's inconvenient," Joe agreed with a trace of his old sardonic smile. Then his face softened, eyes alight. "You *do* love me."

"I wasn't going to admit that," Janessa said. He reached for her, and she felt his hands move down her ribs. "But I love Charley, and I've made my life with him. I can't play you off, one against the other."

"Choose, then." His arms tightened, and he pressed his body against hers until her heart hammered.

"I have chosen." Her face was against his throat, her hands on his arms. "I'm sorry. I never meant to hurt you."

Janessa felt his shoulders sag in defeat. She looked at him in misery as he stood back from her. His face was dark and reckless looking again.

"Odd, the way life works out," he said. "Do you think someone somewhere is laughing at us?"

"Maybe."

"Say good-bye to me, then." He stepped back toward her.

"You aren't going to make it easy for me, are you?"

"No."

He wrapped his arms around her, and his mouth came down on hers, demanding that she acknowledge what she had already admitted, what would hereafter be forbidden, never admitted again. Just this once.

His mouth and arms felt as hot as flame. Her hands crept up his back. The world spun itself into a pinpoint of light and hung suspended.

Charley, coming up the track from the hospital, saw them thus entwined, Joe's dark head bent over his wife's. In a blistering rage, he ran up the path, and as Joe and Janessa parted, Charley caught Joe by the shoulder and spun him around.

"Goddamn you!" he shouted, and swung his fist solidly into Joe's mouth. Joe staggered back, and Charley advanced on him. "The next time you want to kiss somebody's wife, you son of a bitch, it better not be mine."

XI

"Charley!" Janessa screamed.

But Charley wasn't paying any attention, and neither was Joe. Charley swung at Joe again, and Joe hit him back, sending him sprawling in dead leaves.

Janessa picked up her skirts and ran at the men. She tugged at Charley's arm, and he pushed her away.

"Stop it! Stop it, both of you! This is ridiculous."

"Oh, yeah?" Charley lunged to his feet. "I'm going to push the bastard's teeth down his throat."

"You don't understand!"

"The hell I don't!"

They had come at each other again, fists swinging. Janessa circled them. So much for Charley's backing off. She hadn't wanted that, but she hadn't expected this, either. She made another grab at the two men, but they fell, rolling in the dirt, apparently trying to strangle each other.

Charley had his hands around Joe's throat, and Joe was trying to get his knee up to kick him off. Finally he did it, and they rolled apart, both dazed for a moment. As they staggered to their feet, Janessa got between them so that they couldn't hit each other without hitting her. She grabbed Charley's arm and hung on.

"I was saying good-bye!" she yelled at him.

"So am I," Charley said. He was spitting blood, and his coat was in shreds. Joe didn't look much better.

"Joe, go home!" Janessa yelled, wrestling with Charley.

Joe looked at her stubbornly, his hands clenched into fists. He was a fighter, and Janessa knew that his immediate instinct was to punch whoever punched him and worry later about who the aggrieved party might have been.

"Go home, you idiot!" Janessa still had a death grip on Charley. "I'll talk to you later."

"The hell you will," Charley snarled.

"Charley, will you just please let him get out of here?"

Charley stopped struggling with her and watched grimly as Joe climbed into the buggy. He lifted the whip in a sarcastic salute and turned the horse around.

"Thank God," Janessa murmured. "Charley, will you for goodness' sake sit down and listen to me?"

Charley found a downed log and sat on it. He folded his arms in the manner of a man not about to be convinced and looked at her expectantly.

Janessa studied the toes of her boots, trying to think of something to say that wouldn't send Charley running after the buggy in a frothing rage.

"I told you," she said finally, "I was saying good-bye. He fell in love with me. It was partly my fault. I'm sorry."

Charley wiped his mouth with the back of his hand and then poked a finger inside. "I think my tooth is loose."

"You punched him first," Janessa pointed out.

"You kissed him."

"Charley, look, I said I was sorry. I really am. And I'm sorry I've been at you about working. You're a doctor. I can't expect you not to work where you're needed. Not when I know I'd do the same thing and these people need us so much."

"Cheoah, for instance?" Charley suggested. "I know what ails him, Florence Nightingale, and if you don't mind, I'd prefer you confine your attentions to yellow-fever cases."

"I didn't mean him," Janessa grumbled. She crossed her arms, too, and they stared at each other, at an impasse.

"You never ran into full-blown temptation before, did you?" Charley asked. He wiggled his tooth experimentally.

"No. I didn't expect it. It was like having someone throw something at me from behind."

"Well, brace yourself, my girl, because it'll happen again."

"Never. Charley, I promise."

"Horse manure. You aren't a block of stone, and being married doesn't make you immune. Take it from me."

Janessa eyed him with sudden suspicion. "What do you mean by that?"

"If you think I don't notice other women, you have a pretty strange idea of men," Charley said. "I just don't go so far as to kiss them."

"I always thought," Janessa said broodingly, "that when you love somebody, you just aren't interested in other people. Well, you aren't supposed to be!" Suddenly she was annoyed by Charley's admission.

Charley's expression wavered between fading anger and amusement. He held out a hand. "Come and sit down. I didn't think," he remarked as she sat, "that I'd have to explain the facts of life to someone until we had children."

"I am acquainted with the principles of sexual attraction," Janessa said stiffly.

"Sure you are," Charley said. "In mice. And libertines like Sam Brentwood. You happen to be the kind of person who isn't sexually attracted to someone unless you like him a good deal. That's why it's taken you so long to run into this."

"You're being awfully detached for someone who was just trying to strangle a man."

Charley sighed and put his arm around her. "I've got you," he said. "And he hasn't. I can afford to be philosophical. Besides, I think I gave him a black eye." He sounded satisfied.

"Let me look at your tooth."

"I'm a highly trained specialist," Charley said. "I can look at my own tooth. When I get a mirror."

"Your specialty is epidemic diseases. Open your mouth."

"So's yours. Why do you burn to look at my tooth?"

"I'm trying to make amends."

"To prove you're dependable? This shook you up, didn't it? You're not immune. You just happen to be discovering at thirty-one what flirts find out at seventeen. Next time something comes at you from behind, you'll know what it is and can duck." His arm tightened around her. "And if you don't, I'll punch his nose in again."

Janessa giggled and laid her head against his chest. "Sounds reasonable."

Charley kissed her—a trifle gingerly; he had a split lip. "People stay together because they love each other *more* than anyone else, not because they have blinders on."

"And because their husband might punch someone's nose in," Janessa murmured comfortably.

"That, too. Come on, let's go home."

They walked companionably up the path. They passed Steve Jurgen, who took note of Charley's disheveled condition but refrained from commenting.

"I'll mend your coat," Janessa offered contritely. Then, as if to wipe the slate completely clean, "And I'm sorry I said Vernon was slow. I know his work takes time."

"Then, just to be fair, I'm sorry I cast aspersions on old Henry."

"Actually, you weren't so mad at Henry as you were at Yankees and the government," Janessa said. "Oh! I meant to tell you, but I forgot because—"

"You were otherwise occupied."

"Charley, if you're going to throw this at me—"

"All right, I'll try not to. What were you going to tell me before you went berry picking with Cheoah?"

"Charley—"

"Just tell me."

"Uncle Henry's report is going to back up everything

we've been saying about that snake Briggs." She sighed. "He's also going to tell Briggs what's in it."

"Let's hear it for the government," Charley said. "Impartial as hell."

"He can't help it."

"Nope."

They came to their tent, and he lifted the flap for her. "Now about that tooth . . ."

"My tooth be damned." He grabbed her by the waist and lifted her. "I feel a need to assert my territorial rights."

Janessa struggled, laughing. "Put me down, you idiot. You've already exerted yourself beyond your limits."

"I'm going to." He dropped her on her camp bed, a little too hard. Charley, overbalancing, came down on top of her, and the bed collapsed beneath them both.

Janessa found herself thrashing in a tangle of bed-clothes and splintered wood, with Charley trying to unbutton her jacket.

"Let me up!"

"No."

Janessa gave up, laughing so hard she couldn't protest, and let him undo the jacket. His hands crept inside, pulling her shirtwaist out of her skirt. "Damnation," he muttered as they encountered whalebone. "Roll over."

She turned obediently while he undid her stays.

"Women have too much underwear."

"Shhhh." Canvas was anything but soundproof.

"There." Charley pulled off shirtwaist and stays, then put his face against her breasts while he started work on her skirt and petticoats.

"I'd be glad to undress," Janessa said, gasping, "if you'd just get off me."

"Not on your life." He gave up on the skirt and petticoats and pulled her drawers off instead, and then her boots. "My mother always told me it was vulgar to make love with your boots on," he informed her, bending over and kissing her toes.

"Your mother never said any such thing." Janessa

imagined his mother never made love on the floor, either. "And take your own boots off."

Charley was kneeling above her now, unbuttoning his mud-stained trousers. "You're mine, Janessa Lawrence. Mine!" He fell on top of her, and they rolled in the bedclothes, laughing like fiends.

Charley put his hand on her breast and his mouth over hers, and laughter faded into gasping breaths and quiet murmurs. Not quiet enough, Janessa was afraid, and then gave up worrying about it.

Later Janessa sat on a stool at her camp dresser, dreamily brushing out her long hair while Charley sprawled on his own cot, hands behind his head. She felt oddly at peace, almost a little smug. She turned her head this way and that, studying her face in the spotty mirror. She had always dispassionately assessed herself to be a reasonably attractive woman but not a pretty one. Tonight, with her thick hair shadowing her face, she saw beauty as Charley or Joe might have seen it. *No one ever fought over me before*, she thought. Her ethics tried to reassert themselves. *That's medieval. You ought to be beyond that. You'll be dropping your handkerchief next.* But she smiled into the mirror.

Charley stretched lazily, and she realized he was watching her. "I'm not going to sleep in that," she said, pointing at her splintered bed. "That's your fault. You sleep in it."

Charley sat up and began tugging up his trousers. He looked as if his muscles were stiff, but she saw that he had put on some weight, and his skin tone was better. His hair was regaining its old glossy texture.

What would I have done if I'd lost you? Janessa thought.

Charley pulled the bedclothes off the floor and picked up the broken bed. "Yes, O my queen." He went outside with it under one arm.

On his way to the storage tent to filch another cot, Charley encountered Steve Jurgen.

Steve raised his eyebrows at the bed.

"Accident," Charley said. "Flimsy things."

Steve didn't say anything, but a grin spread across his face. He went on, hands in his pockets, whistling happily. Steve's own romantic life consisted of a parade of damsels who ultimately gave up on him because he spent too much time in the field or because, as Janessa had pointed out, he had a tendency to describe, with enthusiasm, the more grisly aspects of his latest case. But he liked his friends to be settled. It gave him a sense of security.

The next night there was a frost, earlier even than they could have prayed for, and within a week the yellow-fever cases began to decrease. In another week they had subsided entirely, so there were only the convalescent and the last handful of the newly sick to care for. Of the formerly sick, however, there were more than three hundred in the graveyard at Yellow Hill and in the family plots among the high hollows of the mountains.

"Sixty percent," Charley said grimly, going over the records. "We lost nearly sixty percent of the people who came down with it. And I still haven't anything to go on."

He was hunched over the laboratory desk, and Janessa rubbed his shoulders. "You wouldn't wish more sickness on them, just for science."

"Of course not. If *I* hadn't gotten sick—"

"But you won't get sick the next time. You'll have another chance at this disease. Probably too soon," she said sadly.

"And the tribal council wants to thank us," Charley said bitterly, "at a special session tomorrow night. Much good we've done them."

Janessa rubbed his shoulders harder. She was used to this. The aftermath always affected him this way. The ones who had survived were so weak, and they still had winter and the Superior Coal Company to fight. There wasn't a family in Qualla Boundary who hadn't lost someone.

"Charley, do you think you could make any headway if

you had more time? To interview survivors, maybe try to backtrack?"

"Who would remember getting bitten by a mosquito?"

"After you got sick and I read your notes, Steve and I did tell everyone to try to keep mosquitoes out. People who caught the fever late in the epidemic might remember." Janessa hesitated. She hadn't seen Joe since their parting, nor had she spoken of him to Charley. How either of them might react to what she wanted to propose, she had no idea. But she found now in the midst of this awful desolation that she couldn't bear simply to pack her bags and let the community thank her, then depart . . . back to her comfortable apartment in New York, where she would make her hospital rounds among people who didn't belong to her, go to parties, and eat healthful food under a roof that didn't leak.

She said slowly, "I'd like to ask Dr. McCallum to let us stay on a little—just you and me. They haven't got another doctor here, and the way things are, Dr. Fentress will be risking his life to come from Ela to treat them. There's so much malnutrition here, half the survivors will probably get sick again with something else. I'd like to just see them through the winter."

"And hold off Superior Coal with a flaming sword?" Charley asked.

Janessa bit her lip. "I can't help the way I feel. But it isn't just that. The people here are going to need us. And they're my family. If I had some breathing space, I might be able to recruit a doctor and talk some of the young ones into studying medicine. Elliot Spray and Walini both say Billy Cheoah has an aptitude for it."

"I suppose if I had more time . . ." Charley mused. He squinted tiredly at his notes. "All right. Wire McCallum and see what he says."

Dr. McCallum had quite a lot to say, mainly about how desperately they were needed elsewhere. But he was intrigued by Charley's theories and knew how stubborn

Janessa could be. They could stay, he said grudgingly at the tail of his lengthy and expensive telegram. But just the two of them. Everyone else—doctors, nurses, orderlies, and equipment—was to return home at once. The service wasn't made of money. He supposed he could continue the Lawrences' pay—at great difficulty. And he was glad to hear that Charley was still among them.

Charley read it and chuckled. "The old devil. He means I'd better have more than an unsubstantiated theory when I get back."

"He's there. We're here," Janessa said vaguely. She would worry about Dr. McCallum in the spring. Right now she was worried about facing Joe. With what had happened between them, it didn't seem right to put herself under his nose all winter. Janessa knew that he was taking pains to avoid her. But she couldn't bear to leave just to stay away from Joe. She felt about these people, her half-blood kin, the way she had felt about Charley when he was sick—that if she didn't take care of them, they would die.

At the council meeting that night, Chief Stillwell Saunooka formally thanked every staff member from doctors down to orderlies. Lottie, instructed by Walini, had presented each with a bouquet of wildflowers from a basket. Steve Jurgen put one in his buttonhole and bent down and kissed Lottie, and she climbed into his lap, which wasn't in the program.

Walini, who knew what Janessa was going to say, had come to argue with anyone who was against it, but there wasn't any need. When Janessa told the tribe that Charley and she would be staying on, a look of relief traveled over all the people's faces. She knew then how much she was needed and that she had decided correctly. Joe gave her a look of startled joy, and then his expression became impassive as if he had revealed too much. Her heart lurched with unhappiness for him, but she clung to her resolution. Joe, too, knew she was needed. He would get by.

The Reverend Nimrod Jackson stood up and bowed his

head. The gas lamps that lit the meetinghouse made his brown hair look paler and less Cherokee than ever, but Janessa had learned that in Qualla Boundary one was either Cherokee or one was not. Nimrod Jackson's white blood went back three generations and had no real effect on his life.

"Brothers and sisters, let us thank the Lord for deliverance from sickness and for these good people who have helped us. Those of us who stand before You tonight are grateful to be alive, Lord. We ask Your blessing on these folk for their journey home and on us in our sojourn here. And we ask You especially to watch over our sister Ka-nessa and her husband, Charley, who have agreed to stay among us in Thy service. I could say a lot about our hour of need, Lord, but You know about that, so I'll just thank You for sending us these good people. Amen."

Eileen Riley sniffled sentimentally, clutching her flowers, and Janessa stared at the floor, embarrassed. She felt hopelessly inadequate in the face of that simple prayer.

The ceremony concluded, the hospital service contingent filed out, leaving only Janessa and Charley behind, and the meeting got down to tribal business. Elliot Spray announced the reopening of the school. Joe Cheoah announced that Colonel Blake had accompanied his report to Washington that afternoon and that Vernon Hughes was staying on to see his efforts through the courts.

"And we know who we have to thank for all that, too, so I won't embarrass her by doing it again." Joe smiled across the room at Janessa, a gentle smile that was most unlike him, but then he went back to business. "We've buried our dead, but the people in Ela have, too, and now things are going to get worse because the whites are going to have time to spend on troublemaking. Superior Coal will have men all over the place now that they aren't scared of getting sick. I want every household in Qualla Boundary to make one more pass at finding old land records: any old scrap of paper that can be found, old bibles, old letters, anything. Whatever you find, bring it to me or to Vernon

Hughes. And if any ignorant jackass doesn't want to bother, you put the arm on him good. There've been some folks who've been too sick to give this any mind, but now's the time. Furthermore—"

He spoke on, eloquently, adamantly, cajoling, threatening, shaking them into action. The bruise around his eye was fading. In time the bruise around his heart would fade, too.

"Lord God A-mighty," Wolf Mooney said in her ear. "I never heard a man go on so." Wolf wasn't a member of the tribal council, but nearly the whole tribe had turned out to say good-bye to the doctors.

"He's right," Janessa said. "You listen to him, Uncle Wolf."

"I got me a shotgun," Wolf said. "Damn sight more use than a piece of paper, if you ask me."

"Not in the long run," Janessa told him.

"You leave Wolf to me," Parker Smith said. "Wolf, you damn ornery bastard, you have Rebecca go through the house again. Lord knows what you got squirreled away. Janessa, you and Dr. Charley are bid to a hog killing Saturday next, and a ball game and a barn dance. We got to have some good times after this summer."

"Why, thank you," Janessa accepted solemnly. "That sounds wonderful." Except possibly for the hog killing. "We would be delighted. Is there anything we can bring?"

"Just yourselves," Parker said cheerfully. "And your dancing feet."

She was being told to act like a guest, Janessa realized. She would bring smallpox serum, she thought. She'd bet that half these people hadn't been vaccinated.

With the rest of the medical team gone, Janessa and Charley moved into an empty cabin near Walini's in Yellow Hill. It had been swept and refurbished for their coming, and it smelled sweetly of Walini's herbs.

"I made you a drying rack, Ka-nessa," Billy Cheoah

said proudly, pointing to a trellis of dowling and two-by-fours by the hearth. "Like Walini's."

There were a newly polished brass bed with a hand-pieced quilt and a trunk for their clothes. Janessa's eyes misted. "I have something for you, too." She produced a tattered anatomy textbook she had asked Dr. McCallum to find in her office at headquarters hospital in New York and send her. "If you're going to be a doctor, this will give you a head start."

Billy clutched it to his chest. Janessa noticed that he had a cut on his face. "What have you been doing?"

"Got in a fight on the way to school," Billy muttered.

"Who with?"

"Couple of white kids. They don't belong here. They just come looking for trouble." From the look of Billy's knuckles, they had found it.

Probably egged on by their fathers, Janessa thought. Enough grown men had been acting the same way, and they were being urged on by Morton Briggs. There were beginning to be regular forays into Quallatown and Qualla Boundary—raids of intimidation.

"Billy, I know it's hard, but try to stay out of fights."

"Uncle Joe says he'll lick me good if I go to Ela," Billy said. "But he says I gotta fight 'em on our own ground. Otherwise, we won't have no pride left."

"Any pride," Janessa said automatically, but she didn't pursue the statement past its grammatical imperfections. Pride was all most of these people had, and that went for the whites from Ela, too. It made fights so easy.

Charley poked his head in the door. "Buggy's ready," he said. "Billy, are you coming to the party with us?"

"I'll ride," the boy answered. His pony was tethered outside. He'd ridden over before Parker Smith's hog killing to see how Janessa liked her drying rack.

They met other buggies and mounted Cherokee on the road. A hog killing was a social event. There was still a frost on the ground, and the morning air was as crisp as cold

apples and smelled like woodsmoke. The women had pans
and baskets of food in their laps, and the men had their ball
sticks over their shoulders or fiddles under their arms.

Parker had set up the hog drum over a fire pit at the
edge of a corn-stubbled field not too far from the house.
Smoke rose from the fire under the hog drum and from the
cabin chimney, where Parker's wife and the other women
would put up the meat. The grunting and snuffling of the
hogs in their pen were lost in the bright chatter of the
guests and the shrieks of children who dashed in excited
circles.

As Charley and Janessa drove up, Parker shot the first
hog in the back of the head and cut its throat. The brilliant
blood poured out all along the ground at his feet. When it
slowed, three men dragged the carcass to the drum and
heaved it up into boiling water to loosen the hair. They
hauled it out again with hooks, and Billy and some of the
other boys were set to scraping the hide. After a second
immersion and scraping, someone cut off the head with an
ax, and the boys put the carcass on a pole between two
trees. The smaller children carried jugs of cider to the men
who were doing the killing, and the older children lugged
tubs of meat up to the house.

Janessa watched queasily as Wolf Mooney hauled hog
innards out into a tub. It wasn't a bit worse, she told herself
firmly, than human innards, of which she had seen enough
in her time. But she got her bag out of the buggy, glad that
she had something to do other than help with the endeavor.
She suspected Charley felt the same way.

"City slickers," Walini teased, her smile friendly and
amused. She handed Janessa a list of names scrawled on
copybook paper. "You just grab them as they go by," she
advised. "You might do Joe first. Then he can sit on anyone
else who gives you any trouble."

"Joe?" Janessa glanced at the list, surprised. She had
thought that if anyone had the sense to get himself vaccinated, it would be Joe.

"His parents never bothered," Walini explained. "He

made sure Lottie and Billy got done a couple of years back, but he didn't pay any mind to himself."

"Well, he's going to now," Janessa announced. "Where is he?"

Walini pointed, and Janessa found him among the hog killers, wearing a pair of ragged overalls soaked with blood. She hadn't even recognized him. He had on an old slouch hat, and he looked as disreputable as Wolf Mooney. She glanced at Charley. "Maybe you—?"

"You," Charley invited. "By all means."

Janessa laid out the serum, needles, and a jar of alcohol on the buggy seat. Charley wasn't going to let her off easy. She marched over to the hog drum while Charley scooped up a passing young boy and scratched his name off the list.

Joe silently watched her. She realized that he had seen her the moment she arrived. She stood a little outside the circle of bloody ground and beckoned to him.

"I want to vaccinate you," she said.

"You sure Charley hasn't got plans to do it with a forty-five?" Joe inquired.

She laughed uneasily. "You'll have to take your chances."

He followed her, rolling up his sleeve, but when he got to the buggy, he held out his hand to Charley first. "I owe you an apology."

Charley looked up from his small, barefoot captive, who was now vaccinated and howling. He popped a peppermint drop from his pocket into the boy's open mouth, and the howls subsided. Charley stood up slowly, while Janessa stood beside them, vaccination needle in her hand, in an agony of embarrassment.

"My wife is sinking with mortification," Charley observed, "and so am I. I imagine you are, too. We're too old for this kind of thing. Let's just not discuss it."

He shook Joe's extended hand, Janessa jabbed the bared arm with the vaccination needle, and Joe went back to the hog drum.

Janessa leaned her head against the buggy for a moment. "Oh, Lord," she whispered, "no wonder people don't misbehave more often. The embarrassment afterward isn't worth it."

"You haven't got the temperament," Charley said. "People who misbehave a lot don't get embarrassed."

"Very funny." Janessa took Walini's list out of his hand and went in search of the unvaccinated.

The hog killing took until late afternoon, and by the time the last of the meat was put up and the last trimmings made into sausage, Janessa wondered how anyone could have any energy left to play ball. But a cold breeze danced down the hollow above Parker's farm, blowing away the overpowering smell of blood, and the men went whooping down to the creek to wash. They came back, bronze skin gleaming, clad only in short trousers, racing each other for the meadow beyond the cornfield. The women came out of the house to watch, bundling their blood-soaked aprons away and straightening their hair.

A Cherokee ball game was a rough-and-tumble affair, short on rules and long on physical contact. It was played with sticks that had a braided bag at one end, and the object was to catch the ball in the bag and get it beyond the opposing goal twelve times. A variety of stakes were put up—belts and scarves, knives and gewgaws—by the players as well as the young Cherokee women, who darted onto the field to give their suitors their tokens. Wolf Mooney collected these and tossed the first ball into the air.

Janessa and Charley sat with the women and the older men to watch. "How do they know where the ball is?" Janessa asked as a knot of some dozen men collided and fell wrestling on the ground, apparently trying to throttle one another out of sheer high spirits.

"It'll turn up," Wolf said.

Janessa watched Joe emerge from the tangle and drag Wesley Calhoun out by the heels. The ball rolled out from under him, and Joe scooped it up with his stick. He raced toward the goal, and the opposition heaved itself out of the

melee in pursuit. Janessa watched them flying down the
field. Their cries were as shrill as the voices of hawks in the
air. Wesley hurled himself at Joe's heels, and the ball arced
against the sun as Joe disappeared beneath a writhing mass
of arms and legs.

Wolf smiled happily. "Good for a man. Proves his
spirit." He shot a glance at his daughter, Rebecca. "I ought
to have played."

"You're too old," Rebecca said.

"Ha!" Wolf folded his arms and watched them wistfully.

A cloud of frying sausage aroma had begun to drift over
the field by the time the game ended and the victorious
team had collected their booty from Wolf. The older
women, who had no suitors in the game, had set long
trestle tables outside Parker's cabin and laid them with
fresh-cooked sausage and cracklings, and the pies and cakes
and covered dishes brought by the visitors. The ball players
hurled themselves into the stream again, then pulled on
dry clothes behind the house while the sun went down and
lanterns sprang to light. There was something magical
about this day, Janessa thought, that couldn't be defined by
the slaughter of hogs or the carefree mayhem of the ball
game. It was a sense of kinship, of belonging, not only to a
family but also to a tribe. It drew her into its easy circle, set
a laden plate before her, and bade her a welcome that by
now needed no words.

As the last light faded and the last plate was scraped
clean, Wolf Mooney tuned his fiddle, and Parker Smith
dragged the barn doors wide. The hay barn had been swept
clean, its wooden floor washed down and its walls hung
with quilts and a bolt of calico. The night was growing cold,
but the barn warmed quickly to the music of the fiddle and
the exertions of the dancers.

They danced to "Chicken Reel" and "Turkey in the
Straw," feet flying in and out of the pattern that seemed to
Janessa, whirling in its middle, to echo that of the quilts
upon the wall. Charley's arm was around her waist, spin-

ning her in and out of the reel, then her arm was linked with Joe's, then with Parker's and young Billy's, and finally, back to Charley. They spread out like the points of a star, then came together again and spun out across the little galaxy of the floor. Charley passed her hand to Joe as the figures crossed again. They spun, arms linked, and Joe caught her eyes with his. As they whirled, lifted on the music of the fiddle, Janessa thought, looking into those bright, dark eyes, *Oh, I do love you, but I can't have you. This is all I can have. Charley won't mind this.* Joe's hand tightened on her arm as if he had read her thoughts and come to some sort of peace. He took her hand up the reel again and gave it back to Charley, and Janessa whirled in Charley's arms, for some reason now perfectly content.

Wolf bent his bow to the fiddle again with hardly a pause.

> Chickens a-crowin' on Sourwood Mountain,
> Ho-dee-ing-dong-doodle allay day,
> So many pretty girls I can't count 'em.

You'll find your pretty girl, Joe, Janessa thought, spinning past him. *You'll find her.*

Morton Briggs bent a gimlet eye on his lawyer. "Just what precisely do you mean, our hands are tied? Supposing you tell me who tied them while you were dozing at your desk?"

Scoggins sighed. When Briggs was in an irascible mood, he was short on logic. "I was speaking figuratively, Morton. I mean they're tied so far as court proceedings go. That Vernon Hughes and that uppity Cherokee lawyer have got things in such a tangle, the judge can't sort out one boundary line from another. The whole map looks like a damned nest of snakes. I tried talking money to the judge, but he's a stubborn old hillbilly and thinks he's honest."

"Well, the head office is getting restless. If they get fed up enough to pull out, my butt's on the line. So suppose you figure out just what the hell to do!" He sighed heavily. "Not that your last idea did us much good."

Scoggins sniffed. "I still say she must have had help. She couldn't have fought off two men by herself. If we could find Eamon Walley, he might have a tale to tell."

"So why don't you find him?" Briggs inquired with elaborate patience.

"I'm looking, damn it!" Scoggins snapped. "In case you're under the impression I've been out picking daisies."

"I did wonder," Briggs said sarcastically. "I figure you must have been occupied somehow, while Colonel Blake's been reporting to Washington how we're all a band of thieves and cutpurses. That's going to look fine in the newspapers," he added.

Scoggins shrugged. "It won't bother the head office. The head office wouldn't care if it looks like Beelzebub as long as it gets its profit. What'll bother the head office is if these Indians win their case."

"Brilliant deduction," Briggs snarled. "If you'll follow it up with a way to get Cheoah out of my hair, I'll give you a plaque to hang on the wall. We should have gone after him in the first place."

"We tried," Scoggins reminded him. "Nobody wanted to, in spite of the money I offered. They all said that laying for Joe Cheoah was like trying to stomp a rattlesnake barefoot. We've got to go after that one another way."

"Very good. You managed to think of one?"

"I may when I lay my hands on Eamon Walley," Scoggins answered. "I've been hearing some interesting gossip about Cheoah and that doctor. Makes me wonder just who she was walking with when Sid had his, er, accident. Old Eamon may shed some real interesting light if we scare him bad enough."

"I thought you couldn't find him."

"I've got a line on him."

"Why didn't you tell me that?"

Scoggins picked up his hat. "I was saving it to cheer you up, Morton."

XII

Honolulu, January 1893

Queen Liliuokalani clinked her teacup in its saucer and smiled at her guest. Annie Brentwood had become a frequent visitor at both the Iolani Palace and the queen's house at Washington Place—a friend and confidante in troubled times. Of course it was awkward not being able to tell her things before they happened, but there was her husband to consider. Sam Brentwood was a member of the Annexation Club, and if the club members thought that Liliuokalani didn't know about them, they were much mistaken. But the club had made another mistake: They had left Honolulu to go back to their plantations a little too soon, before the end of the legislative session. Even the unpleasant minister Stevens had boarded the USS *Boston* for a cruise of the islands. It was quite refreshing, Liliuokalani thought, to have that ship out of her harbor. She had made excellent use of the club members' and the minister's absence.

"Well, my dear, I expect I can count my recent victories on the fingers of one hand," the queen said as her maid poured them more tea. "But I consider them to be an omen. I have gotten rid of my cabinet once more. Disagreeable puppets. Certainly that is a very pleasant accomplishment."

"You hardly had time to get attached to them," Annie

murmured. The new cabinet thrust on her by the planters hadn't lasted much longer than the ones that the planters had spent all year throwing out.

"I shall become very attached to this current one," Liliuokalani said. "I have also successfully managed the administration of the Lottery Bill that the Americans dislike so much. I am all out of patience arguing morality with them. The profits from the Lottery Bill, unlike those from the sugar plantations—no offense meant to you, my dear— will go into general circulation among our people and be spent on public works . . . some little prosperity to match that enjoyed by foreigners here."

"You don't offend me, Lydia dear," Annie said, chuckling. "It's not my plantation. Are you certain about the Opium Bill, though?" That was the third of the queen's victories, and it made Annie uncomfortable. She suspected that it made the queen uncomfortable, too, but Liliuokalani's plump face was determined.

"Morally, I dislike it intensely," the queen confessed, lips pursed. Her small, round hands made a gesture as if to push away the unpleasantness. "But we must have some measures for controlling a traffic that is impossible to suppress—because some of our most prominent haole citizens have made fortunes in it." She chuckled wryly. "That evidence made a splash in the legislature."

"They ought to be ashamed of themselves!" Annie said.

"I would like to think they are, but I very much doubt it. It comes down to this: We have a Chinese population of over twenty thousand persons to create a demand for this evil substance. It has thus become impossible to prevent smuggling or bribery and corruption of my officials. My efforts have been hindered by those who cry so loudly against opium while their ships smuggle it, and I am tired of scandals that make my country look depraved and ridiculous. We will try the Opium Bill for a while. Perhaps fortunes will cease to be made from this depravity."

"It won't look good in the States," Annie warned.

"It won't look worse than the lies that Minister Stevens

spreads about me!" Liliuokalani snapped. "I'm aware of what he's done. He has sent reports to his president calling me—me!—heathen and immoral. Street gossip manufactured by him, about orgies and pagan rituals and I don't know what trash. I would be very pleased if Minister Stevens fell into the ocean."

"Well, he has a nerve," Annie agreed indignantly. "No one would believe such lies." She thought that it would be hard to find a less likely participant for a heathen orgy than this plump queen whose dress and demeanor far more resembled Queen Victoria's than it did those of pagan ancestors.

"It has been my experience that people will believe nearly anything so long as it is salacious," Liliuokalani said. "However, we will put a stop to Stevens."

"So I should hope." Looking at Liliuokalani's deceptively mild and matronly face, Annie thought that the use of "we" was a royal "we" and that Stevens had better look out.

It occurred to neither woman that Stevens's cruise and the Annexation Club planters' absence might not have been the mistake it seemed on first thought; but Sam knew for certain that it was carefully planned, having been left in Honolulu to report on any excesses the queen might indulge in once the haoles had given her enough rope—it was hoped—to hang herself.

Rumors of a new constitution were flying, too, on the heels of the queen's new cabinet, so the information that the queen had so carefully withheld from Annie was already in the hands of the opposition. Sam had sent out several brisk notes while Annie was still hobnobbing over the teacups, so the Annexation Club members, and Minister Stevens aboard the *Boston*, came hurrying back to Honolulu with the metaphorical noose in hand. They roared in moral outrage over the opium and lottery bills, objected loudly to licentiousness and immorality in the palace, and demanded to be notified if any changes in the existing

constitution, forced on the queen by the powerful haoles,
should be attempted.

Three days later Liliuokalani adjourned the legislature
and invited its members and those of the Supreme Court
and all the foreign diplomats to the Iolani Palace for
refreshments. The moment was at hand. She smiled be-
nignly at them and withdrew from the room, knowing that
behind her a Hawaiian member of the legislature bore a
new constitution upon a velvet cushion.

They made a stately procession across King Street and
through palace grounds, which were already thronging with
Hawaiians waiting to cheer their queen's restoration of their
heritage. The new constitution would reenfranchise landless Hawaiians and disenfranchise those haoles who were
not naturalized citizens. Everyone knew the document's
details; in gossipy Hawaii, secrets were hard to keep. The
garden was crowded with citizens in a festive mood. Annie
waited among them, a lei around her neck, ready to cheer
her friend. Koana was with her, in her new guise as lady's
maid.

"Now we'll have a happy time, Miss Annie," Koana
predicted. "A very big party. Where is Mr. Sam?"

"Off gnashing his teeth, I expect," Annie said. "I don't
think he'll be celebrating with us."

Koana giggled. She had developed an intense devotion
to this new haole mistress who was so pretty and wore such
wonderful clothes and was friends with the queen—and
who, best of all from Koana's view, did as she pleased
without consulting her husband.

They watched as the last of the legislators passed into
the palace to be escorted to the throne room. Soon now,
Hawaii would have its constitution.

But in the Blue Room of the Iolani Palace, the queen
was having an unexpected argument with her ministers,
who had proved, as she told them in a low, furious voice, to
have spines of jelly.

"We should have a constitutional convention," one told
her.

"It's most unwise to follow illegal methods," said another.

"This puts us on a par with those who imposed the Bayonet Constitution on Your Majesty's brother."

"Ha!" Liliuokalani glared at them, one by one, with a derision that made them loosen their collars. "You agreed to this constitution."

"We are still in agreement, Your Majesty. Only we have come to feel that such a step must be voted on by a legally elected convention."

"You will bring it all to naught! This constitution is desired by the people. I *will* maintain my right to accede to their wishes in my own name!"

The ministers loosened their collars more. They, like the annexationists, had heard rumors in the wind, and the rumors the ministers had heard were crushing their enthusiasm. The queen's new constitution had seemed a fine idea while the Annexation Club was out of Honolulu. But now the queen's bold move began to foretell political suicide. A sense of having gone too far was overtaking the ministers. Two were hapa-haoles; two were Americans; and they knew very well how far their fellow haoles might be prepared to go if pushed.

In the throne room and in the gardens, the waiting crowd was growing restive. Something had gone wrong— what was it? Gradually the festive mood faded and died while the queen remained sequestered with her cabinet.

It was over two and a half hours later when Annie saw her friend come out of the Blue Room. The triumphant smile of achievement was gone from her face as she came out onto the veranda to address her subjects.

"I have your petitions. I know your wishes and desires, and I shall listen to your views. But I cannot move at this time." She stood so still that she looked as if she truly could not move for shock. Her face was weary with arguing. "So return to your homes peaceably and quietly. Keep me in your love; you have mine. With sorrow I now dismiss you."

* * *

That was the last speech the Hawaiians would hear from Liliuokalani as a reigning queen. In Palace Square the loyalist faction pledged their support for the queen's proclamation, made that morning, to bring about constitutional change only by means of law. It was, however, a proclamation made too late. The annexationists were already seizing their chance, and there would be no going back.

The overthrow of the Hawaiian monarchy began with a meeting of the Annexation Club and its supporters in the armory—a judiciously chosen location from which Lorrin Thurston ironically proclaimed the islands to be in danger of "bloody revolution" and called on all right-thinking men to protect life, liberty, and property in Hawaii.

With a shiver of excitement, Sam listened to Thurston. He liked being part of change.

Thurston's eyes flashed. This was *his* moment, and he clutched at it greedily. "There are rumors of riot and bloodshed. Whose fault is it? Queen Liliuokalani's! But in spite of her wishes, the streets have not run red with blood!"

A lone voice protested that so far there hadn't been any bloodshed at all and that any revolution being proposed was being proposed by Thurston. But the sole protester was shouted down.

"Gentlemen, I say now and here is the time to act! Let Minister Stevens contact the *Boston*. Bring in the marines!"

Sam shouted and cheered with the rest. He stamped and whistled as the stigma of revolution was neatly passed from their own hands to Liliuokalani's.

Annie, at her window, saw the U.S. Marines from the *Boston* march up the street in an efficient column, their uniforms and sabers almost festive among the greenery of Honolulu's perpetual summer. Why was no one distressed?

She ran into the street and saw only music lovers on their way to the evening band concert at the Royal Hawaiian Hotel. The loyalists, after two hours of patriotic oratory, had agreed among themselves that the whole matter had now been settled peaceably and were enjoying their supper.

Annie paced in a frenzy, knowing that she wouldn't be allowed in the palace now with her haole face and her annexationist husband. Sam had had a hand in this—she was certain of that. Sam and his "Committee of Safety," as the annexationists were now calling themselves. She hurried back inside the house. "Koana! Koana, go find out what is happening!"

An hour later, Koana came back looking subdued. "The queen's ministers have protested to the American consulate, but Minister Stevens told them the troops are here at the Committee of Safety's request, and he wouldn't send them away. They're standing in front of the palace."

"Why doesn't someone *do* something?" Annie looked agitatedly out the window again. "Oh, my poor friend."

"They think it will all blow over," Koana said. She brightened hopefully. "The annexationists always make a big noise, but they wouldn't overthrow our queen."

Judge Sanford Dole was arguing the same point, uncertain that he wanted such a central place in history. Should the queen be deposed, Dole knew that he would be president of the provisional government. But events were moving, the current flowing, and it would not flow back. It flowed, after some lengthy discussion, over Sanford Dole.

The queen was not as unaware of events as her supporters were. Her agents had watched the annexationists' gathering and now indignantly demanded her permission to make arrests.

Liliuokalani looked out her palace window at the American marines. Supposedly there to protect American life and property, they were facing *her* and not the street. Hawaiians had been a warrior people, but so very long ago. . . . How could she order them to spill their blood against American troops? There must be some way to solve the problem without bloodshed. And so she waited.

Finally, the following morning, the queen allowed a squad of policemen to assemble outside the office in which the Committee of Safety was still laying its plans. The committee members would be arrested if they started toward the palace, but the queen was still hopeful that the crisis would not come to that. She put her head in her hands. Surely the prospect of arrest would deter the men. Surely the marines wouldn't actually open fire. How had this happened?

For most of the day the situation remained unchanged. The Committee of Safety watched the policemen, who were watching them. The marines watched the palace. And small groups of Hawaiians stood in Palace Square, talking anxiously and wondering what to do. Surely no one would actually take the queen's throne away from her—that, to a Hawaiian, was treason and sacrilege rolled into one.

And then John Good fired his pistol—the single shot fired during the entire revolution. It killed no one, but it set into action a series of events that were, in retrospect, inevitable. John Good's nerves were on edge already as he drove a wagonload of ammunition through the streets, past the angry stares of Hawaiians, to the committee's headquarters. When a lone policeman grabbed his reins, Good lost his head entirely and shot the policeman in the arm.

The sound cracked through the silence in the streets, and everyone nearly jumped out of his skin.

"Who's the damn fool shooting?" Lorrin Thurston demanded.

"Doesn't matter," Sam said, peering out the committee's office window. "Look!"

The Committee of Safety crowded around him, and Thurston pushed to the front. The contingent of palace policemen, who had been waiting nervously since morning, were running down the street toward the sound, with the crowd from Palace Square hurrying after them.

"Come on!" Thurston urged. "Here's our chance!"

The queen's policemen rushed to investigate and found not riot and rebellion but a stunned and irritable officer Leialoha being rushed to the hospital. The Committee of Safety, meanwhile, were now able to cross the street unhindered. They captured, from the few bewildered clerks within, the Ali'iolani Hale, the government's administration building.

They read aloud, mostly to each other, a proclamation abrogating the monarchy and declaring the establishment of a "provisional government . . . until terms of a union with the United States have been negotiated and agreed upon."

By prearrangement, two companies of volunteers immediately occupied the grounds of Ali'iolani Hale and Palace Square. The revolution was effectively over. The queen was informed almost as an afterthought.

Liliuokalani refused to abdicate, but a delegation from the provisional government brusquely informed her that resistance would mean bloodshed—very likely her own. Her lawyers advised her to trust in the good faith of the United States and helped her to write out a protest.

An order arrived from the provisional government that she was to lower the royal Hawaiian ensign from the palace flagpole and strongly suggested that she should retire to Washington Place, for her own safety. The queen was aware that she was being placed under what amounted to house arrest.

She clenched her fists until the nails cut into her palms. She leaned out the window and looked at the soldiers in her yard. With no other weapon at hand, she cursed them.

"I don't want to see your face," Annie informed Sam at breakfast. "I don't want to see your lying, treasonous face!"

"Then don't look at it," Sam growled, and retired behind his newspaper.

Eden looked from one to the other with shocked eyes. "There are soldiers in the street," she whispered.

"They're here to keep order, honey," Sam said. "They're on our side. Don't you be afraid of them."

"They're provisional-government vigilantes," Annie said. "Don't you so much as speak to them."

Eden sank back in her chair and poked unhappily at her soft-boiled egg. Sam picked up another newspaper. He had a stack of them at his elbow and was keeping track of editorial comment. The prevailing wind seemed to be blowing for the PGs, the provisional government, but loyalist papers were advising citizens to write in protest to friends in America to counteract the lurid stories being circulated by the PGs to justify their takeover.

"When the loyalty oath is established, they'll change their tune," Sam muttered, flinging one loyalist paper down in disgust.

"Loyalty oath!" Annie half rose from her chair. "To a bunch of thieving, treasonous, carpetbagging opportunists? *I* know what's happened in the palace! It's been looted from top to bottom by your vigilante oafs. Not content with stealing the crown away, now they're absconding with the queen's personal possessions!"

"The trappings of royalty," Sam said, unconcerned. "Not her personal possessions at all. They belong to the people."

"Well, the people haven't got them! When the President of the United States hears from the queen's representatives, he won't give two minutes' time to *your* delegation."

Sam chuckled. "Don't bet on it. The captain of the *Claudine* has orders not to take on Mrs. Dominis's representatives. Incidentally, she's to be called Mrs. Dominis, not the queen."

Annie's chair shot back and crashed against the sideboard. "I'll call her what I damn well please!"

Sam put down the paper. "Annie, will you just listen to me for a minute? You don't understand politics, and you don't understand Hawaii. This was coming. It needed to come. We've been very patient with Mrs. Dominis for a long time, but she's cut her own throat."

"With your connivance, you lying toad."

"Damn it, Annie!" Sam thumped his fist on the table so that his coffee cup slopped over, staining the linen with a brown pool of liquid. "No one got hurt but one damn policeman who's going to recover. No one's in jail. The blasted woman hasn't even been officially arrested. Now do you think we could have accomplished what we've done without any bloodshed if the people weren't willing?"

"Yes! I watched you do it. That poor woman is the one who prevented bloodshed. She's worth ten of you!"

"That's something else: I want you to stay away from her. No cozy little tea parties. I've got my position to think about now."

"Oh, and which position is that? Are the PGs going to toss out another official and give you his job? I thought they'd already swept clean. Even the royal band, for God's sake!"

"They resigned," Sam said.

"Because they wouldn't sign a loyalty oath."

"We've got to make it clear who's in charge now."

Annie gave him a spiteful smile. "Yes, I understand you've made it so clear that the bandmaster's trying to import musicians from California because he can't find any here who'll knuckle under—not even the Portuguese."

"Where did you hear that? Will you please stop listening to street gossip?"

"Sam Brentwood, don't expect me to do anything you tell me to!"

Eden raised her hands. "Don't. Please."

Neither one of them heard her.

"If it weren't for Eden, I wouldn't stay in the same house with you another minute!" Annie exploded.

Eden dropped her spoon in her uneaten egg and fled.

Sam looked after her, startled. "Now look what you've done," he said.

Annie kicked her chair out of the way.

"Where are you going?" Sam demanded.

Annie whirled around in the doorway. "To my room!"

Sam cast around for some way to defuse her and made a tactical error. "Let's talk this over in private."

"I wouldn't be private with you if you were the last man on earth and the human race depended on it!"

"I didn't mean that—"

"Oh, yes, you did!" Annie was screaming at him now. "That's all you ever think of! You'd make a mink feel undersexed! I'm human, too, damn you, but don't you think you'll get around me that way!"

"Annie—" Sam looked uneasily at the open windows.

"I don't care how desperate I get, I wouldn't go to bed with a lying, sneaking, lecherous, unprincipled traitor who keeps his brain in his *pants*!" She fumbled with the drawer of the secretary that stood just inside the parlor. "And where is my writing paper?"

Sam put his head in his hands. He heard the drawer bang shut again and Annie's furious footsteps retreating up the stairs. He lowered his head slowly to the table. Logical, that was Annie. A shadow moved past the dining room window, and he heard a stifled giggle on the veranda. He groaned and, distracted, never thought about what she wanted with writing paper.

Washington, March 1893

President Grover Cleveland settled into his chair with a certain amount of relish. The American people, misguided enough four years ago to have voted in Benjamin Harrison instead of himself, had come to their senses and returned him to office. Cleveland considered Harrison to have been an aberration, a mistaken hiatus between his own two terms. So much for Benjamin Harrison. And so much for Harrison's last-ditch treaty of Hawaiian annexation, obligingly held up by the Democratic Senate until Harrison's departure. If anyone was going to annex Hawaii, it was going to be Grover Cleveland—but he wasn't about to do it on Harrison's recommendation.

Cleveland pulled the heavy Hawaiian file forward to study it. Certainly a great many people seemed to have opinions on the matter. The provisional government's commissioners had brought with them a letter with numerous signatures, as well as their own pleas. But a letter from the deposed queen and other letters in her support were making Cleveland dubious. So had the appearance of the queen's eighteen-year-old niece and heir, Kaiulani, who had been at school in London. Kaiulani was rapidly becoming the toast of Washington, and in the President's opinion, if this elegant and educated young lady was a "degraded heathen," then he was a monkey's uncle.

Cleveland sighed and looked over the letters again. As he did so, a familiar name surfaced—twice, in fact. He pressed a buzzer on his desk.

"Get me Senator Holt as soon as is convenient for him."

Toby Holt made his appearance in less than an hour, wondering, *What now?* He was tall, with graying sandy hair and the look of a man who had spent a good deal of his life in the saddle. The excellent cut of his frock coat didn't disguise shoulder muscles that made any coat look a half-size too small for him. The mustache he had recently adopted, in keeping with fashion, didn't hide the determined curve of his lips, any more than the spectacles, also recently—and reluctantly—adopted, hid the mingled tolerance and suspicion with which he was accustomed to view the world. Being a senator was probably the tamest thing he had done in a checkered career, but he had discovered that it had its moments. He eyed his president warily.

"What can I do for you, sir?"

Cleveland shoved the file at him.

"I don't know any more about Hawaii than I do about Zanzibar," Toby said hastily. "Less maybe."

Cleveland extracted the letter with many signatures

from the Committee of Safety and pressed his index finger down by the name Samuel F. Brentwood. He matched it with an outraged missive on feminine stationery, signed Annie Laurie Brentwood (Mrs. Samuel). "These folks are relatives of yours, aren't they?"

Toby groaned. "Sort of."

"They seem to be having a certain difference of opinion," President Cleveland remarked.

"So I see." Toby studied the letters with a half smile.

"Well, what's your opinion?"

"Frankly, sir, I think this whole annexation request looks fishy. That's without taking these letters into account. If you want my opinion of the Brentwoods' veracity, all I can say is that going on general moral character, I'd take Annie's word over Sam's any day, even if Annie were dead drunk and Sam were swearing on a stack of bibles. That's just personal opinion. I suppose it's possible he's improved some." Toby didn't look as if he thought it was likely.

"So Mrs. Brentwood is not a hysterical type?"

"No. If she's crossing Sam, it's because she thinks she's right, and she's got something to go on. It's not spite." He thought that over. "At least I don't think so. Of course, he's given her some cause to be spiteful. Hell, I don't know."

"Fat lot of help," Cleveland muttered.

"If you want my political opinion, sir," Toby said, "I think we should investigate further before we take any steps that may embarrass us. My son's sent a reporter out there since this boiled over, and he's been reporting very questionable support for the provisional government."

"Your son owns a newspaper, doesn't he?" Cleveland asked. "There are just as many supporters on the other side, though. Irresponsible so-and-sos, they'll print anything."

Toby chuckled. The press had printed a number of derogatory articles about Grover Cleveland, but he had survived.

"Well, here's something they can print," Cleveland

said. "The annexation treaty is going to be withdrawn from the Senate."

"We hoped it might be," Toby murmured. He was one of the Democratic senators who had managed to sit on the treaty until Harrison left office and Cleveland came in. "Am I at liberty to disclose that to my son? It would be fatherly of me to give him a scoop."

"Just don't quote *me*," Cleveland warned.

"Heaven forbid. He'll have to settle for 'reliable sources.' What *are* your plans for the islands?"

Cleveland gave him a stern look. "They're off the record until I announce them."

"Of course, sir." Toby grinned. He enjoyed letting Tim try to wrestle more out of him than he was willing to give. He thought Tim did, too. It was a form of mental exercise between them and had some of the same elements as the farm boy who indulges in horseplay with his old man to measure how tough he is.

"The queen has sent her own envoys," Cleveland continued. "They're making nearly as much stir as the little princess, so I suppose I'll have to see them." He sounded gloomy.

"The press likes them," Toby said. He pulled a folded sheet from the *New York Herald* out of his pocket and adjusted his spectacles. "I sense a certain swinging away from support for the PGs." He cleared his throat and read: "'Mr. Thurston's threat . . . to deliver the Islands to England if the treaty is not ratified . . . is not quite nice.'"

"First time I heard the press make an understatement." Cleveland grunted. "Well, I've got something for Thurston, damn his blackmailing eyes. I want that American flag hauled down off the government building in Honolulu, and I'm sending a special commissioner to investigate just what Stevens and his annexationists are trying to suck us into."

"Tricky job," Toby commented. "Whom are you sending?"

"Blount, I think," Cleveland said. "He's a sound man, and he won't let expansionist ideas get in the way of good sense."

Toby nodded. James H. Blount of Georgia was a former congressman with a reputation for not letting much get by him. Furthermore, he would be prejudiced by neither the New England connections of many of the annexationists nor by the anguished howls of Louisiana sugar growers in competition with the Hawaiian planters.

"Blount will conduct a thorough public investigation," Cleveland said, "and keep our reputation on the up-and-up. He'll be backed up by an assistant who will conduct a private investigation and report to Blount. I'm thinking about Colonel Henry Blake for that post. I like him. I read his report on his work with the eastern Cherokee last year. Isn't he your brother or stepbrother or something?"

"Something," Toby answered. "Henry's the adopted son of my mother and her second husband. He's married to my sister. We haven't quite worked out what that makes him."

"Never mind," Cleveland said. "You have a highly unusual family, Holt. Like an octopus—tentacles everywhere."

"Yes, sir," Toby said.

"Your daughter's a menace. Not that she's not right, of course, but she's got the Bureau of Indian Affairs running around like a bunch of wet hens. Does my heart good, actually. Well, do you think Blake can do the job?"

"Absolutely," Toby said. "I never saw a man with the ability to melt into the landscape like Henry can, and then emerge somewhere else with something useful. I always said he was a born spy."

"Apparently," Cleveland said with meaning. "I've been reading his dossier."

"Henry's had an interesting life," Toby said, "in the sinister meaning of the word. There's an old Chinese curse that says, 'May you live in interesting times.' Henry's element is interesting times."

"Excellent," Cleveland said. "I'm sure he will do admirably."

"Oh, he will," Toby agreed. He thought a moment. "Although I don't suppose *you'd* like to explain to my sister why he's being snatched from her bosom and sent to Hawaii?"

"Not at all," Cleveland said. He had met Cindy Blake. "You do it."

"I was afraid of that," Toby said.

XIII

"And you needn't think theater tickets are going to buy you off, Toby Holt! I know who's behind this." Toby's sister, Cindy, gave him a glare and a piercing whisper as the houselights dimmed.

"Shhh! Wait for intermission."

Alexandra Holt watched them sympathetically, well aware that Cindy's protests weren't going to accomplish anything. Neither Toby nor Henry had ever in their varied careers dreamed of turning down an assignment from the President. She wasn't even sure that Henry, since he was in the army, could if he wanted to. Which, Alexandra could tell by the gleam in his eye, he did not.

Cindy settled into her seat with an aggravated whisk of her skirts. The people in front swiveled their necks around in annoyance, so she quieted down. But she fixed an accusing stare on her brother's right ear and kept it there through part of the first act.

"Quit staring at me," Toby finally hissed at her. "Look: There's Cathy."

"I'm not through with you," Cindy said, but she gave her attention to the stage.

Catherine Martin, daughter of Toby's friend Rob, had wanted to be an actress and actually run away to New York to pursue it. After a good deal of family hysterics—her parents considered her ambition to be unwise, not to say disreputable—she had been allowed to stay in Manhattan.

The young woman was actually quite good, Alexandra decided, watching Miss Martin in her first starring role, albeit one in a touring company. It wasn't a very good play—some silly fluff about an imperiled heroine and an evil duke—but, as Cathy had informed her ecstatically over the telephone from her hotel, she did have the lead.

The first-act curtain dropped on a swooning Cathy, fainting in her aged mother's arms, with the duke leering wickedly.

"Well," Alexandra said as the houselights came up again, "I do think she's making the most of it." She looked at her son. "Enjoying it?"

"I think it's top notch," Mike Holt said from his mother's other side. Mike was not quite seventeen, and he liked drama with a lot of action, which *The Tarnished Bride* certainly presented. "It was great when they set fire to the hayloft while she was hiding in it."

"Pyrotechnics." Cindy sniffed. "The sets are really very badly done. You can't substitute red lights and a smoke bomb for artistic talent." Cindy ran an art gallery and had high standards. When the group had filed out into the lobby, where lemonade and champagne were being circulated, she put a hand firmly on her brother's wrist. "What do you mean by telling the President to send Henry to Hawaii? He just spent months in North Carolina last fall! The children are going to grow up thinking he's a visiting uncle. I'm out of patience with you."

"With me?" Toby raised an eyebrow.

"She didn't get anywhere with me," Henry explained.

"I imagine not."

Mike touched his mother's arm. "Hawaii, Mama?"

"Yes, dear. To investigate the troubles they've been having there."

Mike fell silent, and Alexandra gave her attention back to Cindy and their respective husbands. She was extremely fond of Cindy, partly because Cindy and Toby were so alike, more so than any two of Toby's own children. It was like seeing her husband in a feminine version. Sometimes that resemblance made Alexandra want to whap Cindy with her parasol for many of the same reasons that made her wish to do so to Toby once in a while. But just now she was firmly in Cindy's corner; she herself was relieved at having Toby settled into a senator's career where she, Mike, and nine-year-old Sally could actually expect to see him at breakfast for the foreseeable future.

Cindy and Henry had been adolescent sweethearts, who had split apart in anger. Each had made another marriage. Later, both widowed, they had come together in a marriage that each had always longed for. They had both been adults and set in their ways at the time, but the marriage had now lasted fifteen years, and they had two children. They wouldn't divorce over Henry's going to Hawaii, but Cindy's anger was no young bride's whim, either.

Perhaps, Alexandra mused, she could think of something enticing to do with Cindy while Henry was gone— take Toby and Cindy's mother, Eulalia, to New York, for instance, to visit Claudia Locke. Eulalia's old friend, recently widowed, had returned from Europe to the old brownstone where she had been so happy with her Howard.

"Henry dear, how long do you expect to be gone?" Alexandra ventured.

"Heaven only knows," Henry answered. "As long as six months, possibly. Maybe more."

So much for that, Alexandra thought. They couldn't possibly spend six months in New York City. Without thinking, she said, "Well, goodness, Cindy, why don't you go with him? You know you're interested in Polynesian art."

Henry gave her a startled look, and Alexandra wished she could take back the suggestion.

Surprisingly, however, Henry stroked his chin, cocked his head thoughtfully at Cindy, and said, "That might be a good idea. Nobody takes his wife and children along if he's up to something disreputable."

"Precisely," Toby commented.

"I want to learn the unofficial story," Henry continued. "No one tells the unofficial story to official-looking people. What do you think, Cindy? Visiting American art collector trailing bored husband on tropical vacation?"

"It warms my heart to be such a useful cover," Cindy remarked tartly. But her expression was thoughtful as a page went through the lobby ringing his chimes to indicate that the second act was about to begin.

"And she's going with him?" Toby's mother, Eulalia, smiled wistfully. She hadn't felt up to going to the theater, but she had waited up for them, with a lap robe, anchored by a cat, over her thin knees.

Alexandra settled herself in a wing chair opposite Eulalia's and pulled off her evening slippers. "She is. Thank goodness. It seems that Mr. Blount is taking his wife as well."

"Frankly," Toby said after a yawn, "I thought Alex had taken leave of her senses. Never get in the middle of someone else's quarrel."

"You were in it," Alexandra pointed out.

"I didn't volunteer. I was drafted."

"Well, it worked out beautifully." Alexandra looked at Mike, who had settled into a chair across from her, eyes brooding. "Are you sleepy, darling? You ought to be in bed."

"I'm just thinking," Mike murmured.

"Well, only another few minutes," Alexandra said. "You know what the doctor says about enough sleep."

Mike's green eyes flashed. "Damn the doctor."

"Michael!" Toby gave his offspring a stern look. "I sympathize with your annoyance with the doctor, but you are not to use that language in front of your mother and grandmother."

"In front of anybody," Alexandra said. Men seemed to

think it was perfectly all right to swear as long as the wrong people didn't hear you.

Mike ducked his head in embarrassment. "Sorry."

"Is Cindy taking the children?" Eulalia asked by way of distraction.

"Yes. They'll have a wonderful time."

Mike looked up suddenly, his mouth set with decision. "I want to go with them."

"What?" Toby shook his head. "Mike, that's not possible. You aren't up to it."

"Dear, they haven't even asked you," Alexandra said gently.

"They would if I asked them to," Mike said. "Frank's fourteen, and Midge is eight. I'd be a help with my cousins."

"That is unarguable," Toby said, "but the trip would be much too hard on you."

Mike looked up at the three of them in turn. "It wouldn't be any harder on me than being shut up here," he said distinctly. "I'm in perfectly good health." His mouth twisted bitterly. "For an invalid. My heart isn't suddenly going to do loops just because I'm on a boat."

His parents and grandmother looked at one another helplessly over his head. A childhood case of rheumatic fever had left Mike's heart scarred and his parents in unending and agonizing indecision over what might or might not be dangerous.

"You'll be going to college in a little over another year," Toby said. "Can't you wait for that?"

"Somewhere close to home," Mike grumbled. "Somewhere safe. We wouldn't want me to be too excited about it."

Alexandra looked at him miserably.

Toby said, "Why Hawaii? If you really want to travel, maybe we could—"

Alexandra caught Toby's eyes. *Eden,* she mouthed silently over Mike's head. Toby cast his eyes upward.

"I want to see Hawaii," Mike offered. "I have the

camera Claudia sent me for Christmas, and I want to try it out." Claudia had presented Mike with an actual moving-picture camera, purchased at who knew what outlandish price (or bribe) through a friend of a friend who worked at Thomas Edison's studio. "Everyone's seen pictures of Washington," Mike added.

The three adults looked at one another again, and Alexandra bit her knuckles. What evil spirit had prompted her to suggest that Cindy go to Hawaii?

"We'll think about it, Mike," Toby said abruptly. "Now go to bed."

Mike stood up, resigned, sensing a family council that wasn't going to take place as long as he was in the room. "Think about it a lot." His voice was tense.

It struck Toby that Mike had grown taller. His face had lost its boyish cast, and he could now almost look at his father in the eyes.

"Oh, Toby," Eulalia said after Mike's thin, wiry figure had stalked up the stairs, "I feel so sorry for him." The cat yawned and stretched, and Eulalia scratched its bony head as if she could somehow comfort Mike through it.

"I do, too." Toby paced in front of the fireplace, then stopped and poked the embers moodily. "He's got my father's temperament and wandering foot, attached to a heart that won't stand up to them."

Eulalia sighed. "Whip wouldn't have let that stop him. Do you really think it's fair of us to try to stop Mike?"

"I don't know," Toby admitted. He sat down in the chair that Mike had vacated. "We'd planned for Mike to be the one to run the Madrona." The Madrona was the Holt home ranch in Oregon. "But the way he feels now, we'd have to tie him up to keep him there, and that stress won't do his heart any good, either. The whole idea of his inheriting the Madrona was to give him a peaceful life. Do you suppose if we let him take this trip, it might satisfy him?"

"Toby, it may be dangerous." Alexandra put her hands

out as if to hold Mike back. "Not just to his heart. I mean the political situation there."

"No. Henry has a better ear to the ground than I do where that's concerned. He wouldn't take Cindy and his own children if he thought it was risky. The Hawaiians have been as peaceable as Sunday school children for years."

"What about Mike's feelings for Eden?"

"That worries me more," Toby confessed. "I don't think Mike ought to marry at all, but I can't bring myself to tell him that. They're awfully young for a case of puppy love to linger, though. If they see each other again while they're still too young to do anything about it, it may blow over." He chuckled. "*I* didn't know what I wanted when I was his age."

"And for quite some time after that," his mother commented. "Toby, you sound as if you're trying to talk yourself into letting him go."

"Maybe I am," Toby said. "If he stays here, pent up and frustrated, it may be worse for him." Just how much of Whip Holt was there in Mike? he wondered. Too much, maybe.

Alexandra curled herself into a ball in the chair and put her face in her hands, while the cat hopped down from Eulalia's lap and batted at Alexandra's stockinged toes. Toby scooped it out of the way and scooted his chair over beside his wife's. He put his spectacles in his pocket and took her fingers between his, holding them against his face. "He's growing up. We can't tie his hands forever. Maybe if he gets it out of his system now, he'll be more willing to recognize his limitations when he's older and we have no control over him."

Upstairs in his bed, Mike was pondering his limitations. He knew more about them than his father thought. Last year on his sixteenth birthday, with a letter from Eden in his pocket, he secretly had made an appointment with Dr. Amos.

"Well, there's been no change in the last six months,"

Dr. Amos had said, dropping his stethoscope around his neck again. "You can't really expect there to be."

"I know," Mike had said, buttoning his shirt. "I want to know what I *can* expect, later on."

"I'm not sure what you're asking me," the doctor said.

Mike gave him a level look, a green-eyed stare much older than the years behind it. "How long am I going to live, for instance? I want the truth."

Amos looked first at the carpet and then at the glass-fronted dispensary case, considering. "There's no way to know," he said finally. "You might live to a ripe old age."

"And I might not?" Mike asked.

"No, you might not. The heart's a tricky organ, and yours is damaged."

"What might set it off?"

Amos sat down in the chair opposite the examining table, where Mike was still perched, feet swinging. "Strain," he said. "Fear. Excitement."

"Can I get married?" Mike demanded.

"At sixteen? You just put on long pants!"

"Of course not. I only want to know what's . . . possible."

"Anything is possible," the doctor said. "All right, I'll be frank. It would be better if you didn't. Marriage itself probably won't kill you. The risk will be on your wife's part. She'll have to understand that you stand a good chance of leaving her a young widow, with fatherless children."

Mike had thanked him and gone home with a new understanding of why his parents were made uneasy by his correspondence with Eden. He had begun to hide her letters. They were innocent letters, full of news of school and the wonders of Hawaii, and signed "Your friend, Eden Brentwood." His letters to her were equally platonic.

But Mike was growing up—and he knew that Eden would be, too. Isolation had made him precocious in some ways. Now, some nine months after that visit to the doctor, Mike lay in bed and tried to imagine how Eden would look. They had exchanged photographs at Christmas, and Mike was gloomily convinced that his made him look like a moron. Eden's looked much the way she had the last time he had seen her, at his grandfather's funeral two years before: gold hair still loose down her back and wide, serious eyes under a schoolgirl's straw boater. But something about her face was gaining definition, losing childhood, growing toward the woman she almost was. Mike turned over uncomfortably. How sinful was it to imagine what the rest of her might look like? When they had first met, when he was thirteen and she was twelve, he hadn't really thought about there being more to her, under those clothes. He had just floated in the rosy light of first love, a light that he had been sure had emanated from Eden. Now, though . . . How stupid was it to think that she might still feel the same way about him? And if she did, how foolish was it for him to go to Hawaii?

Mike sat up and rummaged in the drawer of his bedside table, where he kept Eden's letters and her photograph in a cigar box. He fished out the little gold locket, his secret treasure and talisman. On the back were the initials E.B., and inside was a fine lock of hair. Feeling furtive and a little silly, he closed the drawer and fastened the locket around his neck, dropping it down inside the front of his nightshirt. What would Eden think if she knew he was wearing it? It had been a childish gift, given the first time they had met and parted. He wondered if she had any idea of the significance he had attached to it or the bad times it had gotten him through. According to her letters, nobody ever seemed to ask Eden what she thought about anything, he reflected. And now that included him. Whether or not to become his wife ought to be Eden's decision.

Mike yawned deliberately, trying to make sleep come. *If she still feels the same way, I'll let her decide.* Of course he wouldn't ask her yet; they were too young. . . . Eventually he slept, with the locket pressed against his chest.

The next morning, when his father informed him that

they had, with reservations, decided to let him go with the Blakes, Mike was sure that the locket had somehow worked magic. After that he didn't take it off.

The Blakes decided on traveling by railroad to San Francisco and taking a ship from there, rather than making the tedious voyage around the Horn of South America. Toby, Alexandra, Sally, and Eulalia saw them off at the station.

"I wish I could go," Sally said rebelliously. "It isn't fair."

"You're too young, dear. Aunt Cindy will have enough on her hands."

"She's taking Midge."

"She has to," Toby said. "She's Midge's mother."

Sally stuck out her lower lip and folded her arms across the front of her sailor dress. She was older than Midge, and Sally considered that this expedition gave Midge an unfair advantage. Midge smirked from the window of the Pullman car.

Alexandra put her arm around Sally's shoulders. "I couldn't bear to part with both of you." She gave Toby a frantic look as if they could call Mike back even now. Toby shook his head. The whistle shrieked, and the huge iron drive wheels began to turn. "Mike!" Alexandra called, but her voice was lost in the whistle.

The whole trip took three weeks, counting a three-day stopover in San Francisco to await their ship—and as Henry remarked several times, it seemed much longer.

Cindy merely looked amused and added a Navajo basket to their luggage when the train stopped in Albuquerque. "It's character building, dear," she murmured.

They had an hour's layover to eat dinner in the depot Harvest House, and Frank and Midge were whooping down the platform, burning off two days' accumulated energy. Mike trailed them at a more sedate pace, but Cindy noted that he had his eye on Midge and caught up with her in a flash when she ventured too near the tracks.

"You should travel with your children more often," Cindy said to Henry, "and you'd appreciate the advantage of having Mike with us. The last time I took them anywhere, I couldn't turn my back on them for an instant."

"Where was I?" Henry asked absently, wondering how they were going to fit the new basket in their luggage.

Cindy opened her eyes at him wide. "Heaven only knows," she said sweetly.

"Oh." Henry mulled that over. "I haven't been around much, have I?"

"No," Cindy said. "On the whole you've been worth it, but no."

Midge reappeared. "Mother! That Indian lady has lizards on little leashes for sale! Can I buy one?"

"No!" her parents said simultaneously. They looked at each other and laughed.

What have I been missing? Henry wondered. *How could I have finally married the woman I always wanted, and then spent fifteen years with her not knowing where I was half the time?* He knew, though. It was the job. The army and the other, more sub rosa, assignments that occasionally came from the government. Most of the missions had not been as placid as this one promised to be—certainly no place to take his wife, particularly not after they had had children. It would probably go on that way, too. Henry was a realist. It was what he did, and he was good at it. At the age of sixteen, he had set out on a self-appointed crusade to track down the men who had killed his natural father, and much to everyone's unease, he had done it.

His subsequent stint at West Point, under Lee Blake's sponsorship, had knocked off some of the rough edges and given his headstrong temperament a rein, but it had only further educated him for what was to become his work. If Lee hadn't taken him in hand, Henry reflected, he would probably have become a gunslinger instead.

Henry slipped up behind Cindy, who had gone back to perusing baskets and a pile of Navajo weaving. "We may not get too many chances like this one," he said in her ear. "But I'd like to enjoy it while I have it. I'll try to be underfoot as much as possible."

"Don't feel too guilty." Cindy smiled. "Maybe it's been good for me. I've always been an independent person, as you know. But having you underfoot is what I like best." They linked arms and went to dinner.

Certainly everyone was underfoot on the ship—it couldn't be helped—but the party reached Honolulu in a mood of excitement and camaraderie. The Blakes set up housekeeping in a rented house near the Iolani Palace, now occupied by Sanford Dole's provisional government, and sent a message to the Brentwoods to let Sam and Annie know they had arrived. Just a vacation trip, Cindy had written—Henry had some leave due, and she was planning to take a collection of native art back to Washington with her. And they had Mike Holt with them.

Sam, as it turned out, was in Honolulu already, thick with the PGs. Annie, disgusted, had gone back to the Big Island but returned immediately, prompted by Eden's ecstatic pleas: She had to see Mike, right now. Could she take her new blue silk? Couldn't she pin her hair up, just this once, to impress him? He could visit them on the farm, couldn't he?

Annie hadn't the heart to make trouble, and so the Brentwoods dined with the Blakes in Honolulu a week after their arrival.

Henry, watching Annie and Sam carefully and putting two and two together with marketplace gossip, which he was very adept at overhearing, was beginning to understand their political beliefs and marital strife. James Blount had arrived ahead of him, and Henry had had a meeting with him already, but it had been decided that he would report to Blount only in secret and when he had something solid.

Blount, Henry knew, had enough to keep him busy for the moment, working with Minister Stevens. Blount had ordered the American flag hauled down off the Ali'iolani Hale and commanded that the American marines be marched back aboard their ship.

They had marched snappily, as if on ceremonial parade, and Henry had watched them go with satisfaction. To his mind, it was no part of his country's honor to use its military for its citizens' private ends. Blount had said as much to Minister Stevens, in a conversation that Henry had not been privileged to overhear, but which Blount had reported to him.

"I chewed him out with precision," Blount said, with a faint chuckle. "I haven't enjoyed anything so much since I was in the army."

Henry grinned. "I thought he looked a little wilted around the ears. But maybe that's just his natural expression. We haven't been formally introduced."

"You won't be," Blount said. "You're no use to me if Stevens gets notions about you. He's far too much the PGs' man."

"And whose man are you?" Henry asked. He thought Blount looked like a tough customer.

"I'm my own man," Blount replied. "It helps being an old Confederate. Makes you independent minded."

Henry knew that Blount had also met with the endless stream of both PG dignitaries and representatives of the queen but firmly declined the social invitations that flowed like water. Nor had Blount and his wife accepted the houses and carriages offered by both the PGs and the queen. The couple had settled instead, at their own expense, into the Royal Hawaiian Hotel.

Henry had also been present when the American flag had come down and the Hawaiian flag had been run up in its place. A crowd of Hawaiians had gathered with eager eyes to watch, but strangely there had been no cheering or applause. Blount, puzzled, had asked a Hawaiian why not and received the reply that "It would be discourteous to the

United States, which is so good and honorable. We would not dishonor the American flag."

Blount had remarked to Henry that no one could deny the dignity and good manners of the queen's people. Henry, in a less public position and with an ear to the ground, was given to wonder how long the same good manners would extend toward the PGs, considering what the natives were putting up with. The PGs' "gag law" had actually sent some loyalist newspaper editors to prison, and there were rumors of a PG plot to assassinate the queen.

Henry mentioned both to the Brentwoods over dinner, gently fishing, and got an earful.

"Ridiculous rumors!" Sam snorted. "I assure you no one would think of it. Good Lord, man, we're in the public eye."

"We are indeed," Annie said. "Thanks to you, the harbor's full of warships." Not only the Americans but the British and the Japanese were keeping an eye on their country's interests.

"And the streets are full of reporters," Sam said. "Going off half-cocked and printing the first thing anyone says to them. That reporter of Tim Holt's, Hugo Ware, is as bad as the rest."

Henry thought he might look up Hugo Ware. Henry's son Peter worked for Tim Holt, too—an admirable reason for a social chat.

"Except for the *Star*, of course," Annie retorted to Sam. "The PGs print that."

"The *Star* does seem a little rabid," Cindy murmured. "Speaking strictly as a newcomer."

"Rabid doesn't begin to describe it," Annie snapped. She waved a hand apologetically. "I didn't mean to sound so overwrought. But you've hardly come at a good time for us. I would have liked to show you our beautiful islands as they should be."

"I take it you favor the monarchy?" Henry asked. "Here, let me pour you some of this excellent champagne."

"Annie doesn't know much about politics," Sam offered.

"I know when people are lying through their teeth to Mr. Blount," Annie informed him. "Reverend Bishop, of all people. A man of the cloth! He started out by telling Mr. Blount that it was unpleasant for him to speak evil of anyone and then proceeded to inform him that the queen surrounds herself with sorcerers. Of all the idiotic things, he accused Cabinet Minister Cornwell of being degraded in his personal character, and then when Mr. Blount asked for details, he couldn't come up with anything except that poor Mr. Cornwell had spoken favorably of hula dances."

Sam and Henry both stared at Annie. "How do you know all this?" Sam demanded. "Those are private interviews."

Henry was wondering the same thing.

"I hear things," Annie said airily.

"Servants' gossip," Sam muttered, but he looked uncomfortable.

Henry suppressed a smile. It was obvious that the loyalists, as well as the PGs, had their informers and that Annie Brentwood was liked and trusted by the queen's. "Fascinating," he murmured. His face was carefully open, just an interested tourist, but his eyes were intent. "Tell us more."

"It's all the same," Annie said. "They'll grasp at anything. They've even said Her Majesty is carrying on immoral relations with Marshal Wilson! Wilson's wife is the queen's lady-in-waiting. Wilson's ten years younger than the queen if he's a day, and he loves his wife. It's all spiteful nonsense. None of the Americans believes it, either, except for the PGs. And not all Americans are PGs," she added darkly.

A second table had been set up for the children, and from its vantage point Mike watched his uncle Henry deftly pour champagne and steer the conversation. Frank and Midge were under the impression that they were merely on a vacation. Mike was the only one who knew better, but he was sworn to secrecy and was less interested in politics than in the fact that Sam and Annie Brentwood were plainly still at odds, since that affected Eden. He looked at Eden again and felt a little lurch in his heart that had nothing to do with physical health. Her hair was up in a very adult-looking arrangement, and her slim white neck was adorned with a necklace of vermilion flowers, bright against her blue dress. She had brought a necklace for him, too, and because Eden had put it around his neck Mike had decided that it didn't look silly at all.

"You look very Hawaiian," he whispered. He had contrived to get himself seated next to her. Or perhaps she had contrived it. It seemed to be a mutual wish. *Am I counting on too much?* he wondered, a little frightened now that he was actually there. *Does she feel the way she seems to?* That was a little frightening, too, in its way. He struggled for a casual topic of conversation, with Frank and Midge across from them. "What are those things in your ears? I never saw anything like them."

"Land shells." Eden put a fingertip to her delicate spiral earrings. "They grow in Nuuanu Valley." She gave him a sidelong glance. "I don't suppose you'd like to see them?"

Suddenly Mike could think of nothing he wanted more than to collect land shells with Eden.

"We could take a picnic," Eden suggested.

And without Frank and Midge, Mike decided, feeling adult and breathless. On this picnic he wasn't going to be anyone's nanny. Frank was old enough to look after himself, of course, but he wasn't old enough to know when someone wanted privacy. Mike smiled. He knew that Annie and Aunt Cindy would trust him with Eden, since he was so young, too. A private picnic for an older couple would have been unthinkable. Mike's face flushed as he realized that he would have to live up to that trust and that it mightn't be all that easy.

The next day, after taking classes with the Brentwoods' governess, Mike and Eden climbed Nuuanu Pali, oblivious to any political turmoil brewing below them. Mike's eyes and heart were fixed on Eden as her horse scrambled up the trail ahead of his. They had fruit, sandwiches, and coconut cookies stowed in their saddlebags, and Eden had brought a box to put the land shells in on their way back down from the precipice. The still, hot air was parted every now and then, as the trail changed its angle, by the cool, fresh passage of the April trade winds. Mysterious, giant-leaved trees, as green as emeralds, closed over their heads and then opened again to show a sky spattered with rain dogs floating like translucent butterflies above them.

They passed the mausoleum where the last of the Kamehamehas lay buried. Two tall *kahilis*, the feather plumes of royalty, fluttered at the door. Above the mausoleum the vegetation ceased.

Eden drew rein under the steep crag of Nuuanu Pali. "Look."

Mike, startled, saw the white gleam of bones in the red soil below the cliff.

"Kamehameha drove the defenders of Oahu off the edge of this cliff when he conquered the island," Eden whispered. "They're still here." She kicked her pony in the flanks. "Come up to the top, and I'll show you something pretty instead."

Higher still they rode, to the place where Oahu's doomed defenders had made their last stand. There was no trace on the black volcanic rock of the blood that must have soaked it through, but the precipice dropped sharply to the trail they had just come up. The ponies stood, heads down, blowing in the thin air, and Eden slipped down from her saddle. Mike dismounted, too, and she took his hand, not saying anything. Below them stretched the northern slopes of Nuuanu and green fields undulating toward the indigo waters of Kaneohe Bay. White banners of surf roared over the coral beds, slowed as if the very beauty of the land stole the fierceness from them, and ended as bubbling fingers splayed among the sands.

"It's too windy to eat up here," Eden said, "but I wanted you to see the view." The wind spun her pale hair out behind her in a cloud as fine as sea spray. Mike put a hand out, letting it blow against his fingers.

Eden turned, still holding his other hand, and looked at him. "I'm awfully glad you came," she said, blushing. "Was it to see me?"

"Well, of course it was."

"Good," Eden said contentedly. "Let's go eat."

They remounted their ponies and wound their way down into the emerald valley. They hobbled the ponies to let them graze, then spread their picnic under the tangled maze of a *hau* tree. The soft air seemed to Mike to be charged with possibility. His hand suddenly shook so violently that he spilled the flask of cold tea on the quilt.

He dabbed at it with his pocket handkerchief. Eden produced a napkin from the saddlebag. "Here, silly, a handkerchief won't do it." She blotted up the tea and then glanced at his taut face. "Mike, what's the matter?"

"I don't know," he said. "I thought I had everything figured out, but—I just wanted to see you and didn't think past that," he finished in a rush. "We're supposed to be friends, but now I don't know what to say to you." He stared at her with all the agony of first love. "But we're more than friends," he blurted. "I've been in love with you since I was thirteen. I wasn't going to say that!" He stared up into the knotted branches of the hau tree now. She was even younger than he was. He had no right. . . .

"Is that all?" Eden said, relieved. She put the napkin away and settled next to him, tucking her feet under the folds of her divided skirt. She smelled like lilacs and a little like ponies. "I love you, too," she said comfortably.

"Eden—" Filled with good intentions, he tried desperately to think what he ought to say to beat back temptation. "We're too young."

Eden appeared to be thinking about it. "That doesn't seem to matter, does it?" she said finally.

"You'll meet lots of other fellows."

"I won't want them."

"Oh, damn . . ." Mike said. He put his hands on her shoulders, and she leaned toward him willingly. His mouth touched hers, not a childish kiss like the last one they had shared, but a grown-up kiss between two people who were tangled far too early in a grown-up love. When at last he pulled his head back, it was because he knew he would do something worse if he didn't.

"I know we can't marry for a while yet," Eden said with the guileless assumption that when she was old enough he would ask her. "But I can wait."

Mike steeled himself. "Then we have to talk now. My heart's no good. You know that."

Eden blanched. "Mike, you're not worse?"

"No, I'm just the same," Mike said bitterly. "Iffy, that's how I am. I don't see how I can ask you to marry me, when I might die on you."

Eden let out the breath that was caught in her throat. "Annie said the same thing to me this morning." She gave him a shrewd look. "And I'll bet your parents have, too."

"No, it was the doctor. I asked him."

Eden sat up straight. "Well, the person you should have asked is me, don't you think?"

Mike nodded. "I just want to be sure you really think about it and don't just react."

"I *have* thought about it," Eden said. "I'm scared to death of losing you, but it would be worse not to have you at all. Look at Gran: She had two happy years with Grandpa Howard. What would she have had if she hadn't married him?"

"Neither one of us is eighty-five years old," Mike pointed out. "You could have a lot more than two happy years with someone else." He felt obliged to play devil's advocate, to protect her from himself. "I shouldn't even talk about it—it's indelicate—but what if we have children and I don't live to raise them?"

"I have plenty of money," Eden said simply. Her eyes had a determined glint—like his, older than her years. "Did you ever stop to think," she whispered to him, "that we're *supposed* to be together? If someone gives you that, I think it's wrong to throw it away because you're afraid."

That did it. He pulled her into his arms again and kissed her, burying his hands in the curtain of her hair. She responded eagerly and so trustingly that he was shaken. When he found his fingers moving around her rib cage to brush the fine, pin-tucked pleats on the front of her shirtwaist, he sat back abruptly, breathing hard, and made a stab at the proprieties.

"I apologize, Eden. I'm sorry."

Eden's face was flushed, and her blue eyes were bright. "Nobody saw us, did they?" She handed him a sandwich. "Let's look for the land shells."

Oh, Eden, I love you, Mike thought. *You deserve better than me, but I guess I'm the one you want.*

"Here's one." Eden cupped her hand under a leaf, to which clung a tiny spiral no bigger than her fingertip. It was cerulean blue with delicate brown lines running through it. "They're really snails, but aren't they pretty? Every tree has a different kind."

Mike detached the little shell and held it in his palm. Eden inspected the bark and leaves of the surrounding trees and found more spirals, brown and yellow and green.

"They say if you're very, very still you can hear the shells sing. I never have, though."

They stood silently, listening. It seemed to Mike that there was some faint music in the trees but that it might not be the shells.

He carefully wrapped Eden's treasures in a napkin. "I wish I had brought the camera," he said, looking up at the gray wall of Nuuanu Pali rising out of the trees above them, its jagged pinnacles like the spires of some fantastic church.

He looked sheepish. "I forgot all about it, and I wanted to show it to you."

"Never mind," Eden said practically. "A moving picture camera needs something moving. I'll tell you what: When you visit us on the farm, I'll take you up Kilauea to see the lava. That ought to get Mr. Edison's attention."

Mike's eyes gleamed. "How do you always know what I want?"

Eden considered. "Well, I know *you*."

Mike chuckled. "So you do." He put an arm around her. He would have to be careful, he reminded himself again, but it felt good just to hold her. The years since they had seen each other last seemed to blow away on the trade wind. "I haven't told my father this yet, but I'll tell you since you're so determined to be stuck with me: I'm not going to college. I'm going to get a job in Mr. Edison's studio."

"Have you applied already?" Eden asked.

Practical Eden. "No," Mike confessed. "But I've written him a lot of letters asking about his moving pictures. He's answered them, too. But he's a funny man. I don't think he's really interested in moving pictures. He thinks they're just a novelty. I believe that moving pictures are going to be the new form of entertainment. Mr. Edison is all wrong."

"Then how are you going to get him to give you a job?"

"I'm not sure," Mike said, "but I'll do it. I find that a lot of times if you make enough of a nuisance of yourself, people will give in. I only need to stay long enough to learn the business. Then I can branch out on my own."

Eden laughed. "You sound like your brother, Tim, and Peter Blake talking about automobiles." Peter was Henry's oldest child, by his first wife. At the moment he was managing the business end of Tim Holt's newspaper, but he yearned for the internal-combustion engine the way Mike yearned for moving pictures.

"Automobiles are the future, too," Mike agreed. "The future's going to come so fast, you won't believe it, Eden.

Whoosh, like a train, and nothing's going to be the same. We're almost at a new century. That always makes people restless."

"In 1900," Eden said, counting in her head, "you will be twenty-four. You will be a moving-picture king, and you will take our children and me out for rides in our new automobile." She passed her hands over an imaginary crystal ball. "There, I've told your fortune."

Or I might be dead, Mike thought, because, looking at her bright, confident eyes, he wanted his future with Eden so badly that it seemed almost impossible to him that he might be allowed to have it. A swift prayer went through his mind: *Not so soon, please. Not till I've done what I want to do.*

"Let's finish our picnic," Eden said.

Hand in hand, they went back to the hamper. Eden set out the rest of their lunch and the still half-full flask of tea. She had twined the hamper with scarlet blooms, which she had picked during their ride up from the valley. Mike held the vision in his eyes as carefully as he packed the fragile land shells into their waiting box.

XIV

"Hugo Ware." A pale, lanky man in a wicker peacock chair held out his hand to Henry Blake. They were on the veranda of the Royal Hawaiian Hotel. Ware possessed the lazy accent that Henry recognized as uppercrust British, but Hugo didn't look like a baron's younger son; he looked like what he was, a newspaper reporter—dapper enough but with a faintly raffish aura.

"I'm acquainted with your son, Colonel Blake, and I'm delighted to meet you."

"How is Peter?" Henry held up his hand to a waiter to bring him a drink. He gestured to Hugo's glass. "Can I offer you another?"

"No, thank you. As far as I can tell, Colonel, Peter's going to own most of Guthrie, Oklahoma, by the time he's twenty-one. Unfortunately, I understand he'll be leaving us at that point."

"Peter will come into his inheritance from his mother on his twenty-first birthday," Henry said. "Then he'll have some decisions to make."

"He has an amazing affinity for enterprises that are going to make money," Hugo said. He smiled ruefully. "I wish I had his touch."

"It's his mother's touch," Henry said, smiling. The waiter brought his drink, and he sipped it. "How long do you expect to be out here? Don't you have a wife in Guthrie?"

"Far too long probably," Hugo said gloomily, "and, yes. I miss her like the devil already."

"Newlyweds?"

"Two years," Hugo answered. "But Rosebay's not a woman whose effect on a man wears off." He pulled out his pocket watch and opened it. In the lid of the case was a photograph: a cloud of hair that looked nearly as pale as snow, and a breathtakingly beautiful face.

Henry whistled admiringly. "I should think not."

"She's a Virginia girl," Hugo said. "Mountain people. Came to Oklahoma for the land rush. Every man in town was courting her." He smiled gently. "To tell you the truth, I never thought she'd have me. When she did . . . well, you can see why I'm eager to go home." He put the watch away carefully.

Henry, musing over this oddly matched pair, took another sip of his drink. "Toby Holt told me you were here for the *Recorder*," he said. "I didn't realize it had reached the size to send out foreign correspondents."

"We're getting very big-city these days. Guthrie came up overnight like a mushroom—plenty of pretensions and extremely rapid growth. I don't think Tim and I will be there much longer, though. He has ambitions well beyond Guthrie. All the big newspapers sent reporters here, so here I am, too. And here you are, I expect."

"I'm only on vacation," Henry murmured.

"Certainly. I expect Nordhoff of the *Herald-Tribune* would like to be able to say that. The PGs have threatened to have him shot."

"Regrettable of them. Do I take that as a warning?"

"There is a certain attitude of rope-and-lamppost in the air."

"But so far your neck has escaped?"

"My neck isn't so well-known as Nordhoff's. And my paper's not so large. Also I'm rather a good shot. I hear you are, also."

"Excellent," Henry said with meaning. "So do remember I'm just on vacation." *And anything my nephew Tim has seen fit to tell you about me, you will kindly keep out of your newspaper.* From the perceptive glint in Hugo's intelligent eyes, Henry was aware that he didn't have to issue the warning out loud.

"I shall keep it ever in the forefront of my mind," Hugo said solemnly. "It's an interesting vacation choice just now, of course."

"My wife is collecting Polynesian art for her gallery," Henry said equally solemnly. The two of them were enjoying themselves.

"I wonder if politics can be considered an art form," Hugo mused. "The Hawaiians may be about to take it up rather emphatically. They don't care for the rumors about their queen. One hopes they aren't about to take a leaf from the PGs' book."

"In the form of strong-arm tactics?"

"A certain element appears to be mulling it over," he revealed. "The Palace Square Faction, I've heard they're called."

"You have? Then you might look out for ropes and lampposts yourself, from one side or another."

"I am ever watchful." Hugo smiled. "And ever in the market for reciprocity, of course."

Amused, Henry thought that over. If Hugo was right about open rebellion brewing against the PGs, then the reporter had shared important information. It might be that he could toss Hugo Ware a bone in return, without doing any harm, so as to keep the Englishman useful. "It might be that Minister Stevens is about to be recalled," Henry said casually. "Of course I can't remember where I heard that."

"Neither will I," Hugo responded promptly. "May I attribute a 'reliable source'?"

"You can attribute Attila the Hun if you want to," Henry said, "so long as you don't attribute me."

The Palace Square Faction did not conduct its business in Palace Square—or at least not any business that counted.

It hadn't taken Henry long to figure that out, nor to discover that a number of the faction were haoles. As a haole, however, Colonel Henry Blake was far too recognizable. Accordingly, he made a few alterations to his appearance so he might infiltrate their gatherings. As he was so doing, his wife entered the bathroom, and upon seeing a brown-skinned man clad only in trousers at the mirror, she uttered a gasp of surprise. Then he turned.

Cindy realized that this apparition was her husband. "Henry! What have you done to yourself?"

Henry grinned, his teeth particularly white against his altered skin. "A little judicious application of walnut juice." He looked in the mirror again, inspecting the effect, and combed a lock of black hair into place.

"Of all the—" Cindy let her breath out. "I thought you were a prowler."

"Why would a prowler come in to comb his hair?" Henry inquired. "Hand me my shirt, will you? I think this stuff is dry."

"How do I know why a prowler would comb his hair?" Cindy said indignantly. "To take years off my life, probably. What have you done to your hair? Will it wash out?"

"Well, I hope so," Henry answered. He went into the bedroom, and she followed. "It's supposed to. Do I look like a hapa-haole? I don't want to get too dark, or my eyes will give me away."

"You look like a Mexican bandit," Cindy said. She looked at his chest and arms and then pointed at his trousers. "Does that go all the way down?"

"As a matter of fact, it does," Henry said, buttoning his shirt. "In the interests of verisimilitude." He whistled between his teeth and pocketed a small revolver from the bedside table. "I'm not quite sure when I'll be back. I'll let myself out the back door when no one's looking."

"Someone's always looking," Cindy said. "The whole neighborhood will be convinced I have a Hawaiian lover."

"Nonsense. I've just come to sell you native art." He

gave her an ingratiating smile and bowed over an imaginary offering. "Native kahilis, madam, made from the plumage of rare birds. Taboo to foreigners. Beware the curse that follows." Bowing and smiling, he circled her. "Only three silver dollars, madam. This was made for a mighty chief in the days of Kamehameha."

Cindy turned in the center of the circle, watching him, biting her lip to keep from laughing. He looked totally disreputable, not at all like the man she loved.

"You might knock out a couple of teeth," she suggested. "For versimilitude."

Henry straightened up. "One doesn't want to get too authentic." He picked up a straw hat and jammed it on his dyed black hair. He pulled her to him. "Kiss me. I promise you I'm quite dry."

She kissed him, and when he left, she watched from the window. After a moment she saw him come out into the back garden and move as quietly as a whisper of wind through the shadows of the breadfruit trees to the back gate. Something odd had happened to his walk, too, she noted. She puzzled over it, watching his disappearance down the tree-shaded alley. Something about the shoulders . . . The parade-ground straightness had vanished, shrugged off with the putting on of walnut stain and a straw hat. The stain itself wouldn't have disguised anyone else for two minutes, but Henry made a catalyst of it by shifting his whole being into some alien form, slipping on another skin that fitted him as tightly as his true one. He had done this before, Cindy realized with a shudder. Done it a lot.

Henry, for his part, used the stroll down the alley to draw that new skin around him seamlessly. By the time he had walked to the grove near Waikiki Beach where the Palace Square Faction was gathering, he was what he seemed to be: a disenfranchised hapa-haole citizen who didn't know anything about politics but loved his queen . . . a man who was not a leader but a follower, one of the scores who stood in the

back row while a fiery-eyed Hawaiian harangued them with
tales of PG outrages.

"A box of explosives was found buried near the PG
troop barracks! For which they hold us to blame!"

There were shocked murmurs from the crowd.

"*We* know who planted it to blacken our name and that
of our queen! But since we're already being cloaked in the
mantle of revolt, the time has come to take it on in earnest!"

There were more unsettled murmurs, and then a
ripple began to spread, of halting agreement, and finally
outright cheers. To take matters into their hands and fight
back—as Hawaiian warriors had fought in Kamehameha's
day—was enticing. The idea embued them with a sense of
purpose, of being a part of their own destiny.

"We are Hawaiians! Hawaii for Hawaiians!"

"We must go out to the other islands and be heard! Let
us be heard by the spirits of our ancestors, lest they grow
ashamed of us!"

Cheers and shouting rolled over the beach and met
and mingled with the roar of the advancing surf above the
sand. Caught on the tide, the listeners began to scatter, to
bring the message home to others, to shake them from
docility.

A half mile down the beach, Mike and Eden saw the
gathered Hawaiians moving in scattered knots across the
sand, back toward Honolulu or out onto other trails. They
hadn't heard the angry growl of the cheering crowd, but as
a half-dozen men strode past them, Mike and Eden stared
curiously at the set faces and the eager spring of their feet.
"Why, that's Pilikia!" Eden said, startled. "Sam fired him
when we first came here!"

Mike clutched Eden's arm. The man who walked so
much like the rest, just half a pace behind, was Henry
Blake.

Eden drew in a breath to speak, but Mike shook his
head. His fingers tightened on her arm. Henry's eyes
passed over them like a stranger's, and then he was gone.

"What's he doing?" Eden whispered.

"I can't tell you," Mike said. "But you mustn't say anything." He began to fiddle again with his camera. They had been taking film of the surfers who dotted the long combers off Waikiki. The camera was unwieldy; it had to be mounted on a tripod and could not be moved.

"Do you mean don't say anything to Sam?" Eden asked.

"Don't say anything to anybody," Mike told her, wishing fervently that he had chosen any other location to use as a subject this morning. "Just forget you saw him. It's important."

Eden looked at him thoughtfully. "I'm not stupid," she remarked.

Mike's eyes met hers. "That's why it's important. If you were a bubblehead, I wouldn't be worried about your figuring out what's going on and telling your conclusion to your brother."

A giant wave began to rise out among the combers. The surfers began to paddle.

"He's going to come right in to us!" Mike said, and began to crank the camera, drawing Eden's attention toward the water and not the land.

She knelt in the sand to help steady the tripod, but her low voice came up to him over the *whirr* of the camera. "How can I tell anybody anything? They're all on different sides. I don't even know who's right."

The youthful uncertainty in her voice made Mike feel sad. "They're *all* right, sweetheart. And none of them is right. That's the trouble."

July, 1893

Annie walked past the knot of somber men gathered on the veranda of Washington Place and felt their eyes bore into her back. She could hardly blame them. *I ought to wear a placard*, she thought: *"My husband's opinions are*

*not my own." Or, "I haven't seen the bastard in three days,
so don't link my name with his."*

A maid ushered her into Liliuokalani's reception room,
and Annie saw with relief how the queen's eyes lit up at her
entrance. She knelt beside the heavy carved chair and took
Liliuokalani's hand.

"Thank you for letting me come!"

The queen's brown face was pinched and drawn, like
someone grieving for a death, but she squeezed Annie's
hand and tugged her up off the carpet.

"Sit down. Of course you could come. I would have
sent for you, but I thought perhaps. . . ." Liliuokalani's
voice trailed off.

"That I was in league with the PGs?" Annie's eyes
sparked.

"No, dear. Only that a wife's duty to her husband often
must come before friendship."

"I won't even have them at my dinner table," Annie
retorted. "Consequently, my husband generally dines elsewhere." She took the queen's hand again, and her eyes
softened. "Oh, Lydia, what can I do? There must be
something I can do to help."

The queen sighed. "Help me to have faith. They have
spread such awful lies. I am so ashamed to have things like
that said about me."

"No one believes them," Annie said. "Not even the
Americans in the States."

"America. Such a good country. I must put my faith
in America. That is what my counselors tell me."

"How can you feel that way about America when it
is Americans who have done this to you?"

Liliuokalani looked lost, bewildered, not at all the
woman she had been when she had spoken, eyes triumphant, of turning the tables on the legislature, of giving her
people back their rights. "I can't blame America for what a
handful of her people here have done. What else do I have
to pin my hope on but America and Mr. Blount?"

"They are wicked," Annie said, grieving with her. "Wicked. My husband, too. I never thought he would—"

"Nor I," Liliuokalani said. "Sanford Dole was a friend, a kind man. How could it have come to this? Do we ever truly know anyone? Maybe I am wicked, too. When they brought the marines ashore, I leaned out my window and cursed them." She smiled a little, but it was tenuous. "Cursed them right through my Christianity. But it doesn't seem that Hawaiian curses will work on a haole."

"If I thought they would," Annie muttered, "I would curse them myself."

"Maybe they don't work on anyone anymore. Maybe none of our old ways work. Did I tell you that in Manoa Valley I once saw the ghosts of my ancestors march past? Or I thought I did. They were marching to battle in their red and yellow feather capes and their helmets. They were giants, every one. I was only a child then. I've been a Christian all my life, but sometimes there are things that go beyond spiritual belief, things that go into the blood. Oh, Annie, will we all disappear? Sanford Dole thinks we will; he thinks it's time."

Annie laid a hand on the queen's wrist in helpless sympathy. Her fingers brushed against the bracelet on Liliuokalani's wrist, a heavy gold chain fashioned like a ship's cable, with an anchor as the pendant.

"The duke of Edinburgh gave me that years ago," Liliuokalani said, her attention diverted to the chain and its anchor. "He was Queen Victoria's son, in command of the *Galatea*. They stayed twelve days. Oh, it was so wonderful, nothing but parties and receptions. John and I gave a luau at my house at Waikiki. The duke gave me this to thank me. I've always treasured it."

"It's lovely."

"He was such a handsome, friendly man." Liliuokalani sighed. "I like haoles, you see. How can I be fighting with them now? And how I wish I had my John with me still."

"There are a great many others who are on your side,"

Annie said. "Not just in America, but here in the islands. It is only the planters who want annexation."

"It is the planters who have the money," Liliuokalani said with some acidity in her voice. "Our people have never understood money. They think it is to spend. They don't see it as a form of power, a force like electricity. I think it is money that has brought all this trouble."

"Money can do that," Annie agreed. "People resent it when the wrong person controls it. Or someone they think is the wrong person. Not themselves, anyway." She thought of her life with Sam: resentment and revolution on a miniature scale. Maybe Sam's PG sentiments weren't so surprising, after all. "I'm very well acquainted with the power of money," she said wistfully.

Sam, meanwhile, was discussing much the same thing over dinner at the Planters Club; he had invited Henry Blake along as his guest. Or Henry had invited himself. Sam wasn't sure just how their conversation had arrived at the point of Henry's accompanying him, but Sam was glad to have him. Henry had always disapproved of him, and Sam's black-sheep status in the family still stung. He liked the idea that Henry should see him among the powerful at the Planters Club, a man of action and political sagacity.

"Well, Blake, how are you enjoying your stay?" Lorrin Thurston motioned Henry to a chair beside his. This was an informal dinner, not a political meeting, and interested Americans, especially those with Washington connections, were welcome.

"Very pleasant," Henry said. "My wife has already acquired a collection that will probably cost me a fortune to ship home."

"I heard she is an artist."

"Occasionally," Henry said. "Mainly she is a collector with an excellent eye. Recently she has become interested in native art. She has a gallery in Washington, in which she sells what look to me like mud pots, for exorbitant prices."

Thurston chuckled. "A businesswoman. I'm not sure

how much she will find here of lasting value. The Hawaiian culture is very debased, you know."

"Possibly because we have put it into Mother Hubbards and taught it hymns," Sanford Dole said gravely.

Henry looked at him with interest. So the provisional government's president didn't personally subscribe to the party line.

"President Dole is required to be objective," Thurston said genially with a look at Dole that revealed that this was a bone of contention between them. "But I'm afraid he gives these relics of pagan ways too much credit for innocence."

Henry cracked open an oyster. "You find them dangerous?" he asked, his attention seemingly on the oyster.

"Absolutely." Thurston took a swallow of wine, then set the glass down emphatically. "Everyone in the islands knows that Mrs. Dominis consorts with witch doctors and worse and is the victim of her own repellent sexual appetites. These people are children. They mustn't be led back to heathenism. I'll tell you this: That woman won't live a day if she is restored to the throne. It would serve her well to pray to her pagan gods that the peril of restoration may never come to her."

Dole looked uncomfortable, but he didn't argue.

"Have you heard what Spreckels has done now?" Sam asked.

Thurston and Dole pursed their lips. They were in agreement on the treachery of Claus Spreckels. The biggest sugar producer in the islands, Spreckels had nearly run the country personally during the reign of David Kalakaua, until they had fallen out and Spreckels had gone to live in San Francisco. When the annexation question arose, Spreckels had been firmly on the PG side. But then he had come back to the islands and changed his allegiance.

"He's come out for outright restoration of the monarchy, if that's what you mean!" Thurston snapped.

Sam shook his head. "He's told Blount that his life's in danger, and he's demanding police protection." He leaned toward Henry with a grin. "It seems he found a threatening letter on his gate and got the shivers."

"I cannot believe he took it seriously," Dole said.

"Will Mr. Blount, do you think?" Henry inquired. He looked interested and receptive, as one speaking to the powers of government. If Sam had known him better, he would have recognized the expression.

"It's hard to say what Blount may do. I fear he is completely prejudiced against us."

Henry nodded sympathetically, as well he might, since he had been personally responsible for a good deal of that prejudice over the past few months. "Possibly your choice of music yesterday was incendiary," he suggested with a chuckle. In a fit of pique, the PGs had invited Blount to a Fourth of July reception and greeted him with the strains of "Marching Through Georgia," a Civil War song guaranteed to infuriate any Southerner and most particularly a Georgian who had been a Confederate officer.

Thurston smiled. "Impossible to resist, I assure you. Blount is past praying for. We might as well make our views known, too."

"You have no high hopes for his report then?" Henry asked.

"I don't give a fig for his report. It won't put Mrs. Dominis back on the throne, I can tell you that. She committed an act of revolution against her own country, one in which she still persists. Neither she nor Commissioner Blount is going to turn that fact around or stop the cause of justice." Thurston's eyes gleamed with what might have been the wine he had drunk or a liking for the power he had achieved. "Anyone who attempts the overthrow of the government is a traitor and will be dealt with as such."

"I fear so," Dole said. He looked as if he didn't like it but meant it.

After that, the talk turned to gossip and jokes, but the evening retained an underlying air of veiled threat. Henry mulled over the conversation as he and Sam rode home through the balmy night. Cindy and the children were

visiting Annie and Eden, and Henry was to collect them
there. Cindy was growing uneasy over Mike's attachment to
Eden, she said, and wanted to confer with Annie.

Henry's mind wandered between the two problems. It
was the first time he had found his job complicated by other
people's domestic perplexities, and it was distracting him.
Was Toby hoping for the impossible, that the boy wouldn't
ever fall in love? Was Sanford Dole willing to let Lorrin
Thurston arrange an assassination when Blount made his
report? Falling in love wasn't something you asked to do, as
Henry knew to his pain; it just happened. Blount's report
would be unfavorable to the PGs. If Blount followed
Henry's advice, he would recommend restoration of the
queen. Sam Brentwood was half drunk and didn't realize
how naive he was. Mike could take better care of Eden than
Sam would. How serious was the Palace Square Faction?
Annie was a force to be reckoned with. Family gossip held
that she only stayed with Sam for Eden's sake. A woman of
sharp loyalties. A confidante of the queen's. Was he the
only spy in the family?

Annie greeted them in the parlor, looking like an
outraged wife. *I've been in this business too long*, Henry
thought, *to suspect her of spying.*

"Good evening, Henry. I see you've been consorting
with villains." Her eyes rested on Sam with distaste.

"I've been eating oysters," Henry said, yawning. "And
drinking too much port for a warm night."

"We villains keep an excellent cellar." Sam hung his
hat on the hall tree. "Annie, don't you think you could let
it rest just for the evening?"

He looked a little wistful, Henry thought. Was Sam
falling in love with his own wife, at this late date? It would
serve him right, after how he had treated her, but Henry
felt a little sorry for the fellow.

Mike and Eden were reading a homework assignment
together and had hardly looked up at their entrance. Henry
glanced at Cindy and saw that her expression was ominous.
Gunboats on all fronts. Well, this battle was Cindy's.

Having made a mess of his own love life for years, Henry was more than reluctant to interfere in Mike's. Sam and Annie were going back to their farm in the morning, and he remembered with horror that Mike was to accompany them. Was Cindy going to veto that? The two of them looked too placid for her to have done so already.

Cindy rose. "Henry, we ought to be getting back to the hotel. I'm afraid I'm going to leave you at loose ends for a few days. Annie tells me there are wonderful things to be seen on the Big Island, and she's invited me there."

Henry wrapped Cindy's silk shawl around her shoulders—a purely decorative garment, given the temperature. "Going to play duenna?" he whispered.

"It looks to me as if someone should," Cindy whispered back. "You could always join us—if you run out of things to do here." She gave him an appraising look, as if for lingering traces of walnut stain.

"Very possibly," Henry said. *After I see Blount*.

Only a few days after their arrival on the Big Island, Mike and Eden decided to climb to the volcanic crater of Kilauea, with Cindy's reluctant permission and the inclusion of Koana as chaperon. A pair of burly field hands, Liho and Bill, would manage the cart that carried Mike's heavy camera.

It was dawn when they set out, and as he mounted his horse, Mike noticed his aunt, standing and watching Eden and him. "Aunt Cindy's on to us," Mike whispered to Eden, who was sitting her horse. She blushed and looked shyly at Cindy from beneath a fringe of gold lashes.

Cindy watched the color suffuse the child's face and rolled her eyes heavenward as if she were thinking: Much too young to know what she wants. Toby would be furious. But she didn't say anything. As the whole family was aware, Cindy had known what she wanted at sixteen: She had wanted Henry.

After saying good-bye to Cindy, Mike and Eden and their attendant trio set out at a leisurely pace. The Hawaiians were solicitous of Mike. When the way grew too steep for the cart and the saddle horses and they had to be left tethered beneath a shade tree, Liho and Bill offered to carry Mike. Mike, his face as fiery with embarrassment as 'den's had been, insisted that he was more worried about the camera and made them carry that instead.

Beyond the lower slope where they had left the horses, the sides of Kilauea turned first to drifting, olive-colored sand that sank beneath their feet, and then to conical mounds and ridges of black vitreous lava with channels of sand between them. The group made the trip in easy stages in the cool of early morning, stopping to rest, eat oranges, and drink the water in their canteens. They had all the time in the world, and Liho and Bill far preferred to dawdle on Kilauea than to cut cane.

Mike looked farther up the mountain and saw bushes with scarlet and saffron berries clinging to them, amid drifting clouds of steam. *Ohelos,* Pele's bushes. Mike thought he had never seen anything so forbidding and simultaneously so beautiful as Kilauea.

Sam, rising late, found himself alone and staring at Annie's closed sitting-room door. Annie and Cindy Blake were taking their breakfast in there, and Sam had not been invited. He wondered irritably what Annie was telling Cindy about him and how much of it was true. Certainly, most of it could be, and still leave Annie with no shortage of material—he had to admit that. Philanderer, drunkard, spendthrift. Wrong politics. That last was only in Annie's eyes, but that wouldn't stop her from making the accusation.

Sam knocked on the door, feeling left out and unreasonably sulky about it. When Annie called to come in, he stuck his head around the door and met a pair of ice-blue eyes.

"Oh, it's you," was her opening remark.

"I was going to ride out this morning," Sam said

carefully. "I thought you might like to come with me and show Cindy the countryside."

"Mmm." Annie was noncommittal. "Where are you going?"

"Just down to Harvey Sessions's farm," Sam said. He hadn't wanted to admit that. "You needn't come that far."

"I wouldn't go two feet with you on the way to that PG toady," Annie spat at him.

"Oh, never mind!" Sam bowed graciously at Cindy, who was looking uncomfortable. "Pardon our bad manners." He flipped the door closed with a snap of his wrist so that it banged behind him, then set out for the stables.

"Pele! Pele! Pele comes!" To the south of the Brentwood farm, Pilikia, the same fiery-eyed Hawaiian who had harangued the Palace Square Faction on Waikiki Beach, pointed at the rising plumes of smoke that lifted above Kilauea. "Pele comes back to make her will known!"

Fine talk from a man he had seen piously praying in church that morning in Pahala, Henry Blake thought, but he couldn't blame the fellow. The fire goddess Pele had a reputation in Hawaiian mythology for taking strong steps when she was irate. Pilikia, whose name Henry had learned meant, "Born to Trouble," had taken his crusade to the Big Island of Hawaii, where he had once been ignominiously fired by the PG planter Sam Brentwood. If Kilauea had shown signs of greeting Pilikia's return with increased activity, it was a symbol too useful to be wasted.

Henry, in hapa-haole guise once more, had tagged along to see what was up, and he was beginning to think that a great deal might be. Pilikia was fired with an enthusiasm that burned like the flames in Kilauea's caldron, and the crowd of over five hundred loyalists was beginning to catch it.

"Take the battle to these annexationist planters! The battle should be here, on the land they have stolen from Hawaiians to grow cane for the United States and make themselves rich!" Standing on a black volcanic outcrop, Pilikia waved his arms northward. The morning sun behind him made a nimbus about his head, and he seemed a part of the rock, a force sprung from living rock.

"March on their farms and let them know the will of the fire goddess!"

The crowd surged forward with a shout, flowing like lava, hot and pliable again, their old anger re-erupted. Henry, caught up in the flow, went with them, with a sense of unease beginning to creep down his spine. He had no idea what they might do or if he could stop them if it came to violence. He was absolutely certain of one thing—that to be discovered a spy in their midst would not be healthy.

There were other haoles in the crowd, undisguised— not many but a few, the most violent anti-PG faction—and one other. Henry caught sight of a tall, fair man with a loping stride twenty feet away from him in the press of the crowd. Hugo Ware. Henry glanced away quickly, but not before his eyes met Hugo's. Hugo looked away, too.

The mob surged up the road that wound along the lowest slope of Mauna Loa, and Henry realized, with something that was now approaching panic, that they would pass the Brentwood farm, Aloha Malihini. *Welcome Stranger.* Not these strangers, Henry thought.

He tried to push his way to the front, to see if there was some way to turn them, as the grass-green cane of Sam Brentwood's fields came into view. This year's planting was young, so the crew in the fields was still taller than the cane. When the hands saw what was coming, they threw down their hoes and ran. The white house above the fields would be no refuge against an emotional mob of this size. And Cindy and the children were inside.

Henry pushed harder, elbowing men aside. Hugo Ware put a hand on his shoulder, but Henry didn't stop for him. He nearly caught up to Pilikia when he heard a furious shouting and the explosion of a pistol shot.

Sam Brentwood and another man, whom Henry recognized from the Planters Club as Harvey Sessions, were in the middle of the road, mounted on rapidly panicking horses and swearing furiously. Sam gripped a pistol in his hand.

"Get the hell off my land!"

"Stolen land! Pele knows!" Pilikia pointed at the black plume of smoke puffing to the northeast. "No more will haole thieves steal our islands!"

"You!" Sam spat in recognition. "Pilikia, you don't want any more trouble with me!"

"Go home, you damn fools, before the lot of you ends up in jail!" Harvey shouted. His eyes were frightened.

The mob answered with an angry roar. Pilikia ran forward, and they followed.

"I'll shoot the first son of a bitch who sets foot on my property!" Sam leveled the pistol at Pilikia with one hand and tried to steady his rearing horse with the other.

"Don't shoot!" Henry shouted, but his voice was lost in the rumble of the crowd. Sam couldn't hold them all off. If he fired on them, they would very likely kill him. Still, Sam's teeth were set and his eyes grim as he wrestled with his terrified horse, which was trying to bolt.

The crowd did not stop. Harvey was backing his own mount away. Sam raised his pistol. From the movement of Sam's arm, Henry thought he meant to fire again in the air. But the horse plunged under him as his finger tightened on the trigger, and the shot went wild into the crowd.

Someone at the edge of the crowd stumbled and fell, blood spurting from his calf. With a furious howl, the others leapt forward. Harvey Sessions spun his horse around in the road and put his heels to it.

Sam cast a quick glance between the farmhouse and the road. Very deliberately he aimed the pistol and fired again, inches over the heads of the mob. Then he whirled his plunging mount and followed Harvey. The mob howled after him, carrying Henry and Hugo along, surging northward, leaving the farm behind.

* * *

The horse sank to its fetlocks in dark-olive sand, heaving itself along under Sam's relentless heels. It reminded Sam of a nightmare in which the dreamer is laboring to run through water, pursued by some dreadful menace.

He looked over his shoulder. The pursuers had fanned out, themselves slowed by the sand but driving him as hunting wolves manipulate their quarry toward a place of their own choosing.

Sam felt his stomach lurch as he weighed his options: turn and face the mob and be torn limb from limb or continue up this path, which would ultimately end at Kilauea's active volcanic crater.

Up ahead he could see Harvey on his horse, which was sinking in the sand with every step, flecks of foam from its mouth mottling its sides and Harvey's legs as they drummed against its flanks. Harvey's horse stumbled, slid, and went down on one side, pitching its rider into the drifting sand. The animal righted itself with a frightened neigh, and as Harvey lurched toward it, hand outstretched for the trailing reins, it lumbered away. The horse stepped on its reins, stumbled again, and snapped them. Then, freed of the weight of a rider on its back, the animal began to run, leaving Harvey in the sand. The mob gave voice to this small triumph.

Sam kicked his horse forward again and put down his hand to Harvey, hauling him up behind the saddle. They fled, Sam's horse now doubly burdened.

At last the sand gave way to ancient lava waste, black, compact, and heavy, with a shining vitreous surface thrown up into long ridges and conical mounds taller than a man on horseback. The hollows between were still thick with sand. They might have been on a stormy sea that had been petrified and turned to glass suddenly by some ancient and furious hand.

The reflected sun was blinding, and the wind filled their eyes with needle-sharp fragments. The horse slid and skidded on the polished surface. Looking behind him again as they clambered over a ridge, Sam saw that the pursuers ran along the ridge tops like goats and that they had fanned out still farther, pushing him and Harvey upward toward Kilauea.

"Should have shot them all." Harvey gasped. His hair dripped sweat into his eyes, and he had long ago lost his hat.

"I didn't have five hundred bullets," Sam said grimly. He kicked the horse on. They struggled over another smooth ridge, and the horse went down under them, legs flailing. Harvey was thrown clear, but Sam's foot tangled in the stirrup as they slid down the obsidian precipice to the sand ten feet below. The sharp black rock scraped his hands raw and tattered his shirt, and the horse landed heavily across his leg at the bottom, thrashing but unable to rise. Harvey yanked frantically at its reins.

"Its leg's broken," Sam grunted, wondering if his own was, too. "Get the saddle loose."

Harvey snatched at the girth, one hand up to shield his head from the flashing hooves. The saddle cinch had no buckle but was tightened instead by a long strap running over and under through the girth rings. It was impossible to free quickly, but at last the final length pulled loose, and Sam grabbed the saddle by the horn and pommel and pulled it over the horse's back onto his own chest. His leg had gone numb.

"Try to shift him," he said, gasping.

Harvey kicked the horse in the rump, and it tried to rise again. Sam jerked himself backward, saddle and all. His foot pulled free a split second before the horse's heaving flanks came down hard again. Sam wriggled the stirrup from his foot and managed to stand. His leg hurt like blazes now, but it did not buckle under his weight.

"Can you walk?" Harvey asked. His face twitched as he looked past Sam. The dark, glasslike dunes were alive with men.

"Got to," Sam answered.

"Come on." Harvey pulled at him.

"Wait." Sam pulled the pistol from his pocket.

"Run!" Harvey screamed. He stumbled away, not waiting for Sam.

Sam put the pistol against the horse's head. "Sorry." He pulled the trigger, and the horse thrashed once more and was still. He couldn't leave anything, not even a horse, to die slowly in this glassy wasteland. Then he put the pistol back in his pocket—three shots were left—and limped after Harvey. The pain in his leg ran like a hot iron up his shinbone.

Sam looked back again. He wasn't sure why he was bothering to run. The crazed loyalists were nearly on him, yowling with triumph as they passed the dead horse. He felt numb with fear, and his brain seemed clouded. Only the agonizing pain in his leg gave him a tenuous connection to reality. Another minute, and they would be on him. But they weren't gaining.

He looked back yet again, puzzled, and the truth came on him. They didn't want to catch him yet. They were going to drive him up Kilauea—a sacrifice to the fire goddess.

Sam drew a gasping breath through a throat that burned with thirst and ran on—it was that or sit down and wait for them. He passed a deep chasm through which a column of hot and sulfurous vapor rose. The dark, forbidding bluffs of the north side of the volcano lifted ominously against the brassy sky. As he climbed, he noticed ohelo bushes clinging to the southern slopes, berries glowing ruby and topaz through the drifting smoke. He caught up with Harvey among the ohelos. Harvey was tearing berries from their branches and pushing them into his mouth. Blood-colored juice dripped down his collar.

Sam stripped another bush's berries into his hands and chewed them. They were tasteless but full of juice. He sank to his knees and ate some more. Koana's voice went dimly through his mind: *Always give ohelos to Pele before you eat some. Then she doesn't mind.* Too late for that. He stripped another handful and staggered to his feet. His overstrained leg muscles twitched involuntarily, and he nearly fell. There was shouting behind them. Sam fled farther up the slope, choking down the last of the berries.

One step . . . two . . . three . . . Through sheer force of will and terror, the men dragged themselves upward. Driven by the baying human hounds below them, they crested a rise, and the crater of Kilauea came suddenly into view, a vast sunken plain with a burning red-orange crescent at its center. Sam took a deep breath, and the acrid air seared his lungs.

Harvey gasped. "I can't go on." His face was pale and clammy, and a muscle below his eye was twitching. "I don't care what they do to me."

"You will." Sam bent down, hands braced against his knees, trying to quiet his quivering muscles. "Can't fight here. Got to be a better place. I've only got three shots."

"They've got to be as tired as we are. Maybe they'll give up." Harvey looked down at the men laboring up the slopes below them.

"They won't," Sam said.

"Where can we go?" The precipice dropped sheer beneath their feet. There was no way to climb down the mountainside.

The men below had begun to angle up the slope.

"Where they want us to," Sam said wearily. "For now." The realization that he was going to die began to sink in. He moved mechanically, stiffly, along the ridge.

At the northern end, a steep slide of lava that was banded like a snake, light red and gray, the strata of old eruptions, stretched downward to the plain. Shouting figures pursued them along the ridge, and more materialized before them, demonic apparitions out of the sulfurous smoke.

"I'm not going down there!" Harvey cried with terror. Down the lava steep and into the molten crater was the only way open to them. Sam looked with hunted eyes in both directions and then with mesmerized horror at the burning lake below. It was just visible at this angle as a sinuous coil of flame. It would be so easy just to stop here and let them have him, he thought. Or he had three shots left—he could shoot himself before they got him. He had long since given up the notion that he might talk himself out of this, as he had talked and charmed and wooed his way out of so many situations before. He reached for the gun.

Harvey spun one way and then the other as their pursuers closed on them. His foot slipped on the loose rock, and he tumbled over the edge, rolling, arms around his head. The moment passed, and Sam leaped after him. Sam staggered as momentum drew him faster down the slope. At last he lost his balance and slid part of the way on his back. He scrambled to his feet near the bottom, pulling Harvey with him, and pushed both their battered bodies into a run.

A long triumphant howl pursued them down the slope, and the sunken plain over which they ran echoed beneath their feet as if they were passing over subterranean chambers where hell rose to the earth's surface.

Then Kilauea burned before them. It looked to Sam like hell's gateway, infernal even beyond the imaginings of preachers conjuring damnation in the minds of sinners. The lake of flame's crescent yawned two miles in length and a mile in width—one vast flood of burning matter in constant motion, sheets of flame thrown up like spray above the rolling billows of lava.

Sam stared, almost mesmerized. It seemed to him that since his father's death he had been drowning in one sea or another—his marriage, his father's business, and the more tangible ones: the rolling waters off Waikiki, the glassy black desert just traversed, and now this fearful orange ocean of death hissing just beneath his feet. It seemed to Sam's uneasy soul that the lava hissed his name, and he wondered if he was going to die in it, imitating in fire his father's drowning at sea.

"Pele!" The chant began again in an eerie minor key that set his teeth on edge.

And then he saw her—Pele, where she rose from the caldron. The fire goddess and her handmaidens, burning cones lifting arms of flame, their tresses a fiery cascade of molten stone, their breath the sulfurous vapors of hell. It was Pele who hissed Sam's name, spitting it in fire from her ignited mouth.

Harvey turned away from Kilauea with a look of inhuman panic, with the eyes of some feral thing that sees the dogs upon it; but Sam continued to stare. The pursuing mob loped across the reverberating plain, its echo a low, undulating chant. Harvey dropped to all fours, his mouth working silently, and then sprinted like a rabbit, dodging among the tumbled rocks and upthrust crags fringed with crystalline flowers of sulfur that littered the black ground. He quivered behind one of these, yelping when he discovered that the rock with its arcane blooms was hot to the touch. But no one followed him.

Sam stood still, knowing that because he had fired Pilikia, their leader, and because of his wastrel life, he was the one they wanted.

XV

Mike and Eden, traveling with no particular urgency, had reached the slope where the ohelo berries grew before they became aware that something was amiss. The mob and its quarry were still below them, when they heard their noise—a low rumble like thunder. They looked down and saw the staggering, fleeing men who hurled themselves up the slope.

"It's Sam!" Eden turned frightened eyes on Mike and started to rise.

"Get down!" Mike pulled her back and motioned with a flattened hand for the others to stay out of sight. "That crowd's out of control. We can't stop them. We haven't even got a gun."

"Sam . . ." Eden whimpered. Her brother's desperate, driven face loomed above the jumble of stones that sheltered them.

"We've got to get help," Mike whispered. He thought about possibilities, while his heart skipped a beat and settled. "Liho, stay here with Koana and Miss Eden. Don't leave them. Don't move. Bill, come with me. We've got to get back to the farm."

"Mike, no!" Eden clutched his shoulder. "You can't!" Her face was torn with fear for him and fear for her brother. "You'll—"

277

"I have to," Mike said. "My heart'll stand it. You'd be surprised what a good runner I am." Not under these conditions, though. Never with such a desperate need, which set it hammering in his chest. But he couldn't send Bill and Liho alone. Who knew how they felt about their boss? They might be more willing to join the howling mob rather than save its quarry.

He stood and began to run, with Bill following him. They zigzagged among the rocks, flattening themselves behind an outcrop when the pursuers drew too near, huddling to watch them pass by. Bill might go unnoticed, but Mike knew his red hair would mark him even at a distance. The mob rolled past them, and Mike's eyes widened at one dark face. Henry! Maybe it *would* be all right. But Henry was one against how many?

Mike drew away from the rock and ran again, gasping as the sand bit his throat. He slithered over the slick, immobile waves they had traversed so carefully earlier. His heart was beating erratically. He looked up at the sky, prayed, and ran on, willing his heart to an even beat. *If I get through this, I'll know I won't have to live like an invalid,* he thought. *I'll have something adventurous to tell Dad.* If he didn't get through it . . . well, maybe that was better for Eden, now than later. He cast one final glance over his shoulder at the diminishing figures moving up the slope and ran faster. *Behave,* he told his heart, as if it were some alien creature within his chest. *Just behave until I get to the horses.*

Henry ran with the rest of the mob, not trying to stop them yet. He knew from experience that a rioting pack was long on action and short on logic. When they caught Sam, which was inevitable—Henry, too, had seen how they were driving him—then he might be able to do something. Maybe. He would try to convince them that if they committed murder, they would play into the hands of the PGs—that Sam Brentwood would become a martyr. Blast his self-centered, conniving soul, Sam had brought this on himself—deliberately at the end, Henry acknowledged, to keep the horde from storming his house and harming his family (chalk one up for Sam)—but mainly by conspiring with Lorrin Thurston in the rape of the native population's rights and by thoroughly embarrassing the officialdom of the United States.

Henry had never cared for Sam Brentwood, he reflected as he labored up the slope, and he liked him a whole lot less now. But he couldn't allow Pilikia to toss him into Kilauea as a political statement. Hugo Ware might be of some help; the American press was both respected and powerful. Henry had lost sight of Hugo, but he knew he was somewhere in the crowd. No newspaperman employed by Henry's nephew Tim would back off now, not if he wanted a job when he got back—and not considering who the victim was.

Henry scrambled up the last ridge, trying to stay at the front, scraping his hands raw on spiny shards of volcanic rock, and blessing the fact that he had kept himself in shape. Pilikia was just ahead, bound for the trouble for which he was named.

Cindy was sitting on the veranda of the farmhouse with a shotgun across her lap when she saw Mike's horse gallop up the road. Her hands flew to her mouth, and then she jerked them away again. "*Annie!*"

Annie was in the house, still trying to get some sense out of her terrified field hands. They had no idea where the boss was; they knew only that there was an angry mob on the loose. The hands were frightened almost into incoherence. Hoakina had been translating while Annie tried to piece things together and decide what to do.

She cursed Sam for being who knew where. The last that Annie had seen of him had been that morning when he set out for Harvey Sessions's farm—to plot some further devilment, no doubt. Had the mob gone on to Harvey's farm? Maybe, but Annie was not about to leave the house. With Cindy and her children there, she didn't dare until she knew what was happening. Annie had formed an excellent opinion of Cindy from the moment that Cindy had picked up the shotgun and sat down on the porch with it, but this farm was Annie's responsibility, as was the children's safety. Frank was leaning over the veranda railing, hoping for excitement like all teenage boys who are convinced of their own immortality. Midge was huddled in a frightened ball in the drawing room. Thank God that Mike and Eden were out of the way of harm, picnicking on Kilauea.

When she heard Cindy's frantic cry, Annie ran out onto the veranda, picking up a rifle as she went.

"*Mike!*" Annie leaned the rifle against the wall—even in her panic she knew better than to drop it—and hurried to him. Mike was slumped in a chair, his head between his knees.

"Mike, where's Eden?"

"Eden's all right," Mike said, gasping. "We came to get help."

Bill came galloping up the road, and Annie realized with shock that Mike had outdistanced the field hand.

"What happened?"

Mike straightened up. His face was haggard. There were bright red spots on his cheeks and nose, but the skin around his mouth was white, and his lips were faintly blue.

"Get some water!" Annie shouted, and Frank bolted into the house.

Mike began to rasp out what had happened, pausing only to gulp down the water.

"Oh, my God," Cindy breathed when he told her he had seen Henry, and where.

"Hoakina!" Annie shouted.

The foreman appeared, dodging past Frank, who was now getting water for Bill.

"Hoakina, I want you to come with me. Bring as many men as can ride and can be trusted. And can shoot a gun." Annie paced the length of the porch, skirts swirling about her feet. "And a wagon. And all the ammunition in the house. No! Not all. Leave half here. Cindy, would you stay here with the children? Then, not all the men. Leave a third here, in case. I want my horse, too. Now, Hoakina! Fast!"

"Get me another horse!" Mike called after him. "I'm coming with you!"

"No, you're not," Cindy said. She gripped Mike's arm. "You've done well, but you have to stay here now."

Mike stood up, shaking away her hand. His red hair hung in sweat-soaked tendrils over his forehead, and his lips were still faintly blue, but his eyes were filled with some new knowledge or dearly bought determination. "I'm going. I've left Eden out there." He marched into the house and took a rifle and a pistol from the gun case.

"I'm going, too," Frank said excitedly.

Cindy spun around to him. "You're not!" Her face was so furious that Frank swallowed and backed away.

Mike emerged from the house with the rifle under one arm; he was stuffing the pistol into his pocket. There was a light in his eyes that Cindy had last seen in those of her long-dead father, Whip. Mike stuffed ammunition into his other pocket. "I am going," he said, biting off the words with deliberation. "It may surprise you to know that I can outshoot you."

Cindy had grown up in a wild land and, like the rest of her family, was an acknowledged crack shot. "Have you ever shot at people?" she inquired grimly.

"No," Mike said. With the rifle under his arm, he looked far older than his years. "But I will if I have to. And when I get back, we're going to talk about Eden and me." He looked Cindy in the eyes, and she saw that something important had happened to him during his headlong race down Kilauea.

Hoakina came up with a dozen mounted men, mostly Portuguese and hapa-haole paniolos. A wagon rattled around the house behind him, and he held the reins of two lead horses.

Mike swung himself onto one of them. Annie paused

with her hand on the pommel of the other's saddle. "Do you trust all these men?" she asked tersely.

Hoakina nodded. "I trust them if *you* come. They take *your* orders. Just for love maybe," he added.

"As long as they take them." Annie swung herself into the saddle, bunching her skirts around her. "Damn Sam," she said distinctly. "All right, let's go!"

Pilikia waved his arms in a furious arc over the caldron of Kilauea. "Pele speaks!"

"Pele speaks!" The crowd threw the words back at him in a roar.

Sam stood ten feet away from Pilikia, nearly encircled by the crowd and not moving. There was nowhere to go but over the edge. Beyond the mob he could just see the tip of the rock that sheltered Harvey. It didn't appear that Harvey was going to argue with them for Sam's life. Sam couldn't blame him. Harvey didn't want to end up in Kilauea.

Sam gathered himself for some last stand, unwilling to go gently. He fingered the pistol in his pocket. He could shoot Pilikia and himself before they got him. That might be some satisfaction in the hereafter—providing there was one and that Kilauea wasn't its semblance.

"You won't do yourselves any good!" he shouted. "The government will hunt down every one of you. You'll be shot, and your families will be deported!"

"The PGs will know that we take back our islands!" Pilikia shouted, not at Sam but at the crowd. His face was compelling, and his feet were braced like some ancient kahuna calling down the old gods. "If we do this, we will be committed. I will lead you in triumph through the Big Island and then back to Oahu, where we will put the fear of Pele in the PGs!" His mouth dripped spittle, and his eyes burned like the lava.

Henry pushed himself to the center of the front ring. He turned to face the crowd before Pilikia could stop him. "He has gone mad!" he called out to them. "Will we commit murder? Will we follow a man who urges us to murder?" A few looked uncomfortable at that; some seemed shocked into a sense of reality. Henry rushed on before Pilikia could answer him. "The PGs have spilled no blood as yet. Will *we*? Will we be the ones to begin rioting and bloodshed? What will become of our families then? What will the world think of us?"

"Traitor!" Pilikia shrieked. He leaped skyward like the burning spray. "There is no place for traitors in my army!"

"This isn't an army, it's a rabble!" Henry snapped. "What has become of us?" He held their eyes. "I am ashamed."

"Brentwood spilled blood! Brentwood opened fire!"

"Defending his home," Henry countered. He put his hands on his hips and kept looking at the crowd, not at Pilikia, who was beyond reaching. "Our queen has said she will put her faith in the justice of the United States. Will you let a madman defy her?"

Pilikia lunged at him, and Henry turned to push him away as gently as possible—but it was like fighting with a demented cat. As Henry finally flung him to the ground, he turned and was face to face with Sam, and he saw Sam's eyes widen in recognition.

Keep your mouth shut. Henry tried to fling a silent mental message at him. If Sam spoke to him, they would both be killed. Before Pilikia could recover, Henry played his ace. "Don't think our shame won't be known!" he shouted. "Do you want to give truth to the accusations of heathen idolatry, of savagery? The American press, which favors our cause, will abandon us if we do this!"

"This is war," Pilikia snarled. He crouched to spring again. "Who will run to tell them? You, traitor?"

Henry took a deep breath. "No one will run to tell them. The press is here, among us. Did you think they would not be? Even if we lose our souls and kill this man, we cannot kill an American reporter to hide our guilty conscience!" His eyes met Hugo's in the crowd. *Sorry to endanger you like this, Hugo. I hope I'm right.*

"My editor wouldn't like it, I assure you," Hugo called

out, and they all turned to stare at him. Because there were
a few other haoles in the crowd, no one had taken any
particular notice of this one. "I don't think," Hugo went on,
"that you would care to blacken the name of your queen in
this fashion."

"Who will know what has become of this reporter?"
Pilikia screamed. "Who will know that he was here at all?
Or the traitor?" He pointed a quivering finger at Henry.

"An innocent man?" Henry stood his ground.

The eyes of the mob began to flick uneasily from Pilikia
to Hugo. A quiver of apprehension went through them, but
no one was willing to defy Pilikia. Suddenly the volcano
sent a finger of fire high into the air.

"Pele speaks!" Pilikia screeched. "Pele commands!"
Slowly they began to move toward Sam.

When Annie, Mike, and the hands came to the place
where Mike and Eden had first tethered their horses,
Annie took stock of the treacherous undulations of volcanic
rock ahead. "We can go faster on foot," she decided. "Mike,
you stay with the wagon and horses. I'll send Eden and
Koana down, and you take them back to the farm and out of
here as fast as you can."

"I won't," Mike said. "I left Eden up there, and I'm
going after her."

"Mike, don't argue with me."

"I'm not going to. I'm just coming."

Annie gave up. His lips didn't look blue anymore, and
there wasn't time to fight him over it. "Come on then."

They clambered over the slick ridges and hollows.
Staying in the troughs between was safer, but the sand
dragged at their ankles and slowed them too much. Mike
and Annie saw how the Hawaiians and the Portuguese ran
along the ridgetops, stepping like goats from one ridge to
the next, and began to follow suit. They could keep their
balance, they discovered, as long as they kept moving.
When they passed Sam's dead horse, the bullet hole a
round, red splotch beneath its ear, Annie closed her eyes

for a moment and nearly fell. Then she ran on. He had wasted one bullet just to kill a horse, she thought. He couldn't have had much ammunition to begin with. *Sam*.

They scaled the slopes between the ohelo bushes, and Eden and Koana ran out to meet them. Eden threw herself into Mike's arms and burst into tears.

"I'm all right, sweetheart. I'm all right," he said into her ear. "I told you I'd make it."

Above them they could hear voices, indistinguishable at this distance, but as low and angry as the roar of a landslide. Annie spun around and pushed Koana toward Mike and Eden. "Now will you get out of here?" she said. "Go home."

This time Mike didn't argue. There was no telling what would happen when that mob came back down the mountain. If it was a choice between Eden and Sam, that was no choice at all for Mike.

Eden directed frantic eyes up the slope. "But Sam!"

Annie's voice grew gentle for a moment. "Go home, honey. You can't help." *And if they've killed him, I don't want you to see it*. She turned and started up the slope, through the acrid smoke and low growing bushes, with the field hands behind her.

"Annie!" Mike shouted. "Let the men go. Wait here."

"Like hell I will." These men were here for love of her, not Sam. How much fighting they might do without her was debatable. She concentrated on the simple problem of getting up the hill in the heavy skirts she had not taken time to change. As long as she climbed, Hoakina and the rest would climb with her.

They crested the last rise of the sulfurous hill and saw the dense gathering on the sunken plain below them. It was impossible at that distance to tell who was who or what they were doing. Hoakina pointed along the ridge, and Annie and the men ran toward the lava steep at the north end. Annie picked her way down the rock, praying that no one fell and shot one of their own party.

At the bottom, the plain was thick with people milling,

arguing, as edgy as a herd of cattle on the verge of stampede. "We'll never get through that," Hoakina said, breathing hard. "Too many."

Annie clenched her teeth. She had sent a rider to Pahala for the police, but they would never arrive in time. The crowd rumbled and surged as if in rhythm with Kilauea. "We've got to try." She started to edge her way through the throng, and someone pushed her back.

"Go home, haole wahine," he ordered.

Pilikia, screaming shrilly, launched himself at Henry Blake. Fury and desperation warred in the Hawaiian's face. He nearly toppled Henry, and a handful of men out of the crowd rushed after him. The mob was moving now on its own, keyed up by Pilikia to the point of frenzy. Someone grabbed Hugo Ware by the arms and held him. Hugo struggled against his captor, but two more Hawaiians dragged him to the ground. Henry swung at Pilikia and at the next man to come at him.

As they thrashed on the edge of the crater, Sam suddenly threw himself at the men around Henry. In a moment Henry and he were back to back, fighting, kicking, and clawing at the hands that reached for them. "Get away from the edge," Henry said, gasping. "Try to work your way out from it."

Another hand reached out for Henry and grabbed him by the arm. Henry swung his fist and lashed out with a booted foot. As the man fell back, his hand slid across Henry's chest, clawing at his shirtfront. The man hung on determinedly, and then he staggered back under another blow with a piece of the shirt in his hand.

Henry slugged another man who got close enough. He thought about pulling his gun, but like Sam, he knew a gun would be of no use against so many. The rioters were too close to him for the gun to hold them off. Behind him he could hear Sam swearing steadily under his breath and throwing punches. It wasn't so much a fistfight as a frantic melee, with the men on the fringe of the chaos pushing those in front nearly on top of the combatants.

Henry hit someone else, noting as he did so that except for Pilikia they seemed more intent on getting at Sam than him. Even in this mood the Hawaiians weren't willing to topple one of their own into that fiery lake.

Then there was a scream, and Henry looked up to see a hand held aloft, waving the tatters of his shirt. On one side it was streaked brown, where the sweat had leached the walnut stain from his chest into the cloth.

The shirt fragment was waved like a flag, and a howl of rage burst from every throat. "Spy! Spy! PG spy!"

"Kill him!" Pilikia shrieked. "Pele! Pele!" He ran at Henry again, sure now of his following. His eyes were bright, and mouth was frothing.

With a roar, the whole mob rushed at them. In desperation, Henry snaked his arm around Pilikia's throat and pulled his gun. He jammed it in the man's back.

"I'll kill him!" he bellowed. Pilikia writhed in his grip, but Henry's arm tightened, and the man began to choke. Henry jabbed him with the barrel of the gun. "Tell them to get away."

Sam kicked a man away from him and got his gun out, too. Maybe it would be of some use now, with Pilikia at the end of Henry's.

"Get back, or I'll kill him!" Henry yelled again.

Pilikia's eyes slid wildly over the crowd, his fury warring now with the cold fright that a gun's muzzle against the spine can bring.

The leaderless mob slowed, uncertain, waiting for some order from Pilikia. Suddenly a rifle shot rang out from across the plain, and the loyalists turned their heads and bumped against one another, trying to see what was happening.

Sam put his own pistol against Pilikia's ear for good measure. "Tell them to let us through, or we will toss *you* into the lava." His voice was icy, and Henry realized that Sam was capable of it.

"Of course, *I'd* rather shoot you," Henry said quietly, "but under the circumstances, I'll let Mr. Brentwood decide."

"They'll kill you," Pilikia rasped. "You wouldn't get away."

"They want to kill me anyway," Sam told him. His voice was low in Pilikia's ear, just beside the pistol mouth. "Have you ever been burned, Pilikia? I'm told you don't die right away."

"Tell them to back off," Henry ordered. He could hear shouting in the distance, and another rifle shot. He feared that more rioters had arrived. "Now!" he said urgently.

"Let them go!" Pilikia screamed as Sam began to push the gun against his head. "Let them through!"

"And you," Henry said. "We're taking you. Tell them that, and to let the reporter go."

Pilikia broke down. He babbled his captors' demands, and the crowd backed away, opening a path, their expressions humiliated as their leader dissolved in front of them. There was a scuffle, and Hugo Ware stood up and dusted off his clothes.

"Let's go." Henry and Sam moved through the opened path, pushing Pilikia ahead of them. Sam took his gun out of Pilikia's ear and walked backward, facing the uncertain men behind them. Henry kept his arm around Pilikia's throat. "He isn't much after all, is he?" he said to the men who moved away to let them through. They collected Hugo Ware and went on gingerly, alert to the sea of hesitating bodies around them. The crowd was stunned but not defused. It could be set alight again with one wrong move.

They were nearly through the mob when it happened. Kilauea, perhaps affected by the thunder of footsteps over the underground caldron that fed the burning crater at the surface, roared, and the ground beside the crescent crater began to buckle. A geyser of smoke shot up, and as those nearest it scrambled for safety, a jet of liquid fire spewed into the air.

If Kilauea had spoken with a human voice instead of an

elemental one, it could not have wreaked more havoc. The awestruck mob wavered as Pele's newest mouth burned brightly and the ground fell away from it. The horde turned to recapture the objects of her wrath. If they didn't sacrifice these to her, she might take one of them. The mob took up Pele's cry.

Henry heard the shouting, which flowed like lava through the crowd. Sam, Hugo, and he began to run, dragging Pilikia with them, before the mob's intent reached its outer edges. Hands clutched at them despite the pistol held on Pilikia, and Henry wondered desperately how they would make it up the lava steep, which had to be negotiated on hands and knees.

Another rifle shot rang out as Pilikia and his captors burst through the outer press of bodies. No one was sure what to expect beyond the immediate crush of bodies, but Henry assumed there would be more loyalists. Instead, Annie and a dozen armed field hands were holding off the fringes of the mob. Henry pushed his little group forward, to be enveloped by Annie's men. The Brentwoods' workers closed ranks, and two of them, at a terse order from Annie, peeled off and began to scramble up the lava steep, rifles in hand. At the top they turned and leveled the guns on the plain below. The loyalists, seeing the rifles trained on them, stopped in their tracks.

"We're leaving!" Henry shouted, still holding the gun on Pilikia. Sam swayed beside him, face as white as ash. "Anyone who tries to follow us is going to get shot." He jerked his head over his shoulder at the riflemen on the escarpment, then he turned to Annie. "Get these two up first," he told her, indicating Sam and Hugo. The reporter's pale eyes were still more observant and interested than frightened. Henry wondered what it would take to frighten the Englishman.

Sam was limping badly. Annie and a field hand took his arm, and the four of them began to climb.

"Wait!" A figure scuttled out from behind a rock a

quarter mile away and started to run, lurching across the plain toward them. It was Harvey Sessions.

"Go get him," Henry said, and two more men went off to gather up the terrified Harvey. *And where were you when they were going to put us in Kilauea?* Henry wondered. He imagined that Sam, now halfway up the slope, might feel much the same way. Still, they couldn't leave him. Deprived of any other quarry, the mob would make do with Harvey. Harvey wore the expression of a terror-stricken rabbit as he flung himself toward his rescuers.

The mob's appreciation for the long-range capabilities of a rifle enabled the would-be sacrifices and their saviors to get up the slope. Henry went near to the rear, with Harvey and two field hands behind him. Pilikia literally had to be dragged up the crumbling incline by Henry. When Henry had finally gotten him up, he tied the Hawaiian's hands behind him with his own belt. Then Henry bent, gasping, on hands and knees, just getting his breath back while Harvey and the two field hands made their climb under the protection of the riflemen.

When they were all on the ridge, Henry caught Annie by the wrist and pulled her forward. He cupped his hands to shout down at the men below. "This lady is Annie Brentwood, your queen's friend! She has just risked her life to save you from disgrace—and to save your queen from disgrace. Consider that before you think about committing a dishonor like this again!" There was no need to mention that she had also risked her life to save her worthless husband. Henry saw with satisfaction that a few of the men had hung their heads. Annie was loved in the islands, and Hawaiians had a strong sense of honor.

They began to march down Kilauea in formation, with the riflemen surrounding them. Henry stayed on the alert for pursuit and, with the clarity of consciousness that the aftermath of crisis brought, pondered the subject of honor: The Hawaiians had clearly been provoked by the PGs—about whom Henry would have as many black things to say to Blount as he would about Pilikia—into rebellion against the usurpers; but their sense of honor forbade murder. Thus, patriotism and their regard for human life clashed until both values were left in tatters.

Henry pondered his own honor, which allowed a man to assume disguises to practice deceit. Was he a servant of his government, or traitor to someone else's? It was no new question to Henry, who years before had learned to live with himself and his occupation as a special agent for the United States Army. Truth and honor were relative. Whose truth was the real truth? A question for philosophers to ponder, Henry thought as he scanned the land for more immediate danger.

He dwelt upon the questionable existence of Sam Brentwood's honor. Sam looked like a week-old corpse as the group stumbled along, but Henry saw how Sam's eyes followed Annie, obviously grateful and concerned about her well-being. Henry's family had been at the farm, too. . . .

They reached the wagon and the tethered horses. Annie ordered Henry, Sam, Hugo, and Harvey into the wagon. Mike's precious camera, which they had collected on the way, was handed to the men in the wagon.

Sam put a hand on his wife's arm. "Annie—"

Annie looked at him dully. "Go to hell," she said. "Or get in the wagon. I don't care which."

Wearily, the rest climbed in without argument. They sat Pilikia in one corner and tied his feet, too, but there wasn't much threat left to him. He stared blankly and twitched as the wagon jolted down the mountain.

Not much of a prisoner left for the Pahala police, Henry thought. The PGs might make an example of Pilikia if he wasn't completely crazy by the time he came to trial. It had been Henry's experience that a failed demagogue slid easily into madness. He turned to Sam and asked the question that had been troubling him.

"Why did you shoot over their heads when you met them on the road?"

"Didn't want to kill one of the damn fools," Sam muttered.

"Then why shoot at all? You knew they'd rush you."

Sam stretched out in the wagon bed and laid his battered face on his arms. "Not much choice." His voice was muffled by his sleeve. "They were going to chase somebody. Might as well be me."

Henry sat back and watched the smoky shelves of Kilauea recede. The human heart was unfathomable . . . and those might be words to live by.

XVI

Slowly Aloha Malihini sorted itself into some semblance of normality. Guards were posted along the outskirts of the farm, but no danger appeared. The mob had burned itself out and straggled home in twos and threes. After Henry's children had hugged him with relief—even fifteen-year-old Frank ran into his father's embrace—Cindy took Henry away to have him to herself. Eden inspected Sam for bullet holes and dogged his footsteps until he went to bed. Now that the crisis was over, Annie retreated to her own bedroom. Hugo declined a night's hospitality on the plea that he had dispatches to send—he was not going to waste good copy in exchange for a soft bed and let some idiot get hold of a third-hand report and file it ahead of him.

He rode off, leaving Mike and Eden waving from the porch. The young couple were fed and bathed and in clean clothes, but although weary, they felt restless. Mike took Eden's hand, and they went down the steps looking, by mutual but unspoken consent, for some private place.

They found it in a small trampled spot in the cane not ten yards off the farm road, where Mike discovered with a chuckle that some enterprising field hand had made himself a place to hide his jug of *okolehao*, a potent native liquor distilled from *ti* roots.

"Don't drink that," Eden warned. "It's awful."

"I don't need to. I feel drunk already. Maybe it's you."

"Maybe it's being scared to death," Eden said, but she blushed.

"Maybe it's both." Mike put the jug away in the damp hole that had been dug for it. "Come and sit down. I promise to behave."

Eden sat. "Why do you keep telling me that?"

Mike managed to restrain himself from putting his arm around her. "Whistling past the graveyard," he said. "Afraid I won't."

The cane rustled over their heads, and a fat moon sailed into view through its leaves.

"It's just grass, you know," Eden said. "Cane is, I mean. It's just huge grass. It makes me feel like an ant in the lawn, down here. Do you ever feel very little, as if there's just too much of the world for you?"

"You're shaken, aren't you?" Mike asked. He did put his arm around her. "Bad day." Eden nodded. "Sure, I feel like that sometimes," he went on. "But what a world—all the things out there! I tell you, sweetheart, the way to act in the world is just to go out there and take it on. I feel as if I could take it all on tonight." His arm tightened. "I've got to tell you something, Eden. I thought I was going to die back there on that mountain, before I got to the horses. My heart was jumping all over the place, and I thought I was going to be sick. And then it went away. It just settled down. Maybe it won't always do that, but it's a good sign, don't you think? I think it means we're going to be all right. You and I."

Eden turned in his arm and lifted moonlit eyes to his face, under the whispering cane. "I knew that," she said. The moon bounced from her eyes to his. If Mike knew it, too, then she could tackle anything, even being an ant. Did ants fall in love? Probably not. They just worked all day, carrying bread crumbs. Poor ants. She giggled, but when he asked her what she was laughing at, she shook her head. She lifted her mouth so that he had to kiss her whether he wanted to or not.

They stayed like that for a long while. Despite his good intentions it was really only the intricacies of women's clothing and the lumps of the cut cane stalks in the little clearing that prevented him from making love to her.

No more cane fields, he thought as they walked back to the house.

Fortunately they entered unnoticed. Cindy was occupied in rubbing salve into the cuts on Henry's chest and arms and in picking shards of the glasslike rock out of the lacerations with tweezers while Henry gritted his teeth. The old lava flow had also left his trousers in shreds, and the lightweight, porous stone had rubbed his legs raw.

"You look as if you went through the cane grinder," Cindy said, tut-tutting over his legs.

"Solicitous, aren't you?" Henry grunted.

"I'm relieved to have most of you back in one piece," Cindy said frankly. "You have no idea how terrified I was."

"Well, you can thank Sam that it wasn't worse," Henry said. "I don't like the fellow, and I'll be the first to admit it; but he deliberately set that mob to chasing him to turn them away from the farm."

Cindy raised her eyebrows. "Sam?"

"Sam. Do you suppose Annie's relented enough to pick lava out of him? I haven't seen her since we got back."

"I very much doubt it." Cindy snagged another shard with the tweezers and put it in a saucer. "His hands looked as though he'd put them in a porcupine, but she sent Koana to do it. I'm bracing myself for an explosion in the morning. She's been boiling like a kettle."

Henry closed his eyes. "I have to go see Blount in the morning," he said plaintively. "Can I leave before she gets up?"

Cindy smiled in spite of herself, the fear of the day beginning to fade. "Pudding heart," she teased, and kissed him.

In the morning the explosion was waiting for Sam when he limped down to breakfast. Everyone else had been fed, and Henry, who had a great dislike of domestic scenes, had gone to catch his boat. Annie stood in the center of the dining room, foot tapping, and inspected Sam through the sticking plaster that adorned his face and hands.

He was dressed in clean clothes, and his hair was washed, but he looked ragged and drained anyway. "You look like an illustration," he said tiredly. "*Virtue Outraged*. Why are you lying in wait for me?"

"If this wasn't your house," Annie said through her teeth, "I'd throw you out of it. I don't want to see your disgusting face or your disgusting PG friends again between now and doomsday, and if God is merciful, I won't see them after that! Those children could have been killed up there in the riot you started!"

"I didn't know they were up there," Sam said in what he thought a reasonable tone.

Annie glared at him balefully. Even her red-gold hair seemed to smolder. Sam reflected that by some accounts, the Furies were held not to have been hags at all but possessed of a fearful beauty more relentless than ugliness. In that case, the author of that particular myth might have encountered Annie in a previous life.

"The loyalists started the riot," Sam said grimly. "Do I get breakfast?"

"That's a thin excuse." Annie snorted. "Tyrants breed riots."

"Tyrants!" Sam sat down and angrily began eating scrambled eggs. "All we wanted was a stable government. The tyranny was on the other foot entirely."

"Indeed?" Annie advanced on him. "Then suppose you tell me why your PGs are going to refuse to step down when the queen has agreed with Mr. Blount to reinstate the constitution of 1887? Well?"

"The hell she has. Damn it, isn't there any toast?"

"She has. She told me. She talked with Mr. Blount and promised to do that if she's given back her throne, but the PGs won't allow it. And the toast is cold."

Sam laid down his fork. "Would it be too much trouble

to toast me some more then? If the cook has some spare time? If Liliuokalani's agreed to that, Dole would accept it in a minute. He didn't want this job in the first place." Of course, Lorrin Thurston was another matter, but Dole was in charge.

"Ha!" Annie made no move to get fresh toast. "You're not the only one who knows what's going on. There are plenty of people dedicated to Lydia still working in the palace, loyalty oath or not."

"Will you not call her that?" Sam took a piece of cold toast and bit into it. It tasted like cardboard. He put it down and sighed. In his mood, he was damned if he would say, *I saved your neck before you saved mine, drawing off that mob*. He looked at her angrily. There was a piece of sticking plaster on the bridge of his nose, and it blurred his vision. Or maybe it was just the way he felt about life in general just now. "If you think I'm such a son of a bitch, why did you come to get me?" he inquired.

To his surprise, Annie's eyes overflowed with tears. "I don't know," she said sadly.

Sam put his fork down. He stood up, wincing. "Annie, don't you think there's a chance we could start over? Forget politics. I've been a bastard in a lot of other respects, but I swear I could be a reformed bastard." Her expression wavered, and he smiled, turning on the old easy charm. "I've missed you." He took a step toward her.

She hit him. It wasn't a feminine open-palmed slap in the face. Annie swung at him with a balled fist that connected with the lower edge of his eye socket and had the whole force of her body behind it.

Sam staggered back. Annie raised her fist again, eyes still streaming.

The Hawaiian kitchen maid trotted through, apparently oblivious, and picked up the toast rack. "You want fresh toast, Mr. Brentwood?"

"No!" Sam shouted at her, and she quailed. He snatched his hat and coat off the hall tree by the front door, yelling over his shoulder, "I'm going to Honolulu. Assuming that anyone's interested!"

He marched around the side of the house to the barn. The trade wind that blew down the valley felt like cold water against his burning face. He saddled his horse, called for a stableboy to come with him, and kicked the horse into a gallop toward the coast. Maybe he could catch the same boat Henry Blake was bound for. If it had sailed, he'd take a damned canoe before he went into the house with Annie again.

The inter-island steamer was just untying from the dock at Honuapo Bay. Sam swung off his horse and left it standing there for the stableboy, who was still racing to catch up. Sam shoved his way past the people on the dock and jumped on the gangplank just before they hauled it in. He shoved some money at the ship's officer on deck.

"I don't have a ticket. That's for passage to Honolulu."

"It is required that you purchase a ticket at the company office in Pahala."

"Well, there's nothing I can do about it now," Sam snarled. The gangplank had been run on board, and the steamer was chuffing out into the bay. He pushed through a gaggle of Hawaiian schoolchildren in matching sailor hats and sat down morosely on a bench by the railing, next to an old man with a goat in his lap. Sam gave the ship's officer a look that defied the man to throw him overboard.

It occurred to him that in his dramatic departure from his house, he had neglected to bring so much as a clean shirt with him. But he had money in his pockets and a fat account at a bank in Honolulu. It still struck him as being odd that he did not have to go to Annie for money.

Henry Blake was leaning on the rail, skin scrubbed down to its natural freckled tan. He raised his hat in acknowledgment, but he didn't come over. The schoolchildren stared at them with interest, arguing among themselves in Hawaiian as to whether the two battered haoles had been fighting each other or had been involved in yesterday's riot. The arrest of Pilikia had been the talk of Pahala that morning.

Sam noted that Henry's face and hands were as ornamented with sticking plaster as his own. Women seemed to have an affinity for the stuff. They would stick it on any piece of skin to which it would adhere, so long as the wound had bled as much as a drop of blood. Sam began picking the pieces off his face and dropping them into the water. It made a task he could concentrate on, and the pain it caused was almost enjoyable.

That being done, however, he had nothing further to do but think, and he thought all the way to Honolulu the next day.

As they disembarked, Henry touched Sam's arm. "I don't suppose it would do any good to say I'd prefer you didn't mention my part in yesterday's doings to whomever you're going to see."

Sam gave him an irritated look. "I don't know why you think that. I do have some standards. Contrary to popular opinion." He turned and walked away.

It was a perfect Hawaiian day, bright and perfumed with flowers that seemed to Sam almost sickening in their odor. He walked up to the Ali'iolani Hale and found President Dole in conference with Lorrin Thurston. They looked up wide-eyed at Sam's battle-scarred face.

"I thought you might like to know," Sam said, "that there was a riot on the Big Island yesterday. The only reason I didn't end up taking a last bath in Kilauea is because Blount had some haole spy in the mob, and he saved my bacon for me."

"Good Lord, man!" Dole got up and came around his desk, his eyes concerned. "This is the first we've heard."

"What spy?" Thurston demanded.

"How do I know? I probably wouldn't know him now if he came in and sat on my lap. He'd darkened his skin, and in any case I wasn't memorizing his likeness. A few more police stationed at the Pahala station would be helpful."

"My dear fellow, sit down." Dole offered him a chair. "Let me give you a drink." He poured a shot of whiskey out of a decanter from the cupboard. "We must thank God you're alive."

"I expect you'll read about it in the papers," Sam said. He gulped down the whiskey. "Hugo Ware was there."

"That lying scoundrel!" Thurston smacked his fist on the desk. "We're getting ready to give him a summons."

"This story won't exactly be to the Royalists' credit," Sam said. He held out his glass and let Dole refill it. "You might hold off with your summons, Lorrin, and let the man do you a favor. And I'm a lot less interested in Hugo Ware than I am in more police in Pahala. I've got my family there."

Thurston paid no attention. "This proves everything we've said!" He gave the impression of smacking his lips without actually doing it.

"Damn it, Thurston—" Sam began.

"We can discuss official tactics later," Dole intervened. "Lorrin, this man's understandably worried about his family, and he's had a near escape."

"Yes, of course." Thurston looked more closely at Sam. "I say, you've got quite a shiner, among all those scrapes. You say you fought your way out?"

"Yes," Sam muttered, declining to elaborate on the subject of his eye.

Thurston did smack his lips this time. "This is Mrs. Dominis's doing. You can bet your bottom dollar that she put them up to it. Subversion and sedition. Well, she's just hanged herself."

"Lorrin . . ." Dole gave him a warning look. "We can go into policy later."

Sam regarded both men thoughtfully. "I've heard she's offered to restore her brother's constitution if she's given her throne back."

"Nonsense!" Thurston snorted. "The woman's an autocrat and as rapacious as a shrew. She'll never bend. She's instigating open revolt."

"I honestly doubt she had a hand in that," Sam said reluctantly. "The man they arrested was insane. And he had a personal grudge against me."

"The woman's insane, too! She—"

"Later!" Dole said. "My dear man, thank you for coming to us. Be assured that we will see to providing more protection on the Big Island." He held out his hand.

Sam took it, but he didn't leave. "Tell me this. What if she *should* agree to restore the constitution?"

"Oh, I'm afraid there's no hope of that," Dole said.

"But if she should?"

"Oh well, of course, we will gladly entertain any suggestion Mrs. Dominis makes, but . . ." Dole spread his hands to indicate that it was a false hope. Then he shook Sam's hand again and ushered him to the door. "And now, dear fellow, don't fear. We'll conduct a thorough investigation. Perhaps a committee to study the situation. Thank you for coming." Dole opened the door for him. "Thank you so very much." As it closed behind him, Sam heard the low, urgent murmur of voices on the other side.

I just got the brush-off, Sam thought. It had been very polite but obvious. He wandered through the halls and out into the street again, giving an ironic half salute to the PG guards standing as stiff as toy soldiers outside the door. He looked up quizzically at the Hawaiian flag floating serenely over the building—not Liliuokalani's flag anymore. Then he shrugged and strolled into town.

He wandered into a haberdasher's and bought socks, shirts, underwear, and a linen suit and took them to the Royal Hawaiian Hotel. He didn't feel like setting foot in their Honolulu house; it reeked of Annie, and whether he wanted to trade punches with her or throw his arms around her knees and weep, he wasn't at all sure.

He took clothes and a bottle of whiskey up to his room. The clothes stayed in their parcel, but the whiskey all went into Sam, in a kind of furious defiance of previous good behavior. He woke in the morning with a thundering headache and in a depressed mood. Breakfast on a veranda

alive with bird song and bougainvillea blooms did nothing
to improve his mood, so finally he went down to the
Planters Club to sulk.

It was nearly empty at noon, except for the unlovely
figure of Harvey Sessions, who had arrived that morning to
make his own report. Harvey offered him a drink, but Sam
refused, shuddering.

Harvey, who was almost always a little drunk, didn't
seem offended. He was chatty and affable, perhaps because
he knew that his conduct of two days before had not been
sterling.

"Well, it was a tight squeeze, but it can only work to
our advantage," Harvey said, swallowing more whiskey.
"We finally have evidence."

Sam put his head in his hands. It didn't help his head.
"I really don't believe Mrs. Dominis had anything to do
with it," he said wearily.

"Doesn't matter," Harvey told him. "It's evidence that
we need. There won't be any question of restoration
now—not that there would have been before the riot, but
this makes ours an easier position."

Sam didn't lift his head, but the eyes shielded by his
hands grew thoughtful. "Not even if she restores the
constitution?"

"Hell, no." Harvey was jovial. "Dole as good as told me
himself he won't give in on that. We've got the power, no
matter what Blount has to say. Why the hell would we give
it back?"

"I thought we wanted stability," Sam said. "I don't
recall that power came into it, except to curb the queen's."

Harvey blinked. "You're a babe in the woods, Brentwood. We aren't going to hand it back now, not even if she
does penance in her nightshift. Frankly, it surprises me that
she thinks we would."

"So she *has* offered?"

"Not officially. But she's told Blount she will, and
Blount's told Dole." Harvey chuckled and shook his head.
"Hawaiians. No grasp on reality."

Sam got up slowly. "Have another drink, Harvey," he muttered, and walked blankly back to his hotel.

In his room, he stared for a long time into his mirror, as if trying to figure out who was looking back at him. A certainty sank into the pit of his stomach that whoever it was, he wasn't all that smart. He took the tattered photograph of Annie that he kept in his notecase and propped it up beside the mirror. Not a hard choice between the two of them as to who was the better human being, he thought with a self-disparagement that was new to him—very new, in fact, and it might not last, but it came very clearly for the moment.

James Blount sailed from Honolulu on 8 August to make his official report to President Cleveland and Walter Gresham, the secretary of state. Henry Blake stayed behind, ostensibly because his wife had become enthralled with Hawaiian feather work and was intent upon finding an antique feathered helmet to add to her collection. Henry played his role as a jovial and condescending husband with a facility that mildly annoyed Cindy, but he had his reasons. Blount had made several preliminary reports—his final one was going to be no surprise—but this last one was official, and official action would be taken upon its receipt. What that might provoke in Honolulu was anybody's guess, and President Cleveland had been quite firm about wanting the capable and unflappable Colonel Blake in place, so he could emerge from his tourist identity if necessary and see that the name of the United States was not used by hotheads for their own ends.

The Blakes saw Blount off at the dock, part of a huge throng of well-wishers. The Hawaiians bid him aloha with gifts and flowers and sent both Mr. and Mrs. Blount aboard so laden with leis that their faces could hardly be seen. The PGs, who knew as well as President Cleveland did what was going to be in the report, played "Marching Through Georgia" again.

The Brentwoods were at the dock as well. Each had

come separately, but Sam had gravitated toward Annie.
Cindy watched Sam Brentwood curiously. Something had
happened to him in the last week. Even with all his cuts
healing, he looked haggard, but beyond that, there was an
air about him that he hadn't had before. It was not just a
reaction to a brush with death, Cindy thought, but some
inner anguish that she guessed was connected with Annie.

Cindy decided not to meddle—a resolution roundly
seconded by Henry—except to hope that if Sam and
Annie's marriage blew apart, it wouldn't drive Eden into
Mike's arms. ("Any farther than she's already in them,"
Henry had said.) Then Cindy would most certainly have
some fancy explaining to do to Toby.

Where *were* Eden and Mike? she wondered. They had
been there a minute ago. Cindy gave a final wave at the
departing steamer and went in search of the young couple,
fire in her eyes.

Sam chuckled. "She's looking for the kids. I saw them
looking goopy at each other on a park bench."

"Not such kids anymore," Annie said. "At least they're
faithful and in love with each other." She looked away from
him, her eyes bitter.

"Will you please not snipe at me?" Sam muttered. He
took a deep breath. "I've said this before, and you wouldn't
listen, so this is going to be the last time. Are you paying
attention? I was wrong. I was wrong about Dole; I was
wrong about your precious Liliuokalani. Lydia, all right? I
was wrong. What is the use of learning from your mistakes
if you can't mend them?"

"It may have escaped your notice," Annie said, "that I
didn't leave you because you took up with the PGs. I left
you because you brought a tart home to make love to her in
my bed."

"And it may have escaped your notice that I brought a
tart home because I was being strangled, and it was the
only way I could think of to cut loose. The tart was
irrelevant."

"She wasn't irrelevant to me!" Annie hissed at him.

"Look, could we go somewhere else? People are looking at us."

Annie raised her eyebrows. "You never minded that before, either."

"All right, forget the tart. I apologize for that, too. Annie, you know I regret that foolishness. Damn it, I didn't expect to miss you so much. And I haven't so much as—" Sam tried to think of a genteel phrase but couldn't. "Well, I haven't. And it hasn't been easy, either. I'm human." He gave her an intent look. "How easy has it been for you?"

"Easy enough," Annie said airily. But she appeared to be uncomfortable, as if some admission might be forthcoming if she didn't swallow it down.

"Ha!"

Annie glared at him. "That is irrelevant, too."

Sam threw up his arms in exasperation and nearly knocked the hat from someone's head. "What in the world do you *want*?" he demanded, ignoring the offended gentleman.

"I simply can't think about it now," Annie said. "Your PGs are still threatening poor Lydia, and she's a nervous wreck. I cannot worry about personal trivialities now."

"It's not trivial to me!"

"It's trivial to Lydia, I assure you."

Sam looked at her intently. "All right," he said after a moment. He turned on his heel.

"Where are you going?"

"To get you what you want," he said over his shoulder.

Sam was waiting for Sanford Dole in his office, over the frenzied objections of a secretary, when Dole came back. Dole gave him a glare of distinct unwelcome, but Sam, having slain the minor dragon in the outer office, was fully prepared to take on the major one, scales, claws, and all. Knight errantry had never been his specialty, but if Annie wanted Liliuokalani, then Sam would get her Liliuokalani.

"What do you want, Brentwood?" Dole asked. "Lorrin Thurston told me this morning that you refused to extract a

loyalty oath from your field hands or to canvass the Big
Island for more converts to the Annexation Club." He tried
to soften his expression. "I can understand your hesitancy
to make your political connections too public after your
recent and harrowing experience, but I hope you haven't
had a change of heart. I've ordered a dozen extra police
officers transferred to the Pahala station. Your wife should
feel more comfortable with them on duty."

"My wife doesn't feel comfortable with *you* on duty,"
Sam said frankly.

Dole smiled—barely. "Yes, I understand that you two
have a difference of political opinion."

Sam leaned back in the chair that Dole had not invited
him to take. "What the hell happened to you, Judge? You
used to be accounted a fair man."

"I hope I still am," Dole said stiffly, obviously reacting
to Sam's deliberate use of "Judge" instead of "Mr. President."

"You've let Lorrin Thurston climb up in your saddle."
Sam took a cigar out of his coat pocket and lit it, also
uninvited. "I can practically see him up there now: a
power-mad little cowboy on a horse that's been bred for
better stuff. Disgusting." He blew out a cloud of smoke and
grinned at Dole through it. "Remember Dr. Faust, Judge."

Dole gripped the edge of his desk and his temper both.
"I find your analogy insulting. Why have you come here? I
can have you thrown out." He yielded to temptation. "I can
also make your life extremely unpleasant."

"I'll bet you can," Sam agreed. "Unfortunately, I can
return the favor."

"What are you getting at?"

"I'm considering writing my memoirs. Nordhoff of the
Herald-Tribune tells me I should have no trouble in finding
a publisher. I'm thinking of calling them *Recollections of a
Former Annexationist: How the Sugar Interests Usurped a
Throne.*"

"Now see here—"

"I expect the Honolulu papers will be awfully interested, too. They don't love you anymore, Judge."

"Are you threatening me?" Dole demanded.

"Yes."

"You are aware that you could go to prison for treason. . . ."

"Oh, I plan to stick to the facts," Sam said. "They are disgusting enough to relieve me of the necessity for embellishment."

"That form of accusation against the legitimate government still comes well within the definition of treason."

"As defined by you, I imagine it does." Sam chuckled. "You know, you're going to have an embarrassing time if Hawaii is annexed by the United States. A lot of your handy laws are going to become unconstitutional. Freedom of speech is taken extremely seriously on the mainland."

"Are you willing to sit in prison until we're annexed?" Dole smiled. "I expect not."

"I've never been in prison," Sam said, appearing to mull it over. "I don't imagine I'd like it very much. Fortunately, like you, Judge, I can be bought."

"Are you attempting to extort money, Brentwood?" Dole looked honestly shocked.

"I would not dream of it." Sam put on an expression of seraphic virtue. "I'm deeply wounded that you would even think it of me." He leaned forward. "I'm trying to extort a little justice—a much less tangible currency in this administration, I'll admit, but well within your power."

Dole looked uncomfortable. "Get to the point."

"Her Majesty is the point."

"Mrs. Dominis is going to be very lucky if she isn't deported," Dole snapped. "I should think you would be the first person to cheer that eventuality, considering your recent experience."

Sam put his cigar out. "As I tried to tell you the last time I was here, Liliuokalani didn't have anything to do with that riot. You know it, and Lorrin Thurston knows it—don't try to tell me he doesn't. Nothing that goes on escapes that weasel's notice. You're trying to railroad the woman, but you're going to stop. I want those guards removed from in front of her house, and I want her free to go where she pleases without being hounded and without coming home to find her house ransacked the way her palace has been. I don't want one hair on her poor little head touched, or I'll publish a set of memoirs that will set *your* hair on fire, and prison be damned."

"Why this sudden sympathy for Mrs. Dominis? You aren't a crusader, Brentwood. I know your kind: You're an opportunist. And frankly, your accusations against me may be taken as a case of the pot calling the kettle black. What do you want with Mrs. Dominis, since we've discarded altruism as a motive?"

"A gift for my wife," Sam said. "Annie wants her. I like to keep her happy."

"Buy her a damned diamond ring!"

"She doesn't want one. She wants Mrs. Dominis."

Dole tried another tack. "You don't strike me as a man who lets his wife wear the pants in the family," he taunted.

Sam declined to rise to the bait. "My pants aren't in your jurisdiction," he said, although in the back of his mind he pondered the interesting fact that six months ago that strategy would have worked very well. Now he found he didn't care what the judge thought about his pants. "Take it or leave it," he told Dole.

Dole seemed to come to some decision. "I hope you aren't going to regret this," he said heavily.

Sam knew he had won. Grinning, he stood up. "Given the number of things I already have to regret, Judge, this one will have to get in line."

XVII

Qualla Boundary, August 1893

Janessa had immersed herself all winter in the minutiae of Cherokee life. She had ridden out in the snow to
tend the sick, deliver difficult babies, and patch up the
participants of Saturday-night brawls. While Charley pored
over his notes and interviewed those who had survived the
yellow-fever epidemic, Janessa had spent hours with
Walini, relearning things half-forgotten, cradling to her all
the new/old knowledge, her mother's legacy. Charley and
she had been invited to quilting parties and church socials,
and a barn raising in the spring. And she had seen Joe
enough to grow comfortable with him again.

Over it all, the shadow of the Superior Coal Company
had loomed, as if the company, in the person of Morton
Briggs, exhaled a breath as dark as coal dust to cling to the
trees. But Vernon Hughes was still working on behalf of
the Cherokee and had high hopes for the cases that would
come to trial in the summer.

By late May, when the mountain laurel and the
dogwood made white clouds like lace on the hillsides,
Janessa knew she should be gone. Just for the winter, she
had said, and Charley was growing restless. But still she
stayed.

By July, Dr. McCallum in New York was testy in the
extreme and threatening court martial and military disci-

pline. Janessa bumped into Morton Briggs on the street in
Ela, and he smiled with only politeness and some secret
look of triumph in his eyes. Janessa, in terror, wrote to Dr.
McCallum, claiming that she was not well—dysentery . . .
the water here was bad. . . . She would come back as soon as
she could travel. Charley read the letter over her shoulder
and shrugged but didn't argue, although he gave her a long,
worried stare.

   Now, dreaming over the drying herbs by Walini's fire,
Janessa tried to see in the embers' heart what it was that
held her here. The cabin was hot, and cooking dinner was
a misery. She had shed her shoes and stockings and stuck
tanned bare toes out on the cool stone hearth. Her thin
calico skirts were pulled above her knees. Why was her
desire to stay here so strong? Was it only fear of Morton
Briggs, she wondered, or something deeper in herself?
Was it the call of her blood that made her inhale the
pungent smoke and dream that Charley and she might
settle down and live here . . . where she could still see
Joe? And how much of her desire to stay involved Joe and
how much did it involve being a Cherokee, being the thing
she had never truly been, not even with her mother in
Memphis? The Holts had always been family minded. They
pulled to themselves their far-flung kin and connections by
means of letters and visits and love, then held on for dear
life. Here was another piece of family, and Janessa didn't
feel that she had soaked up enough of them yet to part
again. At least she wasn't a wearisome houseguest still
underfoot when everyone else had gone. She was earning
her keep and more in Qualla Boundary. But she had
overstayed her visit, and she knew it.

   Walini came in, drying her long black hair, which she
had washed in the water from the rain barrel. It was still
midnight color, with only a few strands of gray. She rubbed
it with a towel as she sat down next to Janessa.

   "I have to go home," Janessa said.

   Walini nodded. They had become close enough to
follow unspoken thoughts. She knew Janessa didn't just

mean back to her own house in Yellow Hill. "You have your work. You are an epidemiologist, not a country doctor. So is your Charley. And Joe won't marry while you're here."

They had never spoken of that before. Walini knew about Joe, and Janessa knew that she did, but until now they hadn't talked of it. "I didn't mean for it to happen," Janessa said.

Walini made an amused noise and began to comb her hair. "Does anyone say to herself, 'Well now, I think I will fall in love with some man besides my husband and make us all miserable'?"

Janessa wrapped her arms around her knees and rested her cheek on them. "He fell in love with me," she said wistfully. "It wasn't all me."

"Of course not. And maybe you are both the better for it, too," Walini said. "That happens. You may have broken open something that was dammed up in Joe. He never liked women before you came—not to marry, anyway. His father and mother didn't set him such a fine example. Now he's learned something different. But he won't find another woman till you go."

"I have to go," Janessa said, "if I'm going to have a job left. Vernon Hughes will stay and see you through, though."

"You've done all you could," Walini said. "As a doctor, and to help us hold on to our land here. The whole tribe knows it. Why do you keep telling me that you have to go, as if you thought you must apologize for it?"

"Because I don't want to go," Janessa confessed.

"Ah. Then in that case you had better leave immediately."

Joe Cheoah gave his horse its head, letting it pick its own way down the slick trace out of Painter Hollow. Warm August rain dripped from his hat brim and polished all the leaves to a clear green. Beneath them a redbird darted like a flash of ruby and took shelter on a branch, chirping at him. Joe whistled back at it. He had a pocketful of papers

for Vernon Hughes, and he was feeling cheerfully antago-
nistic. They were only an old survey and a couple of letters
written just before the War Between the States, pressed
forgotten for all those years between the pages of a bible.
But they were all grist for the court's mill. The survey in
particular might provide enough fat to fry up Morton Briggs
and his company lawyers.

As the horse skidded down the end of the steep trace,
Joe slapped his hand onto the rifle case slung from his
saddle. Someone was waiting for him. He had the rifle out
and under his arm before he saw that it was Scoggins, the
coal-company lawyer. Joe leveled the rifle at him.

"Scoggins, you aren't such a dope as to try to waylay
me," he said, thinking of the papers in his pocket.

"Not the way you mean," Scoggins said. "I just thought
you might like to know something I know, before you go
much farther."

Joe reined in his horse. "You don't know anything I
want to know. Whatever's in your mind probably won't
stand daylight, and I always figured a filthy nature was
catching. Get out of my way."

Scoggins grinned. "We found a man who says you
committed a murder—stabbed his boy and threw him
under a train. Now what do you think about that?"

Joe's mouth tightened. His stomach lurched, and he
forced himself to be calm. "I think you'd better be careful.
That same man might just be willing to say you hired him
to kill a woman."

"I don't think so."

"Dr. Lawrence will testify. You be careful what you
start."

Scoggins smiled. It was almost a leer, knowing and
unpleasant. "*Doctor* Lawrence might not want to say much
about what she was doing with you in the woods, when it
happened. A woman like that doesn't make such a credible
witness."

"She wasn't—" Joe bit his tongue. He couldn't refute
that without admitting to the murder. Scoggins was hoping

he would. "From what I hear about *your* witness, he's about as credible as a copperhead," he said grimly. "And he's a mite late to come forward with accusations."

"You know," Scoggins said genially, "we kind of think we'll take our chances on that. The question is, are you willing to?"

"What exactly are you getting at?"

Joe still hadn't lowered the rifle, and Scoggins eyed it uneasily. He licked his lips. "Well, it strikes me that if you were to take yourself off, away from Qualla Boundary and out of the Superior Coal Company's business, there couldn't rightly be a trial, could there? No defendant."

"Go to hell."

"Be a pity for you to have to put Dr. Lawrence on the stand. Might get into all kinds of questions she wouldn't like to answer. A woman's reputation is a mighty delicate thing. Especially a woman that goes around like she does, messing with man's work. Some folks think that's plain immoral to begin with, let alone meeting a man in the woods at night. And with her being married and all."

Joe gritted his teeth. Scoggins wasn't lying about that. The thought of the questions that the prosecution, egged on by Scoggins, would ask Janessa made his skin crawl with fury. He wanted to put the rifle down and strangle Scoggins with his bare hands. But if he killed Scoggins, they *would* hang him. They might anyway. But he couldn't hand his tribe's land over to Superior Coal just to save his skin or Janessa's reputation. The price was too high. *Oh, Ka-nessa, I can't throw my people to the wolves for you, or for me.*

"If we don't see you around again," Scoggins continued, "there won't be much point in going to the law." He gathered up his reins. "It might be best," he suggested. "Women are fickle. Many a man's come to grief counting on one. Your little doctor might get cold feet."

Joe jerked himself out of his thoughts and stared blackly at Scoggins. He kicked his horse forward and pushed past Scoggins on the trail. "Get out of here, you blackmailing snake, before I send somebody after you." He kicked the horse into a canter and rode on, staring straight ahead, face set. If there was one thing he was certain of in the upheaval that had come upon his world, it was that Janessa would testify and never count what it might cost her. He was less certain that it would be enough to save him. Just what was it worth to Morton Briggs to see him hang? And what would it do to Janessa if he did? Joe had no illusions that his death would simplify Janessa's life. If they hanged him, he would be a ghost in her heart forever.

They won't risk it, he told himself, because he had no other choice. *They won't risk it.*

The cabin door banged, and Walini turned. "It is possible, Billy, to come through a door so that it does not rattle on its hinges."

Billy stopped and took a deep breath. He was gasping and wet with summer rain, and his eyes were wide and frightened. "They arrested Uncle Joe!" he blurted. "The sheriff and some deputies from Ela. They say he killed a man!"

Walini jumped up, dropping her comb. Janessa swayed, clutching the drying rack as the room started to go around her. She held on until the swirling ceased, as Billy stammered out what he knew.

"It's Eamon Walley. Sid Walley who fell down on the rail line last year was his son. Now Eamon says Uncle Joe stabbed Sid and pushed him over."

"Just now says it?" Walini demanded. "After a year?"

"I don't know." Billy was near tears. "Eamon hasn't been around since Sid fell. Now he's saying he was too scared of Uncle Joe to come back and tell."

"That is ridiculous. There's no reason for Joe to have done that. The Walleys are no-account trash." Walini had picked up the comb and jerked it through the last of the tangles. Now she reached for her bonnet. "I know Joe."

"The sheriff believed it! They've put him in jail!"

"This is Morton Briggs's doing," Walini said angrily. "He just wants Joe out of the way. We'll take care of him."

She turned to Janessa and stared when she saw Janessa's face.

"Wait." Janessa let go of the drying rack and put out a hand to hold them back. Her stomach was in a tight knot, and she thought she was going to throw up. After a moment it passed. "Wait. Sit down. You too, Billy. You're old enough." She gathered them to her on Walini's rickety sofa and told all.

"I can testify that they were trying to kill me," she said when she had finished with the rest. "But we don't have any proof that they had a reason, that it was Briggs who put them up to it. Eamon Walley won't admit it. Briggs must have tracked him down, he wouldn't have come back otherwise."

She tried to think, to still her stark terror for Joe. "It will be just my word against Walley's. Vernon will help, but he isn't a criminal lawyer. We have to get someone else. Vernon will recommend someone. . . ." Her voice trailed off, and desperate tears streamed down her face. "I have to see Joe. Where is he?"

"That won't make it easier for you to testify," Walini said gently. "You'll give the company ammunition if you go to him."

"*Where is he?*"

"Here," Billy said. "In the jail here. The sheriff wants to move him to Ela, but Chief Saunooka won't let him."

Janessa began pulling her stockings and shoes on. "Go and find Dr. Charley and tell him. And Mr. Hughes. I'm going over there."

"Not alone," Walini said firmly. "We're both going."

"Someone needs to be with Lottie," Janessa said distractedly.

"Billy will find Lottie. Listen to me." Walini took Janessa by the shoulders. "If you go to him alone with tears all over your face, if you make it clear to anyone who has eyes that you love him, you will discredit your own testimony." Walini shook Janessa's shoulders—not hard, but her hands were strong. "Stop thinking of your own fears and think of him."

Janessa blinked. What Walini was trying to tell her hit home. No one would ever believe her if she looked like a woman desperate enough to lie for her lover. "All right." She took Walini's comb and went to the mirror. Mechanically, she unpinned her hair, combed it, and pinned it up again in a neat, tight bun. She put on the discarded straw hat and long white apron that she had taken to wearing in the summer heat instead of her hospital service uniform. She wiped her eyes and picked up her doctor's bag, clutching it to her for both comfort and some symbol of authority.

"Better." Walini nodded.

They walked through the muddy streets toward the jail. Already there was a milling crowd—angry whites from Ela and equally angry Cherokee. The sheriff and Chief Stillwell Saunooka stood on the steps with the Cherokee deputy from Yellow Hill.

Saunooka's figure was impressive, cut into sharp-angled planes by his folded arms, his straight, compressed mouth, and the stubborn, lock-kneed stance of his legs. "Cherokee are law-abiding citizens. This crime—if there was one—took place in Qualla Boundary. He stays in the Qualla Boundary jail."

"Where your Cherokee can spring him loose!" a white man shouted.

"Not from my jail," the deputy said. "Not when the chief gives his word."

"You gonna believe that, Sheriff?"

"Take him to Ela! We want him around long enough to hang!"

The sheriff was a round-faced white man, balding prematurely, with a fringe of slate-colored hair. He looked harassed, but Saunooka was within his rights: Joe Cheoah was a Cherokee, and the murder had happened on Cherokee land.

"You send him to Ela," Saunooka said grimly, "and he

won't be around long enough to try, and you know it. You gonna aid and abet a lynching?"

"Of course not!" the sheriff replied angrily.

"You guarantee that?" Saunooka didn't budge.

The sheriff scanned the crowd. The white faces at the forefront were hungry, almost slavering. In their minds Joe Cheoah was responsible for all their ills, for their disease and poverty, for standing between them and their dreams of easy money out of the ground. Sid Walley had taken on the cloak of a martyr. Morton Briggs and Scoggins were among them, with Eamon Walley between them. Scoggins elbowed Walley, and he shouted, "That bastard killed my boy!"

The white crowd answered with a menacing growl.

"If I leave him here," the sheriff said to Saunooka, "are you going to answer that he stays here?"

"Cherokee don't break the law," Saunooka said. "I don't know what Joe's done or hasn't done, and I'll swear he's no murderer. But he'll stand his trial. I just want to make sure he gets one. You can send some more deputies up here if you want to, but it won't be necessary."

"All right. I'm holding you responsible." The sheriff faced the crowd and held up his hand. "Now you all quiet down and listen to me! It's my job to uphold the law, and that means a man doesn't get tried in the street, he gets tried in a court of law. The chief here is within his rights to keep the prisoner in Cherokee territory."

Janessa felt Charley's hand on her arm and turned to find him staring at her, outraged and bewildered. "Why didn't you tell me?" he demanded. Behind him, she could see Vernon Hughes walking slowly behind, and Billy with Lottie by the hand.

"It happened when you were sick," she said. "And anyway, I couldn't tell you or Uncle Henry. You would have had an armed guard around me and gone looking for Eamon Walley, and then it would have come back to Joe."

"It's come back now," Charley said.

Vernon Hughes caught up with them. "Billy told us

what happened last year," he said. "Legally, you would
have done better to get it out in the open then. You've
tainted your testimony by waiting."

"It would have come to the same thing then," Janessa
said wearily. "We took a chance." She laid her hand on her
husband's arm. "Charley, I have to get in there to see Joe."

Charley closed his eyes for a moment. Then he
nodded. "Yes, I suppose you do. We'll wait for you."

Janessa pushed her way through the crowd to the jail.
The Cherokee made way for her respectfully, and the
whites glared at her. The sheriff looked at her with suspicion.

"I think you ought to know," Janessa said quietly, "that
Joe Cheoah won't deny killing that man, but that he did it
because Sid Walley and his father were trying to kill me.
They were hired to. I can't prove who by, but they would
have succeeded if Joe hadn't come along. You can draw
your own conclusions." She looked straight at Morton
Briggs for a moment.

The sheriff raised his eyebrows. "That's what Cheoah
said, but frankly I didn't think you'd back it up, Doctor."

"Well, I do. And I'll back it up at the trial if you don't
throw him to those hounds out there."

The sheriff put his hands on his hips and shouted at the
crowd again. "Cheoah stays here! And it isn't cut and dried,
because we've got some evidence that speaks for self-
defense. So you all just go on home, and it'll all come out at
the trial."

Scoggins prodded Walley again. "She's his fancy
piece!" Walley shouted. "You gonna believe her?"

Janessa saw Charley start toward Walley, but Vernon
hung on to his arm.

The sheriff beckoned three of his other deputies
forward. "I'm going to arrest anyone who's still hanging
around this jail thirty seconds from now. You folks from Ela,
go on home. And you Yellow Hill folks, get back to your
houses, too. Get!"

"I want to see him," Janessa said.

"Nobody sees him," the sheriff told her.

"He saved my life," Janessa insisted, "and now he's in trouble for it. And I want to make sure he hasn't been hurt." She hefted her bag and tried to took professional.

"They roughed him up some," the Cherokee deputy admitted. "We couldn't help it. Somebody's got to patch him up."

"Let her in," Saunooka said. "What do you think she's going to do?"

"You may inspect my medical bag for firearms if you desire," Janessa said icily. "I won't be long. My husband and my father-in-law are waiting for me." She pointed at Charley and Vernon, who had lingered as the rest of the crowd dispersed, grumbling.

"Oh, all right, damn it. Excuse me. You got ten minutes. Ross, go with her." He jerked his thumb at the Cherokee deputy. "You boys let Dr. Lawrence and Mr. Hughes alone," he shouted at the other deputies. "They won't be long. Billy Cheoah, take your sister and go home with Walini."

Owl Ross led Janessa into the jail. It was a log cabin with only two rooms: Ross's office in front and, through a door, a single cell. Joe was sitting on the bunk. He had a thin trickle of blood at the corner of his mouth and a gash on his head. His black hair was caked with blood.

Ross unlocked the cell and let Janessa in. He clanked the door shut behind her. "You call me when you want out," he said, and went back toward his office, even though the sheriff had meant for him to hang around. "That bastard coal company is after my mother's land, and you pulled my little sister through the fever. I'll be damned if I'll treat you like you can't be trusted."

Joe gave Janessa as much of a smile as he could manage and winced when his split lip started to bleed again. "I got it on good authority that you're ruining your reputation by being seen with me," he said.

"Joe, don't." Janessa touched his face gently and started to open her bag.

Joe took her hand. "Ka-nessa, I know what those lawyers are going to do to you at the trial. I want you to know I would have fixed it so you didn't have to get up there if I could have squared it with my conscience."

"There wasn't any way," Janessa said. "And I'm tough. You'd be surprised." *And you're the one they're trying to hang. How can you be worrying about me?*

"Yes, there was," Joe said stubbornly. "You got to know. Scoggins offered to let the case drop if I got out of town. I made a present of you to those vultures, Ka-nessa. I'm sorry."

You made a present of yourself, Janessa thought. "You were never a hypocrite or a coward," she said. "Neither am I. We'll get through."

"Sure. We'll tar Briggs with his own brush if nothing else."

Even if they hang you. "Vernon's going to get a good lawyer from Richmond. Uncle Henry's in Hawaii now, of all places, but I'll wire Dad and see what he can do." She opened her bag. "Now let me clean that cut. They only let me in here because you were hurt."

"Glad I got hurt then," Joe said. He winced again as she dabbed alcohol on his scalp. "It was my own fault. I fought them. Ow, Jesus! I don't know why. I get mad too easily."

"Don't you just?" Janessa murmured. She clipped some of the hair away from the gash on his head. It was sticky with blood.

"Souvenir," Joe said. "You can put it in your locket."

"Maybe I will."

"Where's Charley?"

"Outside waiting for me, with Vernon. I'm going to have to stitch this. I can give you something to deaden the pain."

"Nope," Joe said. "Then I might not notice you're here."

She stopped, hands shaking as they cradled his head.

"It might be the last time," Joe said softly.

"All right." She took a suture needle and a line of catgut and began, as gingerly as she was able, to stitch the edges of the wound closed while Joe gritted his teeth. "What did this?"

"Somebody's rifle butt."

"How's your vision?"

"Far too clear. I can see the pulse in your throat."

"I'm serious. Are you seeing double? Did you black out?" She finished the suture. "Let me look at your eyes."

She knelt on the grimy cell floor and inspected his pupils. They were even, and the gaze he gave back to her was clear and steady—much too steady. Her own eyes welled with tears again.

"Here, are you crying for me?" He put his hands around her waist. "Don't cry for me."

"I'll cry if I feel like it." Tears slid down her cheeks. "I'm not going to lose you. I couldn't bear it. It will be all right." *And as soon as I see you free, I've got to leave.*

"Sure it will," he said, comforting her. "Sure it will." He leaned forward, and their lips touched. She could taste the blood on them. He didn't seem to mind the pain. He held it to him as if it were a part of her, a part of the two of them. Then he sat back. "You better holler for Ross to let you out."

Only Charley and Vernon had been waiting for Janessa when Owl Ross let her out of the jail. Walini and Billy had taken Lottie home. After Vernon had wired Richmond and Janessa had sent a wire to Toby, Vernon advised that Charley take part in Joe's defense, to help dispel any damaging rumors. Charley had said that he didn't give a damn for rumors, and Vernon had told him grimly that he had better—rumors were going to count for a lot in this trial.

"Everybody's got his own idea of what happened," Vernon had said as they walked toward home, "and the people from Ela won't let go of theirs easily because the idea they've got is the idea they want."

It was as if truth shifted under your hand, Janessa had thought, according to the angle from which you looked at it. No solid ground here—not for Joe to stand on, maybe not for her.

For the rest of the day, she paced restlessly through her house. She was helpless to stop herself, as if the four walls of her cabin mirrored the angles of Joe's cell. Now there was nothing to do but wait and pace, endlessly into the dusk—stopping to light the lamps and then walk again . . . so many steps to the door . . . so many steps to the window . . . so many steps to nowhere. Four more steps back to the table where her uneaten dinner sat.

She picked up her untouched plate and put it on the back porch. Yellow Hill was full of dogs, most of them ownerless. One would come along and eat it. Waste not, want not. Her mother had always said that. *If you can't eat something, feed it to someone else.*

She stood outside in the darkness for a moment.

The air was hot and hung around her like a curtain. Breathing it in was like inhaling glue. The insect chorus shrieked around her, cicadas clacking and whistling, while the fireflies floated silently, little will-o'-the-wisp lanterns flaring and dying. One hung in front of her face, greenish-yellow, and then vanished in a wink.

Janessa went back inside, her hands knotted into tight fists she wanted to beat against the walls. Instead, she clenched her fists against her sides and forced herself to sit down at the empty table.

At Stillwell Saunooka's table, Charley felt nearly as edgy, sitting with the chief, Vernon, Elliot Spray, and the tribal council: the Reverend Nimrod Jackson, Wesley Calhoun, and a handful of others. Joe had saved Janessa's life. No question but that Charley owed him loyalty for that and for the simple facts that he was innocent and a good man. But it wasn't that simple, and Charley felt angry with nearly everyone. His nerves were stretched taut. Not only was Joe in love with Charley's wife, but Janessa had a feeling for Joe

that wasn't going to go away simply because she loved
Charley more. Joe, not Charley, had saved Janessa.
Charley had only been trying not to die at the time; he had
lain there in his fever and done nothing and known
nothing—had known nothing for a year, while Janessa had
kept her deadly secret with Joe.

Were there other secrets she had kept with Joe? No,
that was unfair. He had always trusted Janessa, never
having been given reason not to. But never before had
there been something that she had not told him. Had Joe
hoped that Charley would die? Was he now hoping that Joe
would? Charley, miserable, could find no answer that was
not suspect.

He rubbed his hand across his eyes. Joe was innocent.
Charley owed him Janessa's life. Charley knew he would
even have liked the man had it not been for Janessa's being
between them. In the face of the moment's crisis, he told
himself, other complications didn't matter. They could be
sorted out later, if indeed the issues of the human heart
could be sorted. He sat up straighter and tried to listen as
Vernon outlined courtroom tactics, the possibility of finding
another witness, and the arrival of the lawyer he had sent
for from Richmond.

Outside, a group of men moved silently through the
dark trees, fueled by anger and free whiskey distributed by
Morton Briggs. They stopped at the edge of the field where
the yellow-fever hospital had been, and Briggs and Scoggins stepped back into the trees. If the good citizens of Ela
wanted to make their righteous indignation known with a
hanging rope, the Superior Coal Company naturally could
not approve—not publicly.

Scoggins shoved Eamon Walley forward. "If you don't
want to end up in jail, you better keep them stirred up."

Walley hitched up his trousers. Scoggins himself had
made certain that Walley was fairly full of whiskey, and the
alcohol fanned Walley's natural belligerence into a smoldering hatred for Joe Cheoah. "I ain't waitin' for some slick

Injun-lovin' lawyer to get him off," Walley vowed. "He killed my boy!"

He set out across the field at a trot, and the others followed.

Vernon droned on, listing all possibilities, his voice buzzing in Charley's ears, heard but not comprehended. The cicadas screeched outside, the sounds battering against each other and overlaid with some distant rumbling. The other men were all intent on Vernon's words, so it was Charley, with his divided mind, who first realized what that rumbling was.

He flung his chair back and ran to the window while they stared at him. "Oh, Mother of God!"

At the end of the street, a flood of running figures came out of the darkness and into the faint light from the jail's front window. They nearly blotted it out as they surged up the steps.

"There's a mob out there!"

"Who is it, Charley?" Saunooka went to the window while Nimrod Jackson and Wesley Calhoun jerked open the door.

"Not Cherokee!" Calhoun shouted. "Not even the biggest idiot here would try a jailbreak after you warned them, Chief!"

In an instant he was proved right. A coil of rope, held aloft in someone's hand, passed across a single lighted pane within the jail.

Calhoun began to run, drawing his pistol, and Charley saw that a gun had materialized in the Reverend Jackson's hand as well. Only he and Elliot Spray were unarmed.

"You'd better stay back!" Charley shouted at Spray. The whole street was erupting into chaos as other doors were flung open.

"Maybe I can help." Spray ran on, panting. "Thee stay back."

"No!" Charley outdistanced the portly Spray and set himself to catching the others.

As they reached the jail steps, the door slammed open with such force that it was loosened from its hinges. It smashed into the window beside it. Someone pushed Joe Cheoah down the steps, and Charley saw that his hands were tied behind him. He caught a glimpse of Owl Ross unconscious on the floor of his office.

"We don't want no Injun law! String him up!"

Joe stumbled and fell and was dragged to his feet as the Cherokee of Yellow Hill tried to fight their way through the armed mob surrounding him. The night was nearly moonless, and they struggled with one another in the deceitful dark that masked friend as well as foe and made guns nearly useless.

Charley grabbed a man from Ela who was tricked for a moment by Charley's white skin, punched him in the jaw, and tried frantically to push his way toward Joe. Someone lit a torch, swinging it around his head like a weapon, then another and another flamed to life, ringing a towering pin oak. The rope sailed over one of the huge, spreading limbs and hung swaying like a snake, the noose at its end.

"Get back, you Injuns! This murdering bastard's gonna get what's coming to him!"

"He killed my boy!" Eamon Walley shouted again.

In the torchlight, Charley saw Joe struggling uselessly with his captors. There was fresh blood on his face, and his black hair hung in his eyes.

"String him up!"

The Cherokee howled in rage and rushed the men from Ela as Joe was dragged toward the noose. Charley quit fighting and concentrated on pushing his way into the Ela mob, praying that his white skin would get him through. The circles of torchlight and the black night flowed together and broke apart in a constantly moving, disorienting pattern while the two factions battled each other. Charley pushed closer and suddenly saw, beyond the ring of torches, the bland moon face of Morton Briggs, watching.

Charley jerked his eyes away as if somehow Briggs might feel Charley's gaze and notice him, too. Joe lashed out at his captors with one booted foot and fell again. As they yanked him to his feet, he looked up, head thrown back, and his dark eyes met Charley's in recognition.

"Get out of here!" Joe shouted. It was the first time he had spoken.

Charlie was surrounded by struggling bodies. He lunged, elbowing and shoving his way past the last of them, and flung himself at Joe. He had no weapon but a pocket knife, but before they realized that he was not one of them, he had sliced through the rope around Joe's wrists. Then he was flung away, and a bullet went past his ear.

Charley staggered, then righted himself, trying to reach for Joe as an answering thunder of gunfire burst all around him. Joe swung at the man nearest him, drew his fist back to swing again, and stopped, arms suddenly flung wide. He fell slowly as Charley's hands reached toward him.

Janessa sat with her face buried in her hands, fingers clasped over her ears to blot out the screaming of the cicadas and her own misery. The sound of gunshots cracked through her skull with the suddenness of a physical blow, and she tipped back her chair in startled panic, sending it clattering to the floor. She ran across the cabin and stared wildly out into the night from every window.

Torchlight shone in the distance from the jail, and she heard the angry voices plainly. She had taken off her shoes, and now she ran down the street without them, never feeling the stones under her feet.

The street was full of men, white and Cherokee, running away. Janessa flung herself past them, through them, her eyes fixed on the jail, where the door sagged on its hinges and pale light flowed from an empty room. She was nearly at the jail when she spotted the kneeling man under the tree with another person's head in his lap. Elliot Spray came out of the jail with a lantern in his hand, and the light fell on Charley's bowed head and Joe's scarlet shirt-front.

Spray said something soothing, but she didn't understand. She walked as if through water in a dream to the pin oak and sank to her knees beside Charley.

Joe's eyes were opened wide in his bloodied face, but they weren't looking at her or at anything.

Charley raised his head. There was blood all over his hands. "He's gone," he said. "There wasn't anything to do."

"Thee tried," Spray said. "Thee nearly got killed thyself, trying." The empty noose dangled above them, swaying lightly in the wind.

"Let me have him," Janessa said.

"It's no good, Janessa," Charley told her gently. "He's gone." He looked dully at Spray. "How is Ross?"

"Let me have him!" Janessa batted Charley's hands away from Joe, trying to pull the dead man to her. Her mouth twisted in a silent howl of grief.

"Ross is out cold with a lump on his head," Spray said, "but he's alive. Let her have him. There's something I have to show thee."

Charley let Janessa take Joe into her lap and stood up. He looked down as she rocked the dead form in her arms. Her eyes were focused on Joe's, and choking sobs began to spill out of her.

Spray touched Charley's arm, and they walked around to the other side of the tree. They could hear Janessa sobbing, and Charley put his hands to his face.

"Let her mourn," Spray said. "No one heals without mourning."

"Someone should mourn him," Charley said grimly. He looked around into the empty night.

"They had reason to run," Spray said. He lifted his lantern.

Morton Briggs lay on the ground, with a round, red hole in his waistcoat. His eyes, too, were open in wide surprise.

XVIII

The next morning the sheriff, in a frothing rage, informed the coroner that Joe Cheoah and Morton Briggs had died at the hands of person or persons unknown in the midst of an attempt to lynch Cheoah, and the coroner could hold his damn inquest if he wanted to, but that was all he was going to get.

"Hell, from what I heard from Lawrence and Elliot Spray, Cheoah and Briggs could have been shot by their own side."

"Probably were," Owl Ross grunted, "the way things have been working out." He had a bandage around his head and was obviously in a lot of pain. He was in a smoldering fury, too. His badge was on the desk while he thought about whether he wanted to go on wearing it. The sheriff kept trying to hand it back to him. "I know it wasn't your fault, Sheriff, and Morton Briggs got what had been coming to him, but that doesn't make me feel any better."

"Didn't you see the men who jumped you?" the coroner asked.

"The ones that got me had scarves over their faces. It didn't take long, either," Ross said bitterly. His office had been put back to rights, but the door hinges were still broken.

"They all lit out after they saw who they'd killed," the

sheriff said. "There wasn't anyone left when I got there but Spray and the Lawrences. And they're the only ones I'm sure *didn't* do any shooting. I doubt the men who did shoot those two even know they did it. It was as dark as the inside of a billy goat, and there must have been eighty people out there. You aren't ever going to sort them out."

"You could track down some of the ones who were there," the coroner suggested. "Are you going to ignore folks taking the law into their own hands?"

"Yeah, I could track some of them down," the sheriff allowed. "On both sides. And I could put them on trial for what the whole mob did, when I know that Briggs put them up to it; otherwise, he wouldn't have been there." The sheriff stared at the broken door. "Curse him for being a lying son of a bitch and giving these folks false hope. I wanted this coal company in here, but now I think I'd just as soon stay poor. And if you don't like that," he snarled, "then campaign against me when I'm up for reelection." He picked up Ross's badge and shoved it under his nose. "And goddamn it, Owl, put your badge back on. I'm not going to lose you, too."

The coroner threw up his hands. "All right, it's your call. You're taking some chances, but I can't honestly argue with you. I'm not so proud of our own folks just now, either." He put his notebook in his briefcase, then walked heavily down the steps.

The sheriff turned to Ross. "You're blaming yourself. Don't. It never pays."

"You're just going to let it lie?" Ross asked.

"No. I'm going to pick up Scoggins—and Eamon Walley if I have to hunt him down personally—and charge them with attempted murder. I owe Dr. Lawrence that much, at least." He thought that the memory of Janessa Lawrence cradling a dead man against her bloodstained dress, her face fixed on Cheoah's as if she could somehow call him back, would follow him around for quite a while. "Assuming that she's able to testify," he added. Her eyes had had a blank look that he didn't like.

"She'll testify." Owl Ross tossed the badge in his hand for a moment. "She's tough. Must be the Cherokee in her." He gave the sheriff a crooked grin and stuck the badge through his shirtfront.

Janessa had slept finally, after Charley, without telling her, had mixed a spoonful of laudanum into a cup of Walini's tea. Charley had left her with Walini and a mourning Billy and Lottie and ridden into Quallatown, where he sent a wire to Janessa's brother Tim in Oklahoma. She needed someone, Charley knew, and right now that someone wasn't her husband. Or rather she needed him, but she needed someone else, too, to whom she could pour out her grief without censoring it. Charley had known, too, that Toby would not do. There were things that one might say to a brother, but not a father.

"*Let her mourn*," Spray had said. But the blank look in Janessa's eyes had sent Charley into a panic. She had gone away somewhere behind those blank eyes, and she hadn't said a word from the time that they had persuaded her to let the sheriff take Joe's body until she had finally drifted into a drugged slumber. Tim would be able to get through if anyone could.

In the morning, Janessa woke and dressed, but as far as Charley could see, there wasn't anybody behind those eyes. When she had dressed, she sat down in a chair and stared out the window, while Charley watched her, miserable, and brutalized his conscience with the knowledge that he was still jealous of a dead man.

Tim arrived the next evening, on a horse that he had rented at the livery stable in Quallatown. He was twenty-six and looked very much like a younger edition of his father, blue eyed and square chinned, with the sandy hair that was always referred to by those family members who possessed it as dishwater blond. His hair and clothes were overlaid now with a layer of soot from the train, and traces of it clung to his face as well, accenting the first fine lines beginning to form at the corners of his eyes. He dropped his carpetbag, his only luggage, on the cabin floor, and said, "What happened?"

Charley told him as dispassionately as possible.

Tim cocked an eye at him. "I don't quite see why she's gone off the deep end. A shock, yes, but she sounds catatonic."

"She loved him." Charley folded his arms and looked out the window. "Loved me more, I guess, because she was going to stay with me. But well, I'm not dead, and he is."

Tim's eyebrows shot up into his hair. *"Janessa?"*

"Your sister's human," Charley said. "She doesn't need chewing out; she needs someone to talk to. The funeral's tomorrow."

"I wondered why you sent for me and not Dad," Tim said. He surveyed Charley. "You don't look so good yourself."

"Oh, I'm just fine," Charley said sarcastically. "Just perfect." He pointed at the bedroom door. "Janessa's in there."

Tim nodded. He walked quietly to the door, past Janessa's drying rack. The herbs swayed as he passed and disturbed the air with a pungent scent. "She used to fill the house with these things when she first came to live with us," he murmured.

He turned the knob and stood waiting for her to look up and see him. Her face looked as if it were etched in smoky glass, and all the Cherokee in her showed clearly. When she didn't move, he went in and closed the door behind him.

"I've been on a train for two days," he observed, "and Peter Blake is running my newspaper. He'll probably have sold it and invested the money in automobiles by the time I get back. You might at least say thank you for coming."

Janessa's head turned slowly at the sound of his voice, and her eyes widened until a spark of light began to glow in them. "Tim!" She got up and met him halfway across the room, flinging her arms around him, tightening them so much his chest hurt. "Oh, Tim!"

"You're strangling me," he said, but he grinned, relieved that at least she was speaking.

"How did you know to come?"

"Charley sent for me," Tim said. "You owe him, honey."

"I know I do!" Janessa laid her head on Tim's shoulder and burst into tears. "I'm sorry," she choked. "I can't seem to quit. I never used to cry. Now I do it all the time."

"Maybe it's time you learned. God knows you've had a year that would teach anybody. Here, come and sit down." He led her to the bed and sat on it so that she could lean against him. "You used to comfort me, remember, when I'd been bad?" He chuckled. "A lecture and a kiss. I remember it well."

"Is that what you've come to give me?"

"Just the kiss."

"Oh, Tim, I've been awful. Did Charley tell you what I've done?"

"He told me you're grieving. And yeah, he told me the rest of it. As much as he knows. Is there any more?"

"No," Janessa sobbed. "And now that he's dead, I wish there had been more, so I'd have that to remember. And I feel rotten inside, and I loved him, and I love Charley, and—"

"And you don't feel you have any right to mourn this guy? When you cry for Joe, you think you're hurting Charley, and when you don't cry, you feel as though you're denying Joe. You've got yourself in a state, haven't you?"

She nodded, shivering. "How do you know all that?"

"Brotherly intuition. If this guy had just been a friend, you could have leaned on Charley. As it is . . ."

Janessa's arms tightened around him again. "Please stay till the funeral. If you're here, I'll be able to get through it."

"Of course I'll stay." He looked a little sheepish. "If you won't be offended, I might get a story out of it, too. There are lots of Cherokee in Oklahoma."

Janessa sat up and rubbed her hand across her eyes.

"Do. Write it. Write the whole thing. Give Joe's dying some *meaning*." Her mouth quivered. "Oh, Tim, he's gone, and I can't bear it."

"You've got to," Tim said. "Bear it, and let him go. Don't keep his ghost tethered to you. That won't do him any good."

"Do you think that happens?" Janessa whispered.

"I don't know," Tim said solemnly. "Sometimes I've thought so, that we pull spirits back to us more by our own will than theirs. I do know that wherever he's supposed to go is where he needs to be. Don't hang on to him."

Janessa sighed. "You've gotten awfully grown up."

"Happens to all of us," Tim said.

Janessa managed a weak smile. "Except maybe to me. I'm regressing."

"You never had an adolescence, that's all. You were terrifyingly competent at the age of fifteen. So now you're having it. It had to come sometime."

"Yeah? And when did yours end?"

"While I was trapped at the bottom of a caved-in silver mine," Tim said, "if I had to give it a date. But it was time. And you aren't regressing; you just got the stages of your life mixed up. Somebody shuffled your deck funny." He stood up. "Come on. There's something you have to do."

"I know."

Charley was standing in the front room of the cabin, still looking out the window. His slumped shoulders gave him a weary, defeated look, with his right hand he turned his wedding ring around and around on its finger. Janessa went to him and turned him toward her.

"Thank you," she whispered. "You've always known what I needed."

"Sometimes I haven't wanted to," Charley said.

She put her arms around him. "I can't get by without you, you know. I love you so."

"She wouldn't be in this state if she didn't," Tim observed.

Janessa shot him a will-you-go-away look.

Tim grinned. "I think I'll take a walk. Interview some people."

"He's a wretch," Janessa said as the door closed behind him, "but he's right."

"I guess he is at that," Charley said. He stroked her hair. "Poor baby."

"You never called me that before," Janessa said.

"You never scared me like this before. Are you going to be all right now?"

"Yes."

His finger brushed her cheek. "Not going to vanish on me again?"

She looked at him solemnly. "No, I'm here. You're stuck with me."

They buried Joe the next afternoon, following a morning spent in court thrashing out one of the tangled land-ownership cases, an already-scheduled trial that could not be postponed simply for a death.

Joe was not to have been a witness. He had been only the driving force behind it, and as they gathered to hear the outcome, Janessa thought that he was still there, a presence sensed just over her shoulder. *I will not hang on to him,* she thought, but the presence didn't fade. She could almost see him, first here and then there, a spark flickering among the faces of the Cherokee who packed the courtroom, tense with expectation. If there was anything here to draw him back, perhaps it was not her but this land he had loved so much and the people for whom he had fought so hard.

The white citizenry of Ela seemed to feel his presence as well. They shifted restlessly in their seats, and the men scowled while their wives shot them sidelong glances.

Superior Coal Company was represented by a lawyer who had taken a fast mail train from Pennsylvania, and he looked like a man who had suddenly fallen down a well that hadn't been there yesterday. Morton Briggs's body had been shipped north to his home, and Scoggins was in jail, abandoned by both his company and his replacement. Eamon Walley had agreed to testify against Scoggins as a method of diverting as much blame from himself as possible, and Superior Coal couldn't afford that publicity— particularly not with Tim Holt still hanging around town. Scoggins had wailed almost tearfully to the new lawyer that he hadn't known the woman's brother was a newspaper publisher, and the Pennsylvania attorney had said, well now he did, and hadn't bothered even to try to bail Scoggins out. Scoggins, as Vernon Hughes remarked, had hung himself with the rope he'd meant for Joe Cheoah.

Vernon was in a somber mood and prepared for war. His briefcase bulged with a year's worth of work, much of it painstakingly prepared by Joe Cheoah—a fact of which he informed the judge.

"By rights, Mr. Cheoah should have handled these cases himself, but local prejudice being what it was, I was brought in to help." Vernon gave a long look at the men from Ela on the other side of the courtroom and then at the coal-company lawyer. "Now I'm the only counsel these people have. Please forgive me if it slows me down at times."

"I will." The judge's face was carefully impassive, but his eyes were angry. He had a bony, oblong face and the straight, tight mouth of a man with a bad conscience. This wasn't the first case he had heard on the matter of land over the past year, and like the sheriff and most of the white population, the judge's sympathies had lain from the beginning with his own kind. The judge had grown up in these mountains, a preacher's son who had worked his way through law school and known firsthand the desperation of poverty.

The coal-company lawyer stood up. "Your honor, I have had very little time to prepare for this case. I would respectfully like to ask for a continuance."

"It strikes me," the judge remarked, "that makes you about even. Mr. Hughes has lost his assistant counsel. You still have yours where you can get at him, at least."

"My assistant counsel is in jail!"

"It is far easier to communicate from jail than from the grave!" the judge snapped. "There will be no continuance."

Tim Holt, who now sat in the front row of the spectators' seats, with his notepad open on his lap, had interviewed the judge, among others, yesterday, but the judge, finding that Tim had been a miner, had also interviewed Tim. Tim's description of the bottom of a mine shaft had been succinct: "As close to hell as I ever want to get, Your Honor. And that's on a good day." How would these men from the open ridges and hollows of the mountains fare, under the earth in a three-foot passageway, digging the guts out of their mountains for a pay envelope? How many would be entombed there, and how many would simply die of despair when their world lost its daylight? And what would happen when the coal was gone, as it would be eventually, and the land was scarred above and honeycombed beneath and did not any longer even belong to them?

The judge, whose judicial conscience had been at war all year with his inborn inclinations to side with his own race, now found that the two had settled into accord. A certain suspicion rose in him—the native suspicion of the mountaineer for the motives of big-city newcomers. If Superior Coal was willing to rob the Cherokee for its own ends, how much trust could the white residents put in its promises? The Cherokee were within their rights to keep the land they lived on, and the judge would be doing his own people no favor in the long run by going against that.

When Vernon Hughes and the coal-company lawyer had summed up, the judge drew a long breath. "I'm going to do two things here," he said. "And I'm going to tell you that I don't want to see another one of these cases in this court."

There was an angry mutter from the white spectators, and the judge slammed his gavel on the bench with a crack that rattled the brass shades of the overhead lights and set them humming. From the dark, polished pine of the bench, he looked down at the Ela citizens in cold anger.

"You listen to me for your own sake. This community has come real close to selling out its soul for false coin."

They scowled at him, but they began to look uncomfortable.

"Those of you who were in Yellow Hill three days ago came closer than the rest," the judge continued. "You know who you are, and you know just how close, and you'd better be praying you aren't *past* praying for. But the rest of you are just as responsible. You let greed get ahead of justice. And in your greed, you nearly let the devil give you a shovel to dig your own graves with."

"I object!" The coal-company lawyer stood up again, affronted.

"You can't object. This trial is over. Shut up." As the bailiff took a step toward the lawyer, he subsided. No one else moved. The judge smacked his gavel down again. "You folks don't know it, but I've just done you a big favor. Now get out of here."

They filed out in wary silence. Outside, the Cherokee gathered around Vernon Hughes and Stillwell Saunooka. In a low murmur of voices, too saddened by what they had to do now to be jubilant, they began to thank Vernon.

"We owe you a bigger debt than we can pay," Saunooka said. He turned to encompass Janessa in his glance. "And to you, too, Ka-nessa. You did much for us and at a great price. We will always name you Daughter." He kissed her forehead and shook Vernon's hand.

"Thank the one who's not here," Vernon said quietly.

Stillwell Saunooka nodded. "We'll be doing that now," he said.

They buried Joe Cheoah in the Cherokee cemetery at Yellow Hill, among the past year's graves, now nearly grown over with summer grass and the tangles of wild morning glory. Joe's grave was an open wound in the wet, dark earth, and his casket seemed forlorn beside it.

How long would it take, Janessa agonized, for the grass to lay its blanket over him and the creepers to knot it down? *He will lie here alone, while I am surrounded by my husband and brother, my aunt and cousins, safely enclosed in their warmth.*

Nimrod Jackson preached the service at the graveside. His face was as weary as the rest, but his gray eyes held the hope that only faith gives: that this, too, may be gotten through and will, in the end, prove to have served some purpose.

"Lord, we come here today to give You the body of Joseph Cheoah. He wasn't an outwardly pious man, Lord, but You know all hearts, and You know what was in his. So You know how he loved his birth land and served us, his people. And You know what it cost him. He was willing to pay the price, Lord. Grant us the strength to pay ours when we have to."

"Amen!" It was Wolf Mooney who shouted it, with Rebecca looking up at him, startled. "Well, the war ain't done," Wolf said. "I reckon Joe showed us the way to keep fighting it."

Jackson went on, drawing Wolf's comments into his text, while Rebecca looked up at Wolf proudly. Janessa smiled in spite of herself. It was probably the first time the old reprobate had been at a church service in years. And he was right: In any battle there will be death. It was the living, saved by the dead, who must be counted.

"Joe did what he set out to do," Jackson said. "Lord, we ask You to help us all to do the same."

I did what I set out to do. Janessa looked about her at the sea of faces around Joe's grave. Fully half of them might now be dead had it not been for the hospital-service doctors. *Count the living.* Any doctor realized that to do anything else was to go mad. Silently she began to count, to name them to herself: Wolf and Rebecca, Walini and Wesley Calhoun, and Parker Smith standing beside them in his one good suit, head bowed. The family she had not known she had. She gazed at the other faces, of distant relatives or kin only by tribal blood. Billy and Lottie, standing with their arms around each other. And her first family, dearer now than ever: Charley and Tim and Vernon. Tim stood, top hat in his hands, grown somehow far beyond the little brother she had always visualized him to be. Charley was beside her, solid and comforting, loving and beloved. His eyes rested sadly on the coffin with its wreath of black-eyed Susans, and Janessa knew that Charley had made his peace with Joe, too.

Janessa bowed her head with the almost shamefaced feeling of one who doesn't pray very often and so feels embarrassed to be asking God for something now. *Lord take him to You and watch over him. Give him the peace he's never had.*

Stillwell Saunooka, Wesley Calhoun, Parker Smith, and Billy slowly lowered the coffin into the grave on ropes. Walini put an arm around Janessa, and Janessa slipped her own arm through Charley's on her other side. Nimrod Jackson began to sing, and the rest of them took up the words.

> "O God, our help in ages past,
>   Our hope for years to come . . ."

The coffin came to rest. Parker and Wesley lifted their shovels, and the falling earth blotted out the black-eyed Susans. Janessa stumbled over the words, and Charley pressed his arm closer to hers.

> "Before the hills in order stood,
>   Or earth received her frame,
> From everlasting Thou art God,
>   To endless years the same."

It was half a song of mourning, half an affirmation of faith and hope. Janessa found her voice and began to sing.

> Time, like an ever-rolling stream,
>   Bears all its sons away. . . ."

Their voices swelled together over the graveyard and up to the green hills.

XIX

"Well, Senator, I understand you are leaving us for cooler climes." President Cleveland mopped his brow and looked balefully at the brass grillwork of the White House ventilating system. A steady stream of air, blown across cakes of ice, lowered the temperature no more than a degree or two and made the room more muggy than it was already. "I wish I were going with you."

"Oregon's always glad to welcome you, sir," Toby said. "I'll confess I would have left earlier myself if Theodore hadn't inveigled me into staying."

"The man's a menace," Cleveland muttered. Then he chuckled. "About to investigate *your* civil-service system, is he?"

"He's investigated every one he can get his hands on. That's his job. But I must say I do think he enjoys keeping things stirred up. I'm all for his investigating the conduct of the postal system in Portland. But not before *I've* investigated it, so I can brace myself."

"So you are racing him to the West Coast."

"I'm taking my mother home," Toby said gravely. "The climate here doesn't suit her at her age. And I need to spend more time with the people I'm supposed to be representing. My daughter Sally is developing a Southern drawl you could slice with a knife. Alexandra is, too. When

341

I met her she was pure Kentucky, and it's all come back."

"I'll look for your return in the fall," Cleveland said. "Shed of pernicious influences." He gave Toby a thoughtful look. "When you asked for an appointment with me, I assumed it was not merely to bid me a fond farewell."

"Not entirely, sir," Toby said. "I was hoping to persuade you to tell me what is happening in Hawaii. I'm beginning to feel dubious about having let my boy go over there after reading the dispatches my son Tim's reporter has been sending back—although I have to admit that Henry's letters are calm enough."

"I doubt that you have anything to worry about," Cleveland said. "For supposedly bloodthirsty savages, the Hawaiians seem peaceable enough. To have achieved only one minor riot in reaction to what's been going on out there is evidence of an angelic temperament."

"If I may ask, what are you going to do now, sir, based on Blount's report?"

"Oh, you can ask. I'll have to tell you frankly that I'm blasted if I know. I'm going to order the monarchy restored—that's between you and me, Holt, for the time being—but I am extremely uncertain of how that order will be received."

"What if the provisional government refuses?"

Cleveland sighed. "That is the problem. I really have no authority over there and am reluctant to perpetrate an act of war against fellow Americans."

"Even throne-grabbing, profiteering fellow Americans? I'm not sure we don't have an obligation to prevent our citizens from acting like that."

"It's not exactly a question of putting them over my knee and spanking them. If the provisional government refuses to step down, I would have to shoot them, which is a more drastic form of discipline."

Toby laced his fingers together and contemplated the view out the President's window. Two children driving a pony cart down Pennsylvania Avenue had let it get away from them, and the pony was eating roses on the White

House lawn. The children's nanny scolded it uselessly while two laughing marine guards tried to disentangle it. Toby supposed that things always looked much simpler to the man who didn't have to make the final decision. Those same marines might have to put Liliuokalani back on her throne with rifles if the PGs decided to hold on. A difficult order to give or to refrain from. He was glad he wasn't the President.

Toby stood up and shook hands formally with Cleveland. "I appreciate the information, sir. I'll keep it to myself. But I think I'll tell Mike he's to come home. He has a bad heart, you know, and he's had nearly all the excitement that is good for him."

"It will be interesting to see," the President said, "which of us gets more argument over our order."

Honolulu

"*I'm not going!*" Mike dragged his father's letter out of his pocket, spread it out, and crumpled it up again. He had been carrying it around for three days, talking to it, since he couldn't talk to his father.

"You are going," Eden said. She had been on the listening end of his tirade for the three days. Mike would calm down to a dull simmer, at least outwardly, and then suddenly explode again like an overheated boiler. "You are going because if you don't, your father will come over here and get you. You know he will. And then he won't ever let you see me again because he'll think it's my fault. Also, people are staring at us, and you look demented."

They were setting up the camera on the steps of the church across the street from Washington Place, to film Liliuokalani's expected emergence into public life again. For some reason the PGs had agreed to allow her to go about as she pleased, and a huge crowd was waiting for her appearance. Mike cast a hunted look over his shoulder and lowered his voice.

"Dad can't stop me from seeing you or doing any other

thing I please. In another year I'll be eighteen. I could join the army, or go to sea, or be a bum if I felt like it, and he couldn't stop me."

"Well, you don't want to do any of those things," Eden said practically.

"No, I want to get a job in Edison's studio," Mike said. "Dad's going to look at that in about the same way." His chin jutted out stubbornly.

"You're going to have to wait until I'm eighteen, too," Eden said. "Sam and Annie aren't going to let me go marry a photographer who will probably make five dollars a week."

"I wouldn't let you, either," Mike said. "We'll wait until I'm on my feet."

Eden folded her arms. She looked up at him, her chin jutting out now to match his. "Try to stop me."

"Eden, honey, I can't ask that of you."

"You aren't asking. When I am eighteen, I am going to take the first ship to wherever you are slaving for Mr. Edison, and you will come home for supper to find me sitting on your doorstep." She looked away a moment and then gave him a sidelong glance. "That way everyone will be terribly relieved that you've married me."

Mike flushed. Well-brought-up girls weren't supposed to know anything about sex, but he was becoming convinced that Eden knew more than she let on. Girls weren't idiots. It was all just pretense. He was discovering that his sheltered Eden had a strong unconventional streak. It just hadn't had any outlet yet, except in the adventure books they read together. But she was endlessly curious, and her life had given her an oddly grown-up capability that had blossomed in the months with him. The breeze caught her pale hair and made it float around her face like silk, and there was something in her eyes when she looked at him that had outgrown her schoolgirl dresses. She appeared absolutely capable of doing what she had said.

"Are you sure you'd be willing to live like that?" he asked her.

"Yes. I'm just not sure I can stand it until I can."

"Eden, I love you so." Mike's voice sounded hoarse. He kissed her, not gently but with an anguished urgency, forgetting the people around them, and felt her press her body against his. When they drew apart, a pair of Hawaiian ladies beamed at them sentimentally.

Eden laughed. "Here comes the queen."

The Hawaiian ladies sighed fondly at youthful romance and turned to watch Liliuokalani emerge from her palace in a triumphal procession. She was escorted by an entourage of clerks and secretaries, her deposed cabinet ministers, and a trio of ladies-in-waiting. Nearly half the procession consisted of Hawaiian-born haoles. The division between the Royalists and the PGs was more economic than racial. The PG party was the child of the islands' big sugar planters, with the exceptions of Claus Spreckels and the now defecting Sam Brentwood. Liliuokalani's escort, noses in the air, made it clear that their sympathies did not lie in the PGs direction as they swept past a knot of PG police who stood uncomfortably at attention on the street corner.

Flower-bedecked carts awaited them, drawn in Hawaiian style by liveried servants rather than horses.

"Hold it steady," Mike said, peering into the camera. "This step is wobbly."

Eden knelt on the church steps, cradling the legs of the tripod, bracing it against her shoulder. As the procession came into range, Mike turned the crank with the steady motion that he had finally perfected, and the moving-picture camera whirred and recorded history. The crank was large and unwieldy, as was the camera, and the image through the viewfinder was minute and upside-down. Mike counted "one alligator, two alligators," under his breath to keep the circle of the crank in time and watched the queen enter her carriage, a tiny upended figure with sky beneath her and carriage wheels above. The crowd repeatedly roared out her name— "Liliuokalani!"—bellowing out not her baptismal name and married title but the name under which she had taken her ancestors' throne.

Mike, with the click and whirr of the camera in his ear, heard it only as background sound, like rain or thunder. It was the tiny inverted parade in the viewfinder that held him enthralled. *When Mr. Edison sees this . . .* he thought, triumphant. He was well aware that a storm was brewing between his father and him; but he was fed up with being the focus of everyone's concern, and the life his father had planned for him stretched ahead as dreary as an endless plain. *If my heart gives out, it gives out. I won't die despairing at what I never did.* He could feel Eden's solid warmth against his calf as she steadied the tripod. *Or never had.*

Eden, with nothing to do but hold still, watched dreamily as the carts rolled up the street, the awaiting throng opening before them and closing after them, throwing leis of flowers and feathers, posies of jasmine and plumeria. The queen's own band had begun to play "Aloha Oe," and Liliuokalani sat up straight in her cart, in a gown of bright yellow satin with enormous sleeves, and a wreath of yellow plumeria that looked very like a crown. *More like a crown than he likes,* Eden thought, seeing a scowling Lorrin Thurston on horseback.

The man was caught in the crowd of joyful Hawaiians and trying to push his way through it. Thurston's black beard jutted out angrily, and his face was smoldering. He wore a dark frock coat despite the temperature and resembled a furious crow stabbing with its beak at a flock of bright-feathered birds.

The servants pulled another cart by, singing as they went. Liliuokalani was making as much of a spectacle as she could, her only possible revenge on the PGs. Eden saw Sam and Annie in the cart and stopped herself in time from waving and upsetting the camera. Sam looked cheerful, his old cocky grin back. He gave Lorrin Thurston a mock tip of his panama hat and threw him a flower, one of the many that had landed in the cart. Thurston caught it out of reflex and then flung it angrily away. Sam threw his head back and laughed. For a moment Annie laughed, too. Then her laughter faded, and she looked at Sam with the same puzzled suspicion that had been her expression for the past few weeks.

They don't know what to do with each other, Eden thought. Sam had done something that had made President Dole let the queen have her freedom. That was why Sam was in the cart. But Annie didn't know what, and Sam wouldn't tell her. *It's not fair!* Eden thought, suddenly angry. *They can be married, and she doesn't even want him, but I want Mike, and he has to go away.* She clenched her fingers around the tripod. *Almost two years. How can I stand it for that long with him gone?*

She realized that she had said it aloud when Mike, above her, said, "You can stand almost two years of anything if you have to. I know."

Henry Blake, in search of his wife, found her watching the procession.

"Whom or what are you keeping an eye on? This shindig or our nephew?"

"Both," Cindy said. "It's making me walleyed."

"Well, you don't have to worry about trying to drag him home by yourself," Henry said. "The steamer from San Francisco's just in. The President's recalling me. He's sending out a new minister, Albert Willis of Kentucky. He's an ex-congressman and a reasonably tough old bird. Cleveland seems to feel that with Willis here, he can put me to better use elsewhere." Henry shook his head at her questioning look. "I have no idea where."

"The Cannibal Islands," Cindy said. "Siberia. Someplace inaccessible and dangerous."

"Just as likely to be a desk job," Henry pointed out. "I think I'd welcome one after this stint." His mouth twisted. "I know what's going to happen so clearly, I don't need to stick around and watch it: The PGs aren't going to step down; the President's hands are going to be tied if he doesn't want to fire on his own citizens; and the PGs are going to win by default, blast their lying hides."

"I thought you were an impartial observer," Cindy murmured.

"Officially," Henry said. "I have to be. But that doesn't mean I don't have private opinions. Sometimes I just get tired of keeping quiet about them."

The crowd still rolled past them, singing, letting their queen know they loved her. The air was full of music and the lush scent of the tropics. And how could paradise be so choked with injustice? Did civilization rot everything it touched? It was an implacable force, he thought, that like time could not be turned back. All that could be done, perhaps, was wrestle with it when you could and drag it like an intractable mule back onto the path it should take.

He dug in his pocket for the second letter that had come for him on the steamer from San Francisco. "Janessa's written, too," he said. He handed the envelope to Cindy. It had made its way, growing steadily more dog-eared, from Quallatown to Honolulu as Janessa had packed her bags and made her own way with Charley back to New York.

Cindy read it silently and then with a little gasp of dismay. "That's the young man you told me about, isn't it? Joe Cheoah? The lawyer?"

"Yes." Henry didn't think he would mention the way he had seen Joe look at Janessa and Janessa at Joe. Janessa hadn't mentioned it. The tone of her letter sounded as if she had chosen her words very carefully. "At least someone has won," he said. He felt tired, as if he had spent the whole year involved in dual battles against his countrymen's greed. "Maybe we aren't past hope."

Cindy seemed to follow his line of thought. "In the lump, you mean, as opposed to individual injustice? Oh, I think we're all right in the lump. Janessa's Cherokee won—poor young man, at a great cost—and I think as a whole the country will do the right thing."

"Eventually," Henry muttered.

Cindy chuckled ruefully. "Well, yes, eventually takes

awhile. A collective social conscience is probably the slowest moving force on the planet. But we do get there."

"What an optimist you are," Henry said, but he felt it rubbing off on him. "I suppose it will eventually arrive here, too." He watched the Hawaiians still celebrating in the street and Lorrin Thurston still trying to edge his horse through the crowd.

A gleam came into Henry's eyes. Thurston was hopelessly snarled in a mass of foot traffic, and the more he smacked his horse with his crop, the more the animal balked at the press of bodies around it.

"I'll be back in a minute."

Henry edged his way through the crowd while Cindy watched him dubiously. Henry had been in a vile temper for days over his certainty, which she believed was well founded, that the PGs, with their power, were not going to let it go again, no matter what President Cleveland wanted. Now he seemed less angry but surely not what she would call resigned. Henry had always had a streak in him that grew frustrated when he was unable to take events into his own hands and make them fall out as he thought they should. Just now even the back of his head looked unpredictable.

Henry took Thurston's horse by the reins. "Having a little trouble?" he inquired genially.

"It's this damned crowd in the street," Thurston growled. "We'll put a stop to this."

"How?" Henry asked. "I don't imagine you've got enough room in the jails. Or have you finally come up with another idea for controlling the populace? Like letting them vote on what they want, for instance?"

Thurston's eyes narrowed suspiciously. "I don't discuss the government with foreign citizens."

Henry gave him an evil grin. "I bet you don't. They might go home and report on you. You just tell them lies at dinner."

Thurston tried to snatch his reins back, but Henry wouldn't let go. "You don't trust anybody, do you?" Henry went on. "Dictators can't, you know, so maybe that's wise."

"You're Brentwood's friend, aren't you?" Thurston slapped at Henry's hand with the crop. "You don't know what you're talking about."

"Ah, now that's where you're wrong." Henry snatched the end of the crop and snapped it out of Thurston's hand. "I know more than you think. So here's a piece of advice for you: Never trust anybody, Mr. Thurston, because the time is going to come when you won't be able to trust your own shadow. That's the trouble with telling lies—they build up until they create something real, and sometimes it eats you."

The crowd had finally begun to thin. Henry let go of the reins and smacked the crop down on the horse's backside. It leaped forward with a startled snort, nearly unseating Thurston. Henry flipped the crop after him so that it arced over Thurston's head and landed in a puddle, splattering Thurston's trousers with mud.

"And exactly what did that accomplish?" Cindy inquired as Henry rejoined her.

"I feel better," Henry said, grinning happily. "That's what it accomplished."

"I don't trust you." Annie looked at Sam over a glass of champagne and a plate of crab legs.

"I know that," Sam said. He cracked a crab leg with the pliers and offered it to her. They were at the best table in the dining room of the Royal Hawaiian Hotel, with the summer night breeze blowing gently through the open windows, salt tinged and flower scented, as enticing as a risky love affair. It had taken a good deal of inveigling to get her to join him for dinner.

Annie let him put the cracked shell on her plate. "Then what are we doing here?"

"I'm hoping I'll grow on you." Sam looked blandly cheerful, unwilling to be insulted but unwilling to do much pleading, either. He took the champagne bottle out of the silver bucket in which the waiter had placed it, wrapped solicitously in a monstrous napkin, and poured some more into her glass.

"You aren't going to get me drunk on champagne, either," Annie said suspiciously.

"What a shrew you are," Sam remarked mildly. "I don't know what I want with you."

"Neither do I!" Annie retorted. "Not since your father died and you came into your own money."

Sam played with the crab pliers for a minute, snapping their jaws together while Annie watched him, exasperated. "It may surprise you to know," he said finally, "that what I thought I wanted in the first place doesn't turn out to be what I want now. It took *me* by surprise. Crept up and bit me, so to speak." He pointed the pliers at her and clacked them together.

"That isn't a toy!"

"They seem sort of apt."

"If you mean that our marriage has been painful," Annie said, "I will grant you that!"

"Love seems to be like that," Sam offered. "Look around. Look at poor old Toby Holt and his flame out of the past showing up two years ago, and her husband trying to throw her off a building. Look at Mike and Eden. Look at my father, if you can stand to."

"*You* were the one who couldn't stand that," Annie said. Her expression softened. "Not that I blame you. But you don't love me, Sam, and you know it. You just can't stand not getting what you want." She took a sip of her champagne, a little defiantly.

"Maybe I want you because I love you," Sam said. "You're a hellcat. Why else would I want you?"

"Ha!" Annie dug the crabmeat out of the cracked leg with an expression that indicated she might prefer to use the crab fork on him.

Sam sighed and went back to his own dinner. "You wouldn't be living in the same house with me if you didn't want to," he suggested.

"I'm living with you for Eden," Annie said flatly.

Sam grinned. He didn't look at her, just at the crabmeat he was worrying out of its shell. "Sure."

Annie flushed. "You always had a higher opinion of yourself than—"

She bit off the words with a jerk of her head as the waiter approached them, hovering.

"More wine, madam? Perhaps some coffee or a sweet?" He bent graciously from the waist, back bowed like a dolphin, a fluid pause in his professional circulation of the dining room.

"We haven't finished dinner yet," Sam said. "We'll let you know." Across the room he spotted Harvey Sessions, with his napkin pressed against his lips. Harvey's eyes were crinkled above it, and his shoulders shook. Sam shot him a black look, and Harvey retired to his plate, still chortling. The waiter moved away, and Sam wasn't surprised to see him pause by Harvey's table and whisper in his ear. Harvey slipped a bill into his hand.

It wasn't lost on Annie. "Delightful as hell to be a public spectacle," she said angrily.

"Well, if you didn't look so much like Madame Dufarge waiting for them to sharpen up the guillotine, maybe people wouldn't stare at you."

"Madame who?"

"Never mind," Sam said hastily. "Someone in a book."

Annie leaned forward and glared at him. "That's right, throw it in my face that I'm not educated."

"I didn't mean to. Damn it, I'm not going to edit my conversation to avoid literary references you may not be acquainted with."

"Don't swear at me."

"You said *hell* a minute ago."

Annie gave him a look that said that didn't count.

"Aw, come on, Annie, you're just looking for a reason to jump at me."

"I don't need any more that I've already got."

Sam shifted in his chair and stared glumly at his plate. This wasn't going the way he'd planned. But he could outwait her, he thought. He didn't say anything else until the waiter came floating back to clear their plates and bring the pastry that Annie ordered. He asked for a brandy while Annie took a minute bite of chocolate torte. "You look as if you think there might be snails in it," he observed.

Annie cut a bigger bite and ate it, irritably.

When the brandy appeared, Sam took a fairly big swallow. "Look, I'm going to try this one more time. I love you. I've got a pretty strong suspicion you love me—not that you've ever admitted it since we've been married, which makes me the honest one right now. I want you to come back to me. All the way back. I want to see if we can't start over and make it work right this time. I've grown up some, you know. Don't you think you might be willing to take a chance on that?"

Annie swallowed her torte, then took a sip of champagne. "I haven't the foggiest idea," she said at last, giving him a steely look. "But if that's what you have in mind, I'd say that it's time for Sam Brentwood to start to pay court to his wife."

The bestselling saga of the Holt family
continues with

THE HOLTS:
AN AMERICAN DYNASTY
Volume Four

CALIFORNIA GLORY

by Dana Fuller Ross
author of the popular WAGONS WEST Series

Turn the page for an exciting preview of CALI-
FORNIA GLORY, on sale April 1991 wherever
Bantam Books are sold.

San Francisco, August 1893

"Well, now, Mr. Holt, my health hasn't been good." The owner of the *San Francisco Clarion* looked mournfully at his visitor from red-rimmed eyes that sagged in sympathy with the droop of his dejected gray mustache. The mahogany desk was covered with layers of papers, which he picked up and laid down again apparently at random.

"So I understand from Mr. Howard." Tim Holt nodded at the man who had accompanied him. Waldo Howard was an employee of the rival *Chronicle* but an old friend of Tim's. When Tim had indicated that he was in the market for a paper larger than the one he now operated in Oklahoma, Waldo had suggested that the *Clarion* might be had for a song. Looking at its owner, Tim thought Horace Woolwine looked too dispirited to pick up a copy pencil, much less inspire a staff of reporters to anything livelier than lethargy.

"Not good at all," Mr. Woolwine said. "So many . . . things . . . to attend to. Things all over the place." He picked up a sheaf of accounts and let them drop again.

Tim decided that if Mr. Woolwine finished out the day

it would be a miracle. "Why don't you show me the plant, sir?"

Mr. Woolwine shuffled to his feet. Tim followed him, restraining himself from the urge to herd the old man along. So far, the *Clarion* looked perfect. It was housed in a six-story building on Kearny Street, with bay windows and elaborate decorations of cast iron upon its cornices and, above the main door, a gargoyle with a pencil behind its ear. Tim had fallen in love with the gargoyle and was prepared to love the rest of the *Clarion*.

Within the newsroom, the staff attended to its work on a fleet of serviceable Remington typewriters. A system of pneumatic tubes connected the newsroom with the composing room below, leaving the copyboys to deliver material from reporters to their respective editors and to fetch coffee. The pace of the newsroom seemed to Tim just a shade too slow for the time of day, but with Mr. Woolwine setting the metronome, that was not too surprising.

The news staff looked up at their entrance, and a murmur of interest followed them across the room.

"Who's that?"

"I heard he's some galoot from Oklahoma, wants to buy the place."

"He's got a paper in Oklahoma. He must know—"

"He doesn't know enough to save this rag. What's Waldo Howard doing with him?"

"Probably cadging a free drink."

The city editor, a rumpled man in shirtsleeves, smacked a coffee cup down on his desk and glared at them. "He buys it or he doesn't. In the meantime, it might help if we could get it out on the street this afternoon." He took a bottle out of the bottom drawer of his desk and poured some whiskey into his coffee cup. He picked up a folded length of copy, pages glued together end to end, and gulped down the contents of the cup, apparently to give him the fortitude to read his reporter's efforts.

Tim followed Mr. Woolwine down the stairs, dutifully admiring the brass railings and the ornate brass doors of the elevator, which, Mr. Woolwine explained, they could not ride because it was stuck.

"Anybody in it?" Waldo asked.

"God knows," Mr. Woolwine replied apathetically.

Tim followed him into the composing room where a dozen typographers, perched like frock-coated storks on high stools, were setting copy from long banks of type.

Mr. Woolwine sighed. "I'd like to have a Linotype machine, of course. The *Los Angeles Times* just got Linotype."

Tim's blue eyes gleamed. Ottmar Mergenthaler's typesetting invention was rapidly becoming an obsession with him. The machine cast slugs of type, one column wide, from molten lead, automatically justifying the right-hand margins. One man at a Linotype keyboard could do the work of half-a-dozen typesetters handspiking type.

"Has the *Chronicle* got Linotype?" Tim asked Waldo.

"Wants it," Waldo answered. "Who doesn't? It's a big investment, though, and the public never sees it. Take it from me, kid, and put your dough in reporters' salaries. Linotype just processes what you give it. It won't write you brilliant copy."

"Neither will half the reporters I've got," Tim told

him. He narrowed his eyes at the composing room, mentally replacing the type racks with machines of his imagining.

Mr. Woolwine seemed to find the subject of Linotype depressing. With Tim and Waldo behind him, he shambled through the far door and down another set of stairs to the pressroom. When they were halfway down, the press roared to life, and they could feel its vibrations through the stairs. Woolwine pushed the door open, and the roar enveloped them.

Inside a room two stories tall was a huge, steam-driven, web-fed cylinder press. An iron catwalk ran around its upper level. The noise was deafening. Tim walked around the press and craned his neck to look up into its works. The inside of the pressroom was as hot as a Turkish bath, and the steaming air was heavy with clouds of ink.

"You're in the way, buddy." A pressman wearing a newsprint cap elbowed past Tim, and Tim got out of the way. He spotted the ladder to the catwalk and climbed it, while the pressman shook his head and looked up dubiously, as if expecting Tim to fall in the press and get killed. But Tim had reached the catwalk with no trouble and was prowling along it. Mr. Woolwine squinted up with an expression that said if a prospective buyer fell to his death and ruined the press's workings, it would be in accord with Mr. Woolwine's general view of the way of the world. Tim thought he had never seen such a depressed-looking man.

After he had peered down at the press from all angles, he climbed back to the floor and nodded at Woolwine. "Let's talk."

They went to the washroom to remove the faint overlay of ink that had settled on their hands and faces in the pressroom and then adjourned to Woolwine's office again. Tim looked around, mentally removing the flotsam and jetsam that spilled from Woolwine's desk to the floor and putting himself behind the mahogany desk, which would be quite a lovely piece of furniture once it was excavated.

"You definitely want to sell?" Tim asked.

"Oh, yes." A long-drawn sigh drifted through the room on the heels of Woolwine's affirmative response.

"Then let's discuss business." Tim cocked his head at Waldo. "And you go home to the *Chronicle*. I'll buy you dinner later at the Press Club, but what you don't know about the *Clarion*'s finances, you can't be asked." Not that Waldo would spill the beans on purpose, but he had been known to have a drink now and then.

The negotiations took the rest of the afternoon, partly due to Mr. Woolwine's being prepared to wring every possible penny from the deal, punctuated by lugubrious assessments of the state of his health, and partly due to a general lethargy that caused Mr. Woolwine to produce each new file and record with a tortoiselike slowness. It drove Tim to distraction, and by the time the transaction was concluded, he was jiggling on the edge of his chair, one foot tapping the threadbare carpet.

Eventually they settled on a price consistent with the sale of the *Prairie Recorder* in Guthrie, which Tim had already negotiated, and affected by the substantial amount of the *Clarion*'s outstanding debts. Tim signed a check for the down payment and a promissory note for the balance as soon as the sale of the *Recorder* should be concluded. Mr.

Woolwine signed a bill of sale and a deed to the property and agreed to remain in charge for one month. When they shook hands, Tim thought he detected enough pulse to keep Mr. Woolwine upright for thirty days.

The bill of sale felt almost warm in his pocket, as if it were a living thing. On the front steps, Tim stopped and looked up at the gargoyle with the pencil behind its ear. Had the morose Mr. Woolwine conceived the gargoyle? Impossible. At some point the *Clarion* had had a man with spirit behind it. Tim grinned. He thought the newspaper would take to him just fine.

Tim took a deep breath and looked around in the lamplit dusk. San Francisco had always struck him as a magical place, where ordinary laws of the universe did not apply. The hills, for instance—nobody had bothered to grade the ragged hills that appeared to be pegged to the flatter earth by the houses at their tops. The inhabitants had simply invented cable cars to run straight up and down them. The little cars flowed with apparent effortlessness up each sheer climb and down the other side on gradients that would destroy a buggy brake in a week.

And the air—even in midcity it smelled of raw lumber and fish, much the way his hometown of Portland did, but with the sharp tang of salt overlaying it—the briny scent of the great bay. San Francisco was a seaport, given birth by gold, and its spirit showed in its nightlife. Now at dusk, Market, Kearny, and Montgomery streets were long, gaudily illuminated bazaars, populated by Italian balloon sellers, street-corner drummers hawking stomach bitters and electrical belts, a sidewalk organist with a monkey in a red gypsy vest, ad carriers passing out saloon handbills, and barkers shouting the services of phrenology and palmistry booths. On the corner, a Salvation Army band valiantly attempted to stem the disreputable tide that flowed around it.

Tim hailed a hack and told the driver he wanted to go to the Press Club on Ellis Street. It occurred to him that he had told Waldo to meet him there and that since this dinner was to be on Tim, Waldo might be running up a considerable bar bill. He sat back and noted the illuminated signs as they passed: *Prof. Holmes, Astral Seer . . . Prof. Diamond, Courses in Hypnotism . . . Dr. Ball's Indestructible Teeth. . . .*

San Franciscans were prepared to believe in nearly anything, he decided. It was evident that they still believed in romance. The available ladies who strolled down Market Street in the evening possessed a demure assurance that was a reminder of the West's woman-starved past. Females of any type were still at a premium and were treated accordingly. A girl from a Barbary Coast brothel, Waldo had told Tim, could walk in the shopping district and hats would be tipped to her. And one Kearny Street madam, so Waldo said, had married off six of her girls to millionaires and retired. Waldo seemed to know a good deal about it.

At the Press Club Waldo was awaiting him in the company of a cartoonist who was introduced as Jimmy Warrington. Warrington sported a stiffly waxed mustache and a pair of plaid trousers that a carnival barker might have thought about twice. He was, Waldo explained, between jobs at the moment.

"Bring some of your work around next month," Tim told him, "when I settle in. I'll take a look." He wondered if Waldo was going to supply him with an endless parade of down-and-out journalists. Tim had no idea whether or not he needed a cartoonist.

"I could show you some tonight," Warrington said hopefully. When the waiter paused by their table, the cartoonist looked at his empty shot glass with further hope.

Tim knew perfectly well that if he fell in with these two for the night, he would have the great-grandmother of all hangovers in the morning. "Not tonight," he said firmly. "My little brother is coming in on the steamer from Hawaii at eight tomorrow morning, and I have to meet him." He bought Warrington another drink, though.

When the cartoonist had downed it and gone on his way, seeking hospitality among the other tables, Tim cocked an eyebrow at Waldo. "He any good?"

"Course he is," Waldo said. "Why would I introduce him to you if he wasn't?"

"You owe him money?" Tim suggested. "You're in love with his sister? You lost a bet? Never mind, I'll look at his stuff."

"What's your baby brother doing in Hawaii?" Waldo asked, interested.

"Not a baby," Tim said, chuckling. "Mike's seventeen and feeling his age with great seriousness. He went with my uncle Henry and aunt Cindy to see the islands and visit my disreputable courtesy cousin Sam, who's become a gentleman sugar planter, Lord help us." Tim gave a hoot of amusement.

Waldo grinned as the waiter brought their steaks and a bottle of champagne in a silver bucket—Tim was feeling expansive. "Annie hasn't given him the gate yet?" Waldo inquired. Tim, Waldo, and Sam and Annie Brentwood went back to the wild Virginia City silver days together.

"For a time," Tim said, cutting into his steak. "But Sam's father drowned at sea, and Sam ended up with his half sister, Eden, to raise. Annie came back to keep Eden from growing up as wild as a range colt. My brother Mike's in love with Eden—at their age!—and he doesn't want to come home."

Waldo shook his head. "Puppy love. Very painful."

"It's more complicated," Tim said. "Mike had rheumatic fever as a kid. He's got an iffy heart. Our parents have been inclined to wrap him in cotton wool, and he's starting to kick at it. I'm delegated to meet the boat and take him home to Portland. To see that he *gets* home."

"Fine thing to saddle you with," said Waldo. "I have no living relatives, but when I did, they sapped my energy—energy that could have been better spent chasing a story."

"I don't mind any exertion on their behalf," said Tim. He liked his family and had an itch to loaf a few days in Portland and let his stepmother's servants do his laundry and fuss over him. As the waiter poured more champagne, Tim sat up, alert, ears tuned in the direction of an alcove on the far side of the dining room.

The Press Club was a noisy hubbub of newspapermen, and the cacophony was made louder by a private party in the alcove, where a few adventurous souls were entertaining the cast of a musical comedy revue from the Columbia Theater. They had begun to sing songs from the show, accompanied by a sportswriter with a banjo. He played unhandily but with enthusiasm. Tim could not hear a thing, but his line of sight was clear, and he was startled to see Mr.

Woolwine among the revelers. No longer morose, Mr. Woolwine's thin arms waved like semaphores in time to the music, and his gray handlebar mustache twitched up and down. He appeared to be singing. Bright spots of color burned on his cheeks, and his sunken eyes fairly shot sparks of intensity.

Waldo followed Tim's eyes. "Someone sure stoked his fire."

"I don't like a man who just sold a paper being that happy about it," Tim said uneasily. "I thought he was an invalid."

"Oh, he is," Waldo said. "He just gets off the leash every so often. You made a good deal."

"You don't know whether I did or not," Tim retorted. "And you haven't got any business sense anyway."

"Can't deny that," Waldo said, unnettled. "But I know a paper with possibilities when I see one." He took another bite of steak and studied Tim's square-jawed, dubious face. "Relax. You did all right with the last deal I put you on to."

Tim pointed his fork at Waldo. "You got me drunk and sold me a debt-ridden rag that nearly got me shot."

"You got yourself drunk," Waldo protested. "And I didn't sell it to you; I lost it at poker. Just in the nick of time, too," he added. "I'm not cut out for management."

Tim put his fork down. "If there's something funny about the *Clarion*, Waldo, I'm going to tear you limb from limb."

Waldo crinkled up his face in earnest, champagne-soaked denial, and Tim's expression softened. Waldo was a hopeless businessman, but he knew the news game inside out. Just now he reminded Tim irresistibly of the gargoyle over the *Clarion*'s door. It made it impossible to mistrust him.

Waldo downed his champagne, hiccuped, and reached for the bottle in its snowy napkin. "Tell you what," he offered, "I'll come with you to meet your kid brother. We'll show him the town."

Tim shuddered. "No, you won't. My aunt Cindy wouldn't take to you at all." He watched Waldo pour the last of the champagne. "You won't wake up early enough anyway."

After an evening with Waldo, even one determinedly cut short at midnight, Tim almost didn't wake up. He dragged himself out of his room at the Palace Hotel—too expensive a place for journalists or for newspaper owners, but he was celebrating—and ran down a few flights of mahogany stairs to the patio of the Palm Court. The court was encircled by seven tiers of balconies lined with statuary and palms, rising to a glass roof. Hacks and silver-mounted carriages were already sweeping in through the Montgomery Street driveway, and Tim hailed an empty hack. As he raced down the Embarcadero he put on a pious face of Sunday morning rectitude, which, he feared, would not impress his aunt Cindy one bit.

It didn't. Aunt Cindy, his father's sister, ran an art gallery in Washington, D.C., and was a formidable force in that sophisticated world. Despite her own slightly Bohemian air, she expected nephews to be dutiful and sober. Cindy looked him over carefully, kissed his cheek, and informed him that his cravat was crooked.

Tim shook hands with his equally formidable uncle Henry, who was a colonel in the army but generally accomplished his duties—and hardly anyone ever knew quite what they were until afterwards, if at all—in civilian clothes.

"How were the islands?" Tim asked him casually in the tone of the merely curious.

"Very pleasant," Henry Blake replied in the tone of one who was merely a tourist. Hawaii was undergoing a revolution in which the United States Government was still undecided about how much to interfere. "I met your man Hugo Ware out there. He tells me that Peter is doing well."

"Peter's fine," Tim said, dismissing his business manager, Henry's son. "So you sparred with Hugo. Who won?"

Henry smiled. "I think I should call it a draw."

Tim thought that he would ask Hugo what *he* called it when Hugo got back to the States. There had been some cagey trading of information, he inferred. Talking to Uncle Henry was like dancing with a spider—it was very light on its feet, but you never knew exactly where you stood.

Passengers were streaming past them down the gangplank, and Aunt Cindy looked around and collected her offspring with a blue-eyed glance that could pretty well be translated as "Front and center!"

Frank Blake was fifteen, gangly in short pants but beginning to fill out across the shoulders and show the promise of his father's muscular build. Midge was nine, with more of Cindy about her, but she had the same square-jawed Holt face, waves of sandy-blond hair, and the look of determination that Tim possessed. The Holt blood usually dominated everything else. Both Frank and Midge were freckled from a season in the islands.

Tim hugged them, then held out his arms to Mike, coming down the gangplank after them. Mike was a jolt. At first glance he always looked less like a Holt than anyone else because he was so thin and had his mother Alexandra's red hair. But something else set Mike apart from the other two children now: He was hovering on the edge of adulthood, and maybe, at seventeen, he had already gone past it. Mike's face had taken on definition since Tim had last seen it and had begun to settle into its adult mold. His body was no longer thin but sinewy, as elastic as one of the tough little range ponies that had run loose on the West Coast since Spanish days. And there was something about his eyes—gray-green eyes, the color of water at the foot of the wharf where the harbor seals dove in and out. Tim lowered his arms and held out his hand instead.

Mike shook it. "You look good," he said, studying his older brother. "Respectable."

"Of course I'm respectable," Tim said. "Pillar of the community back in Guthrie. Any day now I'm going to get fat and take up side-whiskers. You look good yourself."

"I am good," Mike replied. "There has not been a jump out of my heart. Not a peep. Not that Dad will believe it." He scowled down at the harbor seals barking for fish heads from the ships' cooks cleaning out their galleys. "I suppose you're the officer in charge. You can put away the hand-cuffs. I'll go along quietly."

"Don't be an ass," Tim said.

"Don't tell me you aren't here to make sure I go straight to the Madrona." The Madrona was the Holt home ranch in Portland.

"I'm just going for a visit," Tim said airily. "I'm planning to tell the country cousins all about San Francisco.

I just bought a newspaper here. So put that in your pipe and smoke it."

"Hmmph," Mike said.

Mike knew what was what, Tim decided as they waited for a drayman to load the passengers' trunks. If Mike did not choose to go to the Madrona, it would be easy to give his older brother the slip, but Tim hoped Mike would decide not to try that.

ELMER KELTON

☐	27713	**THE MAN WHO RODE MIDNIGHT**	$3.50
☐	25658	**AFTER THE BUGLES**	$2.95
☐	27351	**HORSEHEAD CROSSING**	$2.95
☐	27119	**LLANO RIVER**	$2.95
☐	27218	**MANHUNTERS**	$2.95
☐	27620	**HANGING JUDGE**	$2.95
☐	27467	**WAGONTONGUE**	$2.95
☐	25629	**BOWIE'S MINE**	$2.95
☐	26999	**MASSACRE AT GOLIAD**	$2.95
☐	25651	**EYES OF THE HAWK**	$2.95
☐	26042	**JOE PEPPER**	$2.95
☐	26105	**DARK THICKET**	$2.95
☐	26449	**LONG WAY TO TEXAS**	$2.95
☐	25740	**THE WOLF AND THE BUFFALO**	$3.95
